DEADFALL

By Aline Templeton

Kelso Strang Series

Human Face

Carrion Comfort

Devil's Garden

Old Sins

Blind Eye

Deadfall

Marjory Fleming Series

Evil for Evil

Bad Blood

The Third Sin

DEADFALL

ALINE TEMPLETON

Allison & Busby Limited
11 Wardour Mews
London W1F 8AN
allisonandbusby.com

First published in Great Britain by Allison & Busby in 2024.

A CIP catalogue record for this book is available from the British Library.

First Edition

ISBN 978-0-7490-3154-1

Typeset in 11/16 pt Sabon LT Pro by Allison & Busby Ltd.

By choosing this product, you help take care of the world's forests. Learn more: www.fsc.org.

Printed and bound by
CPI Group (UK) Ltd, Croydon, CR0 4YY

For Clare Robertson, my most dedicated publicist,
with much love.

PROLOGUE

2020

The first streaks of dawn were no more than a narrow band on the eastern horizon that highlighted the gnarly roots and rough grasses, then slowly widened as it crept up over bark and branches to gild the lowest leaves with early April sunshine.

In the darkness of the trees and bushes the birds were waking with little mutterings and stirrings until the blackbird's clear whistle, as imperious as the tap of a conductor's baton, signalled the start of the chorus. Then all around responses began – somewhere the croon of a woodpigeon, the aggressive shouting of a wren, then more twittering and cheepings as the light grew.

It was cold still, with patches of ground frost in the shade and even in the open spaces the dew glittering on the grass was icy cold.

But Lachie MacIver was used to that, and to rising early; he was getting old now and his mattress, worn thin with use, pained him so that he was glad enough to rise at first light. He lived in the shepherd's bothy on the edge of the estate; they'd sold off land after the old lady died and there hadn't been sheep for forty years, but when they'd no further use for him they hadn't turfed him out. They'd just let it decay, and now there were cracks in the walls and rain could find its way under the rusted corrugated-iron roof that lifted a little in a high wind.

Do-gooders he despised had tried to move him out, but his answer had been short and to the point. Very short. Here he was his own man, walking the five miles to the village for his pension and supplies and other times living off the land, as he called it.

There was a pheasant shoot across the valley and they were early risers too, and easy pickings. The sun was up by the time he set off, the shotgun broken over his arm – his father's old gun the polis didn't know he had. Plenty folk did know, but round here they wouldn't clype.

He set off to take the short-cut through Drumdalloch Woods. They got nasty if they caught him doing that; he wasn't above taking a fat pigeon if there was no one around – they were daft about birds. By now he'd need to be careful; there were youngsters who'd nothing better to do than checking on wee machine-things they'd set up and writing stuff down.

Lachie paused, listening, as he reached the trees. Even in his heavy boots he could move silently but he'd hear them coming – clumsy, snapping twigs and swearing when they tripped on something. This morning there was only the racket the birds were making and beneath their songs he could feel the deep silence of the woods.

It had a curious power and it was tempting just to stand, losing himself in it, but he needed to get on. He headed for the glade near the middle, crossed by a track leading to Drumdalloch House, the backbone for multiple branching tracks and the route anyone doing the early morning checking would take. He was ready to walk quickly across when something caught his eye.

A huge oak, an ancient giant, stood at the far end and someone was lying across its gnarled roots. He stepped back out of sight. They often made their daft checks from funny positions and there was a rough wooden nesting platform above, right enough, but it had fallen off and the way the person was lying didn't look right.

When he got nearer he caught his breath. It was a woman, and he recognised her – Perry Forsyth's wife. Wearing jeans and a padded jacket, she was lying on her back against the oak with one foot twisted under her, like she'd maybe reached up to the platform and pulled it down on top of her. It looked like it had missed her, but then she must have tripped as she ducked out the way.

This was a right mess. She wasn't moving and he could see a bloody wound on her head. Must have given it a right good bash against the root. Maybe she needed help – but he shouldn't be here, and if he stayed they'd maybe say he'd done something to her.

With an anxious look around, he went to check – not too close, being careful to tread on firm ground. And even from there he could tell she was dead.

The open eyes, glazed, the jaw starting to sag, the little trickle of blood running out of one ear – oh yes. An old soldier, he'd seen enough death before, in battlefields he still revisited on one of his bad nights.

This would be hard on her bairn, but there was nothing Lachie could do for her. Someone would find her soon enough. With another nervous glance he retreated, disappearing into the trees. The pheasants were safe for now and later he'd walk to the village to pick up any news.

He'd like to be sure they'd found her. He wouldn't want to be left like that himself; the flies would find her first and soon other woodland creatures would be running or crawling or more horribly squirming here to perform their interconnected tasks as undertakers.

The white-faced student, who had been doing a check on the data loggers on the trees chosen for the current study, had come stumbling into the kitchen at Drumdalloch House, tear-stained and so shaken she could hardly get the bad news out.

As if he hadn't taken it in, Giles Forsyth stood still as a statue; only the furrow between his heavy grey brows deepened. Beside him his daughter Oriole gasped, almost dropping her coffee mug, and her other hand went to her throat.

'Helena – *dead*? Are you sure? Where is she?'

'I'll show you. Yes, it's – well, sort of obvious.' Her voice broke. 'Fell and hit her head badly, I think. There's great tits nesting in the box above – she probably went to make a recording and overbalanced.'

Giles cleared his throat. His voice was perfectly level as he said, 'You go with her, Oriole. I'll phone the police.' His daughter nodded and went out, her arm around the girl who was still trembling visibly.

He didn't move for a few moments after they left. He wasn't sure he could. A man of his generation, he gave no outward sign of the inner maelstrom of grief, helpless rage at fate and the bitterness of blighted hope. His daughter-in-law, lovely Helena, who had wholeheartedly shared the plan his own children were determined to thwart, was gone, and those children would destroy all he believed to be important the day he was safely dead himself.

His grandmother had dinned into him that these woods were a sacred trust, to be left to him, bypassing his older brother because he'd shared her passion for the glory and majesty of the ancient trees, sanctuary for generations of woodland birds, with records going back more than a hundred years. He'd tried to pass that on to his children but he'd failed. Oh, Oriole paid lip-service but she'd never be able to stand against Perry. The historic legacy meant nothing to him.

He'd called his children Peregrine and Oriole; Perry had always mocked the sentimentality and had raged when Helena had encouraged the son named James to call himself Jay.

Dear God, Jay! A mother's boy, undoubtedly; what would it do to him to lose her, aged ten? Giles would do his poor best for him, but the scar would be deep and disfiguring – and Jay would be all Perry's child, ready to be shaped and no longer a pledge for the future of the woods.

He was old and tired, not fit for the struggle. Perhaps he could train himself not to care what would happen when he wasn't there to see it, but his mental torment felt like physical pain, deep inside him. They said you could die of a broken heart. Perhaps you could.

He straightened his shoulders and walked stiffly over to the phone. 'Giles Forsyth, Drumdalloch House, Kilbain . . . Fatal accident,' he said.

Apart from going into the village where he'd learnt she'd been found all right, Lachie stuck close to the bothy. He could hear activity in the woods and catch sight of folk moving around, but he wasn't going to get caught up. The polis asking questions would mean trouble.

Next morning he took the ferret from her cage, a pretty jill with a brown bandit mask across a silvery face, petting her briefly before she nestled down in his pocket in patient expectation.

He collected the purse nets and the wooden pegs he'd whittled himself, then, a spade over his shoulder, set out for the south-facing slope at the end of the field, honeycombed with rabbit holes. There were no rabbits visible; dawn feeders, rabbits, and if he'd wanted to shoot one he'd have been out at first light. Now, though, they'd be asleep with full stomachs.

There was a small burrow he and the ferret both knew, one that past experience had shown had fewer escape tunnels than the larger ones. Moving quietly, he stretched the net across a tunnel opening and had just started on the pegs when he realised someone was coming up behind him, quiet on the soft grass.

Lachie turned. Jay Forsyth's face was blotchy and his eyes were swollen, but he wasn't crying and Lachie said only, 'Never heard you coming. Make a poacher of you yet.'

The answering smile was fleeting. The boy said abruptly, 'Can I stroke Jill?'

'If Jill wants to be stroked.' You didn't take liberties with ferrets, who tended to make their feelings known in a very direct way, involving razor-sharp teeth and a lot of blood.

But she had poked her head out of the pocket already, inquisitive and bright-eyed. Her whiskers quivered as Jay held out his hand for her to sniff.

'Want to come?' he said softly. Recognising a friend, she came to him and settled as he cradled her, stroking the soft fur.

Lachie watched them silently. After a few minutes Jay, not looking at him, said, 'Have you heard what happened to my mum?'

'Heard she'd an accident,' he said gruffly.

'Yes, that's what they said. She's dead. Did you know?'

'Aye, I heard that too. That's bad.'

He was holding the ferret more tightly and Lachie took a step closer, ready to move in if necessary, as Jay said, 'But do you know what I heard her saying on the phone one day? She said, "They're going to kill me, if I'm not careful."'

Jay's grip tightened further and as the ferret squirmed uncomfortably Lachie took her back in case she would bite and returned her to his pocket. A man of few words, he didn't know what to say except, 'Told your dad, have you?'

Tears welled up. 'He said she didn't mean it, she was just talking about how she was having to deal with people being difficult, that was all. But is that what she meant?'

How would Lachie know? It was the sort of thing folk said, after all, and it wasn't his place to have an opinion. He shrugged.

'He'd likely know,' was all he said. But as Jay looked at him for a long minute before turning away, he felt uncomfortable – maybe he should have told him to tell the polis. But it wasn't his way to look for trouble and after the boy had gone he went back to his task, securing the last pegs around the net so that the ferret could be released to do her work of darkness.

CHAPTER ONE

2023

Oriole Forsyth felt sick, anxiety like a stone in her stomach as she took the winding road to Inverness to see the lawyer. She'd pretty much been feeling sick ever since her father had died, but just now it was the problem of the Drumdalloch Woods that was on her mind.

She'd adored Giles and with his woods seeming almost a part of him she'd tried to love them too, even though she found their shadowy darkness and tangled growth and dank smell oppressive and even sinister; she had nightmares about being lost in rain and darkness with trees creeping closer and closer. Hungering for his affection, she'd hoped showing enthusiasm would bring them closer together, but she was afflicted with a sort of awkwardness that had got in the way of real closeness – and perhaps that went for him too, though it hadn't been a problem for bloody Helena.

Her sister-in-law had been blessed with the gift of

charm, sadly denied to Oriole. She still bore the scars from coming in with the exciting news of herons nesting in the small remnant of the Great Caledonian Forest on the edge of the estate.

She'd known what it would mean to Giles and was looking forward to enjoying his pleasure, but it was Helena who had visibly glowed, grasping Giles's hands in delight and crying, 'Come on, we have to go right now to see!' He'd laughed and let himself be led, not waiting to hear Oriole say it would probably be better not to disturb them too much. She really hated Helena at that moment.

After the accident it should have been Oriole's time, but it seemed Giles had been broken by it. Grief took away his interest even in his birds; he lost appetite, dwindled before her eyes. She'd often thought sadly, as he pushed away a meal she'd laboured over to tempt his appetite, that if she'd died instead he'd hardly have minded provided he still had Helena.

Helena's husband had grieved less visibly–imperceptibly, really. Perry had always worked in Edinburgh through the week and often didn't make it back at the weekend; Oriole had often wondered about the state of their marriage, but that sort of thing they didn't discuss in their family, even if the locals might. Now he was just going on as he always had.

When it came to Helena's son, though . . . Jay had become frankly impossible. He was traumatised and deeply unhappy and seeing his pain she'd done everything she could to reach out to him, but she couldn't break through his unremitting hostility. He seemed to exude hatred, as if blaming her for being alive when his mother was dead.

When he was born she'd been enchanted; he'd been a bright, attractive toddler and they'd been great pals, the two of them – him and his Auntie Rorie. He had been a joy, in a life of duty where joys were scarce. It was later he'd become difficult, perhaps because Perry had been an absent father and Helena had spoilt him, inclined to laugh when he was just plain rude. She'd become 'Aunt Oriel'; losing the childish nickname was painful. She'd been sorry for him, too; he wasn't the happy child he'd been.

After Helena's death Jay had begun refusing to accept limits of any kind, often disappearing for hours on end; once or twice they'd called the police and then looked stupid when he sauntered back in. He would climb trees and scare researchers by dangerously dropping down on them, but any rebuke would result in a temper-tantrum that wouldn't have disgraced a two-year-old – and Jay was quite a big lad. Talking had no effect; he wouldn't listen and since he didn't scruple to hit her when he was in a temper she'd begun to be physically afraid of him.

Perry had made no concession to the changed circumstances, and with Giles depressed and helpless, the problem of Jay landed squarely on Oriole's shoulders. However hard she tried, whatever she did, he only got worse and when she'd got a black eye trying to get him into the car to take him to school when he didn't want to go, she'd given up. She let him do whatever he wanted, hoping he wouldn't kill himself, or someone else, before Perry came for the weekend.

She confronted him as he stepped out of the car. 'Your son – your problem,' she'd said. 'He badly needs help but he won't accept it from me,' and shut herself in her room.

Perry hadn't reacted well, but at least he'd taken Jay back with him, then sent him to board at a private school. He'd settled there all right, she assumed, since Perry hadn't said any more about it.

She wasn't expecting good news from the lawyer. It was well over a year since Giles had died and all that Muriel Morris could say was that probate hadn't yet been granted, despite HMRC demanding death duties be paid before she and Perry had seen a penny. They'd had to borrow to pay and now interest was mounting up she was struggling.

It was all right for Perry with a well-paying job, courtesy of family connections with the wealthy Forsyths, the senior branch of the family who owned an Edinburgh property business. Oriole, with so much time having been given over to looking after Drumdalloch and her father, had only a part-time job as receptionist at Steve Christie's spa hotel in nearby Kilbain.

Giles's estate had been left to his children equally, the house and woods to be shared and always there to provide a home for them both. Perry was determined to ignore his wishes and sell to the highest bidder for development; her loyalty to Giles made her baulk but she could see they'd have to sell up or starve. Anyway, until they were legal owners there was nothing they could do.

Perry, in Edinburgh full-time now, had been happy for Oriole to make it her home meantime, on the assumption she would look after it, along with the woods. Her attempt to get him to pay towards upkeep had failed; he'd pointed out she was living there rent-free, making considerable play of the cost of renting his flat in Edinburgh's Northumberland Street.

She could have said this was one of the smartest streets in Edinburgh, while she was living in a house with a wing abandoned after being ravaged by fire long ago and now spreading rot into the rest of it, allowed in her father's time to crumble quietly. But since she'd never won an argument with Perry, she'd saved her breath to cool her porridge and come up with the idea of an Airbnb.

The trouble was people had high expectations now and she hadn't the money to provide luxury, but she'd managed to carve out two bedrooms and a living-room-kitchen on the first floor to be an acceptable flat that brought in a useful, if sporadic, income.

But she'd had another idea too. The Scottish Institute for Studies in Biological Sciences had been having free run of the woods for decades without contributing, and while Giles had never considered charging them for access, it seemed only fair to Oriole.

It didn't, apparently, seem fair to the Institute's director, Dr Michael Erskine. When she'd approached him to negotiate a suitable fee, he'd been dismissive.

'We're operating on a shoestring as it is. What do you need money for?'

Eating, keeping a roof over my head that doesn't need buckets to sit under the leaks . . . She didn't think he'd be interested in that; 'Costs,' she said.

He sneered openly. 'What costs? The place is just left to run wild.'

Giles had believed in letting nature do its own thing, as being better for wildlife and the trees too. He had this theory that they looked after themselves, and even each other – the 'Wood Wide Web', he called it, and there were pioneering studies in train on that as well as the ornithological ones.

It had been all very well for Giles to be a sentimentalist. He'd inherited a lot of money from his grandmother, but he'd no interest in finance – or indeed, any other boring practicality – and it had drained away over the years; now, with death duties and rampant inflation, there wouldn't be much left to trickle down to Oriole and Perry.

After that bad-tempered meeting she'd been determined not to go on being a doormat. She'd called the lawyer to arrange an appointment to talk over her plan, but the response had been guarded, much as it had been when she'd phoned Muriel Morris after Giles died to hear how much – or as it had turned out, how little – they were likely to inherit after the government had exacted its pound of flesh.

Which was why Oriole's anxiety was feeling like a stone in her stomach as she drove to Inverness.

Muriel Morris glanced at her watch, then got up to fetch a thick folder from a bookshelf. Then after a moment's thought, she took a key from a drawer and went to the huge old-fashioned iron safe that had stood in the corner of the senior partner's office since she was a little girl – and come to that, since her father had been a little boy. She couldn't vouch for her grandfather, but it was certainly possible.

She was a neat, precise woman in her fifties, always smartly groomed. As she took out a heavy metal deed box bearing the painted legend 'Drumdalloch House' and set it down on the desk she looked with disfavour at the dust it had left on her fingers and took a tissue to wipe it off. Its key was attached to the handle of the box and she sneezed as she opened it and more dust wafted up from the documents inside.

Her father had gone over the Forsyth papers with her when she'd stepped into his shoes as the first female senior partner of Morris Soutar – still so-called though the last Soutar had been killed in the Second World War – and she knew more about the family's history than did any of its present members.

Morris Soutar had looked after the estate on the Black Isle, in Moray, since its purchase by Ralph Forsyth in 1883. He was doing well in property in Edinburgh when it was the thing to have a hunting lodge in the north, but Ralph was more inclined to the fleshpots of Edinburgh than to the stalking of stags across moors in what was usually shockingly bad weather, so Drumdalloch became mainly somewhere to send underoccupied children to run wild during the long independent school holidays.

When his son Robert had inherited in 1918, his wife Isabella, a minor heiress in her own right, chose to spend more time with the wonderful exuberance of the Drumdalloch Woods than with her admittedly dull husband – and, wicked gossip had it, with a certain young forester. When Robert died in 1946, she retired to it as a dower house with the ready agreement of her son William, Isabella having, apparently, a famously forceful personality. Ownership was transferred to her as part of her marriage settlement, and she had left it to her second grandson Giles, father to Oriole who was the next appointment in Muriel's diary.

She sat down to wait with a sigh. There were difficulties ahead, and she couldn't see any good news to offer. She was sorry for Oriole, who'd been left dealing with all the estate's problems on her own; she was gauche and awkward, almost childlike sometimes in the black-and-white way she saw things, but she'd been very good to her father and done her best with her troublesome nephew. She was much more likeable than Perry, who always seemed to come in with chin stuck out and looking for a fight. Neither of them had inherited their father's pleasant, easy manner and though Muriel had never known the mother who had died when Perry was five and Oriole three, she had dark suspicions about the woman's character.

She'd had long talks with Giles Forsyth before his daughter-in-law died. His main concern had been the future of the historic woods; he was under no illusions about his son's intentions. Helena had convinced him that in her hands they'd be safe, with Jay to tend the flame right into the future, and he'd told Muriel he planned to change his will in her favour.

It wasn't her place to express an opinion, but she'd met the lady and assessed her charm as carefully calculated. Under tactful questioning, it had emerged that Giles knew nothing about his daughter-in-law's background and Muriel was also extremely doubtful that Helena would be any more likely to preserve his beloved woods than his children were; indeed, it was hard to see where she'd get the money to do it. Giles had few extravagances, but his answer to any shortfall had always been to draw on the dwindling capital.

She was only doing her duty when she said, as tactfully

as she could, 'Any such bequest would undoubtedly be challenged, which always inflicts disastrous costs. Even leaving that aside, by the time death duties are paid and the bairn's part deducted, there wouldn't be enough money to keep the place going.'

He had looked startled. Giles was not a man who had ever permitted himself to be concerned about money and now he looked bewildered.

'I don't understand. I know about death duties, obviously, but "the bairn's part?"'

It took some time for her to explain that by Scots law, half of a sole parent's estate must be left to the offspring. He was both indignant and angry at this restriction, but agreed to think it over.

Then Helena had died. The next time Muriel spoke to him, she didn't recognise the quavery, old man's voice as being his. He'd called her to discuss bequeathing the woods to the Scottish Institute for Studies in Biological Sciences and she had again pointed out the problems; when he sighed and said, 'I'm sure you're right,' he'd sounded defeated, and he'd died weeks later.

Now Oriole was coming in, proposing to charge the Institute for continued access and again she'd have to explain to a Forsyth about the unreasonable nature of the laws of the land. She sorted through the papers in the deedbox and lifted some to lay out for Oriole to read.

Her client came in late and frazzled. She was small and slight and somehow looked as if she were diminished by her problems. 'There were roadworks on the Kessock Bridge,' she said. 'They just seem to be digging up the whole of the Black Isle. You wouldn't believe the tailback, and the weather's getting worse by the minute.'

'Come and sit down and I'll ask Mairi to bring coffee. I could do with it – these papers are so dusty my throat's dry.'

The suspicious look Oriole gave them suggested she saw them as a threat – and she wasn't wrong there. Like the sins of the fathers being visited upon the children, decisions by her great-grandmother were now about to burden the present generation.

Over coffee, they moaned about the injustice and inefficiency of the tax system, until Muriel said, 'So tell me how I can help you,' though she knew what she was going to say wouldn't be helpful at all.

'The Institute is being totally obstructive. Michael was positively unpleasant to me when I pointed out the woods now belonged to us, and I wasn't prepared to let him and his students go on using them for nothing. You know how strapped I am for cash. Can you get something drawn up to deal with this?'

Muriel never liked having to break bad news. 'Well, I'm afraid there will be some problems with that,' she said, and saw Oriole's face sag into dismay.

'But why?' she cried. 'They're our woods. Why shouldn't I charge for access?'

Michael Erskine had appeared in Muriel's office after his meeting with Oriole, a tall, confident man in his early forties, with the arrogance she'd often noticed in academics when dealing with lesser mortals. He'd talked about the importance of the research; she had responded with suitable platitudes. Then he had talked about the legal side.

Now, Muriel said to Oriole, 'I'm afraid he's prepared

to play hardball.' She sorted through the papers on the desk, stiff with age, and pulled out one. 'He says your great-grandmother, Isabella Forsyth, gave the Institute permission to use the site and this is the document giving unrestricted access.'

Oriole looked at it with distaste. 'Well, I knew that. But this was long ago. The woods are ours now.'

'Indeed, but during your father's time there was no suggestion the situation had changed. Evidence of customary practice, what was known as "use and wont", over a period of years with no objection may convey certain rights.'

Oriole went very still. 'You mean Michael can just tell us what we have to do?'

'He's prepared to go to law. If you contested it you might win, but it would be an expensive business and in my professional opinion a favourable outcome would be very unlikely.'

Tears came to Oriole's eyes. 'You know we can't afford that,' she said bitterly. 'Are you saying that this will go on tying us down for ever? I'll tell you one thing – I'll stop organising the Friends of Drumdalloch Woods so the paths can grow over, and if trees fall I'll just leave them there . . .'

Muriel cleared her throat. 'Er – I think you'd have to be careful. I was going to mention taking out insurance as protection against any possible injury claims.'

The tears had started falling and Oriole dabbed at her eyes with a tissue. 'But where can I find money to pay for that? What can I do?'

'Perhaps Perry—'

Oriole's response was to give a disgusted snort. 'Perry? He won't lift a finger. He'll just say Drumdalloch is my responsibility until we're able to sell it.'

She stood up, blowing her nose. 'There isn't any point in going on with this, is there? I'll just have to do what I can. At least I've a few bookings lined up on Airbnb – it's all that's keeping my head above water.'

Muriel let her go. There seemed no point in depressing her further by telling her she strongly suspected that Erskine would try to get a preservation order put on the woods as a Site of Special Scientific Interest. They'd escaped having one earlier since, apart from a protected small group of ancient Caledonian pines, it wasn't native woodland; Isabella had consistently treated the place as if it was only a very extensive garden and, in much the same spirit as a collector choosing exotic stamps, she had overwhelmed the straggly native birch and ash with trees like the monkey puzzle, to be admired by the pergola, and a magnificent redwood to add definition to the skyline.

The only time Muriel had visited, the pergola had been reduced to a ramshackle pile of struts and the only reason the place wasn't totally overgrown was because the deer, like the Institute's students, had unfettered access, but there were also impressive ancient trees, like mahogany and walnut, which Giles had informed her were difficult to grow even in the rich black soil that had given the peninsula its name, and succeeding had been his grandmother's proudest boast.

It might once have been Isabella's pleasure ground, but it wasn't much of a commercial asset as it stood – and if Michael Erskine did manage to get the order, all the

Forsyths would realistically have to sell was a house well past any sort of renovation.

As Muriel tidied the papers back into their strongbox, she sighed. Oriole might lack her sister-in-law's charm but she'd given up a proper life of her own to look after her father – and his wretched woods – quite devotedly. Some people didn't have much luck.

Perry Forsyth sat in the Edinburgh New Town office of Forsyth Property across the desk from his cousin Edward, staring at him blankly.

Edward shifted uncomfortably. With his bespoke suit and well-cut hair, he had the gloss of good living about him, financed by his position as senior partner in a successful and long-established firm, but he was only five years older than Perry and it was an interview he would have been happy to dodge. In the circumstances, though, there was no alternative to wielding the axe himself.

'You have to understand times are really hard, Perry. I absolutely hate having to do this, but with inflation and the slump in the property market we've got no alternative but to retrench.'

'Well, of course I know that. I work here, remember? And I'm family, Edward – oh, all right, I know we're only the *junior* branch. I've never been allowed to forget it, after all.' There was a hard, bitter edge to his voice. 'And I've built up all this expertise over the years – surely that's worth something?'

'Certainly, certainly,' Edward said. 'We'll miss you, of course.' He was lying; they'd been trying for years to find an excuse to elbow out the cousin who was always on the verge of provoking formal complaints from staff about bullying and from clients about inefficiency, and the downturn had at last offered the opportunity.

Perry was scowling now. 'I can't believe what I'm hearing. And what happened to the principle "last in, first out"? Nick Mackintosh only came six months ago. Why are you saying this to me and not to him?'

Mackintosh was a bright, enthusiastic young man, good at his job and popular with everyone, but Edward could hardly say that. 'I know, I know,' he said. 'Life's a bitch, isn't it? And it's hard for me to do this too, blood being thicker than water.'

Perry's darkening expression suggested this line wasn't going down very well. He hurried on, 'The thing is, we're at the mercy of the accountants. We have to cut right back and with your salary reflecting your status and experience, they picked on this as a very significant saving. Naturally, there will be a generous redundancy payment and you'll have time to find something else that makes the most of your skills. And you can pretty much write your own reference.'

Perry searched his face as if he was looking to find a different meaning for the words being said. There was a note of desperation in his voice as he said, 'Look, I don't think I'm overpaid, but I can see that there's a problem. In the circumstances, I'd be prepared to take a pay cut.'

Edward almost groaned aloud. 'I'm afraid the accountants wouldn't accept that. As you said, you're entitled to what you've been paid, and it wouldn't be right. Thanks for the offer, though . . .'

He should have known that it wouldn't be long before

Perry's notoriously short temper erupted. 'Bloody hell, you really think you can get rid of me, just like that? I've never been properly valued. You've run a hopelessly sloppy operation, but when I did my best for the company and tried to get staff you failed to train properly to do the job they're well paid for, did you back me? No, you didn't. You allowed chippy little girls to get away with downright cheek to a senior manager.'

Edward had one more try at cooling it down. 'Of course, I know you were trying to do what you thought best—'

He wasn't allowed to finish the sentence. 'And you didn't agree,' Perry shouted. 'Oh, I knew that – it was bloody obvious. You've been looking for a chance to elbow me and the downturn's given you an excuse. Well, I won't go quietly. I'll sue for wrongful dismissal.'

Little as Edward liked it, he had to take the gloves off. 'If you did, we'd have to disclose the complaints of bullying and harassment. You remember we had to talk about this several times and after the most recent discussion we realised your attitude hadn't changed and complaints were on the point of being made formal. We couldn't have avoided sacking you and the downturn has actually worked to your advantage in allowing us to ease you out. But if you want to run with it . . .'

There was a long, angry silence. Then Perry got up.

'OK, you win. Your lot always win. I don't suppose this dirty trick will even trouble your conscience. What do I have to sign?'

When at last his kinsman had gone, Edward took out his handkerchief and was wiping the sweat off the back of his neck when the door opened and one of his partners appeared.

'How did it go?'

'Ghastly – but he's gone.' He fetched a bottle of Glenfiddich and a couple of glasses from a cupboard. 'Join me? I know it's early, but by God, I need this!'

Perry walked out into North Castle Street, lurching slightly, light-headed with the shock. It had never occurred to him that the position wasn't his for as long as he chose to occupy it. In some hazy way he'd seen it as reparation due from the branch of the family that had grabbed most of the goodies inherited from their mutual ancestors.

Edward he had simply despised – weak, lax, ruled by the juniors – and if he, Perry, had been in charge he'd have run a tight ship and made it a more successful business, one that wouldn't be having to make economies and sack staff.

Staff – like him. Without the job, he was nothing. If he applied for anything similar, he'd be offered a fraction of his current salary – and whatever gilded reference Edward provided, everyone in the property business would know he'd been sacked. The faint buzzing in his head could almost be the sound of messages whizzing around the internet.

The rain began as he emerged, typical Edinburgh rain: not dramatic, but politely steely in its persistence. His umbrella was in his office, but they'd escorted him out; they'd send everything round, probably in a black plastic bag, with an office girl smirking as she dumped it on him.

All he could do was go home to lick his wounds and

he set off downhill towards Northumberland Street. But it wasn't going to be home much longer, was it? Indeed, given the rent, he'd have to pull every string he still had to get out of it immediately; the redundancy money would have to keep him until they could flog Drumdalloch and God only knew when that would be – God and the sodding Inland Revenue.

And then there was James. He couldn't afford school fees; removing him would be catastrophic, not because of the effect on the boy – that didn't cross his mind – but because James would be permanently around, sulky and aggressive, which was painful enough during wretchedly long holidays. Claudia would walk out, for a start.

Anyway, she wouldn't stay if he was penniless. She worked in Space NK in George Street; she'd sold him perfume for a girlfriend and then somehow the girlfriend had gone and she'd moved in. She was high maintenance and even if he ignored Oriole's refusal to take responsibility and packed James off to Drumdalloch, it probably wouldn't help. Even the most dismal flat in Edinburgh was expensive and Claudia wouldn't settle for dismal.

He had to face up to it; in one day he'd lost income, home and girlfriend and acquired the ongoing problem of a son who looked at him daily with eyes narrowed in hatred.

There was only one thing for it. He'd have to go back to Drumdalloch himself.

CHAPTER TWO

Kelso Strang looked out of the window of the fisherman's cottage that stood across from the harbour in Newhaven. It was a shame it was a dreary day, with heavy clouds and a blustery wind coming off the Firth of Forth; it was a very attractive view when the sun was shining, with the lighthouse at the end of the protective curve of the harbour wall, the colourful small boats at anchor and the view of Fife on the other side. He'd so much wanted the house to look nice for Cat – not that she hadn't seen it before, but this was an important day.

He'd met Catriona Fleming only a few months before when their paths had crossed in the Sheriff Court; as a police officer he was giving evidence in a criminal prosecution and she was the advocate's devil, working for nothing while her pupil master trained her. Despite an immediate attraction, Kelso, very conscious of the twelve-year age gap, had wanted to take it slowly but circumstances, and a certain determination on Cat's part, had accelerated the pace of the relationship.

It was, though, important to him that she should have time and space to change her mind; he couldn't bear to think that one day she might feel trapped with an ageing widower. He'd been anxious, too, to reassure her parents, Marjory and Bill Fleming, that he wouldn't pressure her into an early commitment, even though Marjory had said sardonically that if he ever managed to pressure Cat into doing something she didn't want to do, would he please tell her his secret since she'd never managed it.

And indeed Cat, for all that she was young, had shown no sign of drawing back from the decision she'd made well before he had. She felt he was being ridiculously scrupulous. 'I just knew, right from the start,' she told him, adding reproachfully, 'You were very slow, actually.'

Of course, they'd talked about his wife, Alexa, so tragically killed in a car crash along with their unborn baby. Cat's eyes had filled with tears when he first told her.

'Poor Alexa,' she said softly, 'and poor, poor you. You loved her very much, didn't you?'

Kelso found that his throat was constricted so that he couldn't speak and she went on, 'Don't ever feel you can't mention her. I won't be jealous and I promise I'm never going to do the "do you love me more?" bit – that was then and this is now. And I think I'd have liked her – after all, she had good taste in men. But, of course, if you want to see jealous, try so much as glancing at another woman and I'll scratch her eyes out.'

They'd ended up laughing and kissing and deciding that when her pupillage finished, she'd leave her shared flat and move in with him.

'I warn you, I'm going to be just as broke as I am now when I put up my plate and have to wait for clients to come to me,' she said. 'Frankly, I'm going to have to be a kept woman and they'll be saying I snared you for your money.'

'I rather like the thought of being a sugar daddy,' he said. 'But once you get going on the big cases and police salaries are frozen for yet another year, it'll be the other way round.'

And today she was moving in. He'd offered to fetch her but she'd said she'd just chuck the few things she'd kept at the flat in a taxi and come round. At about eleven, she'd said.

Kelso looked at his watch again. Almost half past, but then Cat was seldom punctual. He was nervous – not about Cat, of course not, but about how he would actually feel having changes made to his comfortable bachelor existence. He liked this room, but Cat would naturally, and rightly, have her own ideas about décor and arrangements and he was remembering, uncomfortably, how he'd resented his sister Finella's reorganisation of the cupboards when she had briefly moved in with her small daughter Betsy. Would he find he couldn't help minding when things were different?

There was the taxi now, turning into the paved square beside the house. From the sitting room, he hurried down the outside stair and had the door open before she could get out.

There was only a suitcase and a couple of carrier bags.

'Is this all your worldly goods?' he said, smiling.

She beamed back. 'No, this is just to lull you into a false sense of security. All my real stuff is at home. Mum wondered if we'd like to go down to Galloway for lunch next Saturday and you can see the full horror then.'

'Sounds good,' he said, following her up the stairs. Lunch at the farm was always a treat; he had a lot in common with Marjory, who'd been a senior police detective too.

Cat drifted over to the window. 'Shame it's such a rotten day. This is such a special view.'

'Yes,' Kelso said, then added awkwardly, 'Of course, you do know you can change anything you want – redecorate, anything . . .'

She gave him a level look. 'That's very kind and proper, but you know you'd hate it if I tore everything out and changed just for the sake of change. I told you, I think it's a lovely room – clever colours and I like the paintings. But there's one thing I do want – another comfy chair at the window opposite yours so we can both look out on a good day.'

He felt the tension ease. 'Go and sit down now and I'll bring another one across once I've got the champagne out of the fridge.'

'Oh good. I hoped there would be champagne,' she said.

She sat down with a contented sigh and he looked over as he removed the foil from the bottle. He'd always liked this room but now he realised there had been something missing all along; that other chair by the window, for her to fill.

* * *

It was a scary drive back from Inverness, especially when you were feeling helpless and profoundly depressed. Driven on a tearing wind, the storm was building and as Oriole Forsyth crossed the Kessock Bridge on her way back to the Black Isle the wind snatched at her elderly Kia so that she had to wrench it back into line, while from the inside lane lorries threw up bow waves of water; the squalls of rain were merciless so that even the wipers on their highest setting couldn't cope and she was driving all but blind.

She found herself thinking there would be worse things than a crash that finished it all. What was there to go home for? The roof would be leaking and while there were basins placed under known leaks, a storm always opened up new ones in unused rooms that she probably wouldn't find until they'd done more internal damage. She'd have to check out the Airbnb flat; she'd spent money she could barely afford to weatherproof it but when it was like this nothing was safe.

She dreaded arriving back. Her father had always enjoyed dramatic weather but when the trees roared like the ocean and lashed themselves into a frenzy of whipping branches, she'd always felt terrified even when he was there beside her, but she'd pretend to be brave. Now she was alone, driving along the avenue to the house below trees under siege by the elements, and no one knew better than she how little had been done to ensure that none of the great oaks would simply topple.

The forecourt was empty and the red sandstone Victorian house with its pointed eaves and fire-gutted wing falling into ruin was gloomy in the gathering dusk, even though it was only four o'clock. She parked as close as she could and leapt across to the cover of the rickety wooden porch and in the front door. It wasn't locked; there wasn't much worth stealing and the students and Friends of Drumdalloch had always had access when she wasn't there if they wanted to use the loo or the kitchen, or just wanted shelter from the elements. They'd all have given up and gone home long ago.

The hall was very dark. Oriole had to grope for the switch as, shaking her head to release a shower of raindrops and wiping down her face with her wet hands, she made for the kitchen to get a towel and make a cup of tea. It would be warm there, at least, from the ancient Aga and she draped her saturated jacket over the top.

But when she put the light on, her low mood changed to sheer rage. The kitchen was a complete mess, the table covered with dirty mugs, plastic sandwich packets and the remnants of someone's lunch; there was a pan on the side of the Aga that had been used to heat soup, presumably from the tin left empty on the surface beside it. No one had made the smallest effort to clear up, merely leaving everything for her to deal with when she came in.

Not that it was unusual. When she was at home, she might nag mildly but she'd usually just put used mugs in the dishwasher and rubbish in the bins in passing, so if she was out at work as she had been today their detritus did tend to accumulate. It was admittedly irritating but she'd never got up enough of a head of steam to take a stand.

So she'd only herself to blame for letting them get away with it, but particularly after Giles died she'd rather enjoyed doing a bit of mothering; they were mostly little more than kids and it was company in this big empty house.

Today, though, it was simply too much, on top of all that had happened. As of tomorrow, she was going to harden her heart because it had to be different. If the Institute wouldn't pay to use the woods for their stupid research, they'd have to pay for the privilege of parking at the house. And if they wanted what might be termed use of the facilities, they could pay for that too, or drive the five miles into Kilbain and find a café with an indulgent owner, always supposing they could find one.

She'd go on looking after the Friends who voluntarily did so much, of course, but there would be no concessions for the students, and particularly not for Michael Erskine when he rolled up in his lordly way, as he did from time to time to see how they were getting on. What was more, she wouldn't allow him just to pop in to charge his ostentatiously eco-friendly electric car when it suited him, even if he offered to pay, which often he didn't. Calling out the Kilbain garage to get it going again would be both expensive and time-consuming for him.

She didn't look forward to telling Lars, though. Lars Andersen was working on a PhD in evolutionary biology, a black-haired, black-bearded giant who took himself and his work very seriously indeed, a Norwegian whose English, Oriole always felt, was probably more correct than her own even if occasionally awkward. She had never understood what it was all about, except that it had something to do with fungal networks that established themselves underground and nourished the trees in exchange for the sugars they needed in some sort of symbiotic relationship – or roughly like that, anyway.

He always worked as if he was running a race and was determined to bulldoze everything aside on his way to the winning post. Giles had explained to her that he probably felt he was, since scientific papers were a competitive business and being the first to get a new theory published in *Nature*, the science journal, could have career-changing consequences.

Oriole was, to be honest, afraid of his temper. Delays of any kind bought on his black mood, and she would go out of her way to avoid him on days like today when it was simply too stormy for outdoor work. He'd establish himself in the kitchen, moodily making notes and scanning tables and drumming his fingers while he checked out of the window every ten minutes to see if it was brightening up.

Well, he'd have to go and drum his fingers somewhere else. She was under no obligation to put up with his bad temper. When he'd first arrived two years ago, she'd actually rather fancied him – he was good-looking if you went for the rough-hewn look, with those intense brown eyes, but from the start he'd behaved as if he barely saw her. When it came to Helena, on the other hand . . .

Oriole had thought of saying something to Perry about what she saw going on, but she didn't think he'd appreciate it, and they most certainly wouldn't.

She'd appointed herself a voluntary student, though, ready to help with the ornithological studies and doing checks for Lars on the trees, which had not only allowed them to spend a lot of time together but had given Helena an excuse for not doing her share around the house.

Not that they didn't have their rows. She'd hear them yelling at each other sometimes, and when Helena's smiley persona slipped she could be quite a hellcat. The vicious row she'd overheard in the woods shortly before Helena died had been something to do with the preserving of what he definitely saw as his own personal woods, but it was odd that they should be arguing, given Helena's frequently expressed enthusiasm for precisely that; it had made her think, not for the first time, that her sister-in-law was as two-faced as they came and was playing a deep game. She'd certainly had Giles exactly where she wanted him and Perry had been afraid his wife would convince him she'd protect the 'legacy' of the woods when he wouldn't, and that his father would leave everything to her.

The estate was theirs now, but they were living in limbo with the struggle over the future still ahead. Even if she could never love the trees, she would badly miss the delights of the birdlife they sheltered, and she dreaded too the guilt she'd feel if she couldn't persuade Perry to respect Giles's wishes. And what was there for her anyway, once it happened? This place was all she'd ever known and even thinking about . . . well, afterwards, sent a shiver down her spine.

She shook herself out of it. Standing here going over ancient history wouldn't help the untidy kitchen and she sighed, then went to stack the dishwasher and clear up with a bad grace.

By the time she'd finished, the wind seemed to be dropping as quickly as it had blown up. The trees were much less agitated, so she didn't feel so nervous about the dangers of the drive, and since it was still only five o'clock she'd be facing a long and lonely evening here. She wasn't on duty at the hotel but it would be company and Steve would be pleased to see her. She liked to think that the warmth of the hug he always gave her when she turned up unexpectedly showed genuine affection, though a cynical little voice at the back of her head tended to point out that with staff so hard to come by and so unreliable, an extra – unpaid – hand behind the bar would make any boss feel affectionate.

She wasn't self-delusive; everybody loved Steve, always so personable and charming, so why ever would he be specially fond of Oriole, who was reminded by the mirror every morning of the heavy eyelids and deep-set eyes which, along with the downturned mouth, made her look depressed even when she wasn't. Her father had always said she was very like his grandmother, and she'd worked out quite early on that this wasn't a compliment.

After everything today, she was feeling as gloomy as she looked but seeing Steve was always a tonic. She mustn't show how she was feeling; other people's woes and complaints were very boring so she must put on a big smile and do her best to look cheerful.

Steve Christie was standing in the front hall of the Kilbain Hotel and Spa when Perry Forsyth's phone call came through. Aware that the loud tirade that began the moment he answered it was clearly audible to the receptionist and the guests checking in, all trying not to look as if they were listening, he grimaced and stepped through to the office.

Perry Forsyth, thick and arrogant, wasn't his favourite

person; they were 'mates', theoretically, but he'd have choked him off long ago if there hadn't been powerful reasons not to. Perry would one day have the Drumdalloch estate, while Steve had nothing beyond the grandly named Kilbain Hotel and Spa whose future was uncertain to say the least.

The hotel was distinctly shabby. The 'spa' consisted of a small indoor swimming pool, a room with weights and a treadmill, and a beauty salon that was meant to be offering treatments and hairdressing but couldn't since the beautician had left for a better-paying job. Guests were very sophisticated nowadays and it was only keeping up a constant, exhausting charm offensive to deal with complaints that kept it going at all; he didn't have the money to upgrade, and he'd be stuck with that for ever.

The grand project Steve had been involved in planning long ago had fallen through disastrously, but they'd moved their feet now to concentrate on Perry instead, drawing him in, talking about the killing they could all make together and the returns they would get on their investment. The worry was that once Perry, with his nice cushy job, got his mitts on the inheritance, he might simply blow the money – and of course Oriole's opinion wouldn't count.

So he heard what Perry was saying with sudden excitement, realising the big moment had actually arrived; with the man clearly shaken and vulnerable, it was the perfect time to lock him into a rock-solid business that would make all the difference to future prosperity. He was happy to make sympathetic noises as Perry's fury talked itself out, while he tried to finesse his response.

He was genuinely surprised at the news because he'd always got the impression Perry only had the job at all because of some kind of family arrangement – Perry had bent his ear often enough about the wealth of his cousins compared to what he termed his own penury, even though that had allowed him a pretty cushy lifestyle.

If that wasn't right, then Perry being sacked wasn't surprising in the least. It was amazing he'd lasted there as long as he had; he'd always stigmatised the boss and his fellow-workers as incompetent fools and knowing the man, it was unlikely he'd have kept his opinion to himself. From Perry's accounts, too, of run-ins with junior female staff, he'd often thought that with the spread of the 'MeToo' message he was living dangerously. And now it had happened.

'God, mate,' he said when Perry paused for breath, 'that's rough. Hope you're going to take them to the cleaners.'

'Using what for money?' Perry said bitterly. 'They've said they'll fight me every step of the way and they've only to bribe one of the totties to invent some kind of damaging allegation and I'm toast. They're giving me what keeps them inside the law but unless I settle for that they'll play dirty.'

That gave Steve a fair idea of the situation, but he said brightly, 'Of course, with your contacts and experience you can land another job in Edinburgh, no bother.'

'You think? With them going around bad-mouthing me? No, I'm finished. I've managed to get out of the rental contract – a favour, the man called it, even though he's got people queueing up to take it on – but I'll still be wiped out. I'm going to have to come back north, God help me.'

Steve stiffened. He could sense what was coming next; he'd been privileged to hear Perry's views on the domestic inadequacies of Drumdalloch House, not to mention the shortcomings of his immediate family – which had even included his late wife. But he said, 'Probably wise. Presumably you can live free at Oriole's house—'

'It's not her house, it's our house,' Perry snapped.

'Oh – oh yes, of course, ' he said, though he had also heard Oriole bemoaning Perry's refusal to take any responsibility for it. It had needed fancy footwork to listen to, and apparently sympathise with, the complaints from both sides.

'But actually,' Perry went on, 'I was going to ask if you could find a corner for me in the hotel. I've kind of got used to civilisation – and a bit of good company!' He gave an awkward laugh.

Steve seized on a way of stalling. 'And what about Claudia? How's she feeling?'

'Claudia! Can't you guess? Not really the stand-by-your-man type. She was off so fast it would make your head spin. What about it, though? You can't abandon me to Oriole.'

He was almost ready to offer him the small back room on the third floor, with a proviso about paying for food, when Perry said, 'And of course James would be a problem. They don't get on at all.'

He'd forgotten about James, who would presumably be removed from the posh school. There was no way Steve was having James in the hotel, causing trouble wherever he could; the antics that had frequently scandalised Kilbain were legendary.

'Mate, I'd be ready to, but I couldn't spare the rooms. Like you, I'm frankly skint and there's the Easter break coming up – I need to take every booking I can to keep the place solvent.'

There was a silence, then Perry said heavily, 'I was afraid you'd say that. OK, OK. We'll just have to slum it at Drumdalloch – not that Oriole will like it.'

She wouldn't. Steve had heard about Oriole's struggles with James, or Jay as he liked to be called, and she would certainly be dismayed. 'I'll probably see her shortly. Want me to – er – tell her about what's happened?' The word 'warn' had nearly slipped out there.

'No, no, don't do that. Better I just arrive and explain it myself. Easier that way. I'll see you when I get there.'

Easier for Perry, probably, Steve reflected, but hardly for poor old Oriole. She was conscientious if a bit downbeat for front-of-house, but she was a good soul and one way and another she'd drawn the short straw.

As he came out of the office, Oriole herself was coming in the front door. 'Well, well! Look what the wind's blown in!' he said, giving her a hug.

Her sad-spaniel face brightened immediately. 'I was at a bit of a loose end and I didn't feel like sitting in an empty house. I thought I might sort of give a hand in the bar if you've a lot of people in.'

He smiled at her. 'Actually, you're an answer to a prayer, bless you. Tricia hasn't turned up and we've got a party booking for dinner this evening. Come and let me buy you a drink now and we can have a chat.'

Beaming, she followed him. Oh dear, he thought, it

won't be long before a peaceful night in an empty house will be a wistful memory.

As usual, Oriole threw herself into the job, which meant that for once there were no complaints from the diners and Steve was able to thank her with another hug, send her off home with a bottle of wine and lock up earlier than usual.

He retreated upstairs to his flat with excitement still fizzing through him, excitement it was tempting to share. He glanced at his watch – not midnight yet. He picked up the phone.

'Hope I didn't wake you. It's just I've got what may well be the best news we've heard for a long time.'

CHAPTER THREE

It would have to be one of Lars's fieldwork days, Oriole thought gloomily as she got up and looked out of the window. There was his ancient Jeep, parked on the drive just below – and it would have to be him she'd be trying her hard-line policy on first. She'd known that was likely because he always arrived before everyone else to make the most of the daylight, and she'd given herself a pep talk last night before she went to sleep: *tomorrow is when you stop people walking all over you, and don't make excuses and put it off just because it's really, really hard and you're frightened of conflict.*

It had taken her all weekend to summon up the courage to put her plan into action and now, in the cold light of day, it was tempting to make an excuse. It was a glorious morning, the sun was shining and the trees were barely swaying, as if still exhausted by the violence of Friday's rage. The birds were singing their heads off; now with the breeding season well under way they were constantly busy, flitting among the leaves and making swooping flights from branch to branch.

A pair of thrushes was nesting in the honeysuckle that grew thick around her window; they'd done that the previous year, and, delighted at their return, Oriole had been watching as twigs, leaves and moss were flown in for the renovation project. They were so neat and deft as they tucked and shaped the raw materials into the cup-shaped hollow, with even a few soft feathers added ready to receive the precious eggs that should arrive any day now.

It was idyllic, really – a pity to spoil it with rows and unpleasantness, but it had to be done sometime if she wasn't going to add to the frightening debt growing by the week. Oriole turned away with a sigh and set about preparing for what was bound to be a difficult day ahead. As she went to the stairs, she heard movement in the kitchen and froze; she didn't fancy confronting Lars there, where she couldn't walk off when he turned aggressive, as she was sure he would.

Then a cheerful voice called, 'Oriole? Good morning! Coffee?'

Thank goodness! It was only Nicki – Nicki Latham, the most dedicated of the Friends, young and enthusiastic. She'd recently taken a job in the holiday flat rental agency that Oriole used and as a keen member of the RSPB she'd been interested in getting involved at Drumdalloch. Oriole had never forgotten her reaction when she'd shown her round that first time on a day like today.

Nicki had followed her along the paths between the trees, immediately sensing the need to be quiet. 'It's – it's like the Garden of Eden,' she had breathed. 'The birds – just incredible! They're so tame, they let you get right up to them, don't they?'

'I suppose it's because they've been left alone for more than a hundred years,' Oriole had told her. 'In fact, there's usually a robin around the old pergola here who'll probably come over to check us out.'

He had done just that, sitting on the ruined frame with his head cocked to one side and favouring them with his sharp little song.

'He had me from "Hello",' Nicki always said. 'Making Things Better for Birds – that's my motto.'

She had, indeed, been ready to turn her hand to anything from checking recordings to clearing access paths when necessary, with a speciality of laying about fallen timber with enthusiasm and a power saw. There were a number of other volunteers, but Nicki, who'd fallen into the habit of staying on after the day's work or dropping round of an evening, had become a good friend.

Now she had set out mugs, the kettle on the Aga was starting to boil and she was measuring out the coffee when Oriole reached the kitchen.

'Any eggs yet?' she asked eagerly.

Oriole shook her head. 'Can't be long, though. They were fussing about a lot yesterday even when the rain came on again.'

'Last night I really thought we wouldn't be able to get out today but look at it now – perfect peace!'

'Hmm,' Oriole said. 'I wouldn't count on it.'

Nicki looked up sharply. 'Really?'

She was the only person Oriole confided in; she was

always so ready to listen that she didn't make Oriole feel she was trespassing on her time, as so many other people did.

'You know I said I was going to make the Institute pay for using the woods for research?'

'Yes, you said. Seems reasonable.'

'Not to Michael Erskine, it doesn't. He's flatly refused and apparently there's some old document that allows him to do that and I haven't got the money to challenge it.'

'But that's so unfair!' Nicki exclaimed. 'He's such a snooty sod and he totally takes advantage. Just tell him it's your property now – well, yours and your brother's, and I guess Perry'll back you up, even if he's busy taking advantage of you too. What can you do?'

'Oh, I know I've taken the easy way out till now – I really hate aggro – but I'm determined to tell them they can't park here and I'm going to lock the house so they can't use it unless they pay me for the privilege – oh, you and the Friends can have a key, of course.'

Nicki stared at her. 'Oh wow! They'll go berserk. They've always done that – and it's miles from anywhere, out here.'

'That's my point,' she said.

'Are you sure you can make it stick? You're far too kind-hearted and you've always been too soft with them, never making them clear up or anything.'

She sounded doubtful and Oriole made herself sound more confident than she actually felt. 'Yes, I am. In fact, I'm going out right now to tell Lars to move his truck. Want to come and watch the fun?'

Nicki thought for a moment. 'Not sure about that

– I'm not really into blood sports. Leave the kitchen door open and then I can thunder to the rescue if you scream.'

'Coward,' Oriole said and walked to the door as she took a deep breath. 'Here I go.'

There were twigs and even saplings still littering the place after the force of Friday's storm. Natural pruning, Giles always called it as dead limbs and weak branches were torn away, creating breathing space for new growth. There was no sign of Lars near the house and Oriole had to pick her way along the obstructed paths, skirting the deepest puddles, ploughing through mud, and even dragging one enormous branch, thick as a man's thigh, to one side so she could get through. There'd be plenty of work for Nicki and her saw today; she could only hope one or two more volunteers would turn up to help since any students would be busy with checking what their recorders could tell them about the after-effects of the storm.

The small stony streams and rivulets that seamed the woods were running fast and high today, the water darkened by the rich soil – like arteries of black blood, she always thought, and today in her nervous state that gave her a small cold shiver. The smell of sodden vegetation was rank and the unrestrained anarchy of the trees that blocked her free passage was intimidating. Not helpful, when she so needed confidence.

She mustn't give in, though. Doggedly she persisted along the path to the southern edge of the woods where undergrowth was stunted because of the heavy shade cast by the huge canopies of the tallest trees and there was a viewpoint over a small loch below, where a Victorian wrought-iron bench stood. It was rusted now, but she remembered with a pang picnics there with her father on sunny days like this.

And there Lars was at last. She heard him before she saw him, standing cursing in front of a tree, an ancient walnut with a splash of white paint on the trunk showing it was earmarked for his study. There was a case with testing equipment lying open, with an auger for soil-sampling on the ground beside it, but in the storm a sapling had been uprooted and had blown right across the roots where he needed to work.

He heard her approach and turned, saying, 'That is good! You can give me a help here. I cannot get on with my work till it is moved but here there is a branch catching. Come to this end and pull it round while I drag it back.'

A blunt 'Try saying "please",' was on the tip of her tongue, but there was no point in being provocative and she did as she was told until the obstruction had been moved.

He did admittedly say 'Thanks' in an offhand way and turned immediately to pick up the auger.

Oriole cleared her throat. 'Lars, I need a word with you.'

The dark brows came together as he swung round. 'Oh? Well, can you make it quick? I have a lot I must do today.'

His rudeness made it easier. With her nails digging into the palm of her hand, she said flatly, 'It won't take long. In future you'll have to find somewhere else to put the Jeep. I've decided that the Institute can't go on using the house and the parking area as if it belonged to them.'

Lars looked at her blankly. 'What the hell is this?'

'I had a meeting with Dr Erskine about fixing an appropriate fee for your access to the woods and he refused point-blank. I gather I'm unable to impose a charge for that, but the house and its environs is private property and as of now I'm withdrawing permission for its use.'

'You cannot do that! I am using the kitchen in bad weather – what do you expect me to do?'

Oriole was trembling now and it was hard to control her voice. 'It's your problem, not mine.'

'You expect I will go back to Inverness when I cannot work and then wait for the weather to be better to drive back again – and probably find the effing weather had changed again? Do you not understand how much of my time this would be wasting?'

She backed away a little – with the long steel auger in his hand he looked actively threatening – but she managed to say, 'I'm not going to discuss this. I suggest you speak to Michael and tell him to get in touch with me about some suitable financial arrangement,' and walked off.

She heard a thump, as if the auger might have been thrown to the ground, but she didn't turn to look. She could hear him swearing again as she walked quickly away down the path.

As Michael Erskine walked to the Scottish Institute of Biological Sciences in Inverness his mind was running on the PowerPoint presentation he was about to make to the Board. He must get his pitch right; it could mean a significant improvement to the Institute's academic status in the scientific world – and, most importantly, to his own too – but what would be more convincing to hard-headed board members would be its financial potential. For a start, it would enable them to attract more postgraduate students, particularly the lucrative foreign variety, and further down the line groundbreaking research on tree nutrition would be eminently sellable, not only to timber companies but also to government agencies, at home and abroad.

He was pleased with what he could show them; the last time he was at Drumdalloch, while Oriole Forsyth was out, he'd photographed the aspects of the site that were relevant to the points he wanted to make and it had, if he said it himself, made an impressive portfolio.

Passing the plate glass window of the Institute he paused to glance at his reflection, passed a hand over his hair to smooth it and straightened his tie as he went in. There were some sticklers on the Board and he'd taken trouble over his choice of clothes – a lovat green tweed jacket that hinted at the natural world where the eco-friendly work was being done but was sufficiently well cut to suggest a hard-headed professional approach to it.

'Not quite ready for you upstairs yet, Dr Erskine,' the receptionist said.

'Oh,' he said. 'Bit of a nuisance, that.' He was irritated – even if they were the bosses, surely as director he merited punctuality? 'Will they be long?'

'Talking money, I think,' she said, pulling a face. 'Could be some time.'

That wasn't good news. That suggested there might be financial problems and persuading them to make further investment might be an uphill struggle.

He scowled. 'I'll be in my office – buzz me when they're finished.'

Erskine sat down and opened up his laptop. He might as well do another run-through of the presentation, pinpoint areas where he could emphasise a possible increase in the revenue stream . . .

When his mobile buzzed he looked at it with irritation. He was wanting to concentrate and he was tempted just to ignore it when Lars Andersen's name came up. A very demanding student, he was far too apt to come to the director with every little problem, often one he could well sort out for himself. On the other hand, his research was key to the very programme Erskine was promoting today and if Andersen felt ignored, he could build up a head of steam that would mean precious time being spent calming him down later.

So Erskine picked up the phone, sounding resigned as he said, 'Well, Lars, what is it today? Is it urgent? I'm due in a meeting.'

A moment later he sat bolt upright in his chair. 'She said *what?* She can't do that. We've always had access.'

But even as Andersen went over the top about the implications for his research, Erskine was mentally reviewing the papers granting the access to the woods, papers he'd studied meticulously when he'd had qualms about problems that might arise after Giles Forsyth's death, and had been greatly reassured by what he found. Now, though, he realised there had been no mention at all of access to the house or its immediate grounds; it was, in fact, extremely unlikely that Isabella, a very old-fashioned *grande dame* by all accounts, would have granted any kind of open-door policy. For many years the ornithological research had been just informal records casually kept and it was only with the recent emphasis on conservation and the upsurge of interest in the Wood Wide Web that Drumdalloch Woods had become of much greater significance.

Giles had been so easy-going that granting requests was automatic and increasingly the house had been in constant use by everyone. When the daughter got stroppy and raised the question of payment, he'd given her so little attention before that it was as if a worm had suddenly bitten his ankle and he hadn't hesitated to stamp immediately on this presumptuous behaviour.

But her being difficult had prompted the idea which he was hoping would impress his Board. He had little doubt the Scottish Government would be delighted to put the woods under a protection order as a Site of Special Scientific Interest, and at that point the house – pretty much a wreck already – would become virtually unsaleable. In his estimation, making a suitably modest offer to the young Forsyths before they were in a position to put it on the market, accompanied by a warning about the devastating effect of the SSSI order on the value of their property, could deliver a field station that, given the unique qualities of this particular site, would be a magnet for the top minds in an increasingly important discipline. All it would need apart from renovation would be a couple of proper labs and basic accommodation for a few students, as well as accommodation more suited to his entertainment of influential foreign academics, the sort of hospitality that would bring him international invitations to lecture, though he didn't plan to mention that part at this stage. The word 'world-leading' must certainly feature.

Andersen was still ranting on, as if all that mattered was his own convenience. He really was a bit of a diva and right at this moment Erskine wasn't inclined to indulge him.

'Tell the bloody woman I'll come out tomorrow to speak to her. No, I can't come today. You'll just have to cope.'

He felt like ranting on himself. He didn't need this, and what rankled was that she'd actually got one over on him when he thought he'd seen her off. He'd have to agree to some sort of payment after all; he could beat her down, of course, but if he wanted to buy the property later he'd better keep it civilised. He'd have found money in the budget to contest any case she brought about access, so meantime he could offer what should be enough not to upset the status quo.

The phone on his desk buzzed. 'That's them asking for you now,' the receptionist said.

'Thanks.' He closed his laptop, got up and took a deep breath. There was a lot riding on this one.

Lord McCrae looked round the boardroom table, saying tentatively as the door shut behind Michael Erskine, 'Well, what did you make of that?'

He didn't know the first thing about science. When he'd told his wife he'd been asked to be chairman, she'd said '*You?*' in a frankly hurtful way, then laughed. 'Oh, they all do love a lord, don't they!' He'd pointed out stiffly that he'd chaired several quangos with some success – largely because he never went against the view of the most forceful person there.

Today that was undeniably Emeritus Professor Bernard Crichton, who had been nodding quite a lot as Dr Erskine talked. 'Very able man,' he said now. 'And there's no doubt about it – what we're discovering about the saprophytic fungi's role in the nourishment of trees is an area of research that is growing exponentially. I was also most interested in what he was saying about the unusual character of these woods. Of course, much has been done already on the extent to which trees form social networks that cooperate on threats and necessary support through the fungal network. But this would be, as the director pointed out, a unique opportunity to study such evidence as there may be of interaction between the historic non-native and exotic trees and the native woodland species also to be found in Drumdalloch Woods.'

This seemed to gain general agreement, and with rather more confidence Lord McCrae said, 'Indeed! Very impressive, I thought,' as Annette Davidson – a headmistress whom he was reprehensibly inclined to think of as the token woman – made supportive noises.

'It's not my field, of course,' she said, 'but I could see that as well as the undoubted educational benefits, this could, as Dr Erskine said, have very promising commercial applications. Given our earlier discussions, we must consider ways to improve our finances, even if it involves increased investment.'

The proposal was enthusiastically discussed. The

accountant was ready with cold water to pour and pitfalls to point out, but the feeling of the meeting was strongly in favour of taking the proposal further. The mood, which had been gloomy after the budget report, was now at least cautiously optimistic.

Lord McCrae said cheerfully, 'Then that's splendid. I'll leave it in your hands, Professor, to liaise with the finance committee and report back next week, since time may well be of the essence, with a view to commissioning a feasibility study. Everyone agreed? All right. Thank you very much.'

'It was a very successful meeting,' he said a little defensively to his wife later, 'with an excellent presentation from the director and then the Board coming together. That's what a good chairman can do, you see.'

'I'm sure it is,' Lady McCrae said heartily, but he still suspected there was something faintly cynical about her smile.

Perry Forsyth put another pile of shirts into the suitcase and forced the lid shut – though God knew when he was going to need a formal shirt again. They weren't exactly *de rigueur* in the backwoods of Moray.

He'd always rented fully furnished, so there was just the suitcase and a few boxes to put in the boot of the car. The only problem was that he hadn't actually yet told his son what was going to happen today.

He'd informed the school the previous evening. Perry didn't care that the Head's expressions of regret at the news seemed less than heartfelt, but the man's firm refusal to agree an immediate rebate had been very annoying indeed, since it was hard to see how money could be dislodged from the school's bank account without legal fees he couldn't afford.

He'd been braced for trouble from James, but when the boy had collected his stuff and come out to the car, he'd only looked at his father with cold eyes, saying nothing as Perry explained that 'the arrangement' with Forsyth Property had come to a close.

He gave a short laugh. 'Sacked you, did they?' was all he said, and then, after Perry had tried unsuccessfully to put a more favourable gloss on it, 'So we're broke, are we?'

Brat, Perry thought. 'Not exactly, no. We'll have to draw our horns in for a bit till the government decides to pull its finger out and give us access to what's ours. And of course there's the house, too.'

'Thought that belonged to Aunt Oriole. Turfed me out pretty quickly when she decided she'd had enough of me.'

'You could ask yourself whose fault that was. But no, it's not her house, we share it. There's a lot needs sorting out so it won't be in quite such bad repair when it comes to selling it.'

The boy had turned his head sharply. 'You're going to sell it? Just like that? Grandad said you couldn't, that it was to be handed on like it is . . .'

Perry ground his teeth. That could have been the boy's mother talking – not that he'd ever believed she'd meant what she said. 'Grandad was running the place into the ground. He was spending the money he'd inherited in a reckless way and if it had gone on like that there'd be nothing left.'

His son's silence was so icy that Perry could almost feel

the draught on his skin. Then James said, in a low voice, 'So did you kill him as well, before that could happen?'

Perry had erupted. 'Don't be ridiculous! The sheer impertinence of that is breath-taking. What do you think you mean – kill him as well? Are you actually daring to suggest that I had something to do with your mother's accident?'

'Not her *accident*, no.'

He'd muttered that so that Perry couldn't be sure that he'd actually stressed the word and he wasn't ready for a slanging match. After letting his own chilly silence develop, he said, 'We'll have a talk tomorrow about what's to happen now. It's late, so I'll order pizza and then you can just get straight to bed.'

James didn't reply. They had driven in silence all the way back to the flat and it had been only as they went inside that he'd looked round and said, 'Where's Claudia? Gone, has she?'

Was there to be no end to his humiliation? Perry said stiffly, 'We decided it wasn't working out.'

The sneer on his son's face as he'd said, 'I figured that's what she'd do,' had made Perry's palm itch and it was lucky the boy had gone straight to his own room.

Perry's movements the following morning didn't seem to have wakened him. It was nine o'clock; he couldn't leave it much later to explain they were leaving now. Vaguely feeling the discussion might go better over a bacon butty he put rashers in the pan and went to get him up.

'Time to wake up, James,' he said heartily, then realised that the boy wasn't asleep, just lying on his back staring at the ceiling.

He turned his head and looking darkly at his father he said, 'Jay, not James. OK?'

Perry swallowed hard. Was this how it would be every morning – his authority constantly challenged? The stand-up confrontation would have to come, but he was focusing on the midday deadline for leaving the flat. He left the room, in token defiance saying over his shoulder, 'We'll see about that. Anyway, there's a bacon butty ready when you are.'

The bacon was clearly more acceptable than what Perry was telling him now. Glaring, James/Jay said, 'You mean you're taking me to Drumdalloch today? To stay? Away from my mates here?'

'No time like the present,' Perry said. 'You'll be going to school there. You're at an age where you can't afford to get behind.'

For the first time the boy showed signs of animation. 'What if I don't want to go there? They hate me, you know.'

'Again, it would do you good to ask yourself whose fault that was. In any case, it's not the same school, it would be the senior school in Fortrose. You can make new mates and try for a better reputation.'

'You think?' he said.

'Oh, for goodness' sake!' Perry snapped. 'Just finish your breakfast and get your things packed up. I want to get up there and settled in before it's dark.'

And hopefully, while Oriole might still be out at work. He wanted to move into his father's spacious bedroom without an argument about its sacrosanct nature; that would establish that there was a master in the house again, even if she'd find it hard to accept having had the place to herself for so long.

There'd have to be changes, big changes. He'd spent his time doing some fairly desperate thinking about his future, before the idea came to him as something he'd read somewhere and the talks he'd had with his father walking in the woods came together in a blinding flash. The preliminary research was promising and could even be way better than promising. He wasn't as reluctant as he had been to go back to Drumdalloch House.

CHAPTER FOUR

'He was round the pub with her last night, Sandy said. Cradle-snatching, according to him – bit of a looker, leggy blonde type,' Angie Andrews said from her perch on the edge of a table in the CID room.

'Never!' said DC Mairi Brown. 'Wouldn't have thought he was that kind.'

Not one to miss out on the gossip, DS Livvy Murray emerged from her favourite seat in the corner behind a filing cabinet. 'Who are you talking about, then?'

'Himself – the DCI,' Andrews said. 'Sandy thinks she's maybe a lawyer – reckoned he'd seen her around the courts somewhere.'

'Had to happen sometime, I suppose,' Murray said, managing somehow to sound nonchalant despite feeling that her stomach was descending in a broken lift plummeting to the ground. 'Hope they'll be very happy, then. And I've got desk work to do, if you idle lot haven't.' She retreated to the corner, to her safe space, as wounded animals do.

Andrews and Brown mocked her, but since there were no more dainty titbits on offer it wasn't long before they drifted away.

'*It had to happen sometime*,' she'd said. She'd known that all along, of course, and Livvy had known, too, the sort of woman the lucky one was likely to be, so there was no reason why this should have come as a shock.

Leggy and blonde . . . Well, she'd done blonde herself once but it hadn't suited her and the only thing she could say for her legs was that they kept her off the ground. And of course she'd never thought for a moment that Kelso Strang would think of her except as a colleague – not really. But lurking somewhere at the back of her mind had been the treacherous phrase, 'You never know.'

And their professional relationship had got closer latterly, since she'd stopped her naive attempts at impressing him with maverick ideas, and police officers often did end up together, because only other officers got it about the job. Kelso wouldn't be happy with some dumb blonde kid.

If she was a lawyer, she wouldn't be dumb, though. She'd have a degree, and if she worked around the courts, she'd understand his job well enough.

Then, of course, it clicked. That time she'd been at Kelso's house during the last investigation – the first time, and likely the last too – he'd taken a phone call from someone called Cat.

Livvy had known who that was: a trainee advocate, devil to the notorious Vincent Dunbar, KC. And it had been a good while ago now, so if she was still around this wasn't a passing fancy.

It was starting to rain and she stared at the drops trickling down the glass as she had done so often before, trying to sort out her life. What she'd heard this morning hadn't changed anything, she told herself firmly. She had the same job, the same prospects, the same chance of being included in the next Serious Rural Crime Squad investigation with all its challenges and rewards.

But she couldn't deny she was hurting. 'You never know,' could have no place in her thinking any more, because she knew now.

Oriole Forsyth was having to work longer today because Senga had called in sick. There wasn't anything wrong with Senga's health; she just took an extra little holiday when she felt like it and poor Steve couldn't call her out because he was short of staff and she could just leave and go on benefits – no doubt making up any difference with a bit of moonlighting somewhere.

She'd been pleased to have a reason not to be at home. Lars had appeared the previous afternoon, not to move his Jeep but to carry on arguing about her decision. She had held firm; even if she wasn't sure she could make that stick, she could certainly see to it that he couldn't commandeer her kitchen any more.

He'd announced Michael Erskine would be coming to sort it out the following day, with the air of one who knew this would put a stop to her nonsense. Perhaps it had been naughty not to tell him she wouldn't be there, but she was tired of being someone who didn't matter. If Michael chose to turn up without consulting her, he'd find the house securely locked.

The Kilbain Hotel was on the outskirts of the village and Oriole drove into the high street and parked outside the Co-op, going through her mental list: milk, bread, eggs, pasta, tea, biscuits for the Friends. There wasn't a lot she needed now she lived on her own, but they sometimes had a delivery of fish caught locally and she could fancy a mackerel for her supper.

It was a good night of telly as well; *QI* was on and she was looking forward to her evening as she shopped. It would take her mind off the showdown with Michael Erskine that was bound to come, tomorrow if not today.

Oriole was taking milk from the chiller shelf when she heard her name spoken and turned. Keith Drummond, all six foot two and fourteen stones of him, was standing behind her and fractionally too close.

'Haven't see you for a while,' he said. 'All right, then?'

She smiled weakly. 'Yes, I'm good.' She hadn't missed him – the detective in charge when Helena had died, who'd seemed to take a pleasure in his power to intimidate. She couldn't forget how hard he'd been on poor Giles, who had felt he was under some sort of suspicion, just as she had herself, though to be fair in the end Drummond had dealt with it all extremely efficiently and they had been spared any sort of protracted police enquiry. Seeing him was still a sharp reminder of those days of distress.

'What's Perry doing these days? Don't see him round much.'

'Oh, the usual. Still in Edinburgh.' She put the milk in her basket, manoeuvring it between them so he had to take a step back. 'Well . . .'

'And the boy? Getting on all right, is he?'

She could feel herself going pink with embarrassment; she hadn't enjoyed the visits caused by the various problems with Jay, which Drummond always described as 'just a word from a friend of the family'. He might be a friend of Perry's; he certainly wasn't one of hers.

'Yes, I think so. He's away at school so I haven't seen him recently.'

Drummond nodded. 'And I hear you're the only thing that's keeping my pal Steve's hotel going. He was just saying to me the other day that he didn't know what he'd do without you.'

She coloured up again, with pleasure this time. 'Oh – I don't know. It's just these girls are so unreliable, I'm happy to help out. But I must get going.'

''Course. Good to see you, anyway.'

He was still in her way, though, and it was a moment before he stepped aside. She couldn't think why he should want to suggest she needed his consent to leave; perhaps it was just a work habit he'd developed.

As Oriole went back to her car, she was annoyed to realise the encounter had made her forget to get the fish, It wasn't worth going back and running into Drummond again. She'd eggs for an omelette, and if she felt like pasta there'd be onions in the fridge and a tin of tomatoes in the cupboard for a sauce.

It was nearly dusk now and she was hoping that Lars and Michael Erskine would both have given up and gone; certainly there was no sign of them in the parking area. Just beside the house, though, there was Perry's Audi.

It was ages since he'd visited and she was surprised he hadn't said he'd be coming. She was also surprised to see lights not only downstairs but in her new Airbnb flat – surprised, and then worried.

He'd obviously discovered the key to let him into it. It would be late for him to drive back and she just hoped he didn't think he was going to sleep there tonight; if he did, she'd have to change the sheets, which was a real nuisance, and she didn't trust him not to drop something on the new carpets and spoil the look of the place.

Oriole grabbed her shopping bag and jumped out in a hurry, to disabuse him. There was nothing wrong with the room he'd shared with Helena, apart from the bathroom being down a long corridor, and he could sleep there, like he always had. He should be used to the rust stains on the bath and the primitive plumbing by now.

When she opened the front door, she stopped and stared in dismay. The hall was littered with boxes and there was a sports bag half-open, disclosing dirty kit that could only belong to her nephew. This wasn't what you brought for an overnight stay.

There was dismay in her voice as she shouted, 'Perry! Perry!'

Michael Erskine had set off from Inverness in the early afternoon in a thoroughly bad mood. He'd waited for the call he'd been expecting from Professor Crichton; it had told him the finance committee were enthusiastic and a working group to discuss commissioning a feasibility study had been set up. It was exciting news, but the situation at Drumdalloch meant he couldn't get on with that at once – quite incredibly annoying.

Andersen would be there today, clearly expecting him

to put Oriole Forsyth back in her box and stop her wasting his – Andersen's – precious time. There was more heavy rain forecast and he would need somewhere to work until the system had passed through to let him complete his observations.

Erskine had realised he must do better with Oriole. Perhaps she was merely farouche, but she'd shown signs of being stubborn for the sake of it and for the success of his precious project he must smooth things over until it was time to talk about the house sale. She couldn't expect much for parking and access they'd always previously had, but he decided to up the offer he'd first thought of, so she'd be pleased and grateful when it came to the more crucial negotiation.

Reaching Drumdalloch House he was well prepared. The minibus used by the ornithology students was parked by the side of the road; she must have told them the new restrictions. Andersen's Jeep, though, was parked in its usual place, defying Oriole, which wasn't helpful just when he needed her goodwill.

Her car should have been in the paved area in front of the house, but it wasn't. Where was she, then? Andersen had told her he'd be coming; had she deliberately decided to be out so he had to hang about waiting for her?

Muttering, he parked, then went to the front door, more in hope than expectation. For form's sake he knocked, then tried the handle – the house was never locked. Except that today it was.

He could drive straight back to Inverness, to show he wasn't going to be jerked around. It would mean another visit, though, and she could come back any time. Andersen or the students might know, so with a bad grace he took the path into the woods.

Erskine wasn't really familiar with the layout. Trees were not his own subject, and he only came to observe progress in the field studies and someone would escort him to the sites. He quite shortly came across a couple of the students beside a large oak with a nesting platform built on it. One student had climbed the trunk far enough to peer in.

'Signs of activity, nesting box 14. Nothing at 15,' he called down to the girl, then jumped down as she made a note.

'There's a pair of great tits fussing around watching us from that tree – looks promising,' she was saying as Erskine reached them.

'Afternoon!' he said. 'How's it going?'

'Oh – Dr Erskine!' she said. 'I didn't know you were coming or we'd have been looking out for you.'

Her companion was making apologetic noises too and Erskine was quick to reassure them that he wasn't on an inspection today. They didn't, though, know anything about Oriole.

'We haven't seen her today. Yesterday she came to say we were not allowed to use the house any more – she was a bit huffy,' the girl said. 'Don't know what it was all about.'

'Probably annoyed about the mess in the kitchen,' the youth volunteered. 'But she's never gone on like that before.'

'Do you know where Lars is working?' Erskine asked.

'I think he was right down at the far edge of the woods

where the exotics are mainly. Do you want me to take you?'

'No, no, I know where you mean.'

The paths Erskine followed were muddy but passable, though the signs of the recent storm were still evident. Andersen wasn't where he'd expected to find him but he heard his name being called and he saw him coming from a small group of larch saplings.

Never one to waste time on pleasantries, Andersen launched straight in. 'This is important stuff, right here,' he said. 'Too early to say, but you know my theory—'

Erskine did indeed know Andersen's theory and didn't fancy hearing it again. 'Yes,' he said flatly. 'Oriole isn't at the house. Do you know where she is?'

Andersen frowned. 'She should be. I told her you were coming.'

'Yes, but she isn't.'

'How would I know? Haven't been near the house all day.'

Exasperated, Erskine burst out, 'This is quite ridiculous! I shouldn't have to come here at all let alone be forced to play games with this stupid woman, particularly at the moment. It's under wraps, but we're on the verge of a very dynamic development – looking at establishing a field centre here for dendrology, with labs on the spot and accommodation for overseas researchers, and having the site designated a Site of Special Scientific Interest. So there's a lot of spadework I should be doing right now.'

He knew he shouldn't have mentioned it, but it was all he could think about at the moment and the temptation to boast was strong. What he certainly hadn't expected was Andersen's reaction.

'What!' The man's face darkened. 'A field centre? You cannot do that – bring in outsiders who base their studies on the back of my research – my unique, groundbreaking research – and at every stage dilute its impact! Impeding me, infesting my woods—'

He was shouting now. Stunned, Erskine had taken a moment to understand what he was on about but at 'my woods', he interrupted. 'They're not *your* woods,' he said icily. 'They're not even our woods, unfortunately, but any decisions about them will be the business of the board. And you should perhaps realise your personal academic success is not a priority for them – or indeed for me. Now, go and move your damn Jeep. There's no point in making things worse.'

He turned and walked off, hearing Andersen cursing and a thud that sounded as if he'd thrown something in a temper. This was another unnecessary complication, and when he'd said Andersen's work was not a priority for him it wasn't even slightly true; it was his golden ticket, the whole basis of his pitch for the field centre that would make his name in the wider academic world.

So he'd have to smooth things over, but he was too furious to be prepared to do it at the moment. If Oriole hadn't appeared, he was going to go back to Inverness and phone to arrange a meeting – perhaps even persuade her to back off until it could be sorted out.

When he reached the end of the path, though, he could see there was a car parked by the house – not Oriole's humble Kia, though. This was an Audi, but whoever owned it might well know where she was.

Erskine went to knock on the door. It was opened

by a short, stocky man who looked at him silently for a moment, as if resenting the interruption.

'I was actually looking for Oriole,' he said. 'I'm Dr Erskine.'

'Ah, the backwoodsman!' he said. 'I'm Perry Forsyth.'

That had been meant as a put-down, hadn't it? Erskine didn't like it, but hoping he might prove easier to deal with than his sister he said only, 'Well, I suppose you could say that. I'd forgotten that Oriole had a brother.'

He smiled. 'Oh, indeed she does. Why don't you come in? I'm afraid it's all in a bit of a muddle. I'm just moving in.'

Perry had just laid his shirts on the shelved side of the wardrobe in the larger bedroom of the flat when he'd heard Oriole calling from downstairs. She didn't sound altogether overjoyed.

She pounced before he had even reached the bottom of the stairs. 'You didn't warn me to expect you! And what are you doing in the flat? Where did you get the key?'

'Not, "Oh welcome, dear brother, such a pleasure to see you!"?' he mocked. 'I didn't know I needed to *warn* you, as you so charmingly put it, that I was returning to my own home. And the key to the flat, since you ask, was neatly labelled and hanging from a hook beside the Aga. Nice job you've done, I have to say – almost like civilised living. Not what we're used to at all.'

Oriole had always coloured up when stressed and her face was starting to flare up now. 'You can't sleep there, Perry. I've a family booked in for next week.'

'Good gracious, you are getting het up! You should

see your face – you could give a beetroot a run for its money. Well, you'll just have to cancel them – unforeseen circumstances, you could say with perfect truth.'

She had turned even redder at his words. 'That's my income, apart from what I get from Steve, and it's barely enough to live on, with the loan interest piling up. So you can't use it, but you can sleep in Dad's room, if you want. And I gather,' she said with a glance at the sports bag, 'that Jay's with you.'

'His name's James,' he snapped. 'Why are you calling him Jay?'

'Because he doesn't reply if I don't.' She took a deep breath. 'Look, why don't you come through to the kitchen and tell me what all this is about. I need a cup of tea – I encountered Keith Drummond in the Co-op.' She gave a little shudder.

'Keith? Nothing wrong with Keith. He's a good mate.' He sat down as she dumped her shopping on the table and went to make tea, then rummaged through the bag until he found the biscuits she had bought and opened the packet.

Oriole sighed. 'There's some already in the tin,' she said. 'You'd better use those up first.'

'Oh, you won't have to worry about using them up. I'm surprised James didn't come through at the first rustle of the packet.'

The kettle was boiling but she ignored it. 'What's happened? Have you lost your job?'

Perry hesitated, then swallowing his pride said, 'Bluntly, yes. Edward's an incompetent arse and having to shed staff because he's running the company into the ground. I was picked on because I told him long ago where he was going wrong. I can tell you that now I've gone it'll sink like a stone. Kettle's boiling, Oriole.'

'Oh . . .' She moved to push it off the plate but didn't start making tea, just stood looking stricken. 'Perry, I told you, I'm on the breadline. You can't come here and expect me to support you. And your son.'

'Never liked him, did you? You could have made allowances for a child that lost his mother in tragic circumstances.'

'That's not fair!' she cried. 'Of course I did, constantly! I loved him, you know, right from when he was tiny, and I tried my level best while you swanned off to Edinburgh. I hope he's more civilised now, because he must have grown and I was frankly afraid of him then. Is he going to the local school?'

'There's no money for fees so he'll have to, won't he? I guess there's a school bus to take him – or there's a bike in the garage.'

'That's in your hands,' she said coldly. 'But can we talk about money? And can you move your things out of the flat now, please?'

'Well, I'm all for talking things over. I'm not completely penniless at the moment, in fact, and I've a plan that will have us sitting pretty once we get probate. Trust me!'

Oriole seemed unreceptive. 'Why? You've never given me any reason to. And "once we get probate"? Could be months and months. I have to live meantime, and I've been paying for all the upkeep you've never contributed to.'

'Ah!' Perry said. 'I've got some good news for you. Michael Erskine appeared, looking for you this afternoon. I gather he's not taken with your idea about payment for services received. He was actually quite cross when I told him that the amount he offered was derisory.

'He also seemed to think he could render the property worthless by getting a protection order for the woods and that when we could sell, his Institute would buy us out for another derisory offer. I disabused him and something tells me I'm not his favourite person, but you'll be amazed what I managed to screw out of him.'

Oriole's eyes widened when he told her. 'How did you manage that? It'll certainly help. But Perry, I still need the money from the flat.'

'I was generous enough before to let you treat the property as your own, but I can't afford to go on like that now. But I hear what you're saying – how about I rent it from you instead? Of course, I wouldn't expect to pay what you'd get from a stranger – I'd be entitled to half of it in any case – but it'll cover the utilities and I'll pitch in with the food bills. Jay's a growing lad!'

He laughed. She didn't. He recognised the drooping, helpless look on her face; she'd never managed to stand up to him and he intended to keep it that way. But over the next bit, it was going to be useful to have her on side, so he changed his tone.

'Look, sis, I promise you it'll be all right. I had a word with Muriel Morris a couple of days ago and it looks as if things are moving at last and we may get probate any day now. Then our troubles will be over.

'And, speaking of the growing lad, what's in the house for supper?'

* * *

Michael Erskine was in a towering rage as he drove back to Inverness. The man had been positively insolent and earlier Andersen had been impertinent too – a shock when you'd become used to the sort of respectful attention the Director of the Scottish Institute for Studies in Biological Science was naturally accorded.

Andersen was an irritation rather than a problem; there were a thousand ways Erskine could make things difficult for him, and he was intelligent enough to realise that once he calmed down. The man was neurotically aware of the pressure on being the first to publish when it came to cutting-edge research and he couldn't afford to waste time on arguments with the Institution.

Perry Forsyth was a different matter. He'd had the upper hand in their exchange because he could bring the whole field centre plan crashing to the ground if he refused to see sense and agree the sale when the time came. Erskine had been forced into offering twice the amount – the revised amount – he'd been confident that Oriole would settle for to use the facilities, and even after that there had been no indication that the Forsyths would look favourably on the Institute's offer. Indeed, when he'd explained that once the woods were protected they'd find it hard to sell at all, Forsyth had actually laughed in his face.

'Could take years, couldn't it, with the speed civil servants move at.'

It had taken Erskine all his time to control himself when what he most wanted to do was smash his fist into the man's sneer. His hands tightened on the steering wheel thinking about it now. But beneath his anger, there was fear. That little bastard had the power to wreck the precious, beautiful plan that had been coming together in exactly the way he had hoped it would.

Jay had been unimpressed with the pasta, and frankly disbelieving that there was no pizza delivery on hand. He retired to the sitting room with a handful of biscuits and commandeered the TV to watch a film about vampires.

Perry got up from the table and announced that he was going off to catch up with Steve at the hotel.

And Oriole went up to her own room and wept angry, helpless tears.

CHAPTER FIVE

There were several people in what Steve Christie liked to call the Kilbain Hotel Cocktail Lounge but Tricia had deigned to turn up tonight so he could sit in the corner of the bar, in earnest conversation with Keith Drummond.

When Perry Forsyth came in, he muttered, 'Ah! Thought it wouldn't be long before he appeared,' then got to his feet and went over to slap him on the back. 'Return of the prodigal! This one's on the house. Scotch, is it?'

'Make it a double, then, Tricia,' Perry said to the waitress with a wink. 'Hi, Keith – how's business these days? Pocketed any good bribes lately?'

'More or less have to, don't you? It's not crime that doesn't pay – it's law enforcement. But it's good to get the three of us back together again,' Keith said heartily. 'Let the good times roll, eh?'

'Come on over to the window seat where we can talk properly,' Steve said, picking up his own drink and indicating to Tricia to bring Perry's across. 'So – how are things back at the family mansion?'

He was ready with the reassuring 'We've got your back, mate' speech that he'd reckoned Perry would be needing, but he was looking a lot more chipper than expected, actually sounding quite cocky as he said, 'Better than I feared. Much better. I've strong-armed Oriole into letting us use the Airbnb – it's quite a novelty having a bathroom that isn't a health hazard. Makes it pretty much bearable to put in the time to get the place into shape.'

Steve felt a pang of pity for Oriole. The flat was her baby: the idea was all her own work and the business – small, admittedly, but successful – was her one personal achievement. Perry really was a total sod; she should have told him to shove it, but she'd never had the guts.

'Certainly needs it,' Keith said. 'Last time I looked the whole place was a health hazard. Can't think where you'll start – demolition, probably. Any word of when you'll get the nod from HMRC? Idle bastards, doing WFH in Tenerife, most of them.'

'You can say that again. But it's looking as if things are moving now.'

Steve caught Keith's eye. 'That's good news. We need to have a proper meeting about where we go from here. We've been working on it – I think you'll be excited when you see our ideas.'

'Really?' Perry said, taking another sip of his drink. 'Interested to hear about it, of course.'

But there was something off about that response. Keith's eyes had narrowed; he must have sensed it too. Perry had been despairing when last he'd spoken to Steve, and surely ready to grasp at the lifeline that was being thrown to him.

What had happened? Perry was an arrogant beggar, of course, quite capable of fancying himself as a brilliant entrepreneur, but Steve knew enough from Oriole to be sure there was little coming to them beyond the value of the property – which given its problems was bound to be low – and he knew enough about Perry to be sure that left to himself he'd screw up. If he wanted to capitalise on the inheritance, he'd need their backing.

While Steve hesitated, Keith said bluntly, 'Got ideas of your own, then?'

Perry grinned. 'Oh, I've always got ideas. Not fully formulated yet, but I think I can see the way forward.'

'Care to share it?' Steve said.

Keith leant forward. 'We're in this together, right?'

Steve glanced at him uneasily. His own professional instinct was always to defuse aggression; taking people on was seldom constructive.

But the cocky grin faltered. 'Yes – yes, of course. Didn't mean – it's just I need a bit more research to get my ducks in a row. Then, of course, we'll work it out together. Like we said.'

'Good,' Keith said, sitting back. 'When do you think you'll be ready to talk it through?'

'Oh, can't put a precise date on it, of course. But I won't be dragging my feet.'

'I'm sure,' Steve said hastily. 'Look, I've got to do a round of the dining room. See you later on, if you're still here.'

Keith finished his drink and got up. 'I'll just get back. I'm on an early shift in Inverness tomorrow.'

Perry looked uncertain, then followed suit. 'I've had a

busy day. See you around.' He went out as Steve gathered up the glasses.

Keith hovered. 'What's that about, then? I don't like it. He's up to something.'

'Oh, for God's sake, lay off. He's touchy, and the sort of pig-stupid that could mean he digs his trotters in and makes everything more difficult. He's got something we want, remember.'

Keith scowled. 'And the other way round. Let's not forget that either, OK? And how would we explain it to the other lads this time if someone else rats on us? They're getting very twitchy – we all are.'

As Keith went out, Steve groaned inwardly. Perhaps he'd been too optimistic about the effect of Perry being unemployed. There could be storms ahead.

Oriole got up feeling headachy and depressed. She was on an afternoon shift today, which meant spending a morning avoiding her brother and her nephew. There was at least something to be gained by letting them use the flat; it gave them their own space and it might even let Perry build the sort of relationship the poor child needed, create some sort of home comforts. It wouldn't happen if she let herself be appointed unpaid cook-housekeeper and she'd spelt that out – though she suspected that if there was anything in her fridge or cupboards that Jay fancied, he'd just take it anyway.

He didn't seem to have improved. He'd barely spoken to her, apart from complaining about the food, but he'd glared a lot. He'd grown, too. She was 5'3" and he was not much shorter, and solidly built like his father. She could see how unhappy he was – miserable, in fact. There were marked shadows under the dark blue eyes – Helena's eyes – and she felt heart-sorry for him, but she couldn't see what to do about it if he wouldn't engage.

Perhaps things would improve once he got settled in at school, made some friends, even. Perry said he'd arrange it, so with any luck that might take them all morning, and then she'd be going out to the hotel.

It wasn't helping that it was such a gloomy day. The weather seemed to be determined on sullenness, with heavy purple-grey skies and mist that hung in the tops of the trees. Enough to depress anyone – but at least this morning when she checked the nest there was a thrush brooding there, plumply settled.

She'd laid the eggs, then. Oriole smiled and her mood lifted; there would be scrawny little babies she could watch getting fatter by the day as the exhausted parents wore themselves out at the never-ending job of filling those great gaping yellow beaks. No matter what happened, nature would always be there to offer these moments of uncomplicated delight.

There was no sign of Perry or Jay; perhaps they'd gone already. As the kettle boiled for coffee, she went to fetch bread for toast but there was none left in the bread bin. She'd given them most of the loaf to take upstairs last night but presumably that hadn't been enough for the 'growing lad'.

She made do with yoghurt and honey, then settled down to plan her morning. She was worried about explaining to the agency boss about the problem with the Airbnb, but at least it would be a chance to see Nicki and tell her about the thrushes – and about the cuckoo in her own nest gobbling up her breakfast and all the biscuits!

She began making a shopping list, hoping Perry would get their supplies while he was in Fortrose. She certainly couldn't afford to keep them.

It was as Oriole was finishing her coffee that she became aware of a series of intermittent thuds coming from outside. She was puzzled: with Perry and Jay out at the school, it could only be something one of the students was doing, but it seemed odd. She went out to look.

Just as she stepped out, a stone whizzed past her and she ducked as it bounced off the wall, only just missing a window. As she turned, another one hit further along: Jay was standing there, with a few stones lying at his feet.

'What the hell do you think you're doing?' she shouted.

He looked at her as if he couldn't think why she should be making a fuss, then shrugged. 'Oh – bowling practice, you could say. Cricket, you know?' He said it as if he didn't care whether she believed it or not.

She didn't. It was blatantly no such thing; the body language as he threw had screamed anger and frustration. She walked over to him. 'Stop! For heaven's sake, Jay, that last one only just missed the sitting-room window.'

He laughed. 'I was working up to that.'

'If you really want to practise I'm sure you could find a ball in the house and there's plenty of lawn space in the garden.' She knew that sounded feeble, but she went on, 'Anyway, I thought your father was taking you into the school this morning.'

'So did I. But he wasn't around when I got up.'

Oriole frowned. Where could he be? Now she looked,

Perry's car was still parked in front of the house; how like him, to forget his date with Jay! No wonder the boy was having problems.

'He must be in the woods,' she said. 'Why don't we go and look for him and find out when he's planning to go? And you have to stop that, right now.'

Jay shrugged again, then shied one last stone at the house. Oriole looked back in time to see it hit just below her bedroom window, right into the honeysuckle. A thrush flew out in panic, the nest teetered and then fell. Tipped out, four pale blue eggs with brown freckles smashed on the ground while the distressed bird flew around frantically, screaming alarm calls.

There was a moment's silence, then Oriole burst into tears. Jay stood biting his lip, then turned and ran off.

There was nothing to be done, except tidy up the pitiful debris. Oriole wiped her eyes and did that, seething with fury, though not at the child's casual vandalism; it was pretty obvious why Jay was doing it and she felt for him. She could write the book when it came to anger and helplessness.

She needed to find Perry while she was high on pure rage. He must be in the woods, though she wasn't sure where to start looking for him. There were no students around today, but Lars's Jeep was outside and since she knew where he usually worked she headed there; he might at least have seen Perry.

He had indeed. Oriole hadn't gone far before she heard the voices echoing through the trees: Lars's deep, Perry's lighter, but both were shouting and it was getting louder and louder.

Oriole hesitated, then stopped. She didn't want to butt in on their barney; it wouldn't achieve anything. She could feel the adrenalin draining away and she turned slowly and retreated. Once Perry came back, she'd have her own barney with him – only she knew that somehow it wouldn't work out quite like that.

Lachie MacIver had returned to the bothy, ready for a tea and a smoke. He'd walked into Kilbain as he did on most dreich days; life had always just been what happened to him, without his ever getting fully engaged. As he got older and couldn't do his long foraging walks in all weathers, time could hang heavy and the latest craic in the village shop gave him something to think about.

This morning it had all been about Perry Forsyth coming back. He'd been in the hotel bar with Christie and the policeman; 'thick as thieves', Tricia's mum had said, adding darkly that she wouldn't trust any of them as far as she could throw them. Since her favourite expression was 'There's no flies on me', this wasn't surprising, but even so, Lachie was inclined to think she had something there.

Tricia had taken to not turning up until she'd been paid for the previous shift, and everyone knew how long Christie was taking to settle invoices. Drummond lived in the village but there was no official police presence on the Black Isle at all now, and he worked in Inverness. They'd dealt with that Helena Forsyth's accident; he'd fairly thrown his weight about and he'd a reputation for scaring the living daylights out of anyone crossing him. Then there was Perry – and Lachie had his own thoughts about him as well.

There was trouble brewing over the Drumdalloch Woods too. The students that came in to buy their dinnertime piece had been full of the rows going on: not really knowing the personnel, Lachie couldn't work out who was having them or what they were about, but as a seasoned observer he reckoned it'd build up to a real stramash before long.

So he'd plenty to think about as he spread the tobacco sparingly along the cigarette paper, rolled it up and licked it. Once upon a time he'd have had a wee bit of the wacky stuff in with it, but though it helped the rheumatics he couldn't afford it now. Anyway, the last time it had been new stronger stuff and he didn't need to be seeing monsters in the shadows of the bothy. The lurking problems of old age were bad enough.

As he lit it and took the first puff, there was a tap on the door. He'd never exactly been one for encouraging neighbours to drop round, so after what he'd heard this morning, it wasn't hard to work out who it might be.

'Come away ben,' he called, and Jay Forsyth's tousled fair head appeared round the door. The boy had grown; he couldn't be more than twelve or thirteen but looked older than that, with lines of strain marked on his face and smears on his cheeks as if he could have been crying.

'Back home, then?' Lachie said.

Jay gave a short, harsh laugh. 'That's funny, really – "home". I don't have a home now, you see. I have to live with my father and my aunt and both of them wish I wasn't there. Maybe I'll just make a shack in the woods and live there instead.'

Lachie felt acutely uncomfortable. He wasn't used

to soul-baring; he could count the number of personal conversations he'd ever had in his life on one hand since his mother died – and she hadn't been a great one for those either. He cleared his throat.

'You'd not be very comfortable – it's gey cold at night, even here in the bothy. And what would you have to eat?'

'You could show me how to catch things. Like with that deadfall trap you showed me a while ago – you know, where the animal knocks over the prop holding up a plank and gets squashed.'

'Oh aye, that,' Lachie said uncomfortably. 'You're not needing that – you couldn't cook anything beside the trees without maybe setting the whole place on fire.' It wasn't likely, given its sodden state after a very wet winter, but Jay's idea had an unpleasant kind of resonance. 'You're needing just to go off now to have a wee chat with your dad and get it sorted.'

Jay ignored that. 'Can I sit down?' he said, going over to the three-legged stool that was the only seat apart from Lachie's ancient armchair, and to his host's dismay did that without waiting for permission. He was jerky, a bit disjointed, as if the stress that showed on his face was affecting his movement too.

In the corner of the room a soft chirping – along with a powerful, musky smell – indicated the presence of the ferret in a rough cage with a bit of sacking draped over it and Jay's face brightened immediately.

'That's Jill, isn't it? Can I see her?'

Lachie wasn't sure if that was a good idea; ferrets were sensitive to atmosphere and if he could sense Jay's unease she likely would too. He'd be standing close by, though, and if she showed signs of discomfort, he could take her back quickly.

'All right,' he said, going to the cage. Jill was definitely pleased to see him; her little noises had been requests for attention and now she went into what was almost a dance of pleasure.

'She's so cute, isn't she?' Jay said, smiling. 'Do you remember me, Jill?'

It looked as if she did. She sniffed the boy's hands, then climbed on to his arm and up to his shoulder, sniffing at his neck then pausing, with her head cocked. She made a slightly harsher sound.

Lachie stiffened. Was she reacting to the scent of tension? 'Maybe you'd better give her to me for a minute or two, till she gets used to you again?' he said.

Jay's face changed. 'You don't need to. She remembered me fine,' he said, grabbing for the creature to stop him taking it away.

With a scream of anger, the ferret sunk its small, razor-edged teeth into Jay's hand. Jay echoed the scream and Lachie, his own heart beating fast, grabbed the ferret by the scruff, shaking her to make her loosen her grip, then bundled her into the cage where she paced around, hissing her displeasure.

Blood was dripping on the floor. Sobbing with pain and shock, Jay said, 'So she hates me too! I thought she was my friend.'

Lachie said, 'Och, it was just a wee misunderstanding. She got a fright and they're nippy kind of beasts. We'd better find something to mop it up, though.'

It was hardly the first time he'd had to deal with the

reaction of an irritated ferret, but he was used to it and casual about hygiene anyway. The boy ought to get proper attention, though, and going to a cupboard to fetch a clean, if threadbare, towel he said, 'Away and get your aunt to clean it properly and she'll likely have a bandage. Here – let me hap it up for you.'

Jay held out his hand, still dripping blood. It was a vicious bite, right into the fleshy pad below his thumb, but at least it wasn't through to the bone. He stopped crying but he was still shaking as Lachie clumsily swathed the towel round it. 'It'll stop in a minute. There you are – off you go, now.'

The boy said only, 'Right. Thanks,' and walked out.

Lachie looked after him with a bad feeling in the pit of his stomach. He'd always been content with his own company; other people always seemed to want something he didn't know how to give, and he hated how that made him feel. He'd been sorry for the laddie and somehow he'd got drawn into a personal relationship with him, then it had worked out just like it always did. He'd ended up feeling guilty and he doubted if Jay would ever come back.

His ciggy had burnt out and the tea was cold now. As he went to make another cup, he passed the cage where Jill was still chuntering balefully.

'All right for you, isn't it? No shame,' he said to her with a certain wistfulness.

Jo Melville the letting-agency manager had been less difficult than Oriole had feared she might be. It was still low season so there was a local replacement available and she suspected too that Nicki might have told her boss about her problems. She'd also agreed to Nicki taking her break early and they'd gone off to the café round the corner.

'No! Really?' Nicki said when she told her what had happened. 'I thought he was settled in his job in Edinburgh. You mean he's actually back to stay?' She seemed almost excited.

'So did he,' Oriole said. 'Bit of a shock, I think, but he's full of himself at the moment. But oh Nicki, the thrush . . .'

She told her what had happened, and her friend had listened with her usual patience. 'Poor you,' she said. 'That's miserable. But oh! the poor boy too – he must be in a right mess psychologically. Maybe the school will help with counselling or something.'

'That's the next problem. They were supposed to have signed him on today, but Perry basically stood Jay up. I'm furious with him – it's actively cruel. Whenever I get back I'm going to tear into him.'

'You tell him, girl!' Nicki said. 'Actually, I'd better get back to work – don't want to try the boss too far. But I could come round tonight, if you like?'

Oriole seized on that. 'My shift'll finish at six. I've a bottle of wine Steve gave me and I'll make supper. Perry will be off to the Kilbain again, no doubt, and Jay will probably be upstairs glued to his mobile, so we should have the kitchen to ourselves.'

Nicki had cheered her up, as ever, but even so she was feeling a little sick about 'tearing into' Perry, as she had so boldly claimed she would. She would try but she had to accept she'd never succeeded before.

There was no one around when she arrived back. Perry's car was there, so he wasn't taking Jay to the school, and heaven knew where he was. She'd shopped for Nicki's supper on the way back and headed straight into the kitchen with her shopping.

She stopped short on the threshold with a gasp. The checked oilcloth on the table was marked with bloody smears, a bowl full of pink-tinged water was sitting on it, a pile of bloodstained tea towels beside it.

Dear God! What on earth was going on? Then she noticed that Jay was sitting in the chair by the Aga, his face white and with another dish towel wrapped round his hand.

'Jay! Are you all right?'

'Oh, terrific,' he drawled. 'Haven't bled to death, so far.'

'I suppose it's good to be positive,' she said doubtfully. 'What have you done to yourself?' As she spoke, she knew she'd said the wrong thing even before she saw Jay bridling – stupid!

'Of course it's always my fault, isn't it?'

'Jay, I didn't mean it like that. Let me take a look at it, anyway.'

That he held it out to her meekly told her he was probably in pain and a bit frightened. He was studying her face as she exposed the wound – nasty enough, jagged and quite deep, but it had stopped bleeding.

'How did it happen?'

He didn't want to tell her. 'You could just say I fell on something?'

'Even if it wasn't true?' It looked like a bite; she could almost see toothmarks.

'Oh, what does it matter? Can you just fix it up? It hurts a lot.'

There was no point in pursuing it. She went to where she kept first aid stuff for injured workers and got out disinfectant and bandages. Though he winced when the disinfectant stung, he didn't make any sort of fuss and she could sense that he was still young enough to be grateful for adult reassurance that it wasn't that serious.

'You'll be fine. It'll just be a bit sore while it heals.' She was taping a bandage into place when Perry came in, to repeat the whole sequence.

'For goodness' sake, James, what have you done now?'

Seeing the stony look on her nephew's face, Oriole hurried to say, 'Oh, it looks worse than it is. Hands always bleed more than you'd expect. Anyway, Perry, where have you been? You said you were taking Jay to get registered at the school and he was waiting for you.'

It was hardly 'tearing into him' but even so her brother snapped, 'Oh – did I? Well, I will, there was just something I needed to check on and then got set upon by that oaf Andersen. He needs to watch his mouth.

'I've got stuff I need to do urgently, but if you want to go to the school, I suppose we can go now. Sooner we get it done, sooner I can get back. All right?'

With the shrug that seemed to be habitual, Jay followed his father out, leaving Oriole ashamed, yet again, of being cowardly. Jay was clearly still shaken by what had happened and might have been better not being dragged off to an interview – and it had looked much like a bite.

How on earth had that happened? It looked too small for a badger or even a fox – an angry squirrel, maybe, or a small dog, but she didn't know of any on the estate.

Anyway, she was due at the hotel. She drove there, fretting, but at least she had an evening with Nicki to look forward to.

Settling into the familiar routine was soothing after the last twenty-four hours. She'd just taken a telephone booking when Steve appeared and paused by her desk to wait till she'd finished.

'That was two couples,' she said. 'Three days, dinner, bed and breakfast. That's good, isn't it?'

'It certainly is. Well done!' he said. 'Listen, I was just wanting to have one of our little chats. I'll get Senga to take the desk and bring us a cup of tea.'

It was always a cross to bear that Oriole's face too clearly showed her emotions. It was embarrassing to know that she had gone pink with pleasure when she said, 'That would be lovely. Just give me a minute to log this in and I'll be there.'

CHAPTER SIX

Catriona Fleming was feeling nervous. She was working from home in Newhaven ahead of an appearance before the Appeal Court next morning and the papers demanded a huge amount of preparation. The cases for a new advocate don't exactly come flooding in and she'd been grateful to be given the chance by a solicitor, an old friend, and very anxious to do her best for the client – not least because if she mucked up it would be her friend who would have to face the comeback for choosing her.

Her first ever case flying solo had been in the Sheriff Court, in front of the notorious Sheriff Sinclair, famed for his hobby of filleting rookie advocates and gobbling them up. It was something of a rite of passage, and though she hadn't won her case, she'd come through unbowed, if somewhat bloody.

She'd been gaining confidence since and though the Appeal Court was distinctly scary, that wasn't what was making her nervous. It was that this afternoon she was to meet Kelso's niece Betsy for the first time.

She'd met Kelso's parents – his mum who was a sweetie, his dad who was a bit stiff but gradually thawed – and his sister Finella, Betsy's mum, who was bringing her round for tea this afternoon.

Kelso always described his niece as a minx, but she knew that he was devoted to her. Betsy, according to her mother, was inclined to be possessive about her 'Unkie' and Fin had been anxious that Cat wouldn't take any adverse reaction personally. 'She'll just be jealous, that's all,' she said. 'Pretend you haven't noticed and if she's bumptious and obnoxious leave it to me.'

It was well meant, but not reassuring. She liked kids – and doted on her brother Cameron's little Lewis – but she felt there was a lot riding on this and working out what to have for tea had taken up time she should really have spent checking legal precedents. Naturally she was all for healthy eating but she reckoned that unless human nature had changed since she was that age, Tunnock's Teacakes would be more likely to predispose Betsy in her favour than vegetable crudités and it wouldn't matter, just for once.

Kelso had promised he'd try to get there and she was relieved when he appeared; he kissed her, nicked a teacake and assured her they were a favourite with Betsy too.

'She's a great kid, really,' he said. 'I know she's been a bit spoilt but after the problem with Mark the important thing was just to get her through it.'

Cat knew all about the father who had been jailed for embezzlement and had not tried to see his daughter since. 'Yes, of course. Poor wee soul.'

'She's all right, in fact, and Peter's a great new dad for her. Load off my shoulders, frankly!'

He laughed, but she caught a hint of regret in his voice, and felt another nervous twinge. The relationship mattered to Kelso and however difficult or jealous the child might be, it would be up to Cat to make it work somehow.

'I'm just hoping I can manage to get her not to resent me,' she said.

Kelso laughed. 'Don't worry. She'll love you – a glamorous new auntie.'

Men really were insensitive sometimes. He didn't notice her giving him a sceptical look, saying, 'Oh, there they are now. Prepare for the onslaught!' and going to open the door.

Betsy came in, lagging behind her mother. She didn't appear bumptious to Cat; indeed, more tentative and rather sad. Kelso, clearly expecting an excited embrace, looked taken aback.

'Hello, Betsy! How's my girl? Can I have a hug?'

She let herself be lifted up in a bear hug but without obvious enthusiasm – you would almost say she'd submitted to it, Cat thought, and her heart sank. Was it because she felt she'd been supplanted?

Kelso, still looking puzzled, put her down and said, 'Now, this is your new Auntie Cat. Cat, this is Betsy.'

Cat smiled, bending her knees to get down to the child's level. 'I guessed you were. I'm quick like that, you know? And I bet you guessed as well, didn't you?'

Betsy's solemn blue eyes studied her, then a little smile came to the corners of her mouth. 'Yes, I'm quick too. And you're pretty.'

'So are you,' Cat said. 'Two of a kind, really, aren't we? And shall I tell you something else – I think that kind of person might like juice and a chocolate teacake.'

Betsy acknowledged that she would and went to sit at the table while her hostess made tea and chatted to her.

Kelso watched from the other end of the room, frowning. 'Is Betsy all right?' he murmured to Finella. 'Not like her to be so quiet.'

'She's fine. Just ignore her,' Fin said, smiling up at Cat as she took a mug from her. 'How are things? I hope he's looking after you properly.'

'I think it's the other way round,' Kelso said, but his mind was still on his niece. 'Do you think she'd like a story? Betsy,' he called, 'Story?'

Cat had just gone back and was showing a giggling Betsy something on her mobile. 'I'm just showing her a funny dog clip, but I'm sure she'd like that, wouldn't you, Betsy?'

'OK,' she said indifferently, and Cat could see the hurt on his face.

'Put on CBeebies for her,' Fin said. 'Then we can have a grown-up chat.'

With Betsy's attention now focused on Shaun the Sheep and the adults sitting at the window end, Finella leant forward. 'I've got something to tell you.'

She had gone pink and she was smiling. It wasn't hard to guess what she was going to say, and Kelso got in before she could say it.

'Ah! Now I know what's the matter with Betsy!'

'Very impressive!' Fin said, laughing. 'You can tell he's a detective, can't you Cat? Glad to see that all that training hasn't been wasted.'

'Oh, congratulations!' Cat said. 'When's the baby due?'

Fin gave a nervous glance towards her daughter. 'Possibly best not to mention what we've started calling the B word. Betsy hasn't taken it well.'

Kelso grinned. 'I can imagine. She's used to being the star of the show and of course she'd resent having to share the attention. But she'll get used to it.'

'She'll have to,' Fin said with her usual bluntness and the conversation moved on to family news.

Betsy was absorbed in the programme but as Cat watched her, she could see the little mouth still had a downward turn and she felt really sorry for her. She could see why Kelso was so fond of her; she was bright and fun and she and Cat had got on immediately, possibly because any jealousy was now directed at a much more serious rival. Perhaps if they made a fuss of her for the next bit, it might help the poor little thing to come to terms with losing the solo spot.

Even so, she was taken aback when, as they were going, Betsy said, with a sidelong look at her mother, 'Auntie Cat, can I come to live with you and Unkie instead?'

With Betsy reluctantly persuaded to return home with Fin, Kelso was grinning as he shut the door behind them.

'Well, you did a great job of getting on with her. But could I point out that there is such a thing as being too successful?'

Steve Christie had been fretting over the recent developments, but he was by nature a patient man; Keith Drummond, though, was not. He'd called Steve this morning, bending his ear about Perry Forsyth. He'd nothing fresh to say but he'd said it at length.

Yes, sure, the man was a slimy bastard, but Steve had long ago stopped being over-fastidious about his business connections and Perry, for the moment at least, held the trump card; they couldn't stop him doing whatever he wanted, without turning nasty. Keith was ready for that – he was a policeman, after all – but that could go very wrong and there'd be no hope of cooperation afterwards. That could bring their pretty castles in the air smashing down.

When Keith had said, yet again, that they needed to find out what was making Perry look so smug, he'd replied, 'You're the detective,' which hadn't gone down well, but after Keith rang off, it had got him thinking.

If Steve didn't want to spend the rest of his life running a crummy hotel that might well go under with the next maintenance bill, he had to make this work. And now he thought about it, there was only one person in a position to affect whatever plan Perry might have.

They'd been inclined to overlook Oriole. Everyone knew that her male relatives had frankly exploited her; she'd admitted that somehow she could never successfully stand up for herself. But the inheritance would be equally shared, and given someone to back her up, someone to make her feel good about herself, someone to point out that allowing Perry to take on a project by himself wouldn't be in his interests either, she just might manage to resist him. Someone like Steve, say. And he wouldn't feel guilty about doing it, because Perry would take every penny off his sister if it suited him. Admittedly there were risks in their own scheme, but then business was like that;

with any luck it would pay off handsomely and she'd be in a good place.

And now he thought about it, she might even know what Perry was looking so pleased about. They'd give a lot to know that.

Oriole came into his office in a flurry of explanations about the arrangements she had made with Senga. Seeing the tea tray Steve had already fetched, she protested, 'Oh, you shouldn't have had to do that! I could have done it for you.'

'My pleasure,' he said with a little bow, though he was struggling with the temptation to tell her just to sit down and stop faffing. There was important business to get on with but now he'd have to ask her how things were at Drumdalloch as well, and find the patience to listen to that too.

He needed it. Beginning from Perry's return, she covered everything in detail, along with her own feelings and her worries about her nephew. When at last she ran down, she put a hand to her mouth, saying, 'Oh dear! I'm sorry. You wanted to talk to me, and I've been going on and on, wasting your time with all my problems.'

'No, no, don't apologise. That's what friends are for, isn't it? I just wanted to know if you were all right, and I'm anxious to make sure that when decisions are made you've got someone looking after your interests too.'

Oriole looked overwhelmed – it was probably the first time anyone had said anything like that to the poor woman. 'You're – you're far too good to me, Steve,' she faltered.

Tears had come into her eyes, and he went on hastily,

'Oh, nonsense. But tell me, is there any more word about the estate being wound up?'

Oriole blinked and sniffed. 'Perry says it's literally any day now. I suppose that's when we'll have to make decisions.'

Steve edged a little further forward in his seat. 'Has Perry told you what he's planning?'

She shook her head. 'Just that it'll all be fine, and I have to trust him. But the thing is, Steve – I don't! I think if he's decided something he'll do it and no matter what I think, I won't be able to stop him.'

'But you mustn't think like that! You have the same rights as he does, and he can't control more than his own half of the legacy.'

'I know that, in theory. But I'd never manage to stop him.'

Steve gave her a stern look. 'You know your problem? You're too nice. You're a kind, sweet, gentle person and you can't bring yourself to fight back when it's necessary.'

But Oriole was shaking her head. 'Oh, you're so wrong. I'm not nice at all. I'm just cowardly. I have nasty, wicked thoughts. You only think I'm sweet and kind because you are.'

'Naughty girl!' he said playfully. 'Putting yourself down again – I know what I know! But seriously, what you must consider is what you want for your own future.'

Oriole looked at him piteously. 'That's the trouble. I don't know what I want – I don't really see that I have a future!'

It was the ideal opening. 'Do you have any idea what Perry might be talking about?' When she shook her head, he went on, 'You see, I just wanted to tell you something, and to ask what you thought about it. But it's a big secret; you'd have to promise to keep it from Perry for the moment. It wouldn't do if talk got round, either. Of course, you'd have to be brave but if it all works out, you'd never have to worry again about your future.'

Oriole's eyes opened wide and for a moment she didn't say anything. Then she said, as if she were being put under oath, 'Steve, I swear that I will keep your secret. You can trust me.'

Steve laughed. 'Cross your heart and hope to die? Yes of course, I trust you. And drink your tea before it's cold while I tell you all about it.'

'That's wonderful news, Professor,' Michael Erskine said. 'Thanks so much – very exciting. And I'll start processing the information so the feasibility study working group can get started.'

He sounded enthusiastic; he should even be feeling enthusiastic as the stepping stones to the future he had so meticulously planned started being slotted into place. He wasn't, though – he was feeling hollow inside.

He'd seen it so clearly, the way forward that would mean his mediocre record would no longer count against him. Whatever he might like to pretend, his academic career had been less than lustrous, evidenced by the minor university he'd had to settle for and the poor degree that had needed a PhD to compensate.

Self-presentation was one of his strengths, but that the unprestigious Scottish Institute of Biological Sciences had been the only taker for his carefully-honed CV had been another serious disappointment. He couldn't rely on his own research to burnish his credentials; such papers as he had produced had always failed to achieve publication in the leading journals, so he'd had to rely on the occasional gifted student's work to raise the Institute's profile. Since it wasn't where you'd enlist if you were looking for the glittering prizes, these came along very seldom.

He had consistently been patronised by more distinguished colleagues and for some time now the black dog of depression had been stalking him. The Drumdalloch Woods plan was his big – and, more than likely, only – chance. Success was all about contacts and the field centre would be his calling-card. And Lars Andersen, the stand-out intellectual star during Erskine's years as director, was key to the whole thing.

Something close to panic had gripped him after the phone conversation with Andersen earlier. He'd been almost hysterical with rage after an encounter with Perry Forsyth in the woods that morning and Erskine was waiting for him now, to hear the details – as if what he'd been told already wasn't bad enough.

The Norwegian's physical bulk as he strode in was oppressive and the anger showing black in his face seemed to thicken the atmosphere. Without any sort of greeting, he sat down and began.

'You must to deal with this. How can I work with this perhaps making all my work a nothing? You are responsible to stop him.' Rage had affected his normally fluent English.

'Lars, I understand. Believe me, I'm as angry as you are—'

'No you are not!' he bellowed. 'No one is angry like I am. This man will kill my trees, kill my research – he is like a murderer.'

'Yes, I know. It is intolerable, but we have to be practical, think how we can legitimately act to stop it.'

'There are no laws? We have not our right to work there, like you said?'

'Yes, indeed we do, but our problem is that, apart from the area around the Caledonian pines, the Drumdalloch Woods are not protected like native woodland because of the exotics. It has the same status as an extensive garden. We could get a protection order for certain named large trees—'

'It is not only these large trees! The small trees too – these saplings I work with for my thesis – he talks he will clear these.'

It was worse even than Erskine had realised. If Forsyth acted quickly, the great oaks and mahogany could be felled for timber before orders could be issued – always supposing the man would pay any attention to them. He'd thought of asking Lord McCrae to use his influence to try to speed up the process, but that was clutching at straws. All over the country landowners felled inconvenient trees and took the consequences afterwards, usually a laughably small fine, if that. If it was a question of clearing what could be termed undergrowth, there wasn't a chance.

He simply didn't know what to say. The silence lengthened until Andersen spoke slowly and heavily.

'You are useless to help me? Perhaps then, I take my research elsewhere. I am wasting my precious time and others are going first.'

'But you can't,' Erskine said. 'The originality of your research lies in the unique and historic character of Drumdalloch Woods – the ancient relationships of exotics and native wood and saprophytic fungi. Where else are you going to find anything approaching that?'

As each man stared down the barrel of the gun pointed at their heads, the silence went on and on.

Oriole Forsyth drove back to Drumdalloch, clutching her secret to her like a comforting hot-water bottle. She had lost sleep at night, worrying about what would happen, where would she go, what would she do, when the day came that Perry sold up, as he certainly would. This was unbelievably, magically, the answer to all her problems, the dream come true. She would have no difficulty in defying Perry: to have the plan work, and with Steve at her back, she'd be ready to face down a charging lion.

What would be difficult was not telling Nicki tonight. She was the sort of friend Oriole had never had before: a safety valve, listening as she poured out her hurt that her father had loved his daughter-in-law more than his daughter, sympathising with her problems with her brother and his son, and with Michael Erskine too. Oriole had listened in her turn, had enjoyed listening; Nicki had spent time travelling before coming back to her native Scotland and she'd been Oriole's window on the world she'd always dreamt wistfully about seeing for herself.

If Steve's wonderful plan worked, she might even be able to take a foreign holiday sometime – but she mustn't get ahead of herself, and she must be careful to guard her tongue as they chatted tonight.

She'd just had time to assemble a salad and put the quiche she'd bought in the Aga when Nicki's car arrived and she came into the kitchen. Oriole was laying the table.

'Get the wine out of the fridge, can you?' she said. 'It's a screw-top and you know where the glasses are.'

Nicki paused, looking round. 'No Perry?'

'No, I think they must be out for supper.'

'Oh, I'm disappointed,' she said. 'I was looking forward to putting faces to the people I'd heard so much about.'

'Oh, you will!' Oriole said. 'Let's make the most of having a bit of peace now – I've no doubt there'll be some fuss or other when they come back.'

Nicki brought the wine and over their meal Oriole told her about the row she'd heard Perry having with Lars.

'I'd been going to tackle him about the situation with Jay, but he said they were going to the school this afternoon to get him enrolled. Probably they've gone for a pizza afterwards – Jay was pretty ticked off last night when he found you couldn't just phone to have one sent. He wasn't impressed with my pasta, I can tell you that!'

'Poor boy,' Nicki said. 'My heart goes out to him. I know he doesn't make it easy with the way he's behaving, but it's small wonder after all that's happened.'

'I know,' Oriole said. 'Don't think I'm not sorry for him, being taken away from school and his friends and being dumped here like unwanted baggage. I've tried to help, really I have, but he doesn't accept any of my attempts. To be honest, I think he hates me—'

'Ssh!' Nicki jerked her head to the kitchen door. The handle was turning and a moment later Jay appeared.

'Oh!' Oriole said. 'I thought you were out with your dad.'

He looked at her coldly. 'No. When's supper?'

The women looked at each other. 'Did Perry not give you something to eat before he went out?' Oriole said.

'Just dropped me off after we'd been at the school. There's nothing in the flat.'

Oriole looked flustered. 'I'm afraid we've just finished our supper. I know you don't like pasta but —'

The boy's face was expressive. Nicki stood up. 'I'm Nicki, and you must be Jay,' she said. 'Come and sit down and we'll see what we can find for you. Eggs, maybe?' She looked a question at Oriole.

'Yes, there's eggs in the fridge. There's cheese too, and what's left of the salad and bread and some fruit in the bowl, but there's not a lot else. I'm sorry, Jay, but you see, living on my own I just buy what I know I'll need.'

There was no acknowledgement. 'Why don't I make you an omelette?' Nicki said quickly. 'I'm quite good at that.'

He didn't say thank you, just sat waiting as the women fussed around, having an awkward conversation consisting of remarks addressed to him that they had to answer themselves. His only response was when Oriole, looking at the bandaged hand, asked how it was.

'All right,' he said. 'Wasn't much, really.'

'What was the school like?' Nicki asked, tipping the omelette on to the plate. 'Did you meet any of the pupils?'

'No,' he said, starting to eat hungrily. 'Just the teacher. It's pretty basic, in fact.'

Watching him, Oriole wondered when his last meal had

been. Perry blatantly felt no responsibility for his son, and whatever she'd said about not being cook-housekeeper, she couldn't possibly stick to it if that meant Jay being hungry. The problem was that conjuring up unexpected meals wasn't her strong point and now she was feeling guilty and inadequate.

It was just at that moment she saw Perry's car arriving. She didn't want to have a stand-up fight about it in front of her visitor and indeed the child in question, but after her talk with Steve, she was ready for it.

'Perry, where have you been?' she said as he opened the kitchen door. 'You didn't arrange any supper for Jay, and he says there's no food in the flat.'

Perry had come in looking jaunty, but his face changed. 'Oh, for God's sake – there you go, nagging the minute I set foot in the house. You're the boy's aunt – surely you don't grudge finding him something to eat when he's hungry?'

Oriole felt her face flush. As always, Perry had managed to turn things round so that it was her fault, not his. 'Well, no,' she bleated. 'Not exactly – it's just that we had agreed you would do your own catering and when you live on your own—'

He interrupted her. 'Well, hello!' he said to Nicki, smiling. 'I'm embarrassed – I didn't realise we had a guest. Sorry to have inflicted our little domestic difference on you.'

Nicki smiled back. 'Oh, don't worry. We all know about families. Have you eaten yourself? There are still some eggs left.'

Oriole looked at Nicki with some surprise. With all

she'd told her about her brother she'd have expected her friend to be guarded, even politely hostile, but Nicki seemed quite ready to encourage the friendly overture.

'No, no – don't bother. I had a meal with a business contact. But I see you've got some wine there – I'll just get myself a glass.'

Mindful of the conversation with Steve, Oriole said, 'What sort of business was that?'

She didn't get an answer. Jay had just got up, picked an apple from the fruit bowl and gone to the biscuit box; finding it empty he demanded to know if she'd bought any more, and she'd had to go and fetch some for the Friends that she'd hidden. He took the packet and left the room, without saying goodnight to his father, any more than he had greeted him when he had come in.

Perry had refilled Nicki's glass and poured one for himself and now they were sitting talking at the table. He'd always had an eye for an attractive woman, which Nicki, with her mop of honey-coloured hair and lively personality, certainly was so it was not surprising that he should be trying to chat her up, but it was a bitter disappointment to Oriole that her friend should be so responsive.

Oriole poured what was left of the bottle into her own glass and sat down beside them. She didn't say much, though; she was feeling sick at being trapped in a toxic mess that was beyond her control and even the thought of Steve's secret wasn't as comforting as it had been. If she couldn't even make Perry take responsibility for his own son, how could she make him agree to Steve's plan?

* * *

Something had wakened her, some sudden noise. Used to the silence of an empty house, Oriole startled awake, then remembered that of course she wasn't alone any more. It had just been a door shutting. She turned over, ready to drop off to sleep again.

Then another door shut – the front door, with its squeaky hinge. Odd that someone should be going out in the middle of the night – and then she heard a low-voiced male conversation going on just below her window. Who could that possibly be?

She got up to peer out. It was pitch-black outside, a moonless night, heavily clouded with a light rain falling. The conversation had stopped and all she could see were lights, bobbing among the trees; two torches, perhaps, going deeper and deeper into the woods until they were swallowed up in the darkness. There was a sudden harsh call; a bird disturbed as they passed.

What was this about? Something to do with Perry's plans? Something that had to be done under cover of darkness? Something illicit?

Something that Steve might want to know about? Perhaps she should get a torch and follow them discreetly . . .

Oriole shuddered. Even for Steve, she couldn't do it. Out there in the wilderness of the woods, anything could happen. She didn't know who might be with Perry and, horribly, she wasn't entirely convinced her brother would protect her.

The best she could do was watch and wait until they came back. She stood for a long time, but it was cold and she pulled a chair close to the window and sat down with her duvet wrapped round her.

She woke to the sound of a car's engine and then she heard the squeak of the front door shutting again. There was nothing to see except smothering darkness and the only sounds were footsteps crossing the landing to the flat, and that door shutting again.

CHAPTER SEVEN

Oriole got up early and left the house before anyone else was stirring. She was feeling shaky and she needed time to think about the previous night; she wasn't ready to face Perry yet and anyway she could do without the fuss there would be when they discovered there was no more in the house than there had been the night before for breakfast, and they'd have to make do with the rest of the tub of natural yoghurt.

There was a café in Fortrose that did good croissants and coffee refills where she could linger until she could be sure they'd have gone out. She had a busy day in prospect; Nicki was working, but there was a stalwart group of three of the Friends planning a major assault on a stand of rhododendrons that was stifling tree growth in one area of the wood and she wanted to go down there and help. Fortunately, it wasn't raining at the moment, so despite the new arrangement Perry had made with Michael Erskine she wouldn't have to put up with a bad-tempered

Lars squatting like a malicious toad in the kitchen.

Was she brave enough to confront Perry about his nocturnal visitor? She rehearsed introductory lines: 'What were you doing last night? Who was it who was with you? Why didn't they come in daylight?' But somehow she couldn't see him answering.

Perhaps it would be better to say nothing – just act as a spy in the camp? Or was that the coward's way out, telling herself what she wanted to hear? It could wait, anyway; she wasn't needed at the hotel until later but then she could talk to Steve and get his advice.

And she had something to look forward to as well – walking round and reminding herself of what was left of features her grandmother had installed in her woods long ago: the pergola, ramshackle now; the wrought iron picnic bench looking over the lochan; the summer house, grown all through with strangling vegetation; the paved courtyard somewhere deep in the undergrowth; what was left of an ornamental pond of black water that still produced the mockery of a water lily or two in season; the rockery, now no more than a random pile of stones smothered by bracken; the arboretum with the treasured great trees – and likely more that she didn't know about as well, but she'd told Steve there were records her grandmother had kept somewhere. He'd been very excited to hear about it all.

It must have been a real paradise once, with its tended paths and vistas, before Giles had unleashed the power of nature that always made the woods feel to Oriole such a threatening place, as if they were silently stating, 'We can wait. This will be ours long after you have gone.' But it could all, with work and a bit of money, be restored to order, to what it once had been. That was what made Steve's plan such a brilliant, wonderful idea.

The house would have to go, of course, but despite it being the only home she'd known, she'd always hated it; the dead wing, rotting before their eyes, had given her as a child a recurrent nightmare about the monster that lived there and might creep through in the darkness and strangle her – and the grown-up version of The Dream featured the strangling filaments of dry rot that were creeping through day by day into the bones of the house itself.

And at least she wouldn't have to feel guilty about guarding the legacy that had defined her father's life. Even if his principle of untrammelled growth would have to be abandoned, the landscaped woods would be the crown jewel of the luxury destination hotel; a historic garden, with the birdlife and his favourite trees cherished.

Best of all, she'd have a place to live and work, one where Steve would always be around. She'd never had any illusions about a relationship, but not seeing him any more had been the worst aspect of leaving Drumdalloch.

Keith Drummond wasn't her favourite person, but there was no reason to think she'd have to see a lot of him, and his being able to bring in the sort of backing that would, along with the sale price for the Kilbain Hotel, make the beautiful dream come true was so wonderful that she could put up with it.

'More coffee?' the waitress said.

With a start, Oriole looked at her watch. 'Oh goodness, is that the time? Just the bill please.'

She picked up her bag, opened her purse to get her credit card, and stared. The slot was empty. She looked through the wallet; the money she'd had there was gone too.

Her face flared, as the waitress stood waiting. 'Oh, I'm so sorry! I seem to have left my card at home.'

'No problem,' the girl said. 'I know who you are – we'll trust you.'

Scrabbling in the coin purse, she found she did have just enough to pay. But what had happened to her card and the cash? As if she didn't know.

When she arrived back, Perry's car was outside but there was no sign that anyone had been in the kitchen. He might have taken Jay to school and then come back, or Jay might have gone in with the school bus, armed with his aunt's credit card. She had his mobile and she'd tried phoning but he hadn't answered; she could stop it, of course, but that would mean a hassle and going without money until the new one came through, and she could just take it off him when he came home. She knew what he would say, of course: if she wasn't going to feed him, he had to fend for himself. It was Perry he should be blaming, his card he should have taken, but then Perry hadn't been dumb enough to leave his wallet lying around the way she'd left her handbag last night.

Was Perry catching up on his sleep after his nocturnal adventures? She didn't care. Still in the grip of indignation, she hurried up to the flat she had configured out of the upstairs drawing room, unused for years, and the three bedrooms that ran behind it, on the opposite side from the ruined wing.

She knocked on the door. 'Perry! Perry, are you there? I need to speak to you.'

There was no answer. She knocked again and tried the handle, but the door didn't yield. They'd never been in the habit of locking doors, but perhaps Perry had acquired the habit in the city. It suggested he must be out somewhere.

Or else, that he didn't want her going in. Perhaps there was something he didn't want her to see – something that might give her a clue to what he'd been up to last night.

She ran downstairs to the hook where she kept the keys to the flat. Both were gone; Jay probably had his own. She did, however, have a little stash of spares since she'd found that people on holiday had something of a talent for losing them. With a nervous glance out of the window to see if Perry might be coming back, she took one and went upstairs again.

The neat flat showed signs of careless occupancy already: unmade beds, nightwear and shoes discarded on the floors, a sports bag spilling clothes in Jay's room alongside discarded sweet packets that had missed the waste-paper basket. In the sitting room, there was a laptop on the table, closed.

After another look out of the window, Oriole opened the lid. She wasn't hopeful; things needed passwords and while it woke up she searched for more accessible information. There didn't seem to be any paper lying about; in fact, in contrast to the rest of the flat the room was notably tidy. There was a briefcase on the floor beside the table but it was padlocked; if Jay was in the habit of helping himself to anything he thought might be useful, he probably couldn't be trusted not to snoop on private papers – though given what Oriole was ready to do herself she could hardly take a high moral tone.

The laptop had flickered into life, but as she had feared there was a procedure to perform before it would open. She shut it and turned away, disappointed.

Perry might return at any moment. She was on her way out when she caught sight of the 'Shopping List' noticeboard that hung beside the cooker with its black marker pen, wiped clean, of course, after her last paying guests had gone.

There was something written on it now – a telephone number. It could be completely irrelevant, but it was all she would have to show for her activities and she speedily wrote it on the palm of her hand, locked up and went back downstairs.

Just in time! There he was now, emerging from the woods. Best to look busy. She quickly moved the kettle on to the hob and grabbed the cafetière.

Perry came back to the house in a very upbeat mood. He'd completed the list of measurements he needed and mercifully the hulking Norwegian wasn't around today. There had been other people within earshot during their last encounter and even so he'd felt seriously threatened; Andersen seemed to think he could issue instructions about what must and must not be done, and the violence of his reaction when Perry pointed out that he had no intention of taking orders from him suggested an alarming temper.

He could see Oriole through the kitchen window as he went to the front door and wondered what sort of mood she'd be in today. She'd been a bit stroppy yesterday and it would be a nuisance if she didn't snap out of it. She'd always done the housekeeping before, and it made obvious sense for her to carry on rather than expecting him to run a separate establishment when half the time he'd be out and it would only be Jay.

She had the kettle on, and he said heartily, 'Oh good! I could do with a cup of coffee before I go out to my meeting.'

'Who with?'

Her bluntness took him aback. 'Oh, just some business stuff. Won't bore you with the details. Did Jay get off to school all right?'

'Didn't you take him?'

'God, no! Dead to the world – never even heard him leave. I imagine he got the school bus, or he could have cycled if he felt like it – I showed him the bike in the garage. When did he leave?'

'I don't know. I went out for breakfast and he wasn't here when I came back so I assume he'd gone by then. Along with my credit card.'

Perry stared at her. 'Sorry? Did you give it to him?'

'Oh no,' she said. 'He didn't seem to feel the need to bother with that sort of formality. Helped himself and took my cash as well.'

For once Perry looked shaken. 'God, that little bastard! What did I do to deserve him? No, don't start,' he said as Oriole opened her mouth, apparently eager to tell him. 'If you haven't cancelled it, you'd better do it now before he goes wild with it, and I'll pay you back whatever he's spent.'

Oriole sighed. 'Right – you make the coffee while I do that. But you're going to have to take charge. He needs you to look after him – the way you treat him, he thinks you don't care about him at all and to tell you the truth, I think he's right. I don't blame him, to be frank – it's you that's a total bastard, not him.' She fetched her phone from her bag and went to check the number.

Perry brooded as he made the coffee. James had always been a difficult child. He blamed his bitch of a wife for sabotaging his efforts at proper discipline, encouraging the boy to change his given name, teaching him that cheeking his father was funny. It had been a calculated play to convince Giles that his grandson was the future of his beloved woods and that his own children couldn't be trusted.

She'd not been wrong there, of course – though neither could she. Now his luck was changing, and he couldn't help a small smile, despite everything – and he realised, too, that the answer to the James problem was almost within reach, provided Muriel Morris was right in saying they'd get the nod any day now. Then the boy could go back to his school, and he would once more be relieved of his unwanted responsibility; until then, surely he could sweet-talk Oriole into taking up the slack.

When Oriole returned, he had the coffee ready. 'Come and sit down and we can have a chat,' he said, motioning her to a seat. 'Look, I know it's all been really hard on you, and you've been brilliant at keeping the place going – don't think I don't appreciate what you've done. But soon we'll get our hands on the sort of money that I promise will mean we never have to worry about it again. You can have—'

She interrupted him, not looking as eager to hear what he was going to offer her as he had expected she would be. She said, 'Where exactly is this money going to come from?'

He frowned. 'You don't need to know at the moment – it's business, so I have to be discreet. Just trust me.'

'You're always saying "trust me" but frankly, I don't see any reason why I would. What were you doing in the woods last night?'

Damn! The last thing he had wanted was attention drawn to his nocturnal visitor. Quickly he said, 'Oh, I'm sorry. Did I disturb you leaving the house? I woke up and thought I saw a light in the woods and should check what it was – you never know these days. Didn't find anything so I just came back to bed.'

'Really?' Oriole said coldly. 'Where did you see it from? None of the bedroom windows in the flat face that way.'

He had a very short fuse. 'Oh, for God's sake, mind your own bloody business, if you prefer it that way,' he snapped and stood up. 'I'll see you later.'

She didn't flinch. 'Since I own half of whatever comes to us, it is my business and before I agree to anything, I'd have to know what you were planning. Would you like to tell me now?'

FFS, what had got into the woman! He'd never known her be like this. 'No, I wouldn't!' he yelled. 'You could mess it up for both of us. I'll tell you when I can, OK? There's no point in saying any more when you're just trying to be difficult.' He went to the door.

'Perhaps, before you go, you could give me some money since your son has cleaned me out and it'll be a few days before I get my new card.'

He stopped and turned to look at her, shaking his head and sighing, but he handed over three twenties. 'That's all I've got.'

She wasn't even grateful. 'Then perhaps you could get some more from a cashpoint and pick up supper for you and Jay. I haven't time to shop today.'

Perry stormed out fuming. His earlier good mood had evaporated; his plans hadn't made any allowance for Oriole being difficult. It was so unlike her – but of course, she'd naturally been upset by what James had done. Once that had been sorted out, she'd get over it, he told himself.

He called James's mobile to tell him that whatever he'd spent before the card was stopped would be taken out of his allowance, but of course the call rang out. He swore. Typical! James would mess up just when everything had been falling into place.

But he didn't have time for all this, or he'd be late for the appointment that was much the most important thing right now. He'd tackle James later and Oriole would back off when it came right down to it. She always had.

'He's spent a lot of time trotting off to Inverness,' Keith Drummond said. 'I slipped a note of his number to traffic and told them to let me know if they clocked it.'

'So where was he going?' Steve Christie said. This phone call was giving him a nervous feeling in his stomach; being an optimist he'd kept telling himself that Perry would see sense and cooperate, though he knew perfectly well that common sense had never been one of Perry's more notable attributes.

'Can't exactly tell them to tail him. They've got us all

spying on each other now and we don't want attention drawn to this, do we?'

Steve winced. 'No, no, of course we don't. So what do you think?'

'I think the little sod's going out on his own, that's what I think. Any information from your lady friend? You'd think she has to have some idea what he's up to.'

Steve hesitated. It had been a risk taking Oriole into his confidence without consulting Keith, who always liked to feel he was in charge, and it could provoke one of Keith's ice-cold rages, but he couldn't put it off much longer.

'Doesn't have a clue at the moment, but now she's our inside source. I told her what we were planning – just an outline, selling the hotel and using that and the money from you to transform their site – and when I painted the picture of the luxury hotel, she went crazy for it.'

He heard Keith's sharp intake of breath. 'You did what? You know what women are like – she blathers to her friends and then we're in a competitive situation—'

'She's not like that,' Steve said firmly. 'She's a serious person and she gave her word. You have to remember she has equal shares with Perry and she could block him making other arrangements.'

There was silence for a moment as Keith considered that. Then he said, 'I take the point, but I still think we can't let this go on any longer. He said the lawyer thought it would happen soon and the clock will be running from the minute he gets control. He could do something to wreck the whole thing – would you like it to fall through because someone changed their mind like it did the last time?'

No, Steve wouldn't. It had been gut-churning enough

the last time with the way it turned out – and then they'd still had the hope of getting back on track. This time, if it all went wrong, it would mean the end for them.

'What do you suggest we do, then?' he said.

'Can you get him to the bar tonight? I want to just spell things out – a little more clearly, shall we say.'

'He'll probably come anyway,' Steve said. 'There's nowhere else nearby.'

'Unless he's avoiding us. I'll have to take steps if that's how he's planning to play it. Have to go now – see you later.'

Steve was feeling worried as Keith rang off; when it came right down to it, he was afraid of him. He wasn't exactly concerned for his own safety – though he could imagine a situation arising when he might be – but Keith didn't have boundaries in the same places as normal people did. That tone of cold threat just now – any meeting with Perry was going to be very unpleasant, to say the least.

Still, there was nothing he could do except go along with it, unless he wanted to spend the rest of his life in this tacky little hotel – always supposing he didn't go bankrupt, which was a distinct possibility.

Perry Forsyth's phone rang as he walked towards his meeting. He glanced at it and recognising the number, his heart skipped a beat.

'Yes, Muriel?'

He listened, thanked her and rang off. That was it, done and dusted – what he'd been waiting for so impatiently for so long. He heard her warning that it wasn't any very great sum of money, but it would keep him going meantime.

And the news couldn't possibly have come at a better time. He had everything lined up, just waiting for his agreement. He couldn't help beaming as he walked on towards his meeting.

After such a trying morning Oriole was still in a thoroughly bad temper as she pulled on her gardening gear and gumboots and was just leaving the house when the kitchen phone rang. She thought about letting it go to voicemail – she was running late already and if she wanted to help the Friends before going to work, she wouldn't have time for the survey of the old garden features she'd promised herself.

Still, it probably wouldn't take a minute. When she picked up the receiver and heard the lawyer's voice, her legs went shaky, and she had to sit down. She listened to what Muriel had to say without really taking it in. She remembered her manners, thanked her politely and rang off.

So many different thoughts! She'd have money to pay off the loan from the bank – there wouldn't be a lot left over, though, until the house was sold. Muriel had been downbeat when it came to the sale value – of course, she didn't know about the great secret. But Muriel had mentioned she'd told Perry first, so what would that mean? One thing was for sure – it was all going to start moving very fast.

The first thing she must do was call Steve. She could tell him the number she'd written on her hand, too, before she managed to wash it off accidentally. Right now.

He was more than pleased, he was delighted. 'Brilliant

news!' he said. 'At least we can start to get things under way. See you later.'

It felt so much better now that Steve knew. He'd be able to tell her how to deal with Perry, and perhaps they might actually get him to agree with the plan – Oriole certainly couldn't imagine anything that could be better than that.

As she opened the boot room door a sudden blast of wind almost blew it out of her hand and the rain that had come with it had a stinging edge, turning to hailstones as she stepped outside. They'd had weather like this for the last bit – a sunny day then sudden violent squalls, as if this year's winter was spitefully refusing to loosen its grip.

It was tempting to step straight back inside, but the guys clearing the rhodies would still be at it so she pulled up the hood of her waterproof jacket and went on down the path. She really hated the woods on days like this; darkness always gathered among the trees so quickly when the sky went that purple-black colour and already they were thrashing about like tethered monsters, making the roaring noise that always sounded like angry waves, as if only the roots stopped them closing in on her. She heard a crash as a branch came down and jumped, though she should have been used to it by now – with so little maintenance done there was always work for what her father had liked to call nature's husbandry.

There ahead of her now was the tree she always thought of as Helena's oak; she never passed it without thinking of her dead sister-in-law and it was always hard to suppress the awful image that still haunted her. Involuntarily, her eyes went to the nesting platform that had been the cause of her accident.

It seemed to be sitting at an odd angle. That was dangerous; dislodged by the wind it could strike someone and Oriole had been nervous about safety since Muriel had told her that she could be held liable. She stepped up to it, putting her hand up to straighten it.

Without any warning, it came crashing down, catching her a glancing blow on the head that sent her flying backwards onto the muddy path. She cried out in pain and the world whirled about her with a burst of stars. After a moment she struggled to sit up but, sick and dizzy, fell back again. It was cold, cold; the wind swept a spatter of hailstones stinging across her face. Her teeth started to chatter as she shivered convulsively.

'For God's sake, what's this?' a man's voice called. 'Oriole? What on earth's happened?'

'Are you all right?' that was a woman now.

She managed to raise her head this time. 'Yes, yes, I think so. Just my head – that platform came down.'

The woman knelt anxiously beside her and as Oriole's head cleared she recognised one of the Friends; another was hurrying up, a younger man.

It was he who said, 'Thank goodness you're all right. For a minute it looked like history repeating itself,' but as Oriole was helped up she realised it was what they were all thinking, and that she had been lucky. Unlike poor Helena.

She insisted she was all right but she was staggering, so two of them took her arms to steady her as they went back to the house. Her rescuers were implacable; the woman helped her to bed and when she protested that she had to go to her job at the hotel, firmly told her she would do no such thing and called Steve Christie on the spot, gave her two paracetamol and left Oriole to rest.

She hated the thought of letting Steve down but in truth she was grateful. She could hardly lift her aching head from the pillow without the room spinning round and already blessed sleep was creeping up on her.

But there was one thing quite clear in her head: she had put her hand up to support the loose platform so that it wouldn't drop onto someone's head with the next blast of wind. But it hadn't just become loose; from the way it had crashed down it had been detached already and something had been propping it up. Something that, by stepping closer to the tree, she must have knocked away.

She ought to go and see if there was something to explain it, but the mists of sleep were irresistible now. She would look later, she was murmuring to herself as she gave up the struggle.

CHAPTER EIGHT

It hadn't been a good evening. In the taxi that took them back from the retirement dinner for DS Davidson, the atmosphere was strained. Kelso was working hard to make it clear, without actually saying it, that he wasn't blaming Cat, which only made things worse since it was so obvious that it had been all her fault.

He hadn't wanted her to come. More than that, he had told her that she wouldn't want to go if she knew what it would be like, and she had been determined to prove him wrong. She'd wanted to show that she could take her place in his world just as he had in hers where, as an older man with a sexy job and even an interesting scar down the side of his face, he had been seen as something of a dude and had fitted in with no difficulty.

'Look,' she'd said, 'I know lots of these guys! I've chatted to them round the courts while we were waiting for cases to call. And you've told me all about DS Davidson and all he did for you when you were new to the game – I want to meet him. He sounded just like Mum's Tam MacNee.'

'Of course – why not? I'm sure you'd get on fine,' Kelso said. 'Just not in this context.'

'Do you mean they're all going to get drunk? I can handle that, you know, and there'll be wives and partners there too, won't there? I'd like to get to be part of the community.'

She also reckoned that one of the other guests would be the DS he now most frequently worked with, Livvy Murray. He'd often talked about her as a sort of *enfant terrible* only gradually growing up and she sounded intriguing.

He had reluctantly given in. And it had gone fine to begin with at the drinks beforehand; when she came in, several of the officers she knew, male and female, had come over to greet her, and to start with she hadn't realised there was a problem. It was only when she saw that Kelso, in a group of older men, was looking rigid that she started picking up some of the comments. It was the word 'cradle-snatching,' that first caught her attention, then laughter, followed by a sly, 'Checked her birth certificate, have you?' It was only then she had understood why Kelso had been so reluctant.

It had seemed an interminable time before guests were summoned to the table. There were very few women apart from the ones in the force and among those was a DC she'd come up against in court; Cat had got her client off and clearly that hadn't been forgiven. She began to notice that she was seen as the enemy, and not only by that one officer.

Then there was DS Livvy Murray. Cat heard Kelso

hailing her as she approached the group – hennaed hair in a neat pixie cut, middle height and serious-looking – and then saying, 'You must meet Cat,' so she'd turned with a welcoming smile as they came over.

Livvy smiled too, but Cat thought the smile hadn't quite reached her eyes. 'Pleased to meet you,' she said.

'I've heard a lot about you from Kelso,' Cat said. 'Is he a difficult boss?'

'Oh, sometimes,' she said, and this time the smile she gave along with a sideways look at Kelso was genuine enough. 'And divide everything you hear by – oh, about five.'

So she had a sense of humour. Cat laughed and, encouraged, said, 'We must get together sometime and you can give me your side of the story.'

Livvy's withdrawal was immediate. 'Don't want to get myself busted. Anyway, he's all right,' she said, with another glance at Kelso.

Cat's heart sank. She knew from what he said about Livvy that he was impressed by her growing competence as a detective and he had a mild, if exasperated affection for her, but to Livvy he hadn't been just an admired superior officer. That look said it all, and it was a relief when dinner was announced.

Things deteriorated 'with drink taken', to use the police phrase, and there were ribald comments made that even Cat, the veteran of many an inebriated Bar Dinner, found offensive and she was grateful when Kelso caught her eye to go.

She was embarrassed. She'd been quiet as he tried to smooth things over, but as they walked up the stairs to the house, she swallowed her pride and said, 'I'm sorry I put you through that. Come on, you have my permission to say it – "I told you so".'

He turned to kiss her. 'Would I do that? You remember that rhyme about how to have a happy marriage – the one Marjory says has worked for her and Bill – "Whenever you're wrong, admit it, and whenever you're right, shut up"?'

Even as she laughed and retorted that it was still possible to shut up in a very marked manner, she was thinking about the look on Livvy's face and feeling almost guilty about her own luck and happiness.

'Here he is now,' Steve Christie said as Perry Forsyth appeared in the Kilbain Hotel cocktail lounge. 'Thought he'd be in.'

Keith Drummond grunted. 'I'd have gone to get him if he wasn't. Time to lay it on the line. We can't let him get away with this – we need to make him see sense, whatever it takes.'

Steve gave a nervous cough. 'We still want his cooperation,' he said, but he knew it sounded feeble and it made no difference. He hadn't really thought it would.

'We tried it your way,' Keith said. 'Now we'll try it mine.' He stood up from the stool beside the bar and unfolded to his full menacing height as Perry approached.

But just inside the lounge Perry stopped and turned, looking back as if he was waiting for someone and a moment later a young woman appeared – bright-faced, medium height, fair curly hair.

'What's yours, Nicki?' he said. 'Let's get the party started.'

She laughed. 'Oh well – vodka and tonic, I guess. Nothing like it for getting you up to flying speed.'

'Girl after my own heart,' he said. 'I'll have to take it easy with DS Drummond over there watching me but let's make it a double for you.'

'My mum warned me about people like you,' she said playfully. 'Shall I find a table? It's quite busy.'

'Sure – look, there's one in the corner over there.'

'Right.' She made her way over to it.

Thwarted, Keith had sat back down. He couldn't have the confrontation he'd been planning in front of this woman; it was only as Perry reached the bar that he spoke through gritted teeth.

'Evening, Perry.'

'Oh, there you are!' Perry said jovially. 'Two vodka and tonics, one double, Tricia, if you will be so good. Hi, Steve – got a good house in tonight, haven't you? Stave off the bailiffs for a day or two!'

He was, Steve could see, in high good humour. But they had a card up their sleeves that he didn't know about, and Keith was getting ready to produce it now.

'What game are you playing?' he said in a savage undertone.

Perry looked back blankly. 'Game? What do you mean?'

'Cosying up to Williams Timber? Didn't tell us you were going to do that, did you?'

His face changed. 'How the hell do you know that?'

Keith smiled. 'Oh, we have our methods, as you know.'

Perry started gabbling, 'Oh, well, um, I was going to tell you about that. Of course. Yes, well, it's just possible we've got some trees they might be prepared to take a look at, all just very preliminary, naturally. Thought I'd just check it out, you know, so that once I got probate we could move faster.'

'Any word about that?' Keith said, his voice silky.

'Oh, any day now, I understand.' He turned to pick up the drinks. 'Look, I've got a guest—'

'Lying sod!' Keith said loudly. 'You heard today.'

Several nearby drinkers looked round, and Steve said urgently, 'Keep it down Keith!'

He did drop his voice, but if he had shouted it would probably have sounded less threatening. 'We need a long talk, laddie. Like tomorrow? You need reminding of a few things.'

'Yes, fine,' Perry bleated. 'I'll contact you—'

'I'll call in. You won't be going anywhere.'

Tricia had brought the drinks and Perry, glad of an excuse, brought out his card to pay. 'Right, right,' he said, but his hand was visibly trembling. 'Just coming,' he called to the woman who was looking across inquisitively.

'Oh, before you go, how's Oriole?' It was Steve's first opportunity to ask and he was anxious to know; there was a lot hanging on her well-being right at the moment.

'Oriole?' Perry said. 'Fine, as far as I know. You've probably seen her more recently than I have.'

'Didn't you hear she'd had an accident?' Keith said. 'Hit her head and fell in the wood. Struck by that nesting platform Helena pulled down on herself, actually. Bit of a coincidence. You should probably remove it altogether, you know.'

Perry stared at him, his face losing colour. 'I – I don't

know anything about it. I'll see her when I get back. Yes, of course we should. I'll – I'll take that in hand.' He went over to the table to join his guest.

The man was obviously shocked – punch drunk possibly, Steve thought. But there was something off about his reaction, something that Steve couldn't quite analyse. Could he be lying when he'd said he didn't know anything about it? Or—

'Steve,' said a plaintive voice at his shoulder, 'we've been waiting ages for the waitress to bring us the menu. She seems to be . . . otherwise occupied.'

He looked round. Tricia was laughing with a young man at the bar and he turned, smiling to the most difficult of the current residents, a large lady with an unflattering bleach job. 'I'm so sorry, Mrs Meldrum. I'll get that right away.'

As he went to fetch it, he glanced over at Perry's table. He was talking earnestly to his guest and it looked as if the party he'd mentioned wasn't exactly going with a swing. When next he had the chance to look, he wasn't surprised to see they were leaving.

Keith had left too. Steve had serious misgivings about his meeting Perry tomorrow, but there wasn't a lot he could do about it now and he had work to do. He pinned on his professional smile.

'Now, Mrs Meldrum, shall I wait and take your order? I can recommend the lamb.'

If he had to do this for the rest of his life, he'd probably kill himself.

The sitting room of Michael Erskine's upper villa flat in an expensive street in Inverness had a chilling lack of any sort of personality. The walls and surfaces were bare, there were venetian blinds on the windows and the bookcase that occupied one wall held principally scientific reference texts and box files. A state-of-the art TV screen dominated one wall and the armchair he was sitting in matched the other piece of furniture, an expensive brown leather sofa.

He had a glass of Scotch in his hand, even though he'd been warned that it wasn't advisable while taking the anti-depressants he'd been on for some time now, ever since he'd had to face up to the dreariness of his trudge to retirement with his horizon defined by the limitations of the Scottish Institute of Biological Sciences, but tonight they weren't working and Scotch seemed the only answer.

He should have been able to reduce the dose, or even stop it altogether, with the glorious future opening up before him. The Institute board members were excited; he'd been bombarded with enthusiastic calls and emails from them, even sharing references to the Wood Wide Web that they seemed to have trawled from the most doubtful areas of the internet.

It was the most recent call from Professor Crichton that had sent him to the bottle. He was a highly intelligent and highly experienced man; somehow his antennae had picked up some hint of uncertainty in Michael's voice and he had suddenly said, quite sharply, 'Everything going all right, is it, Michael?'

He'd thought he'd managed to sound confident when he said that yes of course it was, but Crichton had gone on, 'Because, as you know, we're starting to commit to considerable expenditure that we can ill afford, so it's vital that nothing goes wrong.'

'Absolutely,' Michael said. 'No problem. I'm in contact with the owner. We're just waiting until the legal formalities are completed to progress.'

'I take it these will be just that – a formality? And do you have the impression that an offer will be welcome?'

He took a deep breath. 'Oh, absolutely. With a protection order on the woods, he'll be grateful for any offer at all.'

'And that's in hand, is it?'

An even deeper breath this time. 'Absolutely,' he said again. 'They'll be pushing it through.' A second big fat lie.

He shouldn't have said 'absolutely' again; it had sounded phoney to his ears but it seemed to have satisfied the professor and he'd said, 'Great job, Michael,' as he had rung off.

As he reran the conversation for the twentieth time, beads of sweat started to appear on his forehead. He'd been a total fool. Pride would be his downfall; he should have started sounding a note of caution, but he couldn't bear to lose Crichton's good opinion – not yet. His instinct to cover up problems was bone-deep and apart from a very few uncomfortable exceptions that policy had worked well enough in the past. In academic life, though, obfuscation was comparatively easy; when it came to property transactions it was different. The outcome of a property transaction was unequivocal; either you owned it or you didn't, and Perry Forsyth had spelt out that he wasn't looking for a quick at-any-price sale. Unless things changed radically, Michael's humiliation had only been postponed.

And 'pushing it through'? NatureScot, responsible for recognising Sites of Special Scientific Interest, would entertain the application for Drumdalloch Woods but it would take 28 days to get a reply to that and it was highly unlikely that anything formal would be in place in less than four months. By that time half the trees could have gone and even an interim order would need an inspection visit – and how likely was it that Forsyth would agree to that? You'd be talking legal action.

The foundations of his plan were crumbling below his feet and his reputation would be shot as well. Unless something happened to change it, he was finished.

He got up a little unsteadily to refill his glass again.

The trouble about sleeping heavily during the day is that it leaves you completely disorientated. Oriole had tumbled into an uncomfortable sleep in the late morning and woke confused in the evening, unable at first to make sense of it; her head was aching badly and when she put up her hand to touch it, she could feel a lump the size of an egg on her temple.

At last it came back to her: the heavy wooden platform striking her head, her fall and even the hailstones. The hand she'd put up to try to fend it off – there was a bruise and a cut on that hand, now she looked. She could have been killed. Like Helena.

Oriole sat up. This time, though, it hadn't accidentally been pulled down, nor had it just worked loose. From the way it came down on her, it had to have been detached yet somehow kept still in place. Had it been deliberately rigged up with a prop that she might have dislodged without realising? She needed to know.

She was still muddy from her fall and once on her feet

she felt dizzy and a bit sick, but a hot shower and another couple of paracetamols helped, though she was so parched that her tongue was sticking to the roof of her mouth.

She went down to make a cup of tea. There was no one around, mercifully. The Friends and any students would have gone home by now, Perry's car wasn't there and if Jay had got back from school, he must be in the flat. She couldn't avoid speaking to him sometime about the theft of the card, but she didn't feel strong enough at the moment.

She sat down with her tea trying to think it through. If it did prove to be a trap and not just one of those random accidents that sometimes happen – and it could be, of course – then someone had to have set it and given Jay's habit of doing stupid things in the woods so often before, it was hard not to have him as chief suspect. But at the very place where his mother died – would he really play a sort of dangerous trick that mimicked what had happened to her? Surely not.

But who else would have? What for? She tried hard to think of another explanation, but cold reason kept producing the one she didn't want to entertain – revenge by Jay. He was hurt and bitter and angry – so angry! She could have been the intended victim, or Perry, and if it came down on someone else instead, he wouldn't care, would he?

Even with her head still throbbing, Oriole's heart went out to the damaged child. Yes, he had lost his mother but worse was the wickedly cruel selfishness of his father. She needed now to go out into the woods and see if she could work out how a trap might have operated – and afterwards, whatever she found, she must turn on Perry and force him to get psychiatric help for himself and his son before something a lot more serious than a bash on the head happened.

She didn't want to go out into the woods as it was getting dark, to go to Helena's oak and find herself reliving her own recent trauma. But Perry's car wasn't there and there was no one else around so if she wanted to know, she had to go alone.

Oriole took a torch and put on her boots and hooded waterproof, even though the rainstorm had passed through. At least it wasn't far from the house and with her mind on her mission she plodded doggedly along through the mud.

There was the oak and there was the nesting platform down on the ground, certainly, but it was safely propped up against the trunk. There was wood – branches, sticks – piled up beside it to one side of the path; the area where there might have been some sort of prop to hold it in position had been cleared.

She shone her torch into the undergrowth below, but she could tell nothing from the site. At first she thought this proved someone had come back to remove any telltale signs, but looking at the neatness of the arrangements she realised that, of course, it would have been the Friends, responsibly making sure that no more accidents could happen.

As Oriole turned, discouraged, to go back to the house she became conscious of her vulnerability. The thought of going out alone had scared her, but now it struck her that she had no means of knowing if she was still alone, or if someone else was hidden in the shadows over there – or over there. Jay, even. She stopped, peering round the edges of the hood that acted almost like blinkers and listening with painful intensity, but all she could hear was the light fidgeting of the trees in the evening breeze.

She dared not run on the muddy path, but she walked as quickly as she could, not looking behind her, until she reached the safety of the house. All she wanted to do was go back to bed and blot it all out.

Feeling as if he'd gone several rounds with Tyson Fury, Perry Forsyth dropped Nicki Latham back at her flat in Kilbain, then drove back to Drumdalloch. He'd been more than ready to drop her; he'd invited her on impulse, partly as a secret celebration of the mind-blowing deal, but the party spirit never quite took off. Then she'd asked too many questions – far too many, none of which he wanted to answer – and persisted in talking about things he didn't want to talk about so that he ended up wondering why he'd liked her before.

In fact, he'd also reckoned she'd be a kind of a human shield. He needed more time and he couldn't afford to have Keith and Steve think he was avoiding them: having her with him would stop any serious discussion.

All that old pals stuff – it had suited him too, God knew, but did they think his head buttoned up the back? The luxury hotel they'd be allowing him to invest in, as a special favour, had never looked to him like a goer. If Steve managed to sell his run-down dump – far from a certainty – it would barely cover his debts, and though Keith might well have money and backers it had been clear from the start that the whole thing relied on his inheriting Drumdalloch and basically handing it over, having been told for years it was a complete white elephant.

He had, to an extent, played along when he was still uncertain of his future, and well aware of his past, but the moment he'd understood the true nature of the Drumdalloch legacy he'd realised he could just walk away.

What he'd been counting on was the speed of the operation he'd signed off on today. Keith and Steve wouldn't even know probate had been granted until afterwards, and by then how much he cared about them could be expressed by one middle finger. Theoretically, at least.

But it hadn't worked out that way. He'd walked straight into a trap, courtesy of his bloody sister. When she'd been behaving so oddly, he should have realised she'd been got at. If she was going to allow herself to be used, it could make things awkward.

Once she knew the scale of the money involved, she'd fall into line with him, surely. He'd always been able to stamp on any of her pathetic little rebellions, but he had misgivings now – look at the way she'd been going on today! And, worryingly, the hotel plan would be her dream come true; there'd be a role for her, and she'd be working closely with Steve whom she'd rather tragically worshipped for years. But there wasn't a lot she could do before tomorrow morning and after that it should be a *fait accompli.*

The final shock had been Steve's story about the nesting platform. He felt faintly sick, thinking about it; was this another of James's antics? He'd always been a problem with his blasted tricks in the woods, but Helena had always laughed about it, calling them practical jokes.

This, though . . . Perry couldn't forget James saying he'd heard her talking about someone killing her – and quite recently he'd made that remark, 'Not her *accident*, no.'

He was too exhausted and stressed even to think about the implications of that. The house was in darkness; at least he wouldn't have to speak to James now and Oriole must be sleeping off the bash on her head.

He tiptoed up the stairs to the flat, set his alarm for 5 a.m. and got into bed. Everything was actually running in accordance with the plan, though tomorrow would be a difficult day. An awful lot of people were going to be very angry but whatever happened, no one could stop him by then. It would be too late.

CHAPTER NINE

Oriole had gone to bed desperate for oblivion, but it didn't work out that way. She would drop off, then jerk awake after ten minutes and lie helplessly tired as the ugly thoughts whirled round and the hours ticked by. Was it really possible that only a couple of days ago her main worry had been meeting the interest payments? It seemed trivial now there were so many more worries that she hardly knew where to start; she was finding herself drawn deeper and deeper into a swamp of confusion and fear.

At last, not long before dawn, she fell into a proper sleep. Shortly afterwards, the noise began – a loud, grinding, buzzing noise that seemed almost to be inside her head.

She was so deeply asleep that she felt as if she was under water and being mercilessly dragged to the surface by the sound, somehow linked to the pain in her head. Still groggy, she was struggling to understand why her head should be making it.

But it wasn't. As she sat up, wincing, she realised that of course the noise and the pain were separate. Her head was sore because she'd hurt it the previous day; the noise was coming from outside, somewhere in the woods where at this time only the dawn chorus should be breaking the silence.

Oriole could recognise it as the noise of a saw, but it was much louder than the power saw Nicki used on fallen branches – and anyway, Nicki wouldn't be here when it was barely light. A chainsaw, perhaps . . .

She was on her feet, heart pounding, almost before she had quite thought it through, pulling on jeans and a sweater and hurrying downstairs. There was no sign of Perry but the front door was open and when she shoved her feet into her boots and stepped outside she saw a large lorry with a very long flat-bed trailer in the parking area beyond the garage.

So that was it! Perry, without consulting her, was cutting down trees and she knew which they would be – the beautiful, majestic ones in the arboretum intended as a star feature of the new hotel. Long ago, when she wasn't paying much attention, her father had talked about how rare and valuable they were; she'd forgotten, but Perry obviously hadn't.

She was crying as she hurried down the main path, so she barely noticed the damage to trees and shrubs on either side where heavy equipment had been brought through. But she stopped with a gasp of dismay as she heard a crash – then another one.

She'd watched diseased trees being felled and knew the procedure. They would be stripping the tree of side branches with axes as they worked, but the background buzz of the chainsaw went droning on as, heartsore at the destruction of her dream, she hurried past the rockery and the overgrown pond that might never now be restored. She was close enough to hear men's voices and then she reached the point in the path where you could look up to see the trees outlined against the sky.

It was the magnificent black ebony that was under attack, its leaves tossing about as if it were writhing under the assault; the characteristic spreading boughs that had looked like all-embracing arms had been amputated already. Oriole cried out; she could almost hear its tortured cries and feel the giant's dying agony in her own soul.

And there was Perry in a hard hat, standing talking to someone directing the heavily manned operation. He saw her approaching and came towards her grinning. 'Sorry, sorry, did we wake you? But they're doing a great job – it won't take long. And then we can celebrate!'

She launched herself at him. 'You bastard!' she shrieked. 'You rotten bastard!'

He was actually laughing as he held her off. 'Oh, yes, I know. I should have warned you, explained, but I knew you might get a bit wrochit up and there wouldn't have been any point in arguing. It's done now, and what Jim, this nice guy here,' he jerked his head at the man standing beside him, 'is going to give us for it will mean that all our worries are over.'

Oriole, choking with tears, turned to the man. 'He can't do this!' she yelled. 'It's my property too and I don't consent! Stop them!'

Jim was looking as if he was trying to pretend he wasn't there. 'Sorry, miss,' he mumbled. 'Er – it's a bit too late to do anything now.'

There were four men bracing the tree with ropes and as they watched, the saw made its inexorable way through the bole until at last it was only balancing on the stump. They took the strain as the saw was switched off and lowered their victim down to land with a crash on a deathbed of its own crushed leaves and branches.

There was a moment of silence that was almost respectful. Then Perry said, 'Well, it's done now, so you may as well get over it. You can't exactly stick it together again, can you?'

Oriole could barely breathe, let alone speak. She put her hatred into the look she gave him, then turned and hurried back along the path to the house. Steve had to know at once.

Deep in the shadows, Lachie MacIver had been watching what was going on from the start. His arthritis had worsened lately; he'd been turning restlessly when the rough, throaty sound of an engine splintered the silence – a heavy vehicle of some sort, surely? Not the sort of thing you ever heard around here.

He eased himself out of bed with an occasional sweary word, then went in his bare feet to open the door. It was still dark inside the bothy and outside it was very cold, with dew on the grass and light just starting to filter through the early morning clouds. He could hear more engine noise, and car doors slamming, then men's voices coming nearer: it sounded as if they were heading down the main path and going on through the woods.

Once dressed, and with a jammy 'piece' in his hand by way of breakfast, he had stationed himself among the trees on the edge of the woods. He couldn't pinpoint where they all were at first, but then he realised they were heading for the highest point of the garden just beside the straggly Caledonian pines, the place with all the biggest old trees. He could see their tops outlined against the sky.

He'd never gone up there himself. He hadn't been a welcome visitor and he only used the woods as a short cut to where he could pick up a pheasant from the nearby shoot, never paying much heed to the trees themselves, though on a sunny morning he liked the small noises they made – the leaves rustling, the gentle sighs and moans as the wind passed through, so it was like they were breathing. It was company, in a way.

The only felling old Forsyth had permitted was of sick trees but it wasn't hard to work out what the men were about – and sure enough that was a chainsaw starting up. Different times now. The son would likely get good money for it – folk were always needing wood.

They'd be full of it in the village later. A couple of what sounded like big branches thumped to the ground, but he'd been standing there a while and he was getting cold and hungry; he was walking back to make himself another 'piece' before he went into Kilbain to share his choice bit of news when he heard a woman shouting – in a rare state, seemingly. The chainsaw stopped, there was a crash and Lachie gave a gasp as a gap opened on the familiar skyline.

Minutes later he heard someone coming closer, along

the main path not far from where he was standing himself. Lachie shrank back into the bushes, watching the woman through the gaps between the trees as she went back towards the house, sobbing. He could still hear her, even after she was out of sight. He felt shaken himself; the tree had been there on the skyline all his life and it was wicked to do that to it.

Lachie slipped back through the woods to the bothy to make himself a mug of the sort of black tea you could trot a mouse on. There was going to be trouble today, sure as death.

Michael Erskine was working in his office. Professor Crichton had asked for a position paper to present to the board, which was simple enough. He'd always been able to write fluently so there were pages and pages of the sort of stuff they'd enjoy reading – they had their ambitions too. The lists of his contacts in other more prestigious institutions looked particularly impressive.

He read it through, trying to ignore the sick, headachy feeling that was only partly because he'd drunk too much the night before. Perhaps he had mistaken his vocation; he should have turned to writing fantasy novels instead, since pretty much every word of this was fiction. Looked at rationally, what he was doing was quite simply insane; it might well be actionable.

The alternative was to confess that it had all gone wrong. But he didn't actually *know* yet that it had; Perry Forsyth still didn't have the legal right to do anything. Something could turn up; he'd been on to NatureScot three times in the last two days, trying to persuade them to consider this a special case, though the second time the woman at the other end of the phone had sounded terse and the third time positively snappy.

He couldn't afford to think about that now and he returned to his report. Homepages of the various scientific establishments had been very helpful in providing the names of contacts; he was just googling the Max Planck Institute in Germany when his phone rang.

At first, he thought it was some sort of nuisance call. Someone was yelling gibberish in a hysterical way and he almost ended the call. Then he recognised the voice and was suddenly cold.

'Lars?' he said. 'Lars, is that you? You have to calm down – I can't make out a word you're saying. Speak English! What's going on? Take a deep breath and tell me.'

There was a silence, then Andersen said hoarsely, 'It is all over. Finished. He wrecks my thesis. He starts to chop down all the trees. You must stop him, or I must. I do not let him do this – you do not let him.'

It was worse than even his worst nightmares. 'He's doing what?'

'There is a lorry I passed just now on the road, a lorry with the black ebony on it, felled. This is what he is doing.'

The name meant nothing to him – soil science was his field – but what made him feel as if he'd stepped into an open trapdoor and was in free fall was the thought that probate must have come through.

'Was this tree a vital part of your research?' he said.

'A part, but not the vital one. It is what he will do now . . .'

Erskine stood up. 'I'll meet you there. We need to see what has actually happened, see how we can stop him, organise something – a protest, perhaps.'

He switched off his phone, cutting off Andersen who was in full flow again. The trouble was, organisation took time. And even if he applied for an injunction, that would take time too.

Worst of all, if the man had now realised what a valuable asset his timber could be, there was no way he would sell the property at a price the Institute would be able to offer.

With his sister's accusations ringing in his ears, Perry Forsyth silently slipped upstairs to the flat and locked the door, rather in the spirit of raising the drawbridge; he'd prepared supplies yesterday for withstanding a siege, including a bottle of bubbly stashed in the fridge. It would be Oriole, whom he could hear moving around in the kitchen, who'd be left to deal with the onslaught.

He didn't feel like cracking open the bottle yet, though. Despite the extraordinarily comforting balance of his online bank account – checked this morning after the Williams Timber lorry had left – he was nervous. The confrontation with Keith loomed and though he could tell himself there was no way he could be forced into an agreement now, there was always a question mark when it came to Keith.

James's door was shut. He might have gone off to school but if he was still asleep Perry didn't plan to disturb him. It hardly mattered now, given that he'd be going back to his boarding school, if they would take him – and if they wouldn't, there were plenty other schools that would. He didn't need him hanging around; the morning would be tricky enough without that.

From the sitting room he was watching the parking area and the woods beyond. Lars Andersen was an early arrival, leaping out of his tatty Jeep in what looked like a frenzy to run off down the path.

He must have heard already, somehow. There was a group of students arriving too, chatting as they headed into the woods; there'd be a reaction from them too, likely. His stomach was churning, just a bit.

Another car pulled up and there was Nicki Latham getting out and walking confidently into the house. He frowned; he didn't remember her saying she'd be in today, but he'd had so much on his mind that he might not have noticed. Just as well, really – Oriole could let off steam to her.

Restless, he got up to make more coffee and when he got back to his viewpoint there was a man walking fast away from the house, head down, along the path – Michael Erskine.

Ah! Andersen must have summoned reinforcements. He'd keep out of their way until the fuss died down, though later he might agree to see him, just to put him back in his box. Any restraining order would take time to arrange; Williams Timber would be back for the mahogany tomorrow and now Perry could afford an expert lawyer to handle any challenge – not poor old Muriel Morris who'd been so utterly feeble over dealing with Erskine before. Anyway, he'd have no problem with whatever sort of fine they might impose.

But now, much earlier than expected, there was Keith Drummond, striding up to the front door. He glanced up at the house, his face going dark as he caught sight of Perry.

There was nothing Keith could do now, and he was well prepared, he told himself firmly, but he was still on edge as he gestured him to come upstairs to the flat.

'Good gracious! Are you all right, Oriole?' Nicki Latham cried as she stepped into the kitchen.

Oriole patently wasn't, sitting hunched over the table, her head in her hands. When she looked up her eyes were red and swollen and there was a raised lump on her forehead that was a livid green and purple.

'Sorry, sorry,' she muttered, 'It's just so awful . . .'

Nicki took the seat next her at the table and put an arm round her shoulders. 'I came whenever I could. What on earth's happened? Your poor head—'

'Oh that! I think it was probably one of my nephew's little jokes – he's not very thoughtful, but I'll survive. And after all, I was able to cancel my credit card.'

Oriole sounded bitter and Nicki looked at her sharply. 'Has Jay been causing trouble?'

'Oh, I suppose so, but that's not really the problem.' She went on to tell her friend the whole story – the fate of the trees her father had loved because his grandmother Isabella was so proud of having been able to get them to grow here, whose rarity seemed to have made them valuable.

Nicki listened sympathetically, then, in an attempt at comfort, said, 'At least you've got money to fix the roof now. Life here will be a lot more comfortable.'

'Why would I want to stay here? I hate the house, the woods scare me, and what he's done ruins everything. He and Steve and Keith Drummond were supposed to be going in together to build a luxury hotel and the woods would be restored with all Isabella's garden paths and features. I'd have had the dream job for life and now it's wrecked. Steve's so, so angry and Keith will be fit to be tied.'

'My God!' she said. 'That's going to be some dust-up. Where's Perry now?'

'Don't know where he is. I haven't seen him since I came back but he's probably got a price on his head. I saw Lars going out there earlier and he'll definitely be out for blood. Even just disturbing his woods is sort of like sacrilege. And the ornithology students won't be happy either.'

And while she was speaking there was a noise not unlike a flock of birds, as an agitated group of students appeared outside and surged unceremoniously into the kitchen.

A young woman in a brown cagoule who seemed to have appointed herself spokesperson marched across to stand looking down at Oriole with her hands on her hips. 'What is going on?' she said belligerently. 'Vandalism, I call it. Trees and bushes damaged all along the path. I understand this wood is protected, yet everything's in a complete state this morning – birds flying everywhere so that we can't take meaningful observations for our projects. And the nesting platform's been taken down despite there being tree boxes with nestlings we need access to. Perhaps you'd care to explain? It better be good.'

Oriole had never liked her – always entitled, demanding – and she wasn't about to make the expected apology. 'Nothing to do with me,' she said flatly.

'Oh really? They're your woods, but it's someone else's problem, is it, and you're not taking any responsibility?'

'No, I'm not. You're talking to the wrong person. Find my brother if you want to be unpleasant.'

Nicki stepped in. 'As you can see, Oriole isn't feeling very well. All right? Door's over there.'

The belligerent woman was still protesting, 'But who do we complain to, then?' as she was firmly ushered out and Nicki shut the door behind them.

Oriole slumped back. 'Thanks, Nicki. Don't know how I'd have got rid of them. I'm so glad you're here – I didn't know you were planning to come today.'

'Jo asked me yesterday to do a swap with my day off and I thought I might as well come in to see how things were with Jay and everything. Is he at school now?'

Oriole shrugged. 'I don't know. It's just going to be seriously unpleasant, isn't it?'

Nicki was facing the window. 'And talking of unpleasant, there's Keith Drummond now, heading this way. Not looking best pleased.'

'Oh no, not Keith! I don't think I can stand it,' Oriole cried.

They heard him coming into the hall, but his footsteps went on up the stairs and they heard Perry's voice from the landing.

'Morning, Keith. You're bright and early today.'

'Sooner the better,' Keith said, and then the door shut.

'So that's where he is!' Nicki said. 'Tell you what – if anyone else comes to complain, I'll man the door here and send them straight up. I suppose if we actually heard Perry screaming, we could always mount a rescue – though we can't exactly call in the police, can we?'

As a joke it didn't work. Oriole just said bluntly, 'To be honest, I think I'd just leave them to it.'

'Right, you chiselling little sod, you can explain to me what all this is about.'

It was a good-sized room but somehow as Keith Drummond walked in, it seemed to shrink. Keeping his distance, Perry said, 'It's pretty straightforward. I never agreed to anything. You and Steve just told me what we were going to do, and once I thought it through, I realised it wasn't going to work out. Sorry, Keith, but that's the way it is.'

Drummond's face was red with anger and he took a threatening step closer to him. 'I think you're forgetting something.'

Perry held his ground. 'Well, yes, I was grateful to you at that time. My father and Oriole were so stressed—'

'And your head was on the block – oh yes, I remember. In vivid detail. Do you really think you can just dump the agreement? I ended up going through a police investigation thanks to you – are you so dumb that you don't know what I could do to you?'

He'd prepared for this line of attack. 'What you're leaving out is what I could do to you,' he said and saw, with satisfaction, that the shaft had gone home. 'I think we'd better not go there, don't you? You came through it all right, after all, and it might be as well to let sleeping dogs lie.'

'Oh no,' Drummond roared. 'No, no, no.' He brought his great fist down each time for emphasis so that the cheap dining table jumped. 'I'll tell you what's going to happen. Sit down.'

But there was a note of desperation there, wasn't there? Even of fear, that he'd played his trump card and it hadn't worked? Perry was feeling better all the time – high, almost, on the sort of confidence that having serious money in the bank gives you. 'Good idea, Keith. Sitting down we can talk things through calmly. What I suggest is that you and Steve produce a proper business plan and I'd be happy to invest in your company – after professional advice, of course.'

Drummond stared at him. 'That tree,' he said slowly. 'Valuable, was it?'

Perhaps Perry shouldn't have smiled, but he couldn't help it. 'You could say.'

As he spoke there was a knock on the front door, then the sound of voices. 'Just ignore it,' Perry said. 'It'll be that Erskine man, complaining. Oriole's in the kitchen – she can deal with it.'

Then he heard Nicki Latham saying, 'Perry's upstairs in the flat – just go on up.'

Perry swore. A moment later, Michael Erskine threw open the door, looking pale and shaken but clearly very angry.

Ignoring the man sitting at the table, he said, 'What the hell do you think you're doing, Forsyth? You can't just chop down trees like that.'

'Actually, I just have. They're my trees. I can do what I like.'

'I'm warning you!' Erskine said. 'I'm getting an injunction. The woods will be declared a Site of Special Scientific Interest – Lars Andersen's thesis is of considerable significance. You won't be able to ignore that.'

Perry was starting to enjoy himself. 'Can't wait to see it – as you might say!' He was the only one to laugh and he went on, 'The mahogany's going tomorrow. But at the moment, I've other things I need to get on with, if you wouldn't mind?'

'You're playing with fire,' Erskine burst out. 'Andersen is beside himself with anger – if I can't make you see sense, I won't be responsible for what might happen. And it's not just him, there are others whose professional futures depend on this place . . . the students—'

'And you?' Perry said. 'Thought you could walk all over us, tell us our property was worthless, tie us up with fancy orders for this and prohibitions for that. Whatever you do, it's too late now.'

Words seemed to fail Erskine. 'I'll–I'll . . .'

'No, I don't think you will,' Perry said. 'You're wasting your time – and mine.' He held open the door.

The man's face was a mask of hatred and helpless fury as he walked past, shouldering Perry on the way.

Drummond, a silent listener, stood up. 'Looking for trouble, aren't you? In my professional experience, people who do that usually find it. And don't think we're finished with this – I have some people to talk to first.' He walked out, down the stairs and out to his car.

He hadn't been blustering at the end; he'd spoken with

a quiet intensity that was a lot more unsettling. As Perry watched him go, the exhilaration he'd been feeling started to drain away; it was common knowledge that Drummond had some pretty unsavoury connections.

He'd known, of course, that Erskine would get an injunction quite promptly; tree-hugging was fashionable at the moment and there'd be hordes of eco-freaks super-gluing themselves to the vegetation in a matter of days. As long as they felled the mahogany tomorrow and the old walnut the day after, he'd be satisfied. Didn't do to be greedy!

There were just a few more things he'd need to check on before the men came in the morning and he needed to sort out James, but then going off on a well-earned holiday could be a smart idea. He'd even picked up a few brochures in anticipation – he'd always rather fancied South Africa – and perhaps this evening once the hoo-hah had died down, he could crack open the champers and browse through them.

It had been hard to get herself into a fit state to do her early afternoon shift at the Kilbain, but Oriole had managed it, more or less, covering up the bruise on her head as best she could with foundation and powder. She was worn out by the end, though. She hadn't seen Steve – he was away somewhere – and she was worrying that what had happened might end their friendship.

She was determined to stay strong, though, and as she drove home she told herself that she mustn't give in to her stress and exhaustion. There was no point in arguing; tomorrow morning, she had no doubt, they would come for more of the precious trees, but she'd be up well before first light, lying down in the road like protesters did if that was what was needed to stop them. And stop them she would.

Apart from a minor disagreement in the rookery and an owl hooting, the night's peace was unbroken. By early morning, though, the trees were beginning to sway uneasily as again a rising wind stirred the branches and the pale moon came and went behind clouds that were starting to race across the sky.

Its flickering light was mirrored in the black water of the little ornamental pond, in which Perry Forsyth lay sprawled face down with a great bloody gash right across the back of his head.

CHAPTER TEN

It was well before sunrise when the logging team from Williams Timber turned into the drive of Drumdalloch House. It was still dark and a heavy downpour meant they might have to wait a bit until it was light enough to see their way.

Leading the convoy in his Jeep, Jim the foreman said gloomily, 'This is all we need, Chris. And there'll be trouble, I can tell you that.'

His passenger grunted. 'Hysterical bloody woman. Just hope Forsyth's got her agreement – or else manages to lock her in her room.'

The 'hysterical bloody woman' had been sitting at the kitchen table for half an hour before that. Oriole was feeling awful, shaky and light-headed. She had a mug of coffee in front of her but she'd made it too strong and the first sip made her gag and shudder. She should have something to eat but the thought of what lay ahead was making her feel sick. But at the first sound of the approaching vehicles, she leapt up, ran out and stood in the middle of the drive to block their passage as she signalled to them to stop.

Muttering expletives, Jim braked obediently. 'What did I tell you?' he said, getting out.

'Nothing I didn't know,' the other man said, doing the same.

She was shaking as she said fiercely, 'You're just going to have to turn right round and go back. I'm the joint owner of this property and I refuse to let you even enter, let alone cut down trees.'

The foreman said, with what he felt was admirable restraint, 'I can see you're upset about it, miss. But we've a contract with your brother – perhaps he could come and sort this out.'

'It doesn't matter what he says. I wasn't consulted before, or I'd have put a stop to it then.'

'If you could just get him to come and speak to us. Where is he?'

She glanced back at the house. 'Slept in, I suppose. But I'm not waiting till he chooses to come down, just to give me grief. It should be enough for you that I've told you that you can't commit any more vandalism here, and I'm going to stand right on this spot until you go away.'

She might be a small woman, but she was certainly determined. Feeling helpless, Jim looked at his workmate, who looked back at him blankly. 'Look, miss,' he tried, 'we can work all this out once we see Mr Forsyth. If you would just go and wake him—'

'While you take advantage of getting me out of the way and drive on in? I don't think so.'

He tried again. 'I won't move from the spot. You haven't

even a jacket on and you're getting soaked and so are we. None of us wants to stand here like this all day, but I'm not going away until I've spoken to him.'

She eyed him distrustfully. 'Go and wake him yourself, then, though it won't make any difference to me just standing here. It's the upstairs flat.'

'OK,' Jim said. 'Chris, you do that, and I'll go back and tell the guys what's going on.'

He got a dirty look from Chris as he turned away, leaving Oriole standing forlornly, her arms huddled round her against the cold and with her hair plastered to her head. She was trying to stop her teeth from chattering; she'd need to stay quite clear and calm and just go on repeating what she'd said until they realised that whatever Perry's contract with them said, they had no right to carry it out without her permission.

It seemed a long time before Chris came back. 'Not there. I knocked and called, then had a look round but he must have gone out. Could be down there already, thinking we'd just go ahead.'

'Maybe I could go down there, have a word with him?' Jim said looking at Oriole, though not hopefully.

'No.'

The two men looked at each other, then drew back to confer. 'Stalemate,' Jim muttered. 'Nothing we can do unless the man thinks to come back to see why we haven't arrived. I'll try his mobile.'

There was no answer and he pulled a face. 'Give him five more minutes. Then we'll have to persuade her to get out the way – don't fancy backing the whole lot down that drive.'

They waited as the rain found its way through their

allegedly waterproof jackets, then at last Jim said, 'My boss will get in touch with Mr Forsyth later. We'd be grateful if you'd just let us turn.'

Oriole stood back instantly with a sweeping gesture. She didn't say anything, but she gave a huge sigh of relief that somehow it had actually worked, retreated out of the rain and stood at the kitchen window watching as the procession of vehicles turned and drove away.

As they headed back towards Inverness, Jim said to Chris, 'Funny, that. He was dead keen yesterday and it sounded like he was the one calling the shots. And he'd be daft to go away down there to wait for us in this weather.'

Chris agreed. 'It's a big house – maybe he was somewhere else, in another bedroom, or something.'

'Or maybe it was her got him locked up, not the other way round. Wouldn't put it past her!'

'The boss won't be pleased – he was well chuffed with the deal.'

'I'll get him to phone and sort it out.' Then he said, as they crossed the Kessock Bridge out of the Black Isle, 'Funny, though,' and Chris said, 'Right enough.'

With most guests at the Kilbain Hotel booked in for the weekend, only two couples were leaving this morning and unusually there were no actual complaints, even though Steve Christie, manning the front desk, could sense a certain lack of enthusiasm from one of them. Result!

He dreaded to think about the day ahead. It hadn't taken long for the grapevine to provide every detail of what had happened at Drumdalloch Woods the previous day to add to what Oriole had told him in an emotional phone call, and he'd made it his business to stay out of her way until he could see how the land lay.

Keith Drummond's visit to Perry had been meant to put him firmly back in his box, but he'd phoned just afterwards sounding as if he was talking through gritted teeth and Steve had no difficulty in recognising bluster when he heard it.

Somehow Perry, whom they'd seen as a pigeon for plucking, had turned round and screwed them ruthlessly. They were into disaster management or else the whole project would be history.

But he had to forget all about yesterday. What was done was done and it was a question of making the most of whatever opportunities presented themselves – and coping with the new problems too. What he certainly couldn't do was avoid Oriole today, unless she didn't arrive for her shift.

She was due at 9, but at 8.30 she appeared, looking pale and drawn. The bruise on her forehead was still visible under her make-up but she was smiling brightly.

He came forward to take both her hands. 'Oh, your poor head! How are you, love? I was so sorry not to see you yesterday, but it was a meeting I couldn't get out of. Have you been able to make Perry see sense?'

The smile faded. 'Well, not exactly, no. What I did was steal a march on him and got out there before he was up – couldn't believe my luck! The loggers were all ready to start on their next victim, but I just stood in the way like a one-woman protest and they had to turn back.'

'Oh, good girl! That was very brave. And what did

Perry have to say about it?'

'I haven't seen him. The man they sent to look claimed he wasn't in the flat and I certainly wasn't going to hunt for him and give him the chance to yell at me. Once they'd gone, I just drove away and waited for the café in Fortrose to open and then came in to work. I don't want to see him, Steve – not until I've spoken to our solicitor.'

She was looking at him pleadingly. 'That sounds just the thing to do,' he said encouragingly. 'Do you know what his game plan is?'

'Just chop down all the trees and see what he can get for them, I suppose. My father's beautiful trees – and our arboretum.' She had tears in her eyes.

Steve thought for a moment. 'Look, when he finds out what's happened, he might well summon them back if you're not there to stop him. I can see how upset you are – you shouldn't leave him with a free rein.'

Her dismay was obvious. 'But you need me here,' she protested weakly. 'There are the invoices from last night to reconcile—'

'Not a problem. Off you go home and if you get Perry to accept he can't do stuff like this without your agreement, come back with your mind at rest.'

'I suppose I have to go back sometime,' she said. 'It's just that it will be really hard and I'm so, so tired.'

Steve did feel real pity for her. He put his arm round her shoulders. 'You can handle it – look what you achieved this morning, Superwoman! Stick to your guns and keep in touch.'

He watched her go with dragging feet, then went to phone Keith Drummond.

* * *

Lee Williams was an unhappy man as he left Inverness. His foreman had told him what had happened and he was facing the collapse of the most lucrative business deal he'd done in years, the one to make up for all the recent lean ones.

They'd been racing against the clock: once the preservationists got their claws in it would be stopped. The black ebony had been the big prize, but if they could've got even another two or three of the rare hardwoods felled they'd be satisfied – more than satisfied. A delay would be a disaster.

It could be just a question of chatting up the sister and he'd had plenty of experience of talking down tree-huggers. According to Jim, Forsyth had been rude and bullying the day before, which wasn't smart; maybe he could smooth things over and then they could get back on course. Any form of legal wrangling could scupper the whole thing – and the first payment was already in Forsyth's bank account.

There were several vehicles outside Drumdalloch House – a couple of cars, a people-carrier and a scruffy Jeep. No sign of actual protestors, which had to be good, so Williams parked beside an Audi and got out of his car.

He hadn't realised how dilapidated the house was when he'd made his nocturnal visit – one wing pretty much a ruin, in fact. Well, Forsyth had enough already to transform it into a palace if that was what he wanted to do, he thought as he knocked on the door.

The woman who opened it and eyed him distrustfully was quite small and slight, with the sort of face that made you want to say, 'Cheer up, it may never happen!'

'Yes?'

He smiled at her. 'Miss Forsyth? I'm Lee Williams – Williams Timber, you know? I was wanting to have a word with you and your brother. Is he around?'

She made no move to let him in, standing four-square in the doorway, much as she allegedly had stood to stop Jim's men. 'I don't know. I haven't seen him.'

'So he's not in?' As she only shrugged, Williams looked around the parked cars. 'Is he away somewhere? Is his car here?'

'Yes.' She pointed to the Audi.

She was clearly determined to be unhelpful. Suppressing his irritation, he said, 'So he might be somewhere around? Would you mind if I went to look for him?'

'No,' she said. 'Carry on. But I'll tell you now what I told your men – he has no legal right to authorise anything without my consent.'

She went back inside and shut the door before he could say, 'Of course.' He walked off down the path, his heart sinking. That had been a masterclass in passive aggression; there was no way that one would budge. What the hell had Forsyth been playing at?

At least the rain had stopped, even if there was a quagmire under his feet, and he couldn't help admiring the trees as he walked. Some fantastic timber – that oak, there by the path! It was a quaint jumble, though, unlike the well-managed commercial woods and forests he mostly dealt with.

He could hear different birds singing, though he wasn't expert enough to identify them, and he could hear young voices too before he came across students grouped round what looked like some sort of weather station. They were unlikely to be on his side when it came to cutting down trees, but they showed no signs of hostility at present, only looking at him curiously when he asked if they'd seen Mr Forsyth.

They hadn't, so he headed on towards what he thought was the area where he'd seen the black ebony that night, though with all the criss-crossing paths it was hard to be sure. He saw someone working in a small thicket of trees – a huge, black-bearded man, kneeling on the ground with a case of instruments open beside him. He had raised his head at Williams's approach but otherwise ignored him.

'Morning!' Williams called. 'Can you help me? I'm looking for Mr Forsyth.'

The man glanced at him briefly, grunted, 'Haven't seen him,' then went back to whatever it was he was doing – taking soil samples from around the roots of a handsome chestnut, it looked like.

Williams walked further on. He remembered that jumble of rockery stones and then there had been a dark pool that had caught the light of his torch—

A crow flew up suddenly from beside the path with a harsh caw and he recoiled in alarm, then stopped and stared. There was the pool, and there was a man slumped face down in the weird black water, the back of his head a mess of dried blood. There were signs of the crow's interest and he was undoubtedly dead. He was also, undoubtedly, Perry Forsyth.

'Oh my God!' Williams said. His stomach heaving, he turned and stumbled back along the path, groping for his mobile.

* * *

Kelso Strang was sitting round the big kitchen table having coffee after Saturday lunch with Bill and Marjory Fleming in their house, converted from two farm labourers' cottages. They had moved into it when they handed the Mains of Craigie farmhouse on to their son Cameron, his Aussie wife Annelise and now little Lewis, who could carry on the Fleming farming tradition into the next generation – at least according to his doting grandfather, though his more cynical, if equally doting, grandmother did tend to roll her eyes when he said that.

At least, he reflected, lunch as provided by Marjory, though tasty enough, didn't poleaxe her guests for the rest of the day as Annelise's lunches up at the farmhouse tended to do; she'd always said bluntly that slaving over a hot stove wasn't her thing when there were professional chefs prepared to do the hard yards with better results than she would ever achieve herself.

Cat had gone to do what she described as a final edit of her stuff before they packed it into the car to take back to Newhaven, a pile that was currently occupying most of the floor space in the little hall.

'I'll bring in one of the bins for you so you can "edit" it straight in there,' Bill had suggested. 'Cut out the middleman.'

She'd pulled a face at her father. 'You should be glad I'm taking as much as I am. Kelso's done a brilliant job of clearing space for me.'

'I found it therapeutic, in fact,' Kelso said. 'It was mostly things I should have chucked out years ago, like old army stuff – can't imagine why I kept it.' He didn't mention the other, more personal things that had been more painful to give up, but they had gone earlier before Cat moved in.

'Well done you,' Marjory said. 'Cammie's attitude was that he could just leave anything he didn't immediately want with us, so it's a sort of karma that the house it's cluttering up is his now.'

Cat put her head round the door. 'Mum, I don't think it will all fit in the car. I'll have to leave stuff, but I'll come back for it another time.'

Bill groaned and Marjory said, 'I'll believe that when I see it! Oh, all right then, as long as you stow it away properly.'

She disappeared again. Kelso accepted more coffee and leant back in his chair. It was a very pleasant room; it wasn't very big but somehow it managed still to have the feel of a farmhouse kitchen with Scott the Border collie – his behaviour much improved – dozing in front of the Rayburn.

'I gather you're pencilled in for a spot of baby worship after Lewis wakes from his nap,' Marjory said. 'He's really—'

She broke off as Kelso's phone rang. He pulled it out of his pocket, looked at the number and said, with a grimace, 'Sorry, I'm afraid I'm going to have to deal with this.'

'Take it in the study,' she said quickly, and he nodded, walking past Cat, who stopped what she was doing to stare at him, then went through to the kitchen.

'Does that mean what I think it does?' she asked her mother.

'Given that he's off duty, I don't think it's someone asking if he's filled in the form to claim his expenses,' she said. 'It may be something he can deal with on the phone, but you'd better be braced for having to go back.'

Cat sighed. 'Oh, and I did so want to see Lewis! Still, it's his job, isn't it? You know all about that, Dad.'

'Indeed I do,' Bill was saying with some feeling as Kelso came back in.

It was clear from his face what the message was.

'I'm sorry to be a killjoy, but I have to get back to Edinburgh now. Sorry to spoil your day, darling, but can we get the car packed up at once?'

Marjory said, 'Look, why don't you set off straight away and I'll drive Cat up tomorrow with all the clobber. It would work better for both of you and I don't mind.'

Cat was reluctant. 'I don't want to abandon Kelso when he might need support. I'll be quick.'

But even she could tell from his face that he'd approved the suggestion and then, in a flurry of farewells he was gone.

'He'd left already in his head, hadn't he?' Cat said. 'I could tell it was giving him some sort of buzz.'

Marjory nodded. 'I remember that – a sort of a mixture of exhilaration and tension. It's addictive – it's what keeps us doing the job despite all the downside.'

'Like getting ready to make your closing submission to a jury,' she said, then sighed. 'I'll be glad to see Lewis, but I still wish I'd been going back with him. I'll miss him tonight.'

'Ah, young love,' her father said, laughing.

Feeling his heart pounding in a most alarming way, Lee Williams emerged from the woods and reached Drumdalloch House, where the police would presumably soon be arriving. The woman who answered the emergency call hadn't been very specific.

He'd had the nasty thought that he might be expected to stay with the body but had told himself he'd need to show the police where it was. He'd also thought about telling the young people he'd spoken to earlier and warning them to keep away from the site, but again that really should surely be a job for the professionals.

What he couldn't wriggle out of was breaking the news to the man's sister before police cars started arriving. It was hard to know how she'd take it; there was obviously no love lost between the two of them, but you never knew with families. She might be grief-stricken, but on the other hand she might even be pleased. Or might even . . . surely not!

Cutting down trees was his business, and handling delicate social situations was above his pay grade. He found himself walking slower and slower as he reached the house and had to steel himself to knock on the door.

It didn't help that when she opened it she had a 'what-is-it-now?' look on her face. He said, 'Look, miss, I'm afraid I have some bad news – very bad news,' and he saw her go pale. He was afraid she might faint – maybe he hadn't done it right?

But she said, 'I think you'd better come in and tell me the worst,' and as she spoke, to his immense relief, a police car appeared up the drive.

Oriole couldn't think straight; her mind was going round and round, whizzing off in one direction and then another like a pinball.

Her first clear thought was that she must talk to Jay. There was another police car driving in now and before long, Keith Drummond would probably appear and start grilling everyone like he had when Helena died, and the whole ghastly circus would start up again. Jay had the right to be given time to prepare himself.

She got to her feet, but her legs were feeling leaden as she plodded up the stairs to the flat. Jay was never an early riser and she'd been in the kitchen since she got back from Kilbain House so she didn't think he could have gone anywhere without her seeing him.

Oriole knocked on the front door and then went in. 'Jay!' she called, but there was no answer. She put her head into the living room then tapped on his bedroom door.

When she went in, the room was empty. Last time there had been a sports bag on the floor with its contents scattered round about but now, though there was a pile of mainly dirty clothes, there was no bag.

Jay had gone.

CHAPTER ELEVEN

Nicki Latham found a place to park outside Drumdalloch House, in between the police vehicles, and hurried inside. Oriole had sounded quite desperate on the phone and since they were quiet her boss had let her come at once.

Oriole was in the chair by the Aga, huddling close to it as if she was chilled, though it was now a fine sunny morning. She'd been crying and Nicki went over to give her a hug.

She tried to smile. 'Oh, you are so good to have come so quickly. I hate to drag you into this—'

'Nonsense! Glad to be here for you. Now, I'm going to make coffee while you tell me all about it.'

Oriole took a deep breath. 'Right. Like I said on the phone, the tree man found Perry this morning and the police came, then Keith Drummond arrived to grill me. He's so scary, Nicki! The way he looks at you – so cold and hard! And the way he asks questions is sort of brutal, like he thinks you're guilty. He was the same when Helena died

– I felt sick for days until they found it was an accident.'

'It's probably just his way. Did he tell you how it happened?'

'Just said Perry was struck on the back of the head and he fell into that old pond. That was all.'

Nicki grimaced. 'Simple as that! Poor Perry – and poor you, too.'

Oriole's eyes welled up again. 'I'm just thankful Dad was spared this. I know Perry wasn't exactly the best person but – my brother, after all.'

She patted her hand. 'I know. And what about Jay?'

'Oh God! You know the trap when I was hurt? I thought then he must really believe we killed Helena, and I was quite honestly afraid of him. Now I'm afraid for him – he was so damaged, you know, and they may believe he did this to Perry in revenge. What will happen to him if they do?'

Nicki was just bringing over the coffee, but she froze for a moment with the mug in her hand, before she handed it to Oriole, took her own and pulled over a chair to sit beside her. 'You didn't say that to Keith, did you?'

'No, of course not. He didn't even mention Jay. He was only interested in getting answers to what he asked so all I told him was exactly what I'd done yesterday, nothing else. He was called away because some crime officers had been helicoptered up from Edinburgh.'

'So have you told Jay? How has he taken it?'

Oriole shook her head. 'That's the thing – I don't know. He's not in the flat. Nicki, I think he's run away. There's a bag missing.'

Nicki looked horrified. 'But . . . but that's awful! That's

like an admission of guilt. When did he go?'

'The last time I saw him was when you were here for dinner. I had a set to with Perry about treating Jay so cruelly and dumping his responsibilities on me and when Jay didn't appear looking for food, I just thought Perry must have taken it on board.'

'That was Wednesday night. So he could have gone before all this happened. He's not just hiding somewhere in the house?'

'I checked everywhere – and he's taken his bag.'

'But does he have any money? You said he'd taken your credit card – has he still got it?'

'No. I blocked it. I don't know if he has any money of his own.'

Nicki got up. 'Let's go up to the flat and see if we can find out anything that might be useful.'

'We can't. The police are all over it now and they won't let anyone in.'

She looked dismayed. 'Oh, the poor kid! And of course they're going to have to be told, sooner or later.'

'Yes,' Oriole said. 'But at least we can wait a little bit to give him a chance to come back of his own accord. It would look better.'

Nicki agreed doubtfully, but there was nothing more they could do.

DCI Strang paused in Newhaven only to collect the overnight bag he always kept ready packed and drove on to Fettes Avenue to be briefed and agree the orders for the SOCO squad.

The case was, apparently, a murder in the Black Isle,

and there being no police presence on the peninsula now, it had become the business of the Serious Rural Crime Squad, with backup from Inverness, the divisional headquarters for Police Scotland Highlands and Islands. With a bailiwick the same geographical size as Belgium they were permanently stretched, but a DI had already been dispatched from there and was apparently at the site to liaise with the SOCOs.

Angie Andrews, the Force Civilian Assistant assigned to the SRCS, was off duty today, unfortunately. She was hugely efficient, but the young FCA who was on the shift seemed thrown by Strang's request for somewhere to stay immediately, at least until he could assess the situation.

It could easily be needed for longer than that if it wasn't an open-and-shut case; he'd never minded before but now it worried him that Cat, used to a busy household of flatmates, would find it lonely on her own.

That would certainly give him an incentive to get the whole thing wrapped up quickly. Most murders are solved within twenty-four hours and reading the report that had been filed, this sounded straightforward enough: male victim found in woods with a blunt force trauma to the head that had felled him so that he toppled into a pond and drowned. A blow struck in temper, opportunistic rather than planned?

Working on the basis of motive was risky; officers were susceptible to confirmation bias as they became wedded to a pet theory. But if it was indeed an opportunistic crime, that might have to be the way forward since crimes committed on impulse tend to offer much less in the way of hard evidence. In a small place it should certainly be possible to establish who'd had a grudge against this Peregrine Forsyth.

It certainly wasn't interesting enough to bring the media flocking – always a relief – and if the DI was any good a lot of groundwork could be left to him, rather than importing familiar staff from Edinburgh. That wasn't ideal, but they had a straitened budget this time and Detective Chief Superintendent Jane Borthwick was under a lot of pressure to economise. She was, if you thought about it in those terms, his line manager – a good boss, but demanding.

If he could get up there in time, he could work on a sitrep to be on her desk tomorrow and he set off armed with the postcode of the Kilbain Hotel and Spa. It sounded a bit luxe for police digs and he hoped it wasn't going to blow any savings they might make by relying on local staff. At least it was near the crime scene.

The notorious A9, the longest and most deadly road in Scotland, leads from Edinburgh to Inverness and carries a dangerous mixture of commercial traffic with delivery schedules and tourists impatient to get on with their holiday. It has remained unimproved despite years of political promises, and it is a rare day when there isn't a traffic incident.

With his personal history, it was a route Strang hated. It was, as always, congested today and he saw three accidents only narrowly averted when idiots chose to overtake in places where anyone with half a brain would have held back. He'd had to brake hard himself to avoid hitting the car in front that had been without warning seized with a sudden desire to turn right.

It had taken him well over the estimated three hours and when he drew up outside the Kilbain Hotel it was after ten and dark, but even so it didn't take him long to realise that the reality did not match the promise of the name. The outside paintwork was overdue for a freshen-up and whoever was responsible for cleaning apparently suffered from myopia when it came to the finer details.

The owner, introducing himself as Steve Christie, was expecting him. He smiled a lot and greeted his guest with implausible warmth; police investigations were bad news for anyone forced to become involved.

He could imagine his professional manner going down very well with guests, though – 'Such a charming man!' – but there was nervousness in the jerky hand movements as Christie registered him and found a key.

'Now, we've given you a room with a table and a bit more space to work. Your office arranged for sandwiches and coffee to be provided so I'll get them sent up. The Wi-Fi code is on the card beside the TV. Of course, if there's anything else you need, don't hesitate to let us know.'

'I'd actually like to speak to the officer in charge – DI Drummond, is that right? Is he still at the site?'

Christie immediately looked flustered. 'Oh well, no – it's nearly eleven, you know. DI Drummond left a message half an hour ago to tell you that the site has been secured and he'll see you there in the morning.'

Strang raised his eyebrows. 'I'm anxious to get a report off to Detective Chief Superintendent Borthwick tonight. Have you a direct contact number for him?'

Alarm showed in the man's face. 'I-I don't know . . .'

Strang didn't reply. Christie gulped, then said, 'I'll try to find it for you,' and disappeared into an office at the back.

Strang waited, unconsciously drumming his fingers on the desk. He was tolerably certain that a warning phone call had been made before the man came back holding out a note.

'Thank you,' Strang said curtly. 'I'll deal with this in my room. Goodnight.'

It did not bode well for the investigation.

DI Keith Drummond was in a thoroughly bad mood when he arrived at the hotel at eight o'clock the next morning. He wasn't used to being summoned like a kid to the headmaster's office by a phone call in the late evening when he was just relaxing with a beer after a busy day.

Steve Christie, looking anxious, was waiting for him at the front desk. 'What did he say last night?'

'Oh, pulled rank, dressed me down for dissing him by not hanging around until he deigned to show up. Then he kept me on the phone for half an hour getting background – all stuff that could have waited till today. Apparently, he's expecting a DC to be assigned to him but he's got another thing coming – I've made sure there's no one available.'

Christie looked alarmed. 'Is it wise to get on the wrong side of him?'

'I'm just making sure he has to rely on me for the information he's going to need – or at least, what I consider is appropriate for him to get. I'll be able to see he isn't told anything I'd rather he wasn't told. He won't know where to start otherwise, and I can make things very difficult for him indeed, if necessary.'

Christie said unhappily, 'Just be careful, Keith. Don't go too far. He's got pals in high places, right?'

'In Edinburgh, yes. But this is my patch. So where is he – the bridal suite?'

He coloured. 'I suppose you could call it that, but you might be wiser not to make a joke of it.'

Drummond smiled. 'Oh, leave it to me. I'll get him sorted.'

Christie watched him take the stairs two at a time. He certainly wasn't lacking in confidence but having met Strang, it was a confidence that he himself didn't share.

DCI Kelso Strang was awaiting DI Drummond's arrival without enthusiasm. The man had been resentful at being disturbed at home and seemed to feel no urgency about getting the inquiry under way. The golden hour, when evidence is fresh, had passed without any real progress being made.

The SOCOs had completed the preliminary investigation at the site and had been taken back to Edinburgh by chopper; they would be brought back today to investigate Drumdalloch House where the victim had lived. Presumably that would be the starting point and he could take in a visit to the site at the same time.

The SOCOs' report hadn't been encouraging. Firm evidence was going to be in short supply, but they had established the basics and Forsyth's body was now in the mortuary in Edinburgh awaiting a post-mortem. It was unlikely there would be any surprises there: visible debris in the wound suggested the blunt instrument had been a piece of timber; assessed time of death, though as usual imprecise, pointed to the body having lain in the pond for some hours, with drowning as the official cause of death.

The evidence recorded around the site was mainly footprints in the muddy ground – a confused mass of these – and there would have to be searches of the woods by uniforms to try to find the murder weapon. As the officer in charge had complained, 'You're talking about finding one particular haystalk in a haystack here!'

None of this was helpful. But the information he would need to drive the case forward was being channelled through Drummond, and he didn't trust him.

However, when Drummond appeared, he got up from the table he was using as a desk and greeted him with a smile and a handshake, indicating that he should take the pink velveteen chair he had set beside it.

Drummond looked round the room with a grin. 'Hope you're enjoying the bridal suite,' he said sitting down. 'Not feeling too lonely?'

Strang, surprised, said, 'Oh, is it?' He had noticed the over-elaborate curtains and the piles of cushions in varying tones of pink, but it still looked rather a dismal room. Drummond seemed to be waiting for some reaction, so he said, 'Well, it's perfectly satisfactory. Now, I imagine we will start at the house? I want to touch base with the SOCOs and then take a look at the crime scene. At least the weather's better today.'

'So far,' Drummond put in, sounding as if he hoped it would rain.

Ignoring that, Strang said, 'Right. Let's just run through

who I am likely to see. The sister, presumably.'

'That's right. And there's a student who's worked in the woods for years doing some sort of thesis about trees – Norwegian, an obsessive, bit of a roughneck and aggressive with it, thinks he owns the place. He's not there every day but if he is we'll make it a priority to talk to him. Given that it looks as if that tree being felled precipitated all this, he's our prime suspect.'

It had always gone against the grain with Strang to grade suspects, and he didn't enjoy being bounced. 'You know him, obviously,' he said. 'Has he got previous?'

'No – just come across him once or twice. You'll see what I mean.'

Was Drummond disappointed he couldn't assign a record? Strang said, 'Right. And who else figures on your suspect list?'

'There's the big man at this Institute place that uses the woods – Michael Erskine. Thinks he's God's gift – went radge over this tree being felled. Has plans for the woods and he'd run-ins with family before, so certainly worth taking a look at.'

Drummond was clearly well-informed, but Strang wasn't going to take time now to establish the information's source. 'Who else? The obvious question – who benefits from this? The sister, I suppose?'

'Well, you'll meet her. I've known the family a long time. Oriole, nice lady, dedicated daughter, works hard at keeping the show on the road. Admittedly there were arguments – she wanted everything left as it was, her brother was realistic. But they'd compromised over the years – no reason to suppose she'd suddenly get violent.

And there's a boy, of course – twelve, maybe thirteen now. A bit of a troublemaker – I've had a word with him a couple of times. Just throwing his weight about, though.'

The 'nothing to see here, move along' message was coming over loud and clear. Was Drummond really arrogant enough to think Strang wouldn't recognise the blatant attempt at manipulation? He looked at the man who'd been slouching back in the pink chair with his legs stretched out and thought, yes, he was.

Now Drummond made to stand up. 'Well, we'd better get on with it. I'll drive you over. It'd be good if Andersen's there – having to go after him would take time.'

Strang didn't move. 'Have you managed to find me a DC? I want to get on with interviews as soon as possible.'

Drummond sat back down again. 'Oh, yes. You said that, but I'm afraid there's no one available. With the area we have to cover, we're stretched beyond what's reasonable and this morning there's a couple off sick as well. The one I'd pencilled in was DC Andy Munro – nice lad, bright spark – but he's stuck with an assault in Kinlochewe. But don't worry – I can sit in with you. I was a DC once and I'm not proud.'

At that manifestly false statement, DCI Strang got up abruptly. 'We'll take it as it comes. Now, I need to make a phone call. Wait in the car park and I'll follow you in my own car.'

Drummond looked about to say something but as Strang turned to get his phone he went out, frowning.

Angie Andrews had just come on duty when Strang's call came in. She hadn't realised he was on a new murder investigation and she flipped rapidly through the log to find out the details as he told her he wouldn't be able to rely on money-saving local support to the extent he'd hoped.

'It seems fairly straightforward, and if there's a competent detective available right now, it shouldn't be a big problem. Doesn't matter who, as long as they can come at once.'

'Leave it with me, sir,' she said. 'I'll get back to you when I've checked the rota.'

He'd sounded stressed. She thought immediately of DC Livvy Murray, but she was on a day off. Oh dear! Livvy would be gutted if someone else snaffled the role she'd come to think of as her own; she'd been a bit down, for some reason, and if she knew Strang hadn't asked specifically for her she'd be hurt.

It only took a minute to decide, quite unprofessionally, that she'd call Livvy. Sunday morning, 9 a.m. – she was probably having a long lie.

The voice that answered, on the fourth ring, was sleepy and unwelcoming. 'What the hell, Angie—'

'Thought you'd like to know – the boss wants immediate backup on a murder in the Black Isle. Want to do it?'

Suddenly Livvy was sounding wide awake and ready for anything. 'Didn't know there was one. Did he ask for me?'

'Oh, didn't really have time,' Angie said diplomatically. 'Sounds as if the situation there's a bit fraught. Can you do it? No overtime, mind, even if it is your day off.'

'Penny-pinching as always,' Livvy said, sounding brighter every minute. 'Send me details and I'll be on my way.'

'I'll tell him. And if you'd a heavy night last night, for heaven's sake check your levels before you drive.'

The approach to Drumdalloch House was oppressive, shadowed by rank upon rank of trees that met overhead and encroached on the drive, showing no sign of the sort of maintenance needed to make sure that dead branches, like the huge one DCI Strang could see on an elm on the left, didn't suddenly fall on a passing car, which might be his. In addition, ominous black clouds seemed to be ready to oblige Drummond with a downpour and when the house itself came into view round the turn in the drive it was almost comically dreadful – Victorian brick that had weathered badly and a ruined wing with boarded-up doors and glassless windows looking like sightless eyes.

There were a lot of vehicles of one sort and another in the car park, including a people-carrier that Strang guessed had brought the SOCOs from wherever the chopper had been able to land – certainly not around here. There were crime scene tapes in place and a uniform with a clipboard was standing beside the front door.

Drummond had found a space with just room enough for another car to edge in beside him. As Strang was getting out, Drummond came over, pointing out an elderly Jeep.

'That's a lucky break,' he said. 'That's Lars Andersen's so we can catch him before the rain gets so heavy that he decides to pack it in. I know where he'll be – and maybe if we throw our weight about he might crack and confess immediately and we'd all get home to our tea!'

It was clearly meant as a joke, but Strang let it fall flat. Who was it who had said, 'By their jokes you shall know them'? It wouldn't surprise him if it indicated the Drummond technique, and it was time anyway to disabuse the man of the notion that he was in any sense calling the shots.

'I'm going to talk to the SOCOs first. You may want to come in on this – unless you should be elsewhere?'

'No, no,' Drummond said hastily. 'I'm detailed to lend support while this is ongoing—'

Before Drummond could finish, Strang was checking in with the constable and putting on a coverall and overshoes.

Directed upstairs, he looked around the hall. Judging by the moth-eaten stag's head on the wall, a display of ancient swords and a few items of good antique furniture, it had once been a shooting-lodge with some pretensions to gentility, but the damp stains marking the William Morris wallpaper suggested serious problems with the roof.

Just as he reached the top of the stairs, his phone rang. 'Livvy Murray's on her way,' Angie Andrews' voice said.

'Angie, you're a marvel. Thanks.' Strang's heart lifted. He'd wanted someone now, rather than waiting for Murray when that could be arranged, but it was a real bit of luck that she was available. He could rely on her to have his back and her talent for ferreting out information was second to none. He could also look forward to seeing Drummond trying to patronise her.

The flat where the SOCOs were working was bright and modern, though, and he recognised the Airbnb style he often came across nowadays. He'd been hoping the team would be the one he was most familiar with; it wasn't, but they seemed to be organised and purposeful.

However, the message here too was that useful evidence would be thin on the ground. 'Seems the guy has recently arrived here,' the leader said. 'There's been a kid as well, from the clothes, both living out of suitcases. We've bagged up a locked briefcase and a laptop for forensics to have fun with and there's not much else. Nice bottle of fizz in the fridge, though – Bollinger, would you believe!'

'Interesting,' Strang said. 'He's not a visitor, though – he was joint owner of the property. There are probably papers and records somewhere in the main house, but we'd need a warrant and I'm reluctant to extend the search for the moment. Fingerprints?'

'Kev's on it now.' He gestured towards another man in white coveralls. 'Be nice to get some hard evidence for a change. Next to nothing from the crime scene so far, I'm afraid.'

Strang sighed. 'No. I saw the report. Never mind – bricks without straw is our business. Will you be long?'

The man glanced around. 'Not a lot more than an hour, probably. Oh, good morning, sir.'

Strang turned to find Drummond, also suitably garbed, at his shoulder. 'I'm just leaving,' he said to him. 'If you want to stay and check things out here, that's fine. I won't need you for the next bit.'

Drummond looked stunned. 'But the interviews—'

'Don't worry about them,' Strang said, walking down the stairs, unfastening his coveralls as he did so and handing them, with his shoe covers, to the duty constable at the bottom. 'You've told me the heavy demands the size of the division makes on your team and I don't want to add to them. We'll be relying on uniform backup, of course, but DS Murray will be arriving from Edinburgh shortly. I'm just going to have a word with Oriole Forsyth.'

Drummond had hastily followed him down. 'You could miss your chance to interview Lars Andersen,' he said with a hint of desperation. 'With the rain, he could take off at any moment.'

'I'm sure I'll manage to track him down when I'm ready,' Strang said, turning to the constable. 'Is Ms Forsyth in, do you know?' Assured that she was, he walked across to the kitchen door and knocked, leaving Drummond looking black with temper as he hopped, struggling to remove a shoe cover.

When Oriole opened the door, she gave a quick glance over his shoulder, as if expecting Drummond to be with him. Was she hoping he would be there as a friend of the family, to protect her from any awkward questions?

He introduced himself and she stepped back immediately to admit him.

'Ms Forsyth, I'm sorry for your loss,' he said as he took the seat she had indicated at the kitchen table.

'Oh,' she said, biting her lip. 'Yes – well, thank you. And just Oriole is fine. I-I suppose you've got a lot to ask me?'

'If I may. I know it's hard at a time like this.'

He could see her bracing herself. 'It's OK.'

'Thank you. For a start, am I right that you and your brother were joint owners here?'

'That's right. My father left it to us equally, with the proviso that it should always be a home for both of us.'

'So, what is the present situation?'

A very straightforward question, he had thought, but for some reason it had thrown her. 'Oh goodness – I hadn't really thought about it, but I guess his share will come to Jay – that's his son, you know. Well, he's James, really, but he likes Jay. Of course, he'd be welcome to make this his home as well – it's part his now too, isn't it, and it's certainly what his grandfather would have wanted if he'd ever thought of it happening like this. He was a very kind man, my father, devoted to the family . . .'

She had started rambling on, almost as if she didn't know how to stop, looking down at her hands as she pulled at her fingers.

At last he took pity and stopped her. 'Oriole, you're very nervous about something. It might help if you just told me what it was.'

She looked at him with startled eyes, then gulped. Her head dropped as she said, 'Of course I knew I was going to have to tell you, but I hoped it wouldn't be quite so soon, to give him a chance – I don't want you to jump to any conclusions . . .'

Provokingly, she stopped. 'Yes, go on,' he said, trying not to sound as impatient as he felt.

'It's-it's Jay. I think he's run away. I haven't seen him since Wednesday night and his bag's missing.'

Strang gaped at her. The straightforward case that he'd been confident could be dealt with by standard procedures had just blown up like a roadside bomb.

Whatever the boy's aunt said about not jumping to conclusions, it was what everyone would immediately do. He was going to find himself pinned out like a frog on a dissection board as he contended with the problem of a child who was missing from home, who might, or equally might not, have killed his father, always under the relentless glare of the media.

He said, ‘Then I think we have to get on to that immediately. Can you describe him – height, hair colour, a photograph, perhaps . . .’

It was surprising how coherent you could sound, even when you felt as if you’d been punched in the stomach.

CHAPTER TWELVE

For once there were no significant delays on the A9 and DS Livvy Murray arrived, as instructed, outside Drumdalloch House around midday. She wasn't taken with what she saw – all those creepy trees, and a building that suggested one of the Addams family might open the front door – and something major was clearly happening. She'd been overtaken just before the Kessock Bridge by a badged car in full emergency mode, and when she arrived she only managed to park because another car drove off. There were uniforms everywhere.

There was no sign of DCI Strang, and she approached the duty constable at the front door to ask.

'Not here,' he said. 'Likely back at the hotel – know where that is?'

'No. My orders were to come here, so I'd better call to find out what he wants. What's going on?'

'Misper,' he said. 'Thirteen-year-old boy, missing

since Thursday probably, but no one seems sure. They're pulling out all the stops.'

Missing thirteen-year-olds were not uncommon but – no one noticing for a couple of days? What did that tell you about the Addams family? She went back to the car and called Strang.

'Livvy! You're the only bit of good news I've had all day.' He sounded stressed. 'I'm working from Kilbain Hotel. I'll want to brief you asap, but before you come, talk to Oriole Forsyth at the house. Her brother's the victim and it's his son James Forsyth who has made off.'

'Oh. Sharp intake of breath,' Murray said, wincing,

'Exactly. The media will be in full cry any minute now. What I want you to do is to get her talking – it won't be difficult. Find out everything you can about the set-up – family relationships, history – everything. Be gentle – she's a nervous creature.'

'No wonder! I'll do my best, boss.'

The woman who opened the door to her was no Morticia and she did, indeed, look nervous; she was practically twitching, a slight, almost wispy figure with the sort of face that suggested she'd never expected life to be easy and had resigned herself.

As they both went to the kitchen table to sit down, Murray said, 'I'm DS Livvy Murray. First of all, can I say I'm sorry to put you through all this when you've had such a loss – and the worry about your nephew too.'

'Oh yes,' Oriole said on a long sigh. 'So dreadful.'

'Look, this isn't a formal interview, just a chance for me to get clear on what's happening. Is James's mother here?'

'He calls himself Jay, not James, actually. He changed it to please my father who liked bird names – Peregrine and Oriole, you know. And no, she isn't here. She died in an accident a while ago.'

Even so, surely someone should have noticed he wasn't around? 'So are you his guardian?'

'No, no!' It was an explosive denial of responsibility. 'Perry is – well, Perry was . . .' It brought her up short. 'Maybe I am, then – I don't know—'

She was becoming distressed. Murray said swiftly, 'Don't worry, no one's expecting you to deal with this right now. May I call you Oriole? Tell me about yourself, how things are for you, what's been going on.'

She put her hand to her head for a moment as if she was collecting her thoughts and Murray noticed a large, green-purple lump on her temple – she must ask about that, but she didn't want to interrupt Oriole who had started to talk, and talk, and talk.

It was nearly one o'clock before she started to run down and Murray felt she had learnt as much as she could hope for.

'Thank you. You've been most helpful,' she said, getting up. 'By the way, what happened to your head?'

Had she asked that a little too abruptly? To her surprise, Oriole jumped, her eyes widening in shock.

'I-oh, I can't,' she stammered. 'Wouldn't be fair – I can't . . .'

'So this is something you don't want to tell me,' Murray said. 'I'm sorry, but I'm afraid you must.'

Oriole stared for a moment, gulped, and then began again.

* * *

Steve Christie had spent the morning hovering around the hall. DCI Strang had returned already and gone straight to his room without saying anything other than 'Thank you' when the receptionist gave him his key, but there was no sign of Keith. He'd claimed the man wouldn't be able to do anything without him – surely they should have come back together?

It was an hour later when Keith appeared, looking grim. 'All hell's broken loose,' he said.

Steve felt the first twinges of panic. 'What's gone wrong? You said you had it all under control!'

'Never mind what I said,' Keith snarled. 'I'll tell you—'

Suddenly becoming aware the receptionist was all ears, Steve said, 'Come into the office,' where, to her disappointment, he shut the door. Even so, she could probably hear the torrent of rage and obscenity that Keith let loose; he could only hope it wouldn't actually blister the paint.

'For any sake calm down,' he said. 'Tell me what's happened.'

'Oh, I'll tell you all right. The sodding kid's run away. So there's an All-Points Bulletin with every cop in the north of Scotland looking for him and no doubt the press will be picking over all the old stuff again. Not only that, but the bastard just flatly told me I wasn't needed – he'd be working with a woman DS brought up from Edinburgh.'

His tone sharpened by worry, Steve said, 'I told you not to play games with him. You could have got one of your own in there so he could report back but now we won't even know.'

'Not playing it that way, is he?' Keith said with a

dagger look. 'Just went in to talk to Oriole by himself.'

Steve couldn't conceal his dismay. 'But the whole point was that when he did, you'd be there to protect her, keep him busy asking about stuff that didn't matter, stop her saying anything she shouldn't! You know what she's like once she gets talking!'

'Of course I know! The minute Perry's death was public knowledge, you should have told her to keep quiet. Did you even speak to her?'

Keith had him there. Of course he should have spoken to her. Steve's had always been the shoulder she liked to cry on; she must be in quite a state by now and expecting him to call to ask how she was coping, at the very least. He'd chickened out because he didn't want to be drawn further into the whole mess, but that could prove a costly mistake.

'Wouldn't have known what to say to her,' he said feebly. 'But I could do it now, I suppose.'

Keith said coldly, 'I hope you don't find the horse has bolted. You're quite sure she understood that the hotel plan was a total secret?'

'Of course. Crossed her heart and swore to die.' He didn't voice a worrying suspicion that she could have taken the oath to mean that she would never tell Perry; whether she would consider it applied to other people – like the police – he didn't know.

'The immediate problem is the boy – that's what's driving it. Did Oriole ever tell you anything about him – friends, places he went to?'

'She didn't have much to do with him – always said he hated her. Are you going up to see Strang now?'

'No point. He's definitely taken against me. I might as well go back to Inverness – find out from that end what's happening. See if I can steer the lads who're involved in the right direction. Best I can do.'

Of course, Keith had a lot of pull there, a lot of friends. But Steve couldn't help remembering that if all this went pear-shaped then he'd have a lot of enemies too – as would Steve himself, by association.

All in all, it wasn't surprising that when the receptionist greeted him brightly with, 'Well! What's going on, Steve?' he snapped, 'Perhaps you could just mind your own business,' in a thoroughly uncharacteristic way.

DCI Strang was on the phone to DCS Jane Borthwick when Murray came in, with his laptop open on the table in front of him. He pushed it towards her, mouthing, 'Get up to speed on this,' and went on with his call, detailing the steps being taken.

'Inverness is getting round the locality, of course, and searching the woods here. No details of a phone for him, but presumably he has one – they're trying to track that down. Oriole Forsyth gave me the name of the boy's school in Edinburgh so friends can be questioned, but I think that's all we can do at the moment, boss. We've had a photograph circulated and there's an APB so we just have to hope for a sighting soon.'

He finished the call and sat back in his chair with a groan. 'Please tell me you've got some solid information from the sister, Livvy. I'm groping in the dark here, and I'm wondering why the local DI feels it necessary to try to control my actions, frankly to a rather worrying degree.'

'Oh, trust me, I can,' she said with a self-satisfied grin. 'Like you said, getting Oriole to talk was no problem and I'll give you a potted version but I'm going to start big: Jay Forsyth had a good shot at murdering his aunt earlier.'

'He *what*?'

'Yes, I know. Sounds a bit extreme, doesn't it? She didn't want to tell me what he'd done. She's inclined to make allowances for him because she reckons he thinks that she, and/or his father, murdered his mother.'

'That seems remarkably generous of her in those circumstances. I have to ask – had they?'

'According to Oriole, the students who use the woods for their research have a platform with bird boxes on it attached to an oak, and Jay's mother Helena was maybe having a look and dislodged it. It didn't hit her, but she hurt her foot or something and cracked her skull as she fell. It was pronounced an accident and she was cremated.'

'So if it wasn't, there's no subsequent way of checking. Any indication of why they might have wanted to kill her? Or why Jay might have thought they had?'

Murray shook her head. 'Didn't really elaborate – just an impression she had from his behaviour – bad, apparently, behaving like a sort of Tarzan in "his" woods and his mother encouraged him. Hinted there were marriage problems as well. Anyway, the attempt on Oriole: same tree, same nesting box, same platform. It fell on her head and knocked her out. Friends found her and hustled her to bed so she only thought later that it could have been a deliberate trap – platform detached, then propped up with something that got pushed away as she stepped towards it. I think that's what she said.'

Strang nodded. 'A deadfall trap. I've known that done to kill vermin – old gamekeepers' trick.'

'Right. The Friends had tidied everything up to make it safe, so she hasn't any proof – stressed that, and kept trying to shield him. But I reckon she probably believes he did it and that he killed his father, and the basic message was that Perry was asking for it – totally selfish bastard, apparently. And not just towards Jay, either – plenty of people had reason to hate him. Including her, not that she admitted that.'

'Drummond gave me a couple of names he was pretty determined to push. Did Oriole mention a student, Lars Andersen, or the Director of the Institute that uses the woods?'

'Oh yes. That's Michael Erskine. Had a run-in with Perry on Friday morning and according to her, Andersen exists in a state of more or less permanent fury, totally possessive about the woods. And the tree being felled caused all sorts of trouble.'

'Ah, the tree at last! That is where I came in. There's a statement from the boss of the timber company – did you have a chance to read that?'

'Skimmed it while you were talking. Black ebony – no idea what that is. According to Oriole it was very special, and Perry was going to go ahead and cut down more of what she called her "father's trees", despite her not agreeing. She was determined to stop him.'

'Was she, indeed. You know how much I distrust establishing a narrative ahead of the evidence—'

'Mmm,' Murray said.

He had the grace to smile. 'Yes, OK. But on the face of

it this looks like an impulse killing and most of what we'll get as proof is flimsy, so you have to start somewhere. And what you've just told me would put Oriole squarely in the frame, despite Drummond assuring me she shouldn't even be considered a suspect – which is curious in itself. I'm worried I'm going to have to waste time I can't afford on preventing him hampering me at every turn.'

Murray grinned. 'Oh, you can relax on that, boss. Drummond and Steve Christie and Oriole herself wanted Perry to join a consortium to create a luxury hotel and Perry went out on his own instead, selling off the trees. Which definitely makes Drummond a suspect who will have to be taken off the case.'

'That's quite a considerable relief. Let's get him removed at once, then. You can be the one to tell him, Livvy. I'm only sorry I won't be there to see his reaction, but for the moment at least, I've got to focus on the boy – he's the headline news.

'JB will be issuing a press statement tonight. We've got social media drooling already – it's perfect clickbait, of course. She's been in touch with DCS Anderson in Inverness who's a mate, and we'll have any support we need. He recommended a DI to organise backup – interestingly, it wasn't Drummond.

'I'll give you the name now, and you can get across to the headquarters in Inverness and liaise. Get him to set up an incident room locally, and I'll hold a briefing for you both whenever I can. Boost the profile – I'm relying on you to show we're pursuing several lines of enquiry so they can't claim we're assuming the boy did it. Perhaps—'

His phone rang and he answered it with a wild hope

that they might have a lead, might even have found Jay himself. They hadn't, of course; it was a routine query which he dealt with and then turned back to Murray.

'I think that's all, then. Good luck!'

'Right, boss,' she said. 'But there's something else you need to know. I just Googled black ebony. It's known as the "Million Dollar Tree". Unbelievably rare, pretty much unknown outside some place called Gabon.'

Strang looked at her with horror. You weren't just talking clickbait on social media here – this was banner headlines and the top of the BBC News at Six, and he felt sick.

They'd been told to expect her, DS Murray realised on arrival at the Inverness Divisional Headquarters. When she introduced herself, the FCA at the desk said, 'Oh yes, of course. I'll just call DI Drummond, if you'd like to wait over there.'

Murray said, 'In fact, it's DI Hamish Campbell that I need to see. Is he here just now?'

The woman looked flustered. 'I've been told it's DI Drummond will be looking after you. I'll just call him and then maybe he can get the other officer for you. Take a seat – he shouldn't be long.'

Murray hesitated. She'd hoped to get a feel for the situation before confronting Drummond but making a fuss was never a good start and perhaps it was best to get that interview out of the way anyway.

'Fine,' she said, and went to the bench seating opposite.

She didn't have long to wait. It was less than three minutes before a tall, harsh-featured man appeared and strode across to her, beaming and holding his hand out.

'DS Murray? DI Keith Drummond. Welcome to Inverness. Pity about the reason for your visit, of course, but I'm sure between us you and I can get it all wrapped up neat and tidy. I'll just take you to my office and we can swap notes.'

He was, she thought, trying to exert charm, but the handshake was too forceful, the smile fake, and he was standing oppressively close. She took an involuntary step backwards as she said, 'Yes, fine,' and followed him through.

He took his seat behind the desk and waved her to a chair. 'Now, let me see if I can use my influence to get them to bring us a cup of coffee. We need to show you some proper Highland hospitality and they do a nice line in shortbread. You'll be hungry, coming up all the way from Edinburgh.'

She was indeed and she had a weakness for shortbread, but she wanted to keep this short. 'Thanks, but no thanks. I've a lot to do so we'd better get down to business.'

His smile flickered a little. 'My goodness, what a very conscientious lady you must be. Well, let's make a start. I live in Kilbain, so I can drive you around and give you all the lowdown, explain the wheels within wheels, you know?'

He laughed, she didn't, and he went on, 'But first, tell me how things are going with my poor friend Oriole. I know DCI Strang was having a wee word with her – was she all right? She's very shy, and I'd thought he might have got more out of her if I was there to be a reassuring presence.'

Murray was bristling; he might not actually have said 'little lady' but she heard it just the same. 'Yes, she was all right. I had a long chat with her too and she was enormously helpful.'

With deliberate malice she had lingered slightly on 'enormously' and saw his face change. 'Oh? Well, that's good, then.'

'Yes, it is. Now, I'm sure your local knowledge could be very helpful, but I understand from Ms Forsyth that you, Mr Steve Christie and she herself had a plan for a luxury hotel on the Drumdalloch property, which needed Mr Forsyth's investment to make it work, but he had refused and begun selling off trees instead.'

A red flush crept into his cheeks. 'Oh, that daft idea! I know Oriole, bless her little heart, believed in the dream, but for the rest of us it was just the sort of rubbish you talk after a few bevvies. Even if Perry had agreed to exploit the site, where would we have got the money to build? He didn't have it, Steve's hotel's so deep in debt he'd hardly see a profit if he sold it, and I can tell you my savings in a sock under the bed would barely buy me a drink in a posh cocktail lounge. No, dear, you're barking up the wrong tree there.'

She gave him a small, tight-lipped smile. 'I've reported on this to DCI Strang and he considers that the bare facts as stated mean that none of you could be eliminated from the list of suspects as yet, and as a police officer you couldn't be involved in the investigation.'

The colour in Drummond's cheeks deepened. 'Are you having a laugh? Look, I know your boss took against me just because I didn't lick his boots, but he can't humiliate me like this – virtually accusing me of murder.'

'Oh, not really a humiliation is it, sir?' she said brightly. 'Just routine, arm's-length police procedure. Recusing yourself as a friend of the family would probably be the best way to do it, so no one could accuse you of wrongful influence later.'

His face was almost purple now. 'Are you really expecting me to accept this? It's completely outrageous – I'm going to take it upstairs and see that Strang's put in his place.'

'Oh, I'm sorry,' she said with a visible lack of sincerity. 'I didn't realise you didn't know about the SRCS, sir. DCI Strang is only accountable to Detective Chief Superintendent Borthwick, and it is only through her office that arrangements for use of the local force are made. In fact, she has been in contact already with your DCS Anderson and DCI Strang has passed on the name of the officer he recommended – DI Hamish Campbell. Could you arrange for me to meet him?'

Murray's enjoyment of the moment was tempered by the worry that he might actually give himself a stroke. Drummond's eyes were positively bulging with rage as he snarled, 'Oh, really! That's the way it's going, is it? You don't give me orders, Sergeant – go back to the desk and sort it out yourself.'

She was getting up to go, when a thought came to her. 'I believe there was another death in Drumdalloch Woods some time ago – Helena Forsyth. Were you personally involved in that?'

It was, she thought afterwards, rather like watching a chameleon change colour as its background changed. The red of anger drained from Drummond's face, leaving a sort of sickly pallor.

'Only very indirectly,' he said.

Easy enough to check, anyway. 'I see,' Murray said, and left. You had to be careful nowadays; they'd got awfully fussy recently about suspects dropping dead after police questioning.

The Institute was always quiet on a Sunday, with only research students working on lab projects and staff catching up with paperwork, and just a janitor on duty.

In his office, Michael Erskine was staring unseeing at the folder on his desk. He'd been struggling for hours with intrusive thoughts about penned beasts being transported for butchery and had hoped that he might manage to come up with a coherent plan in the atmosphere of professional calm.

But there wasn't a lot of that around the Institute this morning. He'd come in late; he'd again resorted to Scotch along with his medication and the hangover this morning had been even worse than the previous one so he hadn't felt strong enough to walk to the office and wasn't crazy enough to drive illegally.

He'd been greeted by a very cross receptionist who said, as coldly as she dared, 'The janitor had to haul me in from my day off to deal with all the phone calls and stuff. I don't know what you've been up to but there's been reporters and all sorts wanting to speak to you. Professor Crichton – he's phoned twice, wants you to call back. Doesn't sound very happy, but then none of us are – me included. I was meant to be going out for lunch today.'

Very much on his professional dignity, Erskine said, 'Thank you, Margaret. Go on fielding calls, please, and I'll call Professor Crichton now.'

He hadn't, in fact. He'd just been sitting there like a zombie with the result that Professor Crichton called first. Margaret was right – he didn't sound happy.

'Oh, there you are, Michael! I've been trying to get hold of you. – I thought I'd have heard from you by now.'

He was obviously expected to explain but he could only offer a reason, not an excuse. Rather than trying to invent one, he just said, 'Yes, I'm sorry.'

'Were you along at Drumdalloch?'

'No, no I wasn't, actually.'

'Oh, I thought you might have been.'

Though he had said, 'might', his tone implied 'should' and Erskine winced as Crichton went on, 'But perhaps you can give me an update on what is going on there, anyway? They tell me there's some very sensationalist stuff on the internet and it was on the news that the man we were dealing with has been murdered. Is that really the case?'

Erskine cleared his throat. 'Er – yes, I believe that is right, though I know no more than you do.'

'Really? I'd have thought with the Institute's long involvement with the woods that they would have been in touch – and they certainly haven't contacted Lord McCrea, who is also very concerned. Anyway, where does that leave us?'

The moment he'd feared so much for so long – having to confess to his lies – had come, but now at least he was able to say, 'It's most unfortunate. In the circumstances,

I'm afraid there's nothing we can do. We'll be going back into legal limbo again.'

'Nothing?' Crichton's voice rose in dismay. 'We've spent good money preparing for this. Was there an agreement?'

'Only verbal.'

'Oh, I see. I hadn't altogether appreciated that.' He was clearly annoyed, but he went on, 'So who is the owner now? You mentioned a sister – can we work with her to reinstate it – and make sure to get it on paper this time?'

Erskine almost laughed at the desperate optimism. 'I doubt it. There's a son who will presumably inherit – all very complicated.'

'A son? The child who's run away? But they're saying on the internet – oh, without reason, I'm sure – that it was he who killed Forsyth!'

He was reaching more solid ground. 'Of course, the internet is famously unreliable, and I wouldn't believe anything I read there, but he was a rather wild boy – we had problems with him playing dangerous and unpleasant practical jokes on the staff.'

'Really?' Crichton said slowly. 'In that case, I suppose we wouldn't want to involve ourselves in anything like that. We can hold a watching brief for the moment, and of course, once the SSSI is approved it will put paid to any developers' plans.

'Anyway, despite this I think you are to be congratulated on coming up with such a bold and imaginative idea, even if it didn't work out as we had planned.'

It was way beyond anything he could have hoped for.

'Thank you so much, Professor. As you say, things may turn out all right in the end.'

He was just savouring the moment when, with a token knock on the door, Lars Andersen burst in.

'You did not answer my calls!' It was accusation rather than statement. 'I am here to tell you the police will not let me into my woods. You must come now and explain to them they cannot do this!'

'For God's sake, Lars, they're the police! You must know I can't tell them to do anything. You'll be allowed back in once their investigation there is complete.'

'But this could be days . . . weeks . . . I need to be there now! I need to see whether there were signs of distress from the murdered tree within the fungal network, perhaps even establish a time frame. It could add a wonderful new dimension to my thesis and they are stopping me. You explain to them that this is dynamic science! More important than that, they waste time on a man who is dead anyway and of no account, a man who took the life of a most precious tree.'

'Lars, the way you're talking makes me think you could have killed him yourself,' Erskine said. 'You were there in the woods, you told me how furious with him you were after he felled that tree. Perhaps I may go and have a talk with the police after all.'

Andersen had not sat down; he came now to tower over him, his voice rising. 'You will not say that! Do not dare! They will arrest me because I am a foreigner, because I told Perry he was evil. But I will tell them you were so angry with him you could nearly not speak, and I will tell them you came back later when I was finished my work. I passed your car as I went home. So – you will help me now?'

Outraged, Erskine said, 'Are you really trying to blackmail me? No, I will not.'

Andersen's only reply was to draw back his arm, punch him in the face and storm out. Accustomed to deference and a stranger to physical abuse, Erskine was left not so much shocked as frankly disbelieving, at least until the pain hit.

CHAPTER THIRTEEN

'Have you seen what they're saying on the internet?' Cat Fleming, at a loose end in Edinburgh, demanded.

At the other end of the phone, Marjory sighed. 'Do I really have to spell out to you how dumb it is to read what's online when your partner's a copper? I never look at anything except sheepdogs in action. Have they started in on Kelso yet?'

'Not really, just the usual "police are utterly useless and won't be able to do anything".'

'It'll be Kelso tomorrow, unless they find the boy. What's he saying about it?'

'Not a lot. He sounds incredibly stressed, poor love, and he says that the place is swarming with media. JB's going up to do the press statement tonight so at least he'll have her to back him up.'

'That's good, at least. And I'll tell you something interesting – when I heard them talking about the Drumdalloch Woods it rang a bell. I remember the name featuring in a committee discussion a while ago – some sort of complaint that had been brought concerning a fatal accident enquiry.'

'Is that your Police Investigation and Review thingy?'

'That's right. I wasn't involved but the Inverness force was definitely scrutinised. Can't recall the details, though I do remember someone thought it smelt a bit but they'd no evidence to go on and there were no further proceedings. It might be helpful for Kelso to know that.'

'Why don't you tell him yourself?' Cat said eagerly. 'He might open up to you – he certainly won't to me.'

Marjory laughed. 'Forget it – I'm not going to be your stooge. I may not actually be his mother-in-law but I'm not going to get a reputation for interfering now. Besides, I don't know any more than I've told you – he'd better check via official channels where there will be more detail anyway. No doubt you'll speak soon and you can tell him then.'

'All right, if you're going to be like that.' Cat sounded glum. 'It'll all get worse for Kelso in any case, won't it?'

'Yes, it certainly will. And whatever they say about him, for heaven's sake don't go into battle for him and reply.'

'Oh, I'm not totally stupid, you know. What age do you think I am?' Cat said, trying not to sound huffy and failing. 'Anyway, I'd better go and put a wash on. I've nothing better to do.'

Marjory smiled, then shook her head. It wasn't going to be altogether easy for her daughter, or for Kelso either. Criminal defence lawyers and police officers have an adversarial relationship and it's bone deep on either side not to give succour to the 'enemy' – and sometimes the inverted commas aren't even there.

This case – the possibly murderous kid on the run – was going to be hard on Kelso and he could use the kind of support she'd always relied on Bill to provide when the going got rough. There was nothing she could do about it – advice always threw Cat back into teenage mode, and anyway it wasn't as if she thought she had the answer. Cat was all grown up now and they'd have to work it out for themselves.

There was a gentle tap on the kitchen door. Oriole, who had been sitting by the Aga feeling awful for what seemed like hours now as she looked at her laptop and read what was appearing, sounded infinitely weary as she said, 'Come in.' How many times was that, this morning?

Certainly, police officers didn't usually tap gently but even so she was astonished and delighted when Steve Christie put his head round the door, saying, 'How are you, sweetie? Still standing?'

She got up, tempted to throw herself into his arms, and when he held them wide, she did just that. She'd started to cry again. 'Oh Steve, Steve, I really needed you! I don't know what to do.'

'They've let me come at last,' he said, patting her on the back. 'I'd have been here long ago, but they were refusing to let anyone in. If it hadn't been for Keith pulling strings, I wouldn't be here now.'

'Oh, thank him for me,' she said. 'It's been dreadful, though I have to say the officers from Edinburgh have been very kind and considerate, but they keep asking questions I don't want to answer. Of course, I understand – someone killed my brother and whatever I might have felt about him recently, I can't help thinking how much my father wanted us to be a family.'

'Well, of course,' Steve said. 'Families are really important, and I like to think of myself as part of yours.'

Oriole could feel her cheeks glowing. 'Of course you are. I was just so sad that Perry wouldn't agree for us all to work together. When I told DS Murray about what we were planning, she agreed that it would make sense and Perry was just being pig-headed.'

She moved back so that she could look at him. For a moment she thought he looked annoyed and said hesitantly, 'It was all right to tell them, wasn't it?'

'Of course it was, sweetheart,' he said, releasing her. 'Now, see here, I don't think you've been looking after yourself. Have you had lunch? No, I thought not. Bad girl! Sit down, and I'm going to make you the special Christie scrambled egg on toast. Eggs in the fridge, bread in the breadbin? Right, just wait for the experience of your life! Not for nothing did I go to catering college!'

It was like a dream come true. It was the first time ever that Steve had come to visit her; the only time they'd talked was at the hotel, with both of them having to break off when they were needed elsewhere. This was so kind and caring – it melted her heart. She'd always known that Steve was way beyond her, but perhaps with this situation neither of them could have imagined, things might even be different.

'Tell me about Jay, though,' Steve said, lifting a lid on the Aga and putting bread in a toasting rack. 'Poor kid – any idea where he might have gone?'

'They keep asking me. Not the faintest, I'm afraid. I've told them there was a bike in the garage and that his only friends were in Edinburgh – Perry only got round to enrolling him in the local academy on Wednesday.'

'Do you have a phone number for him? I guess he has a mobile, doesn't he?'

'Oh yes. On it all the time. But I tried phoning and it just went to voicemail.'

'Not much use, then. But remember when he stole your credit card? I know you stopped it, but what did he use it for? Have the police asked you about that?'

'No. I don't know, actually. If they want, I suppose I could go on to the computer and find out.'

'Have your lunch first, madame!' Steve produced a plate of fluffy scrambled eggs with a flourish. 'I'll look it up for you while you eat, if you trust me. Then we can decide if it's something useful we can pass on.'

'Of course I do!' He brought the laptop, and she tapped in the password.

He called up the account, then swivelled it towards her. 'Supermarket,' he said. 'Sweets, crisps maybe – something like that from the amount. Then he went to that scruffy café in Kilbain and it looks like he had breakfast. Not worth wasting police time with that, is it?'

'Not really,' she said, indistinctly. 'Steve, this is delicious. You're so kind.'

'You need someone to look after you, now you're on your own. And I'm volunteering for the position.'

'Oh Steve! Yes please,' Oriole said. Despite everything – the horror of it all, the worry – she felt a tiny, warm surge of happiness.

* * *

DS Murray hit it off at once with DS Hamish Campbell. He was middle-aged, grey-haired and burly, with an open face, and best of all he was a Weegie.

'Great to hear the Glasgow accent,' she said as she sat down in his office. 'I've spent far too long in Edinburgh.'

'I always think they speak as if they've a mouthful of pebbles and they're always feart they'll drop one, poor souls.'

They dealt with the important stuff first – slagging off the Rangers manager – and then Campbell said, 'We were told Keith Drummond was in charge, so I didn't think I'd get a sniff at it.'

She registered his tone, but only said, 'DI Drummond is very matey with the Forsyths, and Oriole mentioned this plan they had, along with Steve Christie, to convert Drumdalloch into a luxury hotel, but when probate came through Perry dumped them and started selling off the trees. Obvious motive there, so of course Drummond couldn't be involved.'

'Wouldn't like that,' Campbell said bluntly.

'No, you're right there. Anyway, your Super recommended you to our DCS Borthwick as the best for us to work with – and that was before we knew about DI Drummond's connection, so I think you can take that as a pat on the back and maybe a wee gold star.'

She'd thought he'd laugh, but Campbell said, quite seriously, 'More a relief, to be honest. He's fairly new and I've never been sure how much notion the man had of what goes on at grass roots level. I'm going to say flat out that Drummond's running his own show here, and there's a lot that go along with his ideas. I've been long enough here to hold my own, but I've an Asian constable who gets a hard time from a lot of them.'

Murray, sadly, wasn't surprised; they always talked of 'rotten apples' when there was a scandal, but in recent years there was no doubt that the rot had spread.

'Drummond's "own show" – what's that about?'

Campbell grimaced. 'Repeat this and I'll deny I ever said it, but it's an open secret that money changes hands in return for a blind eye turned or a lead not followed up – but try proving it! There's a sort of brotherhood in Police Scotland that sees things the same way – built on taking it ill that we're not properly paid or appreciated. Well, we're not, but there's still some of us old-fashioned enough to think we're here to lock up the neds, not to join them, but there's plenty around here would always cover up for a brother if needed.'

'It chimes with a lot of other stuff, too, right?' she said. 'Racism towards your constable, seventies sexism towards me. DI Drummond seemed to think I'd appreciate being called "dear".'

'Brave man,' Campell said, adding with a laugh, 'Gave him his head in his hands and his lugs to play with, did you?'

She grinned. 'Pretty much. Anyway, do you know where we are at the moment? Any progress on the boy?'

'Not that we've heard,' Campbell said. 'Apparently the house has been searched, including an abandoned wing, and they're out searching the woods now, too – so far nothing useful. They've checked the boy's phone but it's switched off and hasn't been used since a call in Edinburgh five days ago. But there's a bike missing, so it's more than likely he's away off somewhere. There's a coastguard chopper out as well. We don't know if he's got money and there's no record of a credit card. He may show up when he's hungry.'

Murray knew how that felt – it seemed a long time since her breakfast roll – but these days shoplifting wasn't as hard as it used to be. She said, 'My boss wants to spell it out that we're by no means assuming the boy did it. He's tied up with that at the moment, but he wants a murder incident room set up too – at the hotel, possibly?'

'I've had a drink there – there's certainly space. Leave that with me, and I'll circulate the details and trigger an appeal for information.'

'That's great,' Murray said. 'He wants to meet you and brief us both there whenever he can get time. DCS Borthwick's making a flying visit to do the press statement, so he'll want to have something to tell her. There's a list of suspects we'll need questioned to establish their movements – obviously that includes Drummond, which won't go down well.'

Campbell shrugged. 'His problem. I'll arrange that.'

'I'm hoping the public will bring us the dirt on Perry Forsyth. Not a popular man, apparently. I'll link you in so you can get access to whatever comes our way.'

Campbell stood up. 'I'll get on with that and you can flag me when we've a time for the briefing.'

'Thanks,' Murray said. 'That's a load you've taken off my back. See you later on.'

The Co-op, with a post office attached, was what passed for a commercial hub in Kilbain and today even though it was a Sunday it was seething with customers, most of whom were doing more talking than buying. Gavin Sinclair the manager was having his work cut out to keep till queues moving for the sake of people who didn't have all day to spend discussing the most sensational local event they could ever remember as their purchases were scanned, but it was clear that both operatives and customers felt that not being allowed to exchange their theories came close to suppression of free speech.

DI Drummond was a well-known local character and when he appeared a noticeable silence fell, before the chat, murmured now, swelled up again. He looked round, spotted Sinclair and strode towards him, the press of shoppers parting for him rather as the Red Sea had for Moses.

'Big problems for you today, eh Keith?' the manager said. 'Anything I can do for you?'

'Got a minute, Gavin? Through the back?'

Sinclair nodded and turned. In the little office, Drummond said, 'Needn't ask if you know about Jay Forsyth – and no, we haven't found him yet. But through a credit card he was using, we've established that he made a purchase here last Thursday – nothing major, just sweets or stuff, around eight. Can you check who was on duty?'

'No problem.' Gavin went to a board on the back wall and ran his finger across it. 'That would be Linda. She's on at the moment. I can call her in now.'

He bent forward to switch on a speaker by his desk and made the announcement.

'Thanks,' Drummond said. 'Don't suppose there's been anyone else reporting a sighting?'

'Not to me. Ah, Linda!'

The woman came in looking distinctly nervous and Drummond said hastily, 'Don't worry, there isn't a problem. I just wanted to know if you remember a laddie you'd have served early on Thursday morning – maybe buying crisps or something?'

Linda thought for a minute. 'Oh, yes! I think there was one, early. Usually, we get a bunch of them in on their way to school, but he was on his own. Bought a big packet of Haribo—' She broke off and her eyes widened. 'Here – was that him?'

'We think so,' Drummond said gravely. 'Did he say anything to you about where he might be going?'

'Didn't say anything. Not even thank you – not very polite, really. I suppose if he's done what they're saying, he wouldn't be, would he?'

'Now, don't go jumping to conclusions. Have you seen him since? No? But would you recognise him if you saw him again?'

Her eyes were bright with excitement. 'Oh, I'm sure I would! So would I tell the police if I do?'

Drummond said firmly, 'You tell Gavin here. He'll have my number and I'll come round at once to follow up. Thanks, Linda.'

After a chat with Gavin, Linda went back to work, clothed in an aura of importance. From the next door till, another assistant said, 'What did he want?'

Linda smirked. 'Well, I only served that actual boy – the one that's missing! I'm to look out for him. Tell you later, or I'll have Himself on at me.' She took her time getting herself settled again, then keyed in her code and said, 'Right, sir, sorry to keep you waiting. Oh, it's you, Lachie! All right, then?'

She started checking through the old man's groceries. She was glad to see he'd bought a bit more than usual; she often thought he didn't eat enough, but it was against company policy to make a comment on what was in a customer's basket, so all she said was, 'You go and have a nice day, then.'

He said, 'Aye, right. Thanks, Linda,' but even so, she thought he was looking a bit down, poor old boy.

It was hard to think clearly when the only thing on your mind was your stomach. Having called Strang to touch base, Murray had time to pick up a sandwich and she drove into Kilbain. It never did any harm either to get a sense of the local gossip; she was an expert eavesdropper and as yet she wouldn't be a marked woman.

She'd just parked outside the Co-op when DI Drummond, the last man she wanted to see right now, came out. It wasn't surprising; someone had said he'd a house in a small development just off the main street. She sank down as low as she could in her seat, though she wasn't hopeful she'd escape unnoticed. Your car is a proclamation of your identity and it's every cop's instinct to notice them; she couldn't be sure he hadn't clocked hers in the car park outside the Inverness headquarters earlier.

But he powered off without looking to left or to right, like a man on a mission. It might be worth finding out what that might be, so she got out of the car and tailed him a discreet distance behind.

In fact, he only walked a few yards, then went into

a rather basic-looking café, which she certainly couldn't follow him into. She turned back and went to the Co-op, wondering what he was doing.

He should have been reassigned, but it almost looked as if he was working on the case anyway – why else would he be here? Then of course, she remembered – perhaps he was taking the day off to lick his wounds and had done a shop, then gone on to the café for lunch.

He wasn't carrying anything, though, and he hadn't struck her as the type to patronise the local greasy spoon either. Murray filed away that thought as she went in.

She picked a cheese and chutney sandwich and a Diet Coke from the stand by the door, then went off round the shelves pretending to be choosing something else, but there was nothing she heard anyone say that was in any way interesting or surprising.

She went to the till, joining the queue behind an elderly man wearing a duffel coat that had definitely seen better days. He had red hair, greying now, and faded blue eyes – typical Celtic colouring – and he was slowly counting out his money in cash. The assistant was having a kindly word with him and as he left with his shopping in a tatty backpack she caught Murray's eye and smiled. 'Oh, that's Lachie – he's a character! Lives in a bothy on the Drumdalloch estate and we're aye worried something'll happen to him, but he's thrawn – refuses to do the sensible thing and get a bit of help. Not above helping himself to a pheasant if it crosses his path, mind!'

They both laughed, and Murray paid and left. A bothy on the Drumdalloch estate – it might pay to check that out.

* * *

Lachie plodded back home feeling the weight of his years. This was too much; all his life he'd looked after himself, not asking anything from anybody, but now he'd somehow been landed with an unasked-for responsibility. Contact with people had always made him uneasy and now he was feeling constrained and irritable, as if he was wearing a scratchy tweed jacket next to his skin and buttoned too tight.

And it was only going to get worse. Jay Forsyth would be waiting for him, hungry and miserable, endlessly wanting to discuss himself and his problems; used as Lachie was to silence, the constant yap, yap, yap felt almost like a physical assault. He'd told the laddie the only thing to do was go back home but that wasn't the answer Jay wanted.

The other answer was that Lachie could turn him in to the authorities, but clyping was kind of a dirty thing to do – and he'd no love for the polis anyway. He'd had many a run-in with them himself and even as a young man had done time for poaching, which had taught him to avoid all contact where possible.

Until this morning, he'd known nothing beyond what Jay had told him – that he'd run away but then his credit card wouldn't work – so the stushie that was going on in the town was a shock – police cars everywhere, Drummond strutting around, everybody talking about Jay having killed his dad and then run away.

Lachie knew fine that he'd be in big trouble if they tracked Jay down to the bothy – and it was when, not if. This couldn't go on; apart from anything else, he was tired of sleeping in a chair instead of a bed and his pension wouldn't stretch to feeding him. No, he'd need to spell it out – Jay had to go home.

When he reached the bothy, Jay was ensconced in his own armchair, prodding moodily at a mobile. From the cage in the corner, the ferret started chirruping when she heard his voice; she'd been very unsettled, complaining that he hadn't taken her out, but after her last encounter with Jay he hadn't dared. If the boy was bitten again when there wasn't disinfectant on hand, he could get blood-poisoning and that would be a whole new mess.

Lachie set down his backpack on the table and as he started to get out the food Jay got up and came over, looking disparagingly at what was there.

'Did you not get crisps or anything?' he said.

'Crisps don't fill you up. Fishcakes and beans for our dinner.'

Jay pulled a face. 'You could have got pizza,' he said.

With considerable annoyance, Lachie said, 'That costs a lot. And they're all out looking for you now. Everyone. Not just the polis. There's even a poster up on a lamp post.'

Jay looked shaken. 'But they won't know I'm here – I'm safe enough.'

Lachie put the last of the shopping into the cupboard. 'They'll find out. Saw how the woman at the till looked at me when I'd so much in the basket – she'll work it out next time. I got the jail when I was young. I'm not going back. I'll give you your dinner, and then you can just be away back home.'

'But you don't understand!' he cried. 'They're saying I killed Dad. It'll be me in jail, if they catch me.'

'Likely not if you didn't do it,' Lachie said. 'Running

away just makes it worse.' He got out the old black frying-pan, put in a slice of lard and unwrapped the fishcakes. 'After, you'll go back home, eh?'

Jay didn't reply and he was very quiet as he ate. When he'd finished, he got up and without saying anything, packed up his bag and left.

Lachie watched through the window as the boy disappeared into the trees. He was feeling bad. He should have asked, 'What are you going to do?' but he was feart that Jay wouldn't say the right thing, and then he'd get sucked in all over again.

Had Jay killed his dad? There was no doubt he hated him – he'd talked about little else – but he'd said he hadn't. Could Lachie believe him, though? He couldn't forget that after his mother died the laddie had told him he'd heard her saying, 'They're going to kill me if I'm not careful.' Was this revenge?

He wasn't sure – but anyway, it wasn't his business. He washed up the pan and the plates, then took the delighted ferret out of its cage.

'We've had a bad time, the pair of us,' he said, ruffling her fur, 'but we'll away out now and see if we can maybe get a rabbit to our tea.'

When he opened the door, there was a man just walking up the path and his heart gave a thump of shock.

DI Keith Drummond said, 'Where's the boy?'

Lachie's face was blank as he said, 'What boy?'

'Oh, don't waste my time,' Drummond snapped, pushing him aside and, ignoring the ferret's scream of annoyance, stepped in to look round the bothy. There was a tall press in one corner and he almost wrenched the door off the hinges, to find only shelves holding Lachie's meagre belongings.

'Where's he gone, then?' he said.

Lachie's shrug tried to suggest at once ignorance and indifference, but he was scared. Drummond was a bad man to cross.

His face was red with temper and frustration. 'Tell me if he turns up, then. And I wasn't here, right? God help you if I find you've lied to me.' He stormed off.

Mechanically stroking his pet to soothe it, Lachie waited until he was out of sight. That wouldn't be the end of it, though. There'd be more trouble ahead.

CHAPTER FOURTEEN

'Infested' was the only way to describe it. As DI Strang looked out of his bedroom window, all he could see was reporters seething like ants just beyond the hotel, which was being policed by a couple of uniforms he could only hope wouldn't be overpowered by a sudden surge. He took care to stand well back; catching sight of him last time had provoked a chorus of shouted questions, all variations on the 'Have you found him yet? Did he do it, then?' theme.

He was waiting now for Murray and DI Hamish Campbell to arrive for the briefing. Murray had been enthusiastic about him and Strang had already seen uniforms arriving with equipment for an incident room on the premises. It looked as if one way and another they were getting a grip of the situation, although so far none of the searches for the boy had turned anything up.

When they appeared, DI Campbell made a good first impression on Strang, just as he had on Murray.

'I can see the incident room taking shape,' Strang said. 'I'm grateful that you've got it moving so fast.'

'Just the job, sir,' Campbell said. 'We've got the laddie's photo up on the internet as well and circulated in the town, and I've lined up officers ready to act on instructions once you outline the priorities.'

'Excellent. The search for Jay Forsyth has to be number one, obviously, but we also have a very basic list of suspects for Perry Forsyth's murder. DI Drummond features, unfortunately, along with two others who were in on a luxury hotel scheme – Oriole Forsyth and Steve Christie, the owner here. Then there were two that DI Drummond mentioned – Dr Michael Erskine and Lars Andersen who are both connected to the Biological Institute in Inverness. We'll need formal statements taken from them all as a basis.'

Campbell said, 'After I spoke to Livvy this morning, I sent PC Maggie Stewart round to the Institute and she managed to speak to them both – she's writing up the statements of their movements now. Interestingly, she said that Dr Erskine had quite a shiner – walked into a door, allegedly. She did also happen to notice that Andersen had a bruised knuckle, but thought we'd want to look into that ourselves.'

That made the other two sit up. Murray said, 'Wow!'

'I'm seriously impressed by your efficiency and her good judgement,' Strang said. 'What can they have been quarrelling about? Livvy, perhaps you might move on that. I'll talk to Drummond myself later, but I'll want a statement about his movements before that – might be awkward, I suppose.'

'From what you said earlier, Hamish, there may be other officers who will confirm his movements as being whatever he wants them to be,' Murray said. 'He's quite an intimidating man.'

Campbell grinned. 'Oh, Maggie's no' feart! She's got the bit between her teeth; she'll go to see him this afternoon, and she'll take in Christie at the hotel here too. I wondered about maybe leaving Oriole Forsyth till later?'

Strang nodded. 'She's a lot on her plate at the moment. We don't want "police brutality" allegations. That should be enough to keep us going – once we get incident room witnesses we'll probably have more to add.

'As you'll have seen, the investigations on the site aren't particularly helpful but I do have a Forensics report hot off the press. They've managed to access Perry Forsyth's bank account and it shows a recent transfer from the timber merchants: £650,000.'

Campbell looked stunned, but Murray said, 'Seems a bit crazy but that's what the internet said about it – the Million Dollar Tree. No wonder Forsyth didn't fancy pitching in with the consortium – and he'd other trees to sell too.'

Campbell's phone rang. He glanced at the number and at a nod from Strang, took the call.

'There's been a sighting.' he reported. 'Someone claiming to have seen the boy in Inverurie.'

'How far away is that?' Murray asked.

'Two, maybe two and a half hours by car,' Campbell said. 'Not likely, to be honest, but we'll get the details.'

'We'll no doubt get plenty of those,' Strang said. 'Great job, Hamish. I'll see you tomorrow, unless something more comes up. Livvy, I guess you'll be going back tonight?'

She pulled a face. 'Suppose so, but I think I might have a chat with Dr Erskine first – want to see the shiner before it's had time to fade.'

After they had left, Strang sat back in his chair, reviewing the situation. They had struck it seriously lucky with Hamish Campbell – the efficiency was stunning – and thanks to that he was feeling more in control of things than he had thought possible earlier today. He'd certainly enough to convince JB that progress was being made.

But the boy, the boy! Jay Forsyth, thirteen years old: a damaged child, disturbed – dangerous, even. First and foremost, a victim, and frighteningly vulnerable out there on his own. Protecting him was his duty, but Jay had deliberately put himself beyond that help.

He sighed. Situations like these took a heavy emotional toll on police officers; long experience had taught him to cope, but how he wished that, like Livvy, he would be driving home tonight!

Even from the window of her flat, Nicki Latham could see the activity in the quiet street and she'd spent all morning checking for news. She went out to get a newspaper and anyone she met was ready to talk about the runaway, and without exception assumed that the boy had done it.

'We don't know that,' Nicki had said, but she was forced to agree that it looked bad and later she headed over to Drumdalloch again.

There were still police officers around, and lots of crime scene tape, but the woman PC on duty was quite chatty once Nicki explained she wasn't a journalist, but unfortunately she hadn't heard anything new. She was sympathetic, though.

'He's just a kid. Losing his mum like that and not what you'd call a proper home life after – no wonder he's been a problem. Poor wee soul! His auntie'll be upset with all this. She's not put her foot over the doorstep.'

'Yes, she certainly is,' Nicki said.

But when Oriole greeted her, she was looking better than she had in the morning. She'd been chopping an onion; there was a tin of tomatoes on the surface, and she gestured towards her preparations.

'It's the dreaded pasta for supper again – I haven't got up the courage to go into the Co-op. You're welcome to join me – it'd be good to have company.'

'Why not? Thanks.' As Nicki sat down at the table, she said, 'Of course, I can get whatever you need. The town's swarming.'

'I suppose I'll have to face it sometime. Apart from anything else, I've told Steve I'm going to ask the police when I can go back to work.'

Nicki noticed that a faint flush had come to Oriole's cheeks as she said that. 'Spoken to him, then, have you?'

She laid down the knife and turned, smiling. 'Yes! Do you know, he came to see if I was all right and he was just so kind. Made me his "special" scrambled eggs – well, I suppose they were just ordinary scrambled eggs, really, but I was starving and they tasted so good!'

'What did he want?' Nicki said, then realised she'd put her foot in it as Oriole turned back to the onion, looking a little offended.

'I told you – he just came to see how I was. And of

course he was asking about Jay, if there was anything to suggest where he might be. I'm afraid I wasn't much help – told him I'd tried phoning, but it just went to answerphone, so he may not even have it any more.

'I'm awfully worried about him, you know. Whatever the truth is, running away won't make this disappear, and I don't think he has any mates, except maybe in Edinburgh, but with everyone out looking for him, I can't see how he'd even get there.'

'The weather forecast's terrible. If he's sleeping rough somewhere he could get hypothermia,' Nicki said grimly. 'And what about food? Has he any money?'

'Don't know that either,' Oriole was saying just as there was a knock on the door.

She went to answer it and Nicki could hear her making some arrangement for the next day. Oriole's phone was lying on the table and she scrolled through the phonebook and memorised the number for Jay.

Oriole came back, pulling a face. 'I'm to make a formal statement tomorrow, to tell them precisely what I did all day Friday after the loggers left. It won't be difficult – you were here when there was all the fuss and after that I did my shift at the hotel, then came home and I've been here since. It's felt like it's been a week – this has been the longest day I can ever remember.'

'I'm not surprised. You've really had a rough time of it. What you need is an early night – I'm not going to stay long. Shall I set the table now?'

It wasn't much after nine when Nicki left. When she got back to her flat, she got out her mobile and dialled Jay's number. It went to the recording.

'This is Nicki. Jay, if you're there, pick up.'

She waited a moment, but nothing happened. She dialled again. 'You remember me – I made you an omelette the other night? I'm on your side.'

Again, nothing. She bit her lip, then rang for the third time. 'I won't tell anyone anything. Get in touch any time.'

Now she could only wait.

What struck DS Murray forcibly as she went into Dr Erskine's flat was the bleak impersonality. There were no pictures in the sitting room, no photos, and the bookshelves that covered one wall didn't have anything on them that looked like leisure reading, only forbidding-looking tomes, neatly labelled box files and stacked magazines. The one on the top, *Nature*, had a cover showing something weird like an atom. There was nothing that suggested a wife or partner, or any family.

It wasn't easy to make him out either. He had the kind of patronising middle-class manner that always got her back up with the way that it suggested there was something faintly ridiculous in a lowly police officer being allowed to actually question people like him. The effect was rather spoilt by the purpled swelling on his cheek and the half-shut bloodshot eye.

Even so, she was clearly expected to be impressed that he was Director of the Scottish Institute for Studies in Biological Sciences and in explaining the working relationship with the Drumdalloch Woods, he mentioned more than once the international significance of its contributions to research.

But under all that guff, he was, she reckoned, scared.

There were a few nervous hesitations and his hands were keeping up a continual restless twitching, and when she cut across him to say, 'Yes, I know enough about the situation there,' he actually jumped.

'I've seen your formal statement. It seems you were one of the last people to see Mr Forsyth alive. Can you tell me about that meeting? Was it previously arranged?'

Murray knew, from Oriole, that it hadn't been and she waited with interest as a positive volley of 'Well, ums' suggested that he was debating yes or no.

'Just tell the truth, Dr Erskine,' she said. 'You'll find it's easier. And quicker.'

He spluttered, 'Well yes, of course! That's an outrageous implication – I was merely trying to get my thoughts in order. I received a distressed phone call from one of my students, Lars Andersen, who had discovered Mr Forsyth's vandalism in cutting down the black ebony. He's a big, powerful man, he was raging mad and I was afraid of what he might do – he is obsessive about his research, you know. So I tried to talk him down and promised to speak to Forsyth and make him understand this couldn't go on.

'When I went to see him there was another man with him whom I didn't know – he didn't speak, as far as I can remember. I told Forsyth I would be getting a protection order to stop him cutting down any more trees.'

'And that was all?'

'Well – um . . .' Another pause, then he said, 'I'm afraid it got a little heated. Forsyth was very aggressive, and I put my case quite forcibly. I could see I wasn't getting anywhere so I just left. That was the last I saw of him – as I said to the constable this morning.'

She reckoned he'd been thinking of the other man who'd witnessed it – DI Drummond, as she knew – and tailored his account accordingly.

'What did you do then?'

'I went straight to find Lars. I tried to explain the situation, but he was being entirely unreasonable, talking wildly about Forsyth being evil, the tree-felling being murder – of course, I know he didn't really mean it. Just, well, you're no doubt familiar with the passion scientists have for their research.'

She wasn't, actually, but what she was familiar with was the oldest excuse in the book: a big boy did it and ran away. If she'd had a fiver for every time she'd heard it, she wouldn't be worried about her next gas bill.

'And you left him after that?'

'Yes, he wanted to get on with his work and I thought the routine would calm him down. So I went home. And that's really all I can help you with.'

His hands had stopped twitching and he seemed to have got his confidence back, as if he felt he'd got through it better than he'd feared. It was tempting to needle him with a bit more probing, but it was getting late and she had the long drive back to Edinburgh ahead of her.

She said, 'Thank you for your cooperation, Dr Erskine. That's all I need for the moment, though it is likely that there will be more questions later.'

Erskine looked alarmed, but didn't respond. As she got up to go she said, 'I have to ask – have you been in a fight?'

'Oh . . . er, this?' He touched his face awkwardly. 'No, no, of course not. Just my own stupidity – I was pulling open a door that had stuck and it sprang back into my face.'

If she'd had another fiver for every time she'd heard that excuse as well, she'd have been able to pay off the loan on her credit card too.

Murray was mentally running though the interview as she set off down the A9. Cold fish, and calculating. She'd sensed, too, an odd sort of insecurity, though he'd got into his stride when he was dobbing in his student. She had no doubt he would be capable of icy rage, but it was hard to imagine him losing it and striking down Perry Forsyth, and he'd been perfectly rational in his response to the tree-felling that all the fuss was about.

She'd always had a tendency to look for the motive ahead of the facts, but this time she'd more or less got the boss's blessing to do so. It was an old principle that if you wanted to understand why someone did something, you should look at the consequences, and she did that now.

She simply couldn't see what Erskine would gain by killing Forsyth, in which case he should probably drop off the list of suspects. Unless, of course, there was a whole other agenda they knew nothing about.

Cat Fleming was feeling down. The weekend was dragging; she hadn't wanted to contact friends who would only ask about the missing child, and housework had failed to deliver the warm glow of virtue she felt she deserved.

The house without Kelso in it had felt very empty. They'd been forecasting bad weather and the rain had started, with a wind that had already set all the little boats dancing and clinking on their moorings. On this north-facing coast they took the full brunt of whatever storm came across the Firth of Forth and tonight it was a bleak prospect.

Cat switched on all the lamps and drew the curtains, trying to make it feel cosy again, but she couldn't shut out her worries. Kelso had told her JB would be making a statement and it was Breaking News on the six o'clock bulletin.

Detective Chief Superintendent Jane Borthwick sounded calm and competent, as she always did, but it couldn't disguise the lack of progress with the search for Jay Forsyth and all they had to offer concerning his father's murder was that they were pursuing enquiries.

Cat sighed and switched it off. No doubt Kelso would phone when he got a moment, but it could be quite a while.

What she mustn't do was go on to the internet. She wouldn't learn anything new, and the ignorance and hostility was like sewage swirling around. A glass of wine, perhaps, and then she could get on with preparation for the case scheduled for next week. She'd been putting it off, but she might as well get started when she was miserable anyway.

Cat was walking over to the fridge when, without warning, the front door opened. She gave a gasp of alarm – but there was Kelso!

'Good gracious! Whatever's happened?' she said, rushing to hug him.

He laughed. 'JB took pity on me and brought me back in the chopper with her. It'll mean an early start tomorrow morning but that doesn't matter.'

She studied his face anxiously. He looked tired, but all right; perhaps she worried too much. 'Are you hungry? I'll send out for a curry, shall I? I need a treat after a dreary day, and I don't suppose yours was a barrel of laughs either.' When they were settled with their curry and beer, he told her about the house in the deep woods and the Million Dollar Tree and the local inspector who was proving to be a great asset and about Livvy Murray who was definitely growing into her role.

It was interesting, but he wasn't giving her any details about the case itself that she couldn't get from the media or what he was thinking about it and she was beginning to feel a little hurt.

'You do know that I don't know any journalists? And I promise I won't gossip at the court about anything you might tell me just in case some of them know journalists, or might have one of your suspects as a client.'

Kelso was taken aback. 'Well, of course,' he said. 'It's not that I don't trust you, it's just that discretion's engrained when it comes to operational matters.'

'You'd tell Mum, though, wouldn't you?' Cat said unwisely, and was kicking herself a minute later as she sensed his withdrawal.

'Not a lot to tell at the moment, in fact. I doubt if either of you would be interested in the details of setting up the incident room or reading the reports that mainly didn't tell us anything much.'

'Mmm,' she said. She'd let herself sound childishly jealous – of her *mother* for heaven's sake – and asking anything more would be pointless. Instead, she said, 'Talking of Mum, she told me to say she remembered some sort of complaint that came up to her police committee after another death in Drumdalloch Woods a while ago.'

Kelso, who had been lounging on the sofa, sat up. 'Really? Did she know what was involved?'

Cat shook her head. 'She said that you'd be better going to the records. All she remembered was that something didn't look good but they'd no evidence to let them take any action.'

'Right,' he said thoughtfully. 'Now tell me about your lousy day.'

She could tell she'd lost him; his mind was elsewhere, and she was quite sure he'd be on the phone to her mother tomorrow, despite what Marjory had said. Cat wanted to be his confidante herself, but it wasn't something she could simply demand. It felt hurtful, though, and she was finding it hard not to let it show.

She said, 'Too boring to talk about. Look, it's getting late and you have an early start tomorrow. I don't suppose there's any more news about the boy?'

''Fraid not. They'd have called me if there was.' He stood up yawning, and took her into his arms, holding her close. 'Let's make the most of our unexpected bonus.'

Steve Christie had left a message on Keith Drummond's phone earlier telling him that DCI Strang had gone back to Edinburgh and asking him to call back, which he hadn't. He had the sort of nervous imagination that Keith not only didn't have, he didn't have either understanding or sympathy for the people who did. As a result, Steve had got round to imagining Keith had managed to get himself locked up and couldn't answer his phone, so it was a relief when he walked into the bar of the Kilbain Hotel later that evening.

It was busier tonight than Steve had ever seen it, with Tricia completely submerged by the orders and service being slowed up by the journalists trying to get her to stop and give them a quote. Steve had been policing that and helping out at the same time but when Keith appeared he abandoned his post to sweep him off into the office.

It was never hard to tell when something hadn't gone well for Keith. He was scowling as he came in and threw himself onto a chair so that it creaked in protest.

'Not . . . not a good day?' Steve said tentatively. He could never be sure that what had happened wouldn't turn out to have been his fault.

'The little bastard's slipped through my fingers,' he said. 'Got a good steer from that café where he'd had breakfast. Waitress noticed he'd a sore hand and he told her he'd been bitten by a ferret, so no prizes for guessing where he'd got it. Of course, I got a flat denial from Lachie MacIver but I knew he was lying. I reckon I just missed him.'

Steve knew better than to say it might have been just as well. He'd been troubled by Keith's plan to get to Jay ahead of the police – he couldn't quite understand how they could benefit from that. He'd even been brave enough to ask yesterday, but Keith had sharply pointed out Jay was coming into big money now and they had to get him to fall into line, and he'd added that the lads were getting edgy; the police purge was becoming worryingly rigorous and having failed to set up a safe haven once before, they needed to succeed this time.

He said instead, 'So what do you do now?'

Keith's face darkened. 'I find him – what do you bloody think? It's savage out there and he's got to be getting hungry. Someone must be sheltering him. I just have to work out who. He can't know many people around here.

'But tell me, how are you getting on with Oriole?'

Steve gave a sigh. 'Oh, you know how she is. Now she's making assumptions that I'd really rather she didn't make.'

'Oh? Well Steve, I think you'll have to encourage them, however little you like it. She's key to the whole thing and it's your job to make sure she doesn't get cold feet.'

He looked at Keith with some dismay. 'But Keith . . .' he ventured, then said, with a sinking heart, 'Oh, I suppose so. Meantime, anyway.'

Nicki Latham's flat was in a little side street in Kilbain and it was to some extent sheltered from the worst of the storm, but she could hear debris being blown around – an evil night to be out in its blast.

She couldn't settle to anything, not even the episode of *Succession* she hadn't seen, and she kept glancing at her phone to make sure it really was switched on. At last she stood up; since there was nothing more she could do she might as well have an early night.

She picked up her phone and was just switching off the light in the sitting room as it rang.

She recognised the number. 'Jay?' she said. 'Jay, are you all right?'

There was silence, then he said, 'Can I trust you? You won't just hand me over to the police?'

She realised he was crying and a lump came to her throat. 'Yes, Jay, you can trust me. Where are you?'

'Will you come for me? I'm scared, so scared,' he sobbed. 'The trees – the trees are all sort of screaming and I don't know what to do. There's branches falling—'

'You're in the woods? Just get yourself out to the edge of the road, right, and I'll come to pick you up. I'll flash my lights on and off. Be careful, and don't go to the house – there'll still be police there tonight. Can you do that?'

Another hesitation. He still didn't trust her, did he? She waited and at last he said, 'I have to, really. There's no one else.'

Tears were trickling down her cheeks as she grabbed a raincoat and her car keys. And she knew whose fault it all was – or perhaps she should say, whose fault it had been.

CHAPTER FIFTEEN

It had been wonderful to have that unexpected night with Cat, though he'd thought she seemed a little subdued; she had a difficult case calling this week so perhaps that had been on her mind.

The storm had not abated overnight. The weather seemed to have got stuck in one of those patterns that seemed to be more common these days and Storm Leonard was lingering like a boring guest, and as he took to the A9 again in atrocious conditions, DCI Strang fretted away at his problems.

He was suffering frustration at his helplessness as he obsessively rehearsed the bleak facts about the search for Jay Forsyth. They hadn't managed to pin down precise timings, but the last confirmed sighting had been on Thursday and today was Monday. The 72 hours within which most missing children were found had passed and every further hour made it less likely he'd be found unharmed. The storm would be cutting the odds still further.

There had been dozen of reports of sightings, as there always were on high profile cases, but none had been helpful and quite a number had been from what you could only call nutters wasting police time. When it came to people who knew him by sight – nothing. The trail was stone cold. However he'd done it, or wherever he was, he'd vanished. Could a child as young as that do that so efficiently, without help? And if someone was helping him, who was it, and why?

He still couldn't make up his mind about Jay. The boy could have run away because he had killed his hated father, he could have run away because he believed he would somehow be blamed, or he could even have run away for a reason as simple as unhappiness and got caught up in the aftermath of Perry's death.

And it mattered. If Jay had done it, he would be safer than if he hadn't.

If he was innocent, running away had played into the hands of Perry's killer and he was in serious danger. He could be found dead, drowned, say, as if he'd been overtaken by remorse, and without evidence to the contrary the assumption of guilt would be made and more than likely there'd be no resources for further investigations.

They had these at the moment, though. He reminded himself he was far from helpless and he'd see Keith Drummond today; there was something rotten there and his task was going to be to drill down like a dentist dealing with a bad tooth and exposing the decay within.

But even if he succeeded in that – there was still the child, out there and vulnerable. Not to manage to bring him back safely whatever he'd done would be a serious blow.

Cat had persuaded him to talk about the unhealthy fear of failure that had haunted him all his life. She had ascribed it to an overbearing father who had demanded success, but he had an uncomfortable feeling that it was just another manifestation of the mortal sin of pride.

But it had in the past spurred him on to making efforts and taking risks that went far beyond professional expectation and so far, at least, that had paid off. Never despise making use of a pathology, he told himself as he reached the Kessock Bridge. He was a soldier by trade and in a battle you use whatever weapon comes to hand.

There was an accident on the A9 and DS Murray arrived late for the briefing and exhausted from battling with the sudden gusts of wind. She got drenched in just the short walk from the car park.

The incident room set up at the Kilbain Hotel was in the spa area and it was busy; at a couple of tables officers were taking statements from witnesses and others were milling around. She was directed into a small side room where Strang was holding the briefing.

The treatment table had been removed but the heavy scent of perfumed oils hung in the air, glamorous posters on the walls promised what could be achieved and there were mirrors everywhere. Murray's rainswept appearance confronted her full on as she came in and she winced.

Strang and Campbell were sitting on kitchen chairs at an imported small table, with spindly velveteen and gilt chairs opposite for visitors, and were already deep in conversation. Officers from other forces had been drafted in and they'd heard a lot about Perry Forsyth's shortcomings but evidence from a student who'd been working in the woods that day had got them at least closer to knowing when Forsyth had actually died.

'She came in last night,' Campbell said to Murray. 'She'd finished up at around 4.30 p.m. on Friday when she saw him coming from the house and walking quickly along the main path – gave her a brief nod but didn't speak. She wasn't surprised – she'd reckoned he was afraid of getting his ear bent about the tree. There was no one else around apart from students working elsewhere or gathered in the minibus ready to go back.

'In his statement, Lars Andersen claimed he'd left the woods by then, but unfortunately she couldn't remember if she'd seen his Jeep or not. We're checking with the other students, and they're running through the CCTV on the Kessock Bridge now but it's a labour-intensive business.'

'If that's the time frame it would rule out Dr Erskine,' Murray said. 'We'd have to verify, but he claims the last he saw of Forsyth was when he left after their barney in the morning. To tell you the truth, he's not very promising – can't see what's in it for him. It all seems to have kicked off when the tree was felled, and I didn't think he cared that much.'

'The one who cared certainly seems to have been Andersen, according to the witness,' Campbell said. 'Possessive about the whole wood, very temperamental.'

'It does shift the focus to him,' Strang said. 'We'll need to up the pressure.'

Murray was waiting for him to task her with it but instead he went on, 'Livvy, I've another job for you. I need your terrier skills. The fatal accident to Jay's mother

Helena – we talked about that before. It seems that there was some complaint about the investigation – it came up before the PIRC committee. I want you to track down the report. As I understand it, they thought there was something fishy and checked but there was no further action they could take.'

'Remember we commented on her being cremated?' Murray said, 'Not much you could prove after that, could you?'

Strang nodded agreement. 'What I want is a list of people interviewed, their statements, the name of the two doctors who signed the cremation certificate and a note of who instigated the complaint. And who was in charge of the original investigation.'

Campbell delicately cleared his throat. 'Er . . . I can tell you that. DI Drummond.'

Strang said, 'Ah. I did wonder if he might have been.'

'Very indirectly, was what he told me,' Murray said. 'Not true, then?'

'Seems not. I'm going to arrange to see him today. Anything else? No? I think that's it. Livvy, you can get on with it now.'

When Livvy stood up she'd dried off but the reflection in the mirror – her hair in a frizz from the damp, mascara washed away, shirt collar drooping – was no less demoralising. Averting her eyes, she went back into the incident room; it was clear from the queue of people that giving a statement had become a Thing.

It was noisy in there, but she found a small room kitted out for hairdressing and she settled down to the task of trawling through the records of the Police Investigation and Review Commissioner. Given the weather, this was a cushy number and the sort of job she relished so she was happy enough to settle down in the client's chair, once she'd draped a towel over the mirror.

It was with some trepidation that Nicki Latham went into work that morning. She could have called in sick, but with Jo Melville being a mate there was no guarantee she wouldn't pop round in her lunch break to see that Nicki was all right.

She'd left Jay lying spreadeagled across her spare room bed, sunk in the profound sleep of the exhausted child. Looking at him her face had softened; it had been well into the small hours before they'd got to bed, and she reckoned he was unlikely to wake before her lunch hour.

Nicki had driven through the storm to Drumdalloch the night before with her heart in her mouth. Would he be able to find his way to where she could see him? Going into the woods in these conditions without knowing where to find him would be crazy; she'd seen at first hand the destruction that could be wrought on the unmanaged woods.

Jay had grown up there, of course, but without shelter or, as far as she knew, serious wet-weather clothing, it wouldn't take long for hypothermia to set in and leave you disorientated and unable to go on, never mind the danger from falling branches, and even trees. What Giles Forsyth had called 'natural pruning' was a brutal business.

As she reached the entrance to Drumdalloch House she could see the lights on and a couple of police cars parked in the drive. She drove past it at normal speed, in case anyone might be watching, but as she followed the road round the boundary of the woods she slowed to a crawl, afraid of missing him – visibility was dreadful and he would hardly be standing conspicuously on the verge.

She had flashed her light on and off as she went. She'd told him not to wait near the house but she was getting more and more anxious driving along, and saw the trees thinning out near the farther edge.

And then, there he was, spotlit in the headlamps, a small huddled figure emerging from the scrubby bushes. He staggered in a savage gust, and she braked sharply as he ran round to the passenger side and got in.

His teeth were chattering – not hypothermia, then, thank God, but his clothes were so wet that a puddle was forming on the floor. She turned the heater up to full and grabbed the blanket she'd brought from the back seat.

'Wrap up in that,' she said. 'It'll get wet but it'll stop you losing heat.'

He hadn't said anything, or looked at her, but Nicki had sensed his tense sidelong glance.

'We'll talk later. Now just rub your arms and legs to get the circulation going, and there's food in the front there, if you're hungry.'

She set off back to Kilbain. After a few minutes, Jay, still shivering, reached into the glove compartment and started to demolish the ham and cheese sandwich.

When he'd finished, he said, 'Where are you taking me?'

There was fear in his voice and Nicki said quickly, 'Just back to my flat, where you'll be safe and warm. Not far now. I'll run a bath to warm you up and if you're still hungry there's a pizza in the freezer.'

That seemed to reassure him. For the first time, his shoulders relaxed and he slumped back in his seat with a long sigh. He had actually dropped off to sleep before they arrived back and when she stopped he jerked awake with a cry of fright.

'It's all right,' she said. 'There's no one around – just follow me in.'

He had nothing with him. 'I had a bag, but it got covered with stuff and I lost it.'

The tears started and she said hastily, 'No problem. You take off the wet things and I'll find a T-shirt and tracky bottoms or something. Here's a bath towel meantime.'

It was only after he was clean and warm and sitting by the electric fire with a mug of hot chocolate and a slice of pizza that she said, 'You're going to have to talk to me, Jay. What made you run away?'

He looked so pathetically young and small in the clothes that were too big for him. 'I was going to leave anyway. Then when I heard about Dad – well, loads of people knew I hated him and I knew they'd be like, "He did it!" and I knew I'd have to disappear. Lachie wouldn't let me stay on with him but I'd a sort of den in the woods and I thought, like I could maybe live there and hunt stuff, but I suppose that was dumb. And tonight, some branches crashed in on it and I had to crawl out.'

'But Jay, couldn't you see that running away was bound to make everyone think you must have done it?' Nicki paused, and then said, 'After all, you laid that trap for your Aunt Oriole, didn't you?'

His pale cheeks flushed and he wouldn't meet her eye.

'Well – sort of, but it wasn't to kill her – just a sort of . . .'

His voice trailed off, but she knew what it was that he hadn't said. He had told himself it was just to give her a fright but if it had killed her, he wouldn't have shed too many tears. Callous creatures, children.

She said, 'Why did you hate them so much?'

Now his eyes were fierce. 'Because they killed my mother! Grandad didn't trust them to look after the woods after he died, and Mum told me he was going to leave it all to her then me so we could do it. So they had to kill her before that could happen. I heard her on the phone – she said, "They're going to kill me if I'm not careful." And then they did.'

There was a long, long pause before Nicki said, 'You know revenge won't bring her back but somehow in a crazy way you got to feeling you owed it to her, didn't you? Now I'm going to have to try to work out the best way of sorting this. Meantime, you can just stay here. Don't go out and for heaven's sake don't run away again while I'm out at work.

'Your eyes are closing. I'm going to pack you off to bed. Wear what you've got on now and your clothes will be dry by tomorrow.'

Jay had looked pitiably forlorn as he trailed off, but he was asleep five minutes later when Nicki checked.

She went back into the sitting room and sat down with her head in her hands, bowed by the weight of responsibility. She knew what she should do – the phone was right there on the table – but she wasn't going to be bounced into making an end to it just yet.

All night, anxiety dreams kept waking her – dreams

where she was trying to find something that was lost or where she knew she was being chased without knowing why, and she had a cottonwool head when she got up in the morning. She didn't put on the TV in case it woke him, but read on her mobile that there were no fresh developments.

On her way to work she got in supplies along with a couple of T-shirts and a pack of underpants from the small children's section at the back of the Kilbain Co-op, then carrying the little pile of purchases she hurried to her car. The frenzy of yesterday seemed to have passed and there was no more than the usual number of people about.

One of them, though, was DI Drummond, and a cold shiver ran down her spine as he came towards her, as if her complicity might be written on her face, but he only nodded brusquely and walked on, presumably to start another day of hunting for the boy at this very moment lying asleep in her spare room bed.

At last, DCI Strang had something to tell DCS Borthwick. A bike had been found in an overgrown area of the Drumdalloch Woods, near to what looked like a roughly constructed shelter that had collapsed. A sports bag with what looked like the boy's personal things was lying in the debris.

Borthwick was incredulous. 'You mean he's been living there? And with the manpower we've expended on searching that place, how come no one spotted anything while he was doing his Robinson Crusoe bit?'

There really was no answer to that. Strang said feebly, 'Well, it's basically like a jungle there. And it's likely he'd made the den years ago when he was growing up here.'

'But living in it for four days? Where was he getting his food? Was he cycling into the village? What about CCTV?'

'No official cameras, and the one outside the supermarket in Kilbain isn't working. But though the bag of clothes suggests he was there until the shelter collapsed, possibly last night, I'm not convinced he actually was living in it. It would have been pretty rugged and there's no sign of food waste or even personal waste round about – and how did he manage to leave afterwards? Not on the bike, anyway.'

Borthwick was quick to understand. 'Someone else involved?'

'Looks like it. Don't know who, can't think why. Opens up a whole new angle. He didn't leave the area anyway until then, so I'm planning more local appeals to look out for unusual behaviour.'

'I suppose that's all you can do,' she said. 'Get me some footage of the shelter and the bike so at least I'll have some red meat to throw to the ravening hordes.'

She didn't sound thrilled as she rang off, but then Strang wasn't exactly thrilled either. He glanced at his watch – half an hour till his interview with Drummond. He was building a lot on that, hoping for something of a breakthrough and earlier he'd asked Campbell to sit in on it; he'd looked surprised and even concerned.

Strang smiled. 'Not up for it?'

'Oh, I'm fine – I've a broad back. It's just I was wondering if it's maybe a wee bit like rubbing salt in the wound.'

'That was the idea. He's not going to succumb to a

charm offensive, is he, so I reckon getting him riled and off-balance is the best way to proceed.'

He was checking through Drummond's formal statement when the phone rang and one of the incident room officers told him someone was wanting to speak to him, a Professor Crichton from the Scottish Institute for Studies in Biological Sciences.

'He says he won't talk to anyone except the top man,' the officer said. 'Will you see him, sir?'

Strang groaned. He recognised the type, but at the moment he couldn't afford to ignore anything that might be useful. 'All right,' he said. 'Arrange a table in the far corner and put up a screen.'

The professor was quite short but had a distinct air of confidence and he came forward holding out his hand before Strang could speak.

'I'm told that you are in charge. Is that right?'

'Yes.' He shook hands then led the way to the hastily screened-off area. 'As you can imagine I'm extremely busy, so if you can tell me what you want as briefly as possible.'

The man looked put out but said, 'Of course. I simply wanted to say I was somewhat taken aback that, given our declared interest in the Drumdalloch Woods, we had not been contacted directly to keep us informed about developments. Our chairman, Lord McCrea, is particularly concerned.'

Strang stared at him. 'I'm afraid we had no idea you were in any sense involved. We knew, of course, that you had an arrangement to use the woods as a research facility for your students and have spoken to Dr Erskine and one or two others, but that was the extent of it.'

It was Crichton's turn to stare. 'You mean that Dr Erskine didn't mention his plan that we should buy it to set up an international research centre?'

'No,' Strang said slowly. 'He didn't. Tell me about it.'

He was late for his appointment with DI Drummond, but then Drummond was late too, sending an apologetic message saying he'd been caught in a traffic jam on the Nairn road after a burn overflowed but it looked as if they were getting cars moving and he shouldn't be too long.

The great thing about official reports was that they collated all the facts in one well-organised file. The problem was always getting authority to access them, and Murray had spent a frustrating half-hour trying to find out who could even give permission. She was exhausted by her efforts to stay sweet and reasonable in the face of the most extraordinary unhelpfulness and obstruction, but in the end, here it was.

She scanned through it. All the information Strang had requested was there: there were familiar names among the witnesses, like Perry and Oriole Forsyth; there was a note stating that the police doctor who had signed the certificate for cremation was dead himself now, though the other signatory had confirmed his agreement to the finding; the complainant, Rebecca Grover, had an Australian address and was described as the sister of the deceased.

She read the summary with particular interest. It said that there was no further information available concerning the cause of death and with no strong evidence of any procedural deficiency, there would be no further action – all very bland and official, but somehow it conveyed the impression that they thought it stank to high heaven.

She forwarded it at once. She could go along and report, but when she asked the desk officer in the incident room where Strang was she was told that he and DI Campbell were just about to interview DI Drummond.

'Oh,' Murray said. 'Right,' and turned away. She'd been tasked with a job that Strang had thought would take much longer so of course it wasn't a deliberate snub. Even so, this was definitely the most significant interview so far and she couldn't help feeling she'd been supplanted. She couldn't go in and join them now; three would very definitely be a crowd.

She stood for moment, thinking. Strang had said they needed to lean on Andersen; she could do it now. She called the Institute to see if he was available and was taken aback when they said he was believed to be working in the woods this morning. The windows of the spa were rattling in the gale and all you could see through them was rain that was almost hail being hurled in swirling sheets.

For a moment she thought of finding something else to do that could legitimately be pursued indoors, but the truth was that she wanted to see for herself the man that Erskine had pretty much accused of being Forsyth's killer. That he could be working in these conditions suggested that he was dedicated at the very least, verging on obsessional, or in her opinion, totally off his trolley.

So she accessed his formal statement, speed-read it and went to the car to struggle into the unwieldy 'weatherproof' uniform that had never, in her experience, afforded any significant protection against Highland weather, getting soaked in the process.

The Drumdalloch drive was all but a tunnel under overarching trees and today they were roaring like a stormy sea, lashing to and fro as waves of wind passed through. Murray was frankly terrified.

Apart from the ribbons of crime scene tape, shredded now and floating wild, there was no sign of police presence at the house apart from an empty badged car. Gone off with some mates for a coffee, no doubt, she reflected darkly.

But there was an elderly Jeep too, so Andersen was indeed working here. Taking a deep breath she got out, staggering as the wind hit her and hard rain slashed at her face. Did she really have to do this?

She didn't, but she didn't want either to have to admit she'd chickened out, even to herself. There was an obvious path; with another deep breath she set off along it.

In fact, once she was in among the trees they gave some shelter from the gale and their canopy stopped the worst of the rain getting through. Now she could hear their individual creaks and groans as if they were being tortured by the whipping wind and she gave a small scream as something crashed to the ground near the path with a tearing noise. There was mud now sucking at her boots, making walking a slippery challenge, and there was running water everywhere with what had been little streams bursting their banks and flowing out along and across the path. Horribly, they were pitch-black, looking like snakes writhing around her feet. There were black rocks as well, and layers of moss and lichen growing on up the tree barks as if trying to smother them and even a stark white dead tree with lightning strike burn marks still scoring its trunk – a sort of witches' wood, deeply sinister.

People always talked about the healing power of trees but here they exuded an almost human malevolence, like an ill-intentioned mob. But she couldn't turn back now, even though she was wondering if she'd even manage to find the man. There were lots of other smaller paths criss-crossing the one she was on and she glanced down them, but she was afraid if she turned off she could get totally lost and wouldn't be found until they came across what was left after the dear little woodland creatures, probably eyeing her hopefully right now, had finished with her.

She gave a shudder, but gritted her teeth and walked on, shouting his name. If she found him, she'd drag him out of this living nightmare to be interviewed at the hotel. Under arrest, if necessary, which might not exactly be best practice, or even legal, but frankly by now she was past caring.

'Expecting a phone call?' Jo Melville said.

Nicki Latham looked startled. 'No. Why?'

'It's just you've been unusually edgy this morning – you've looked at your watch a dozen times and I wondered if you were waiting for one.'

Nicki felt her heart skip a beat. 'Oh, no, not really. Just, it was sort of a long morning.' Then, on an inspiration, she said, 'Well – there was this guy who said he might phone back . . .'

Jo laughed. 'Aha! Come on, what's he like?'

Nicki pulled a face. 'Not worth talking about. I was actually trying to think of the best way of choking him off if he did phone.'

'Doesn't do to be too picky, you know! Anyway, it's nearly lunchtime. Want to go first?'

Nicki picked up her shopping and her raincoat, glancing out of the window. Sounding as offhand as she could she said, 'God, it's horrible out there. See you later, if I don't drown.'

Freed at last, she set off for her car, forcing herself not to run and draw attention to herself.

How would Jay be feeling today? Relieved to have some clothes that weren't an embarrassment, anyway. She could make him lunch and reassure him that they'd talk it all through, but later – she still had a lot of hard thinking to do. Would he even be awake, though?

She hadn't allowed herself to think, *Would he even be there*? so that it was only when she tried to unlock her front door and found that it wasn't locked that panic seized her. With just a glance into the sitting room and kitchen she flung open the door of the bedroom.

The bedclothes were rumpled, but that was the only sign that last night hadn't been another of her disordered dreams. Jay himself had vanished.

CHAPTER SIXTEEN

When Steve Christie's phone rang, he looked at the caller ID and grimaced. Then, with his profession's awareness of the difference a smile makes to your phone voice, he smiled.

'Oriole, love! How are you? I've been thinking about you so much since yesterday. I hope they've been giving you some peace. You've had such a dreadful time, poor sweet, and what you need is space to rest and recover.'

'Oh, a couple of policemen came in to take my statement – just about what I'd done on Friday, so it wasn't difficult and they were very nice. Since then, there's been hardly anyone around. I was just phoning to say not to worry, they said I could do whatever I liked so I'll get in for the afternoon shift.'

Steve's heart sank. 'Absolutely not, sweetie! I'm not having you driving in this weather – even getting from your house to the road is seriously dangerous in a gale like this. Anyway, the hotel is full of media people so it wouldn't take them long to find out who you were.'

'I suppose that's right,' she said reluctantly. 'I need to get in the messages but Kilbain, or even Fortrose, could be terribly embarrassing. But Steve, it's horrible being alone here with nothing to do except worry. I just keep thinking about poor Jay being out there somewhere – I don't suppose there's any news, is there?'

'Not that I've heard, though they wouldn't necessarily tell me. What about your friend Nicki? Won't she be coming round to see you?'

'I don't know. I've phoned her but it's switched off. Steve, couldn't you come to see me?'

'Can't think of anything I'd like more, love, but the blasted police are really demanding – always wanting another area brought into service. I'm pretty much tied down here.'

'Of course.' Her voice had flattened. 'It's just, well, depressing, with the weather and everything.'

'Of course it is. But once the storm blows itself out why not take yourself off to Inverness and treat yourself to some retail therapy? Not before, mind! I'm not having my best girl crushed by a falling tree!'

Oriole giggled a protest. 'Oh Steve! But that's a good idea. And I'll buy a lovely cake to have in the house when you have a minute to come across.'

'Can't wait.'

Christie put the phone down, feeling sick. He despised himself for allowing Drummond to force him into the part he was playing, but the stakes were indeed high for him too – comfort and happiness if they got what they wanted, a life of drudgery here, at best, or even bankruptcy, if they didn't. Jay was known to be a tree-hugger, and his coming into everything his father owned – a very sizeable amount, according to the rumours about what he'd got for the tree – had left the whole thing on a knife-edge. He'd have to be convinced that the best way for the woods to be preserved as his grandfather had wished was to go along with the hotel project.

But they had to find him first. That was what Keith had set out to do this morning, but Steve hadn't had any progress report so far.

He was at the desk telling a hopeful journalist that the hotel was fully booked, and fending off her attempts to extract a juicy quote, when Keith came in, flinging the door wide so that the gust of air blew the papers on the desk onto the floor.

He slammed it behind him, then marched across to the stairs, saying only, 'Up there, is he?'

'No, through in the spa. One of the treatment rooms,' Steve said, acutely aware that the journalist's ears had almost visibly pricked up.

Keith rolled his eyes, muttering, 'Dear God!' then went past them to the spa wing.

'Well, he didn't look best pleased!' the young woman said chirpily. 'Come on – tell me! Is he a *suspect*?'

'No,' he said coldly. 'Just a police officer going to a meeting. And if you'll excuse me, I've a lot to do.'

As she went out, disappointed, Steve leant on the desk to steady himself and took deep breaths to slow his racing heart. Of course Keith was going to be a bloody suspect, as Steve was himself; because of their involvement with Perry the police had questioned him about his movements and even though he'd never left the hotel and could prove it, it gave him a bad feeling. But Keith had been perfectly confident he could handle it, and surely he knew all the tricks when it came to police questioning.

What was really worrying Steve was the look on his face as he came in. Keith could never hide his feelings and he'd looked incredibly stressed. And knowing his intentions, there were only two conclusions: either he hadn't found Jay Forsyth, or he had and Jay wasn't playing along.

From the symptoms Steve was experiencing he could be in the throes of a heart attack, but the last thing he wanted was to draw attention to himself. He held on to the desk a little longer, then went through to the bar, which he'd decided not to open at this time, and poured a double brandy.

He'd said, 'No.' Just like that. A flat 'No'.

DS Murray had first spotted him after passing the crime scene tapes around a black pond, obviously where they'd found Perry Forsyth's body. Andersen was quite a long way off but, she knew, perfectly within earshot and even after she employed the full force of the voice developed for use on Saturday night rammies in Glasgow after an Old Firm game, he didn't react.

He looked like a great black bear, enshrouded in the sort of waterproof coat and hood that could shrug off the worst Scottish weather could throw at it, and bizarrely there was a huge black umbrella beside him, pegged down so that it couldn't be seized by the wind.

Murray ploughed her way towards him and it was only when she was standing right in front of him that he'd paid her enough attention to say, 'No.'

'I'm finding it much too difficult to conduct a proper interview under these circumstances,' she said, feeling disadvantaged already. 'I need you to come to the incident centre in Kilbain.'

Andersen looked up at last and she got the full benefit of the dark beard and the deep brown eyes; he was definitely fit, but with an unsettling intensity of expression.

'You do not understand,' he said. 'The evidence here – it could be vital, and already you have kept me away from my research, away from making crucial observations. You want to remove me now, you have to arrest me.'

For all her brave talk, she couldn't, of course. 'I have no wish to do that,' she lied. 'Do you always work outdoors in weather like this?'

'No. But at this so important time, I must work on.'

'Look, Mr Andersen, you have to realise you're a suspect in a homicide enquiry – and it's been suggested that you are guilty. It's in your interests to convince us that you aren't.'

He gave a great shout of laughter. 'Ha! Erskine, no doubt, who wanted to kill him more than I did. He is no scientist, a nothing, who thinks he's a big man.'

She could see the bruising on his knuckles. 'You had a fight with him, didn't you?'

He shook his head. 'Not a fight, no. I hit him, and then I left.'

The rain that was finding its way through gaps in her rainwear was distracting; she was getting colder and colder and she was losing control of the conversation. 'But you described Mr Forsyth as a murderer after he felled the black ebony, didn't you?'

A light came into his eyes. 'You are ignorant. You are like someone who is deaf and blind. The trees – they are people in their way, individuals in a community, where they support each other, suffer, get scared, ask for help. Or compete, same like we do. Below ground, they talk. They talk endlessly. These tiny filaments, they are everywhere. Mycelium, a fungus – it lives in cooperation with the trees. They feed it, it feeds them. Everywhere, below our feet they grow and grow all the time, thin white worms humming with messages, like telephone wires. You can almost hear them, if you listen.'

For a chilling moment, she almost could. Murray cleared her throat. 'I can see what you're saying. But calling it murder . . .'

'Still you will not see. This – it is like he wickedly kills a tree because he is too stupid to understand and it is only money, for him. When one dies, maybe they all suffer. Maybe only some do. Maybe none. This is what we do not know exactly. And it has just happened right here for me to study.'

He suddenly turned his eyes on her. 'You are investigating, like I am. Here is my chance to observe in real time how quickly these messages are passed. To see if this tree – not native stock – has been connected, if the signals of distress it sent out after being attacked – like a person screaming, you understand – was answered with supplies of sugar.'

He gestured to the case of instruments that was being sheltered under the great black umbrella. 'Here I can record that – like, you know, a 999 call for an ambulance.'

His gaze was mesmeric and Murray, disorientated by

cold and the weirdness of it all, had to make an effort of will to look away. Get a grip, she told herself.

'It's all very interesting, Mr Andersen, but I haven't time to listen to this now. You were allegedly very angry with Mr Forsyth. You are, by your own admission, a violent man. You certainly had the opportunity to kill him – he was seen entering the woods on Friday afternoon—'

He erupted. 'Not by me! I collected evidence of immediate effects of the ebony being felled but I needed tests in the laboratory to tell me what they meant. I was excited, I have to say. What he did was evil, but it gave me this special opportunity. So . . .' He shrugged.

As simple as that. 'So you were all right with it? Not angry any more?'

'Oh, angry – I suppose, but I was too busy to think about it. I went back to Inverness at perhaps four. Now, I can go back to my work?'

'Did anyone see you leave?'

Andersen had moved away from her. Now he turned. 'I don't know. It is not my business to know – it is yours.' Then he went back to bend over the open case that had a screen showing measurements and hieroglyphics that meant nothing to her.

There was little more Murray could do, except to squelch back through the woods, haunted by the white worms writhing under her feet and the trees screaming. And what had it all been for? CCTV would tell them whether he'd left Drumdalloch before the last sighting of Forsyth, but she would be prepared to bet that he wasn't their man. She hadn't been able to believe Michael Erskine would care enough to do it either; her personal list of suspects was shortening rapidly.

And did that include the missing laddie? Only someone with no experience of juvenile crime could think he was surely too young to kill, and Murray had plenty of that; she'd regularly seen for herself the terrible damage inflicted by lack of love. But a child striking down his father in revenge for his neglect? Not so common.

Siblings, mind you – there was certainly good precedent for that. Oriole had been furious with her brother and was not visibly in distress over his death, but then she'd been open about their quarrel when, if she'd killed him, it would have been smarter to keep quiet and pretend to grieve. She'd been a lot more worried about her nephew and had even tried to cover up the attack he'd made on her, when you'd think that, if she'd done it, she'd be only too happy to turn their attention that way.

When it came to Jay, the trail was getting colder by the hour. Feeling depressed, she ploughed on, trying not to think that the restless trees were emitting messages of hate as she passed.

As at last she came in sight of the house, she realised that the wind was dropping and there was a faint lightening in the sky. She couldn't wait to get out of her jacket, now almost as wet on the inside as it was on the outside.

It was just as Murray got back to her car that she remembered the old man she'd seen in the Co-op. He lived somewhere around; she could ask at the house where it was and go to talk to him.

It wasn't appealing. She felt what she'd done already went above and beyond the call of duty. And anyway, there might be new developments and the boss might have other ideas – she'd got into enough trouble in the past doing things on her own initiative.

So she could feel positively virtuous about driving back to the hotel to get warm and dry and find a cup of coffee and something to eat. There'd be time enough to do that later, once the rain went off.

When DCI Strang finished his interesting conversation with Professor Crichton he saw that Murray had sent through the PIRC report and he took time to read it before he went back to the treatment room where DI Campbell was waiting for him. There was as yet no sign of DI Drummond.

'Sorry to keep you waiting, but that was all interesting stuff,' he said. 'I'll brief you later but follow any lead I give you. Anything new?'

'Having a better idea of time of death has speeded up the Kessock Bridge CCTV search,' Campbell said. 'They've been able to stop slow-running earlier tapes and they've already found a clip of Lars Andersen crossing at 16:15, which squares with his statement. It's not to say that he couldn't have gone back later, but it's something.'

He was still speaking when a peremptory knock came on the door and DI Drummond walked in without waiting for a response.

'Apologies,' he said to Strang. 'Traffic problems.' Then he noticed Campbell and his face hardened. He wasn't a fool; the other man's presence was close to a direct insult and his voice was cold. 'Oh. I understood you were bringing in your own people.'

'Given the widening scope of enquiries, I felt it would

be helpful to have local support,' Strand said blandly. 'Take a seat.'

Drummond sat down, his folded arms a classic barrier. 'You've seen my statement, I assume. I've no doubt you know it checks out and I don't think there's much I can add to it.'

'Just a few things I want to talk about. First, could you cast your mind back to the time of Helena Forsyth's death? You were, I understand, in charge of investigating it.'

His eyes narrowed as he looked at Campbell. 'Oh, nice little knife job, Hamish! But if this is some pathetic attempt to drop me in it, Chief Inspector, I would point out that the case was fully reviewed and found perfectly satisfactory.'

'I should make it clear that this did not come from DI Campbell. I've read the report, but I'm more interested in what happened on the ground at the time. I didn't, for example, see anything more than a formal statement taken from Perry and Oriole Forsyth. Was there any further questioning done, or any examination concerning the nesting platform to establish its likely condition before it fell? DI Campbell can probably help you out, if you can't remember.'

'I don't recall anyone being tasked to do that,' Campbell said, adding fair-mindedly, 'though of course it might have been done without coming my way.'

Drummond was clearly having difficulty in controlling his temper. 'The police doctor declared it a tragic accident and the second doctor also signed to permit cremation. The autopsy confirmed that the wood debris found in the wound was compatible with her head having violently struck the root of the tree after she slipped. There was no indication of foul play so there was little point in pursuing expensive, and as the review shows, unnecessary investigations.'

'Perry Forsyth was spending more time in Edinburgh than at home. Were you aware of rumours that the Forsyths' marriage was in trouble?'

'I never pay attention to local rumours,' he said flatly.

Then more fool you, Strang thought. 'Were you also aware Giles Forsyth was planning to leave Drumdalloch to Mrs Forsyth in his will and cut out his own children?'

Drummond was visibly shaken now and it took him a moment to collect his thoughts. 'Nothing to do with me what Giles chose to do with his money.'

'Nothing to do with you, when you, Steve Christie and Perry Forsyth were in a consortium to develop the property as a luxury hotel after his father died?'

At this further provocation Drummond swore, thumping his fist on the table so that the flimsy structure jumped. 'I suppose I have bloody Oriole to thank for all this. Only a moron like Christie could have thought she'd keep it to herself – she's a woman, after all.'

Ignoring that, Strang said, 'I would also be interested to know about your status in the consortium. Mr Forsyth would be providing the property to build on, Mr Christie was going to be selling this place, but what were you to contribute? A hotel of the type you envisaged would be a highly expensive project.'

Drummond's fists were clenched now. 'I'm hardly penniless. Obviously, I have savings, and in any case, felling a few selected trees would go a long way to funding the build—' He stopped abruptly, as if only just realising the implications of what he had said.

Strang left a calculated pause before he said, 'Yes. So you can perhaps see that with Mr Forsyth having decided that he would rather fell his own trees and keep the profits than plough them into a speculative enterprise, it isn't surprising that we are taking a particular interest in you, and Christie too.'

'Then don't forget Oriole,' he snapped. 'She was the keenest of all of us to preserve the trees.'

'We haven't forgotten her, or anyone else who had the means, the motive and the opportunity. Nor have we forgotten that Mr Forsyth's share of the legacy will now come to his son. Have you any information about his likely whereabouts?'

'No, none. You may remember that you made it clear that I wasn't needed.'

He stood up abruptly. 'I'm keen to do my duty as a police officer but I have begun to feel that I would be unwise to answer any further questions without my lawyer being present.'

'That is, of course, your right,' Strang said. 'Thank you for your cooperation.'

As the door shut behind him, Campbell said, 'Didn't see a lot of that, actually.'

'He's in an awkward position, but on the face of it his alibi stands up and unless we have something that puts him at the scene of the crime, we can't take it any further, and when it comes to Helena Forsyth's death we're stymied.

'It's actually the money side that interests me. What you

could save on a DI's salary isn't going to be commensurate with the contributions of the other three . . .'

Campbell gave a delicate cough and Strang turned to look at him. 'Being naive, am I?'

'Wouldn't take it upon myself to say that, boss,' he said. 'But it's been noticeable that there's a lot of nervousness in some quarters about this purge on police corruption. It's been talked about for years, but it's looking like they mean it this time and we've a new boss who's maybe a bit keener than the last one was.'

'I see. Other sleeping partners on the consortium, you think?'

'Might well be. I wouldn't want to name names when it comes to that, but I can certainly tell you which are his closest associates.'

Strang sighed. 'The sad thing is that I'm not even surprised. It certainly widens the scope of our enquiries – and after my chat with Professor Crichton, we'll need to pull in Erskine. I'll get hold of Livvy and see you both here once we've had a break for lunch. In my old sergeant's favourite phrase, my stomach thinks my throat's been cut.'

Steve Christie had hovered around the hall waiting for Keith to come out. He had believed he was as stressed as he could be, but he realised he'd been mistaken when the man appeared, his face almost purple with rage.

'What-what happened?' Steve stammered.

Keith pointed to the office. 'In there.'

Senga, at the reception desk, was clearly fascinated. Steve followed him, bleating, 'Keep your voice down. The receptionist's got ears like a bat and it's not soundproof.'

Afterwards, he thought it might have been better if he'd just let him shout. Keith hurling obscenities at him in a cold, furious undertone was even more terrifying.

'I blame myself – I knew all along you had the intellect of a brain-dead maggot and yet I let you in on this. It's thanks to you that this will go pear-shaped and when we're sharing a cell in Barlinnie for conspiracy to murder I'll make sure you'll long for death every day of your life.'

'For God's sake, Keith! What is that about?' Forgetting his own warning, Steve had raised his voice. 'I haven't—'

'It's not about Perry! It's about that duplicitous bitch Helena.'

'*Helena?* But—'

'Oh yes, but, but, but! There was an enquiry, right enough. What it found was that the procedure was correct. They didn't make any finding about the actual death – there was nothing there for them to find.

'But now, thanks to your criminal stupidity in telling Oriole about our plans, she's swivelled the spotlight on to the consortium, and now they've a reason for opening that particular can of worms you can imagine what might come writhing out.'

Steve opened his mouth, but no sound came out and Keith went on, 'You'd better make sure Oriole shuts up. In fact—'

He stopped abruptly, and Steve found his voice. 'This is a disaster! Where do we go from here?'

Keith said, with sudden energy, 'I'll tell you where we go. You're going to phone Oriole and tell her that you're worried about her safety with that murderous brat still on the loose, and you want to have her here to look after her, and then you can woo her – you remember what that word means? Flowers, lovey-dovey stuff, working up to a proposal. Tell her that there's a police witch hunt and you'll be at risk if she cooperates with them. Right?'

It felt as if the floor was dropping away under his feet. 'But Keith, I don't want to marry her!' His voice rose to an aggrieved wail. 'I've never fancied her in the slightest – in fact I feel exhausted just talking to her after half an hour – or rather, listening to her go on and on about every tiny thing. I can't—'

'Oh, I think you'll find that you can. It's your punishment.'

Grasping at a passing straw, Steve said, 'The hotel's full, Keith. I don't think I can find a room for her.'

'Then she'll have to share your room, won't she?' Keith said with an unpleasant smile. 'That's just a little bit extra added for not making sure she wouldn't talk before. Now get on with it.'

He turned to go. Steve said hollowly, 'I'll see what I can do. And what about Jay? Any luck?'

Keith's smile vanished. 'Working on it,' he said and walked out.

Jo Melville looked at her watch again and frowned. Nicki should have been back from her lunch hour by now – indeed, she should have been here in time to let Jo go and get back from hers by now. There was an appointment in Nicki's diary in ten minutes and it looked as if she'd forgotten about it.

It must be a problem with the guy she'd been talking

about. Jo was an understanding employer; Nicki was very good at the job and she'd come to think of her as a friend, but standing up a client for the sake of someone she'd described as unimportant simply wasn't good enough.

Jo sighed, and dialled her number, but it went to voicemail. She said, 'Nicki, pick up. Your client's due any moment – in fact he's just getting out of his car.'

There was no answer. Jo muttered savagely under her breath, then pinned on a smile as the client came in.

'Mr McMorran? I'm sorry, Nicki's been detained but I'm sure I can help you. Do take a seat.'

Oriole listened yet again to Nicki's voice message, then hung up. There was no point in saying anything when she hadn't replied to the two messages she'd left already. There'd been no response to a text she'd sent either.

She'd thought Nicki was her good friend. She knew more than anyone how upset Oriole was, how lonely, so it was really hurtful that she was snubbing her.

She had a few casual friends in the town – more acquaintances, really, but not a single one had got in contact when all this happened. She'd be in despair if it wasn't for Steve.

Her lips curved. 'My best girl,' he'd said. Not that he really meant that, exactly, but it was more than she'd dared to hope for. And at least she knew he was looking out for her and he, at least, would never let her down.

The incident room had been quite busy earlier but it was quiet when the young PC on reception duties saw a woman coming in, shaking back the hood of her raincoat to show fair curly hair frizzing a bit in the damp. Though she had bright blue-grey eyes, they were shadowed and her face was very pale. She hesitated on the doorstep and seemed to be taking a deep breath.

'Can I help you, madam?' she said encouragingly.

'I want to see whoever is in charge of the murder case.'

It wasn't unusual for public-spirited witnesses to feel it was beneath them to speak to anyone other than the boss and the standard response was, 'I'm afraid he's tied up at the moment and he's a very busy man, but I can find someone else who'll be able to help you,' and she gave it now.

'Then I'll wait,' the woman said.

There was something about the way she said it that made the young officer realise this was one she shouldn't try to brush off.

'If you can give me your name and tell me what you've come about, I'll get it passed on to DCI Strang to see if he can find time to speak to you.'

A strange smile came over her face. 'I think you'll find that he can. My name is Rebecca Grover, and I've come to confess to the murder of Perry Forsyth.'

CHAPTER SEVENTEEN

'It seems that Dr Erskine has been somewhat economical with the truth,' DCI Strang said to DI Campbell and DS Murray as they met in the re-purposed treatment room. 'According to Professor Crichton, he had a very ambitious plan for the Institute to buy Drumdalloch and set up a field centre for international students. I take it he didn't mention anything about this to you, Livvy?'

Murray shook her head emphatically. 'Not even a hint. Said he'd had a set-to with Forsyth about messing up his students' work, but he didn't sound impassioned – not about the felled tree, not about anything, really. Bloodless sort of guy – couldn't quite see him going radge and seizing a lump of wood. Couldn't see what would be in it for him, either.'

'According to the professor, acquiring the site would have fulfilled a dream for Erskine. He's apparently a rather low-grade academic and this would be his path to higher status in the scientific establishment. Crichton had been given the impression that the woods were getting protected status and that the Forsyths would be grateful to have the place taken off their hands and that there was an agreement with Forsyth to that effect.

'With all we now know about his plans, it seems beyond unlikely that he'd settle for a derisory offer, but Erskine seems to have strung the Institute board along. Crichton suggested he'd got so much praise that he'd got above himself and couldn't bear to admit he'd been wrong, especially with them having spent money on it.'

'That's a motive for murder right there,' Murray said thoughtfully. 'With Forsyth dead, Erskine could claim that yes, the arrangement had been going ahead but now, through no fault of his, the deal had collapsed.'

'I'll get them to check his number plate and carry on with the Kessock Bridge screening,' Campbell said. 'It'll take some time to run it through to the morning, of course, but it could maybe prove helpful.'

'He could have hired a car for the purpose,' Strang pointed out. 'He's an intelligent man and he could have worked out the risks. Anyway, we need to pull him in to explain himself. Hamish, can you—'

Just as he said that, there was a knock on the door and a young woman constable came in looking uncertain.

'Sorry to disturb you, sir. It's a female who says she has to speak to you.'

Strang raised his eyebrows. 'Did you suggest she should speak to someone else? What is it about?'

'Yes, I did, sir. But then she told me she wanted to confess to the murder of Perry Forsyth.'

There was a stunned silence. 'She *what?*' Murray exclaimed.

Strang was cautious. 'What does she look like, Constable? Is she – er – someone who might be likely to be confused about this?'

'No, sir. She seems nervous, but – well, you would be, I suppose. She says her name's Rebecca Glover.'

While Strang said, 'Ah,' and Murray added, 'That would figure,' Campbell looked from one to the other, confused.

'Tell Ms Glover I'll see her in a minute. Don't let her leave. Hamish, this is Helena Forsyth's sister. I think you'd better go – three officers is a bit heavy.'

'No problem,' Campbell said. 'I'll do the follow-up on Erskine, anyway – you never know what may happen.'

After they had gone, Strang said, 'We have to be very careful now – with no recording equipment here, her brief could claim we'd beaten the confession out of her. It's all about procedure and the slightest breach could screw up the whole thing. I think we're safe to ask a couple of general background questions, but she will have to be cautioned before we go into any details, and given the opportunity to have a lawyer present. In fact, we will stress that she should have.'

False confessions, for whatever reason, were common enough and though Murray hadn't dealt with one before, she knew the danger of a miscarriage of justice was very real. She said, 'I'll keep quiet. I'll fetch her, shall I?'

The woman who was waiting stood up quite steadily and followed Murray into the little room, but her face was ashen and she was taking short, shallow breaths.

Strang said, 'Come in and sit down. I understand that you told the constable that you wanted to confess to Perry Forsyth's murder.'

'Yes. I killed him.'

'And your name is Rebecca Glover?'

'Yes. Helena Forsyth was my sister and I believe that her husband killed her. That's why I killed him.'

'I don't want to go into details at the moment. Are you perfectly sure you wish to stand by what you have said? I don't suppose I need to tell you that there are very serious consequences.'

'No,' she said. 'I understand and I don't wish to change anything.'

'Right,' Strang said. 'I will be formally arresting and cautioning you, but before I do that I want to ask an important question on a different topic. You are Jay Forsyth's aunt. Do you know where he is?'

'No, I don't. If I did, I'd tell you,' she said, welling up.

Strang eyed her narrowly. The emotion looked genuine enough but there was something in the way she said it that didn't ring quite true. 'Are you entirely sure about that? It would be in his interests, you know.'

A tinge of colour came into that pale face. 'Yes, I know. And I'm sure.'

'And you are still sure about your confession?'

She nodded.

'Then I am arresting you on suspicion of the murder of Peregrine Forsyth. You do not have to say anything but anything you do say will be noted and may be used in evidence. Do you understand?'

'Yes. I killed him.'

Murray noted the words as Strang went on, 'You will be taken to Inverness police station where the process of arrest will be completed. You are entitled to have a lawyer present and I strongly advise that you should.'

'I don't have one.'

'They can arrange there for someone to represent you. Are you ready to go?'

The woman bit her lip, then, 'Yes,' she said firmly.

Back in the incident room, Murray gave directions to two uniforms who escorted her out. She watched them go, then went back into the room.

Strang was looking grave and she could see they had the same thought. 'She thinks her nephew did it, doesn't she, boss?'

'Or perhaps even knows he did.' He groaned. 'What a hideous mess! I'll get on to the DCS – we'll have to inform the media. And the worrying thing is that I'm pretty sure Ms Glover knows more about Jay than she's prepared to tell us. Don't know what, but I'm afraid she thinks she's giving him a chance to get away when it's hard to see where he could safely go.'

'And we can't even grill her on the how and where details of the crime,' Murray said. 'I bet she'd trip herself up if we did.'

'We'll have the chance to do that later but it's frustrating meantime. I think we proceed as if this hadn't happened, talk to Erskine, for instance, and generally keep that investigation going low-key. But with Jay, I can only hope when the interview with Glover is set up, we find out if we're right about what she's doing.'

Then Strang paused. 'Rebecca,' he said thoughtfully. 'So she just appeared and popped into the woods to kill her brother-in-law, just like that – or has she been around for some time preparing the ground, as a student, say?

Might she have been living under a different name? Once they've taken her mug shot Hamish can get it circulated locally.'

'I'll fill Hamish in on what's happened,' Murray said, picking up her phone. She explained, then listened. 'Really?' she said. 'Well, well, well,' and rang off.

Strang looked an enquiry.

'The Kessock Bridge,' she said. 'They didn't have to search any more of the tape. As Lars Andersen was crossing it at 16:14, Michael Erskine was coming from the opposite direction. He returned at 17:27.'

There had been a trickle of locals who seemed to feel they had something useful to tell the police, which the watchful Steve Christie doubted, but more interesting was the woman who'd come in for a drink with Perry that evening – Nicki someone – joining them. What did she have to offer, he wondered? She definitely didn't look a happy bunny.

Steve wasn't a happy bunny either. He didn't want to phone Oriole – he really, really didn't – but he knew he must. Keith would be on the phone before long to check that he'd issued the invitation; he might get away with one more night of freedom but that would be it.

He was talking to a genuine resident, keen to discuss the drama, when suddenly two officers appeared from the spa corridor, escorting Nicki handcuffed between them.

'Excuse me,' Steve said abruptly. 'I must just make a phone call.' Heading for his office, he muttered to Senga, 'Not a word to any of the journalists, mind.'

Keith didn't seem as excited by this news as Steve had

expected. He grunted, 'Right,' and went straight into, 'Did Oriole agree?'

Steve swallowed. 'Er – well, I haven't got through to her yet.'

'You don't mean she isn't taking your calls?'

'Well, I don't know. I've been run off my feet today, but I'll do it tomorrow.'

He had to hold the phone away from his ear at the response and his hand was shaking as he set it down. He had his orders: get her in now and tell Keith that she'd come. He couldn't understand why it was urgent, but he had that 'better not to know' feeling.

Steve went back to the desk where Senga was positively vibrating with speculation, cut her short and took the bookings register back to the office. For once, the hotel was pretty much full, but there was the small back room on the third floor available. With a bit of juggling, he could switch it for a first floor front with more space so he could suggest Oriole retreat there rather than encountering awkward situations downstairs.

He bitterly resented being told to do it now – or indeed, being made to do it at all – but he still picked up the phone again. Remembering the mantra, he was smiling as he said, 'How are you doing, Oriole love? I've been worrying about you, all by yourself out there.'

She told him how grateful she was for his concern several times, while he got up courage to say the actual words to invite her into his daily life. Then he'd to listen to a lot more incoherent gratitude and excitement. At last, she said, 'I'll pack up my things tonight and be with you first thing in the morning, all right?'

Steve knew what he was supposed to say – 'Oh no, come now' – but the words stuck in his throat and he heard himself saying instead, 'That's perfect! See you tomorrow, then.'

Keith wouldn't be pleased, but at least he felt he'd gained some self-respect – and his last night of freedom. Which, when he thought about it, probably only meant sitting in his flat contemplating a bottle of gin.

DCI Strang had been summoned south for a conference with DCS Borthwick. Despite the arrest, with no further progress to announce on the hunt for Jay Forsyth, the heat from the media was still on and Murray had the impression there was going to be some sort of brainstorming session. She wasn't sure what anyone could say that hadn't been said already, but you had to keep the high heid yins happy.

Campbell was arranging for Erskine to be brought in tomorrow and since there wasn't anything else useful she needed to do today, she could make an early start back herself.

She was on the point of heading home when she suddenly remembered the cottage on the Drumdalloch estate. She'd been meaning to go there, but demoralised by Lars Andersen and the storm conditions, she'd quit and gone back to the hotel. She could make up for that now.

Lachie sounded interesting, from what the shop assistant had said. Murray had always had a soft spot for elderly folk who had no truck with earnest do-gooders wanting to make them respectable, even if that did mean extra work for the force sometimes. She had plans to be one of them in due course.

The trees lining the Drumdalloch House drive were in more benevolent mood today, swaying in the light breeze. Almost as if they were dancing to celebrate the sunshine, Murray found herself thinking, then sternly banished the thought. She'd be as weird as Lars Andersen if she didn't stamp on it now.

His Leep was still there, alongside a people-carrier, an Audi and an elderly Kia, but there was no police presence. Murray parked, got out and looked around.

There were birds flittering in the trees, their singing surprisingly loud, as if they were joining in a general shout, glad the storm had passed, just like the trees. Oh dear, another weird thought!

But there were human voices too, over on a path she hadn't taken before. A group of students was peering at what looked like a weather station or something, and though she got some slightly suspicious looks they were quite ready to help.

'If you mean the old guy we see around,' one boy said, 'go down that path until you see the fields beyond the woods. It's a sort of shack he lives in, really.'

Murray thanked them and went on. It was still muddy underfoot but the growth here was scrubby rather than majestic and intimidating like the oppressive Lords of the Woods. Between the slender trunks she could see rough fields that looked as if they might have been grazing for sheep.

But there was only a ramshackle building that might once have been a shepherd's hut, though not one to tempt David

Cameron. She headed towards it, climbing over a wire fence that sagged low in the middle – clearly a well-used route.

The man who opened the warped wooden door half an inch was unwelcoming. 'What are you wanting?'

Murray produced her warrant card. 'I'm DS Murray,' she said, then seeing alarm on his face added hastily, 'There's no problem. I was just wanting a wee chat. Can I come in?'

To say he admitted her reluctantly was an understatement. He seemed to be considering refusing, but then stood aside.

It was hard not to gag on the smell that hit her first – feral, musky – and then there was the shock of the sheer poverty. In these days of the welfare state, you seldom saw a room that had only what were genuinely the bare essentials; a bed, unmade; a small wooden table; a shabby armchair; a stool; a sink with one tap containing unwashed dishes; a small stove; a curtain concealing what was probably a primitive lavatory; a tall wooden cupboard. The basic fireplace was full of dead ashes, and it looked as if the floor hadn't been swept for quite some time. And there was the source of the noxious smell – a rough sort of hutch with wire netting across the front. In it she could see the bandit mask of a ferret peering out.

It was a primitive lifestyle and he actually looked quite frail, walking stiffly as if in pain. With the gaps she could see in the structure, it must be punishingly cold for the poor old soul.

Uninvited, Murray sat down on the stool. After a moment he sat in the chair, pushing it back away from her as far as it would go.

'Don't know what you think I might have to say.'

He sounded belligerent, but she realised that he was actually scared. The ferret, as well as the comment about pheasants in the Co-op, suggested poaching might have caused the occasional run-in with the cops, but this wasn't the standard 'Don't know what you mean' defensiveness. This was something more.

'You know what's been going on?' she said. 'About what happened to Perry Forsyth, and his son being missing?'

'No more than anyone else.'

'But living so close, you must have known them quite well?'

'Always kept myself to myself.'

'You must have known Mr Forsyth, surely.'

McIver shifted in his seat. 'Kept himself to himself too. Never wanted anything to do with me.'

'But Jay – did you never have anything to do with him?'

She'd scored a hit. McIver's eyes went all over the place as he muttered, 'Not so's you'd know.'

Taking a punt, she said, 'But you've seen him since he went missing?'

She could see his knuckles tightening. 'No I never.' He was a bad liar.

'I'm afraid I don't believe you. You could be in trouble – Jay Forsyth being missing is very serious. I'll ask you again: have you seen him since last Thursday?'

'I never,' he said again, then with an attempt at defiance, 'You'll not make me say something that's not true.'

Years of service taught you how to read people's intentions – literally a survival skill – and she had McIver down as one of those that were easy feart and faced with authority would crumble. That little spurt of aggression didn't fit with that.

It was perfectly true that she couldn't *make* him say anything. With a sigh of frustration, Murray looked round the room for inspiration.

And there it was, in the rubbish bin beside the sink, poking out from among the potato peelings. An empty Haribo packet.

'What's your favourite kind, Lachie?' she said.

He twitched at the unexpected question. 'Don't know what you mean.'

'The Haribo sweets. You obviously like them – what's your favourite?'

McIver was starting to look panicky. 'Never heard of them. Don't eat sweets.'

'It's funny you bought a whole packet, then,' she said. 'Lachie, stop this before you get yourself into real trouble. The boy was here. When was it, when did he leave and where did he go?'

He was starting to sweat but he still didn't answer and Murray felt a cold chill. Surely she couldn't have been so badly wrong in her assessment – surely it wasn't possible Jay actually was around here somewhere, lying in a shallow grave? Could this old man, not entirely steady on his legs, really have overcome a thirteen-year-old, by all accounts robust and athletic?

'I'm giving you this straight, Lachie. I'm beginning to think you may have harmed Jay, so if you didn't, you'd better speak up. Otherwise, I'll have you on suspicion of murder.'

He went into full panic. 'No, I never, I never. I'd never do that, not to the bairn. He'd had a bad time, was all, just wanted out of it. Rubbish lot at the big house, he said. You'll need to believe me.'

'I'd like to believe you, but it's looking bad,' she said. 'Talk me through exactly what happened.'

McIver was almost tumbling over his words now. 'He liked the ferret. Talked to me, sometimes – no one else to talk to. Wanted to stay with me when he ran away but when I tried to get him to go home, he said he couldn't because you'd say he'd done it.'

'Killed his father? Had he?'

'How do I know? Don't want to know – didn't want him here either, sleeping in my bed, wanting food I wouldn't be able to pay for. Wasn't my job to look after him. Told him to go back home and he left. If he didn't, it's nothing to do with me. All I ever wanted was to be left in peace.'

This fitted: under pressure, he'd cracked. But why not sooner? Why the uncharacteristic resistance? She sighed.

'Did you really think I'd settle for that? You're still hiding something, Lachie. What is it? If you don't tell me now, the next stage is taking you into the station for questioning, and we'll go over and over that story until you do.'

He bent forward and put his head in his hands. Then he said, 'It's not right. 'Snot my fault. It's your lot makes trouble. You'll have me if I don't do what you want but Drummond'll have me if I do.'

Murray gaped. 'DI Drummond?'

'Aye, Drummond. Came here after the boy had gone. He was looking for him, but he said I'd pay for it if I told anyone that.'

'He threatened you?'

'You could say. He's an evil bastard. Here, you'll not tell him, will you?'

She didn't know what to make of it all, but it looked as if that was the whole story. She got up, alarming the ferret, which started a high-pitched chittering.

'I can't promise, but I won't unless I have to. If you remember anything to suggest where Jay might be now, you'd better tell us right away. That's all for now.'

She left him looking confused at the abrupt ending of the ordeal and went back to her car. Right enough, it would explain McIver's behaviour – Drummond would be good at putting the frighteners on – but why should he have bothered? Admittedly, he'd been taken off the case, but the whole force was involved in the hunt for the missing child, which was no doubt what he'd say if challenged.

But how had Drummond known where to look? He certainly hadn't shared his information. He must have wanted to get to Jay ahead of anyone else, but she didn't know why. Personal kudos? That was possible. She'd succumbed herself to the pulling-a-rabbit-out-of-the-hat temptation more than once, and Drummond had savagely resented being passed over for Hamish. It would be giving the finger to Strang if he could flaunt his professional skill by being the one to find the child the whole of Police Scotland had been looking for.

Pity the boss had gone off to Edinburgh. This was a development that needed talking through, but even supposing he answered his phone he wouldn't have time for lengthy discussion, and all she really had to tell him was that Jay had been at Lachie McIver's hut but had disappeared and that Drummond had come looking for him – as they all had been.

She was tempted just to call in at Drummond's house in Kilbain and ask a few questions. She'd have the advantage of surprise; McIver wouldn't have tipped Drummond off about her visit – indeed, just the opposite.

Once Murray would have done that, but she liked to think she was more mature now. As her superior he'd laugh in her face and then he'd have his story straight for Strang next time. She'd be better just going home.

But she wasn't quite as mature as all that, and as she went back through Kilbain she couldn't resist driving along the street where Drummond lived. She didn't know the house number, but there were only four in the development; very expensive, especially for a man on his own – mostly, her canteen informant had sniffed.

Identifying Drummond's property wasn't difficult. The other three had well-tended gardens and signs of family occupancy: a trampoline behind one, a baseball ring attached to the garage at another, a fancy flowery china plate displaying the number at another.

The fourth garden was just hardstanding with a mercilessly neat square of grass and as further confirmation it had a large black Ford – standard police issue – parked in front of the integral garage. A forbidding-looking house, like its owner.

Light was starting to fade and there was a light on in the hall and behind the closed venetian blinds of the sitting room, so Drummond must be in. These houses looked to have at least four bedrooms and likely a study as well;

expensive indeed, Murray reflected. Even if she made inspector, she couldn't see herself affording anything like this and she remembered Hamish's blunt words.

She was tempted to ring the bell to see what would happen, but she resisted. She could tell the boss tomorrow and it could be taken from there.

People always said gin was a depressive and certainly Steve Christie wasn't enjoying his night of freedom. He had the TV on, but his own thoughts were darker than the Nordic thriller he was theoretically watching.

He'd been coerced into a ludicrous position. He'd never felt anything for Oriole beyond a certain sympathy for her difficult life and he felt sick at the thought of having to fake the romantic wooing she was now sure to expect. Sooner or later he'd have to disengage for his own sanity and she would be left devastated. It was just plain cruel.

Steve wasn't a man who was deliberately unkind. He'd been weak and greedy and somehow he'd got trapped in a situation he was too scared to get out of and he despised himself for letting it come to this. Sooner or later, he'd need to find courage—

There was a knock on the door, but he hadn't time to answer before it opened and Keith Drummond came in. He was beaming, but the smile faded as he looked round the room.

'Where is she, then? When they said you'd taken the night off I thought you'd be having a cosy evening together.'

'Oh,' Steve said, with a sinking heart, 'she needed to get her things together. She's coming tomorrow morning.'

The change in Keith was frightening. Suddenly he seemed

bigger, his face black with temper, his eyes glittering. 'You bloody fool! She's still there?'

'Er – yes, I suppose so.'

'Weren't you listening? *Now*, I said. She was to be here, tonight. It was all worked out. Do you have any faint idea how much you've buggered things up?' He spoke with lacerating contempt.

Steve had talked about finding courage, sooner or later. Without warning, he found it now, and his voice was remarkably steady.

'No, Keith, I don't. What have I done?'

Oddly, it brought Keith up short. He stared at Steve as if he was a stranger, then he said, 'You don't want to know. Tell me once she's actually here.'

He walked out and it was as if air had been sucked out of the room with him, leaving Steve gasping.

It wasn't new, not wanting to know what Keith was up to; he'd said that to himself many times. But he couldn't get away with that ignorance forever and he didn't begin to know what he could do now.

CHAPTER EIGHTEEN

Detective Chief Superintendent Jane Borthwick was looking harassed. Weren't they all, thought Strang a little tetchily. It had been a long hard day and to be told at the end that he didn't seem to have accomplished anything was hard to take.

'Oh, I know you've been doing your best, Kelso,' she said in a tone that he, possibly unjustly, felt was patronising. 'But I'm going to have to go out there and find a form of words to say that we have made an arrest, but somehow phrase it in a way that won't lead to them accusing us of total incompetence when, if you're right, we'll have to let her go, probably tomorrow.' She paused, then said, 'I don't suppose you could be wrong about that, could you?'

She'd sounded wistful. 'Of course I could be,' he said. 'I've no proof, but to be honest I don't think I am. Her confession was really no more than a statement that Perry Forsyth had killed her sister, so she had killed him, with no corroborative details – quite unusual, that, in my experience of genuine confessions. I think she thought if we'd someone ready to put up their hand to it we'd settle for that.'

'If only!' Borthwick sighed. 'So you think, then, that she believes the boy did it?'

'I suspect she may even know he did. But if you're asking me if she was telling the truth when she denied knowing where he is now, I'd have to say I think she probably was.'

'So he's on the run, is he, with every incentive to lie low until she's been charged, when he'll nonchalantly stroll out of the bushes? Presumably this is how they worked it out?'

How did she expect him to know that? 'I'm afraid I don't know.'

She clearly wasn't satisfied with that as an answer. 'Hmm. The trouble is that even if we were in a position to charge her after you'd had a chance to question her, it won't satisfy anyone unless we're able to say the boy's been found. And as I understand it, you've made no progress on that?'

'Sorry, ma'am, no. There have been alleged sightings but under questioning they've all come to nothing.'

'Right, then,' she said. 'Tomorrow is another day. What are you planning to do with it?'

He told her about the new line on Michael Erskine. 'He claimed not to have seen Forsyth after their set-to, but there's CCTV evidence that he went back, at least to the Black Isle, later in the day. Doesn't actually prove anything, of course.'

Borthwick sighed again. 'Story of our lives at the

moment, isn't it. And what about the inspector who's allegedly bent? Where does he fit in the picture?'

Strang pulled a face. 'He certainly had motive – Forsyth did the dirty on him by backing out of a little plan they'd made together for a luxury hotel at Drumdalloch, and I certainly wouldn't put anything past Drummond, but the alibi seems to check out. I suspect the big story there is actually police corruption.'

'That's a problem that in this particular case, I'm happy to say, is someone else's. I think DCS Anderson is well up to speed on that, in fact. Yes, given the unsafe confession I suppose all you can do is go on working on the homicide – broaden out the investigation, maybe? But the depressing thing is that even if you got someone bang to rights, you wouldn't get much credit – it's the boy that's the story. Oh well, I suppose if you were hungry for affection you wouldn't go into this job.'

'No, I don't suppose you would,' he said drily.

'Well, do the best you can, Kelso, and pray for a miracle.'

He left the meeting in a thoroughly disgruntled mood. A meeting with JB usually left him feeling invigorated but now he felt depressed and inadequate. The stories in the media must be getting to her. Well, join the club.

He had to cheer up, though, and not take his worries home. In the past on days like this, he'd return to an empty house to sulk over a Scotch, kick a metaphorical cat and then spend the evening going through whatever evidence merited further thought; now Cat was waiting for him and he'd have to content himself with muttering under his breath as he drove home to get it out of his system.

* * *

Cat took a match to all the little tea lights she'd arranged on the window ledge by the front door to welcome Kelso as he got back. She guessed he might be in a celebratory mood; they'd announced on the news that an arrest had been made and while that wasn't the same as someone being charged, it was progress. At the least it should mean a pat on the back from JB, which she knew always meant a lot to him.

When he came in, she could tell that his meeting hadn't gone like that, even though he put a lot of enthusiasm into greeting her and sounding cheerful.

She said, 'Darling, you just look exhausted. Go and sit down while I get the drinks. How was JB?'

Kelso went to sit by the window and pulled a face. 'Not very happy. She likes results, but she doesn't like the ones I've brought her, so she wasn't exactly complimentary. It's hard for her – she's the one who has to go out and face the world, after all – but I had a good swear about it in the car on the way home and now what I need is a drink and something else to think about. How was your day?'

'Oh, Kelso, you're always so polite, as if you read somewhere that's what men must make sure to do when they come home before they talk about their own, whatever it was like.' Cat bent to drop a kiss on the top of his head as she brought the drinks. 'For the record, it was standard stuff, case went off when our witness didn't turn up – the usual. But tell me what JB was saying – I'd expected her to be pretty pleased with you, after the arrest.'

He laughed. 'Oh dear, guilty as charged. I just didn't want you to have to listen to me moaning on about feeling blamed for something that wasn't my fault.'

Cat spent her days defending people who were, at least theoretically, wrongfully accused and unfairness had always sparked her crusading zeal. 'That's just so unjust! You can't choose what evidence you find. What was she on about?'

'Well, you know how little an arrest actually means, before any charge,' he said. 'And in this case, it probably means less than most.'

She frowned. 'You mean you've got the wrong person?'

She could sense his withdrawal. Ready enough to talk about his own feelings, he'd just realised this was fringing on operational matters and he'd started to feel uncomfortable. She'd have to take this one on, sometime – she wasn't going to spend her life tiptoeing round professional etiquette.

'Er . . .' he said, and she cut in. 'Well, if you like I can tell you what my client said about the missing witness – "Right little cow that one, should have known she'd shaft me", as it happens – as you work at looking interested while your mind is elsewhere. On the other hand, we could talk about what's uppermost in both our thoughts.'

Kelso looked awkward. 'I'm sorry. I just don't want to burden you with my problems.'

'Look,' she said, 'you're looking really stressed. Mum told Dad about her cases and she always said it helped a lot to talk it through. I suppose I could suggest you phoned her for a chat but to be honest I'd be wretchedly jealous. You could talk to me instead. If you can get hold of a copy of the Official Secrets Act I could swear to it, if you like.'

He gave a laugh – embarrassed, she thought, and she was holding her breath as she waited for his reply.

At last he said, 'It's drilled into us, you know. But we're trusting each other with our lives, so being professionally discreet is a bit daft. And yes, it's on my mind to the exclusion of everything else. Pour me another drink and I'll tell you about it.'

Cat jumped up. 'I'll call Deliveroo at the same time. Tapas?'

She'd have to be careful, she told herself. Your job is to listen, not talk, even when you think you have an idea he ought to want to hear. There's a lot hanging on this.

Later – much later, she said thoughtfully, 'That's quite a story. This woman is prepared to go to jail for her late sister's very possibly homicidal son, who would actually get a pretty light sentence given his age and the evidence of his family problems – and you said it was a single blow, likely struck in temper? His case would call in the youth court and there'd be a lot of sympathy. So—'

She caught herself up short. That was just the sort of thing she'd told herself not to do.

But he was looking at her with interest. 'Share the thought.'

'There's a lot of money floating around now, isn't there? If Jay was actually found to have killed Perry, he wouldn't inherit, and it would go to his sister instead. I don't know what impression you had of the aunt's character, but—'

'My God, you're cynical!' he said, and his tone was admiring. 'Hadn't thought of that. Worth serving a short jail term, tempered by mitigation? It's pretty convoluted, if theoretically possible. If you're talking money, Oriole is the one we should be looking at – means, motive and opportunity – but according to Livvy Murray she was doing her best to deflect suspicion from Jay and worrying about him, though I suppose that could be faked too.'

'From what you said about the consortium, she was their goose who would make sure the golden eggs came their way so that would spread the motivation wider, wouldn't it? And it would involve the bent copper you talked about.'

'Certainly should. The trouble is he was actually on a night shift, and we checked out the hotelier as well but he was working all evening and on call all night. Which leaves Oriole – but we've got nothing to go on.

'Still, hopefully tomorrow we'll be able to question Glover properly as well, and I'll look at her with new eyes. I've got Erskine the lying academic lined up too.'

He suddenly gave an enormous yawn and Cat jumped up. 'You need your rest, with a long drive early tomorrow. I've probably kept you up far too late.'

'It's helped, though. I'd have spent the evening going through stuff I've gone through twice already – and agonising about that child. Where is he tonight? Who is he with? He's so vulnerable and it's my job to prevent anything bad happening to him.'

He's blaming himself again, Cat thought. 'It's your job to *try* to prevent anything bad happening to him,' she said firmly. 'You can't do more than your best. Now come to bed.'

Oriole had been rushing round in a positive tizzy ever since Steve's phone call. She could hardly believe what was happening: Steve had been so worried about her, here all on her own, so – well, incredibly enough, *loving* when he phoned, that it was as if the wild dreams she'd always refused to allow herself even to imagine could come true.

The other things hadn't gone away, though, and most of all she was worried about Jay – where could he be? Whatever he might have become, somewhere there still was the child she'd loved before bad parenting had made him so sad and angry. There had been such cruelty and unfairness and she hated to think of him being punished because of it.

Oriole left Drumdalloch House early on a beautiful sunny morning, even before Lars Andersen arrived. That was another thing that made her happy: she'd get no more complaints from him or the students or the aggressive Dr Erskine either.

She could see people looking like journalists hanging around, one or two with cameras, but they paid no attention as she walked into the Kilbain Hotel.

Breakfast was in full swing and there was no one on the front desk. She dumped her two suitcases there, then went along to the dining room, where guests were attacking their Full Scottish. Steve wasn't normally here at this time, but someone would be around to deal with guests wanting to pay their bills.

She went through the swing door into the kitchen, where Senga was chatting to the chef. She looked round in surprise.

'Oh, for goodness sake! Don't say he's brought me in again when you were coming anyway – did that to me yesterday for the desk when he could just as well have done it himself.'

Oriole could feel herself blushing. 'No, I'm not working

this morning. Actually, Steve's asked me to sort of move in. Do you know what room he's given me?'

Astonishment simply didn't cover the look on the others' faces. Senga's jaw had dropped and the chef, after a moment, turned to make a business out of frying some more bacon.

'He's *what?*' Senga said. 'Well, I don't know anything about it – you'll have to go up to the flat and ask him.' Then she stopped, as if something had suddenly struck her, but she only went on, 'Yes, I think that's what you'd better do.'

Oriole agreed and as the door swung to behind her, she heard the two of them starting to laugh and her face got hotter and hotter until she felt it must be shining like a beacon and guests would be turning their heads to look.

She was about to climb the stairs when the man himself appeared at the top.

'Oh Steve!' she called. 'Here I am!'

She could see he was looking taken aback and said uneasily, 'Am I too early? I wasn't going to disturb you, but Senga didn't know where my room was.'

Had she done the wrong thing? But no. Steve was hurrying down to meet her and giving her a big hug.

'Of course not, love! I thought I'd be down to meet you myself. I've put you in the big corner front on the first floor, so you've got a bit of space and somewhere comfy to relax and escape attention.'

'But Steve, I can handle that! You need all the help you can get – I've never seen it so busy.'

'No, I'm not going to let you, I want to feel you're properly protected. Come on up, now – I need to talk to you.'

'My suitcases . . .' she said. Being so unsure what she'd need, she'd basically brought it all, but when Steve saw them he looked – well, sort of surprised, and again she felt she'd done the wrong thing. But he was smiling, making a joke about travelling light and then carrying them up for her.

Oriole had never been in this room before but she knew it was one of the best rooms in the hotel – more evidence of care and thoughtfulness.

'Oh Steve, this is beautiful! You are so kind! I just love the way the chairs are set into the corner there, with a view of the trees – look at that lovely beech with the leaves such a fresh spring green.'

Steve said only, 'Let's sit down. I'm afraid I have something to tell you, something that's a bit worrying.'

The happy bubble burst. She was glad to sit down as her knees gave way. 'Is it – is it Jay?' she faltered.

'No, no, something else entirely. Perry came into the bar one night with someone called Nicki and I seem to remember you had a friend called that.'

'Yes, Nicki Latham. I didn't know she'd gone out with Perry, but I certainly introduced them.' She was still a bit hurt at not being told. 'Is she all right?'

'I don't know. The police are being very cagey. All they've said is they've arrested someone they haven't named, but I saw her going into the incident room in the spa and later coming out handcuffed between two policemen.'

It was hard to take it in. 'Nicki? Are you sure? What on earth could they have arrested her for?'

'Well, murdering Perry, I suppose. At least that seems to be what people are saying.'

'But she hardly knew him! I know he wasn't the best

person, but I can't think she even had time to find that out. They must be making some mistake.'

'Well, the police aren't famous for getting things right. But did she never say anything to you about him?'

Oriole shook her head. 'She mostly just listened while I did the talking – she's such a good friend to me, you know. I'm-I'm really upset about this. Do you think there's anything we can do to help her, tell them she's not like that . . . ?'

'I don't think so. They'll just do what they want and then when they realise they're wrong say sorry afterwards.'

'But that's awful,' she protested.

He patted her hand. 'Don't worry. I'm sure it will all be fine. But you see, there's going to be even more media interest, so you stay up here – all right? I'll get them to bring you up coffee and magazines from the lounge and you can just chill and enjoy the view.'

Steve had gone almost before she'd thanked him. She was feeling crushed. This wasn't at all what she'd expected. Instead of the happy dream of working around the hotel with Steve, with everyone knowing there was, well, something special between them, she was being shut away alone with no companions other than worrying thoughts.

Even so, she didn't feel grateful when Keith Drummond appeared, all smiles.

'Steve told me you were here, and I just popped in to see you were all right.'

'Oh! Yes, I'm fine. Steve's looking after me very well.'

'Glad to hear it. I wasn't sure what that nephew of yours might decide to do next and you'll be safe here. Now, take it easy—'

'Wait a moment, Keith. Steve says they've arrested Nicki Latham. Do you know what that's about? She's a lovely person and this has to be some silly mistake.'

'Don't know anything about that – not my case. It's down to this fancy lot from Edinburgh, so no wonder they're making a mess of it. Nothing to do except wait till they come back with egg all over their face.'

He took out a card. 'But if you're worried about anything, you've got my number there so you can just call me and I'll be round to sort it out. All right?'

And then he was gone, and she was alone again.

Long, slow journeys – which this one certainly was – were a good opportunity to think, Strang reflected as he endured the A9.

Talking everything through with Cat had been surprisingly helpful. He'd talked about his last case to Marjory, of course, but that had felt more like a session with a non-judgmental JB. As Cat listened, he'd felt energised, seeing a new perspective. Her own contribution, too, had sparked off a line of thought he hadn't considered before.

On reflection, her idea about Jay being set up was too elaborate to be likely, though he'd keep it in mind, but it had prodded him into paying more attention to the money – big money, in this case.

Everyone wanted money. The important question was always, why? Straightforward greed, usually, but it could equally be the need for a shield or even a springboard or – the big one – the desire for power. Serious money was the fairy godmother who could grant all your wishes. The more he thought about it, the stronger the stench grew.

Organisation by category. It was a new way of looking at the whole case, and he had the sense of facts falling into place, almost like the little silver balls in a child's puzzle. He didn't have answers, but now he had thought-framing questions burning in his mind.

A call came in from Inverness to tell him the interview with Glover was now possible, and he arranged to go straight there. Livvy Murray was on her way up from Edinburgh but he wasn't going to wait; he got a message sent to her to say she'd be sitting in with him if she arrived in time but if not Hamish Campbell would, and then she should go ahead with the Erskine interview. There would be a briefing when he'd finished with Rebecca Glover.

His fear of danger for Jay was growing stronger by the hour, and if under questioning Glover indicated a new line, this was of course top priority. The homicide investigation was his job too, but it was hard to feel impassioned about getting justice for a man who by all accounts – particularly those of the local witnesses – had been a thoroughly nasty piece of work.

But regardless, if the child had indeed simply been tried too far, he would still have to find the necessary evidence to convict. Punishment was, mercifully, not his to decide.

Rebecca Glover had not realised how shocking she would find her night on remand. The cell was clean enough, if spartan; without a second thought, she'd slept in youth hostels where conditions were much worse and often dodgy with it. It was only as they locked the door that she felt panic.

She'd never been claustrophobic, but it hit her now.

Through the long night while she struggled with her breathing, she had to face what she'd taken on – not just for tonight, but for indeterminate years ahead.

But she had to. That phone call she'd had from Helena, when she'd said they would kill her if she wasn't careful . . . Rebecca had vowed then that if anything happened, she'd come after them. Well, him, really – it was pretty obvious that it was him.

And she'd failed to get justice for her sister. At the other end of the world at the time, she'd been living her best life moving around temporary jobs on a work visa, too broke to have the air fare home. By the time she got back, it was all over and even the review she'd agitated for came to nothing. She couldn't let her nephew shame her, and then suffer for it. She was scared – terrified, really. How much worse would it be for a child?

Rebecca hadn't been impressed by the lawyer they'd found for her. He was a pink-faced youth who seemed unprepared for the situation he'd found himself in. He'd bleated on to her the day before about not answering questions, and when he joined her to go to the police interview, he repeated the advice.

'Whatever they ask, you say, "No Comment", right?'

'No, not right,' she said firmly. 'I want to get on with it.'

He shook his head. 'People always think that if they just explain to the police what happened, it will be all right. But it won't. You'll give away something that will cause you trouble later.'

'You don't seem to understand. I'm not trying to conceal anything. I killed Perry Forsyth and I've confessed. That's it.'

To do him justice, he kept trying to do what he believed was best for her, but when they went through to the interview room and two officers came in and identified themselves for the recording, he still hadn't persuaded her.

It was Detective Chief Inspector Strang's eyes she noticed first. He had a very direct, penetrating gaze and she shifted uncomfortably as he began by asking her to confirm her confession to Perry Forsyth's murder.

'Yes,' she said and heard her solicitor give a faint groan. 'He killed my sister, so I killed him.'

'I see,' Strang said. 'There are one or two questions I want to ask you now, if you are prepared to answer them. First of all, what time was this?'

She had that worked out. 'I went to see Oriole because she was in a state about Perry having chopped down one of the trees. I was with her when DI Drummond arrived and then Dr Erskine from the Institute went up to the flat. After they'd gone, I saw Perry going down into the woods so I said goodbye to Oriole, and then I waited around for a bit until I was sure no one was watching me, and I went very quietly down the path so he wouldn't know I was following him. When I got close enough, I just picked up a stick and hit him with it. He fell over and I checked to see he was dead, and then I left.'

There was something a bit unnerving about the way they were looking at her. Perhaps the 'just fell over' bit hadn't sounded properly convincing. 'It was a big, heavy stick,' she added. 'More like a bough, really.'

Strang said, 'So what time did this take place?'

'Oh, I don't know exactly. I suppose about one-fifteen? I got back to the agency not much after two.'

Strang nodded at DI Campbell. He had a kindly expression and Rebecca almost felt he was sorry for her when he said, 'There's just a wee problem with that, I'm afraid. You see, we've this witness saw Perry Forsyth walking down from the house into the woods at around five o'clock.'

It hit her like a fist in the face, so that she gasped. She hadn't thought it through; it hadn't occurred to her that they might try to prove she hadn't done it. Feebly, she said, 'Well, she must have made a mistake . . .'

With Strang's eyes studying her, she couldn't go on. Biting her lip and trying to force back tears, she muttered, 'Sorry, sorry.'

'Am I to gather that you are withdrawing your confession?' Strang said. Her solicitor sprang in. 'My client is making no comment,' and this time she let it pass.

Strang said, 'There will be a lot to sort out, but the urgent thing is that I need to hear what you know about Jay Forsyth's whereabouts. I suspect you believe he killed his father and are trying to protect him. I also suspect you've seen him since he left home and may even know where he is now. I urge you to tell me, for his safety. He's unlikely to be competent to look after himself and he's very vulnerable.'

Rebecca was openly in tears now. Talking over her lawyer's warnings, she said, 'Yes, I saw him. He was trying to live in the woods and he was hungry and cold and scared. I fetched him and he stayed at my flat overnight, but I left him asleep yesterday morning and when I came back he'd gone again. I don't know anything after that. I only know he was scared you'd say he'd killed his father.'

There was an appreciable pause, and then Strang said slowly, 'And had he?'

'I don't know!' she cried. 'I didn't want to scare him by asking too much. What happens now?'

CHAPTER NINETEEN

Mercifully, the crash just ahead of DS Livvy Murray only involved a great deal of crumpled metal and quite a lot of ill temper as well, but it wasn't life, death and ambulances stuff, and accidents on the A9 never had to wait long before a patrol car arrived to deal with them. Though she spoke to the officers after they'd stopped the traffic, they waved her on with the rest.

It had cost her the chance to be in with the boss interviewing Glover, though. She was longing to watch the unravelling process and it stung too that Kelso saw Hamish as being just as good – which he probably was, but she prided herself on being more likely to come up with a killer question if needed. Increasingly, though, she felt she was losing professional ground when recently she'd been gaining it.

Of course, that had nothing to do with Kelso having moved on personally. Absolutely nothing. Of course. The investigation was suffering because of budget cuts and travelling to and fro, instead of living on the job when there were down times just talking through the case – and just talking, anyway. Was Kelso, she wondered, doing that talking with his Cat? A surge of what could only be called petty jealousy swept through her until, ashamed, she refused to give it head space.

Anyway. He'd given her a free hand with Erskine, so she had to play a blinder. She needed a killer question to draw out a definite answer to the 'had-he-or-hadn't-he?' question. Confirmation bias was her weakness and after her last interview with Erskine she'd come away convinced it showed he simply wasn't the type – big black mark, since he'd lied to her and she hadn't noticed. This time he wouldn't get away with anything, she vowed, as she at last reached Kilbain House and went into the incident room.

It was much quieter now. The natives must be talked out and according to the clearly bored FCA on the desk, no one had come in to offer anything about Rebecca Glover.

'The only thing I've heard is gossip from one of the staff here. She said the woman was calling herself Nicki and was a pal of Oriole Forsyth – stepping out with her brother, allegedly.'

Murray's eyes widened. 'Oh! We wondered about that – had she just suddenly arrived with murder on her mind? Living here under an assumed name would be more likely.'

The woman agreed. 'Almost an admission of guilt, isn't it?'

With what else she knew, she couldn't quite agree with that. 'Mmm. Has Dr Erskine arrived?'

'In the second treatment room. A bit like going in to

the dentist, isn't it? He doesn't look too happy about it.'

Murray grinned. 'Cruel and unusual punishment, maybe, with the added torture of cheap scented products.'

As she came through the door, Erskine rose like a rocketing pheasant from one of the small gilt chairs in front of the imported table. He was, indeed, looking terrified.

'Good morning, Dr Erskine. Please sit down.' She took her place, saying, 'This is not a formal interview under caution, but you may have guessed that the first thing we must talk about is the lie you told me. I need the truth now.'

He gulped, then cleared his throat. 'Well, it was a very confusing time, you see—'

'No, we're not going there. I'm a busy woman. You told me you had left Drumdalloch for home after speaking to Mr Forsyth and that this was all you could tell me.'

Avoiding her gaze, he said, 'That was true, in fact.'

'But . . .' she prompted.

'You've obviously discovered I went back afterwards,' he said stiffly. 'Well, yes I did, but the reason I didn't tell you is precisely because I knew you would think it proved I killed Perry Forsyth, when I can assure you that I most certainly did not.'

'Lying to the police in those circumstances isn't the smart thing to do.'

'I know that, obviously. I'm not a stupid man.' The arrogance had crept back into his manner. 'It was merely a misjudgement.'

Feeling like a cat watching with glee as an overconfident mouse strolled into pouncing distance, Murray said,

'Another misjudgement, was it, when you didn't mention to us how much you had riding on the deal you wanted Mr Forsyth to agree to?'

'How the hell—' Erskine went white. 'Oh God, you haven't contacted Crichton, have you?'

'No,' she said with deliberate malice, adding as he visibly relaxed, 'he came to us.'

It was a flimsy chair and for a moment she thought he would fall off it as it rocked. Then he said shakily, 'That's the end, then. That's it, I'm finished.'

For a moment Murray thought they were going to be presented with another confession. But no; his life story came out – the story of a weak and inadequate man, desperate to grab the status he couldn't earn. She cut across his frantic protestations of innocence to ask, 'So why did you go back, then?'

'I just wanted to start again – suggesting a basis for cooperation in a rational way, instead of shouting at him. I was ready to apologise to try to keep my project alive. I went up to the flat, but he wasn't in. I knocked on the kitchen door and Oriole opened it, but when I started trying to explain, she slammed it in my face.'

Oriole hadn't mentioned that when Murray had talked to her. 'Ms Forsyth will remember this?'

'Yes, of course she will. She may even have seen me going back to my car and driving off. And if your precious cameras caught me on the Kessock Bridge before, they'll have caught me coming back a short time later.'

That was true – they had. What was also true was that it was quite a plausible account – but then he was an intelligent man.

She stood up. 'Thank you, sir. I'm leaving it there, at least for the moment. You will have to make an amended statement.' She left him looking sick and shaken.

Did she believe him? Determined to ignore any gut feelings, she went along the corridor to the hotel and emerged into the hall just as Oriole Forsyth was coming down the stairs.

'Oh, this is a lucky coincidence!' Murray said. 'Do you mind if I quickly ask you something?'

'No, not at all. I'm just coming down to fetch a tea tray to take to my room.' She gave a little, self-conscious smile. 'Steve's asked me to move in here and he's so protective he won't even let me help out in the hotel, with all the media interest.'

Surprised, Murray said, 'Oh, I see. I just wanted to refer to your statement about your movements last Friday. Did anyone come to your door in the late afternoon?'

Oriole's brow creased. 'Came to the door? I don't think—' Then she stopped. 'Oh yes! I'm sorry, I'd completely forgotten. Dr Erskine knocked – around six, a little earlier, maybe, but I'm afraid I was rude and wouldn't speak to him – well, I told you how unpleasant he'd been. I was relieved when he just drove away. But I'm afraid that's made work for you when you were so kind and patient listening to me. I'm so sorry!'

'No, that's all right. Don't worry.'

So it had checked out. Bit of a dead end, really. And there was the boss now, arriving back from Inverness with Hamish. She'd at last have time to talk about Drummond's curious behaviour – and that, she thought, really did have mileage.

* * *

'It's dispiriting that none of this got us any further with the boy,' DCI Strang said to DI Campbell as they drove back from Inverness and reached Kilbain. 'I'd been pinning my hopes on getting at least some sort of steer.'

'Bit of a blow,' Campbell said. 'Especially with her admitting she'd been in contact.'

'Mmm. I take it you've checked nothing new's come in – sorry, of course you have. You know, we're running into the sand. Another twenty-four hours and they'll be calling in another force to take a look.'

'Well, good luck to them. Maybe Livvy's come up with something.'

As they drew up outside the hotel, Strang pointed. 'There she is now in reception. Does she look pleased?'

Campbell studied her as he got out of the car. 'Hard to say. She often doesn't have a pleased face on, even when she is,' he said, and Strang laughed as they went in.

'The laughter's misleading, Livvy,' Strang said as he saw her face brightening. 'That was just a joke, not a breakthrough. Tell me you've got something on Erskine.'

Murray pulled a face. 'Fairly plausible and there's one wee point confirmed. As it stands, nowhere to go. Glover didn't deliver?'

Strang shook his head and as they went through to the treatment room she added, 'They're saying in the hotel she was a friend of Oriole's called Nicki who dated Perry.'

'That's something to get our teeth into, anyway.' Strang said. 'Hamish—'

'On to it, boss.'

Murray called after him, 'Oriole's actually in the hotel – saw her earlier.'

It was good to have something to work on, even something as flimsy as this. After his optimism earlier, Strang was feeling low, aware that when he next spoke to JB it would have to be a smoke-and-mirrors job to make all this sound like progress and she was extremely unlikely to fall for it.

'Not looking good, is it?' he said as they sat down.

'No, but . . .'

He perked up. 'But . . . ?'

'There was this weird thing last night,' Murray said, and she told him about her interview with Lachie McIver and Drummond's odd behaviour. 'I went round to his house after but there was nothing to see there. I could have followed it up, but I reckoned he'd just pull rank on me and it would warn him we knew. Hope you appreciate my restraint, boss!'

'Indeed,' he said absently, then, 'So, Glover said Jay had just run off. We haven't had a sighting. Drummond was hunting for him. How likely is it that the laddie on his own has managed just to disappear? And how likely is it that Drummond won't manage to find him – and what will he do when he does? It's a chilling thought, Livvy.'

'But why should he be in danger? Surely, it's Oriole who matters to the consortium and she's wildly in favour – she told me. Jay's a minor and she'll be his guardian for years.'

He'd told her often enough not to jump to conclusions, so he had to guard against doing just that. He said, 'I suppose I do need to think all around this. How do you see it yourself?'

He heard her talk about hurt pride, and showing everyone up, but his mind was elsewhere, on something

Cat had said, on something he'd thought himself, and he cut in before she was finished.

'You may well be right, but I can't risk your being wrong. We have to move now.'

Murray was obviously surprised at his urgency. 'You don't really think he'd actually harm the kid? That sort of thing's hard to cover up.'

'Maybe, yet it happens all the time.' He picked up the phone. 'Find me DI Drummond.'

The door opened and Campbell came in. He looked from one to the other enquiringly, but then said, 'I've just seen Oriole Forsyth. She confirms the information that links Nicki Latham to Glover, but she was in a bit of a state – been crying for a while, I'd say. She wouldn't tell me what was wrong, but you should maybe just go up and have a word? Room 104.'

DS Murray left the treatment room reluctantly. It looked as if dramatic developments were going to take place and she didn't want to miss out on the action yet again. But she was curious to know why Oriole should be in 'a bit of a state'.

When she'd spoken to her earlier she'd seemed pretty pleased with herself, purring like a kitten about Steve Christie being so protective. In that long original conversation they'd had, it had come across pretty clearly that she was besotted with the man, even though she'd stressed they were just friends, so you'd expect her to be on top of a wave.

Something must have gone badly wrong. Murray found room 104 and tapped on the door. She could hear a muffled sob, but there was no reply and she tried again.

'Oriole, it's Livvy Murray. You sound distressed. Please let me come in and you can tell me how I can help you. Not as a police officer, just as a concerned friend.'

There was a long pause, and then the sobs grew nearer and the door was opened a foot or two to let Murray in while Oriole hid behind it.

The room was in a mess. The wardrobe and drawers had been emptied and clothes were spread on the floor where there were two waiting suitcases but so far not much progress had been made at filling them.

Oriole was a pathetic sight. Few women can cry attractively and she definitively wasn't one of them: her nose was red and swollen, her eyes were puffy and all but shut and her cheeks were blotchy and raw from her scrubbing at them with the tissues that were piled high in the wastepaper basket.

She was shivering with misery and Murray's heart went out to her. 'Oh, goodness! Whatever's happened?' she said.

With a wail, Oriole threw herself at her. 'So cruel,' she kept saying. 'I can't believe he could have been so cruel. I don't know what to do except just go, but I'm so upset I can't get myself organised.'

Patting her back, Murray pulled her to sit down in one of the chairs. 'Who's cruel?' she said as she went over to the basin to fill a glass with water.

'Steve!' She sounded heartbroken. 'Only – only of course, it's not Steve really, it's that horrible Keith. He's made him do this.'

Murray said firmly, 'Then you need to tell me, calmly, so I can understand. Take a drink of this – don't try to say anything more until you're feeling calmer.'

It took a few minutes, but then she managed, 'I told you I was on my way down to get some tea, remember? I hadn't seen Steve all day and I was hoping to bump into him, but he wasn't around downstairs and I didn't like to go up to his flat.

'So I just went on through the dining room and I heard Senga talking to someone in the kitchen, and they were sniggering about something so I stopped to hear what it was. Oh, I know eavesdroppers hear no good of themselves, but I had to know – I was sure she'd be saying something nasty about me.' She started to cry again. 'But I never thought it could be *that!*

'She said – she said she'd heard him and Keith having a barney – shouting at each other, and Keith was saying Steve had to marry me, and – and he – he didn't want to, said he'd never fancied me.' She gave another great sob. 'Then she said, "Poor bastard – said he got exhausted with her going on and on. Well, we know what it's like!" Then they both laughed some more.'

'So I just ran back here. I'm leaving – going home once I get packed. I never want to see him again. But, oh Steve!' Oriole collapsed back into tears.

Mechanically offering her more tissues, Murray thought she'd never heard anything so brutal. She also thought there was a very interesting question that Oriole clearly was too upset to ask herself – why should Keith force Steve to do this when Oriole was wholeheartedly committed to their joint project already?

She bent down and started picking up clothes and folding them. 'Look, Oriole, I'm going to help you. Come on, now, we'll work together. Much of what Senga said could be made up, you know, but I think you should get back home and sort it out from there. You're not fit to speak to anyone at the moment.'

The mechanical task was soothing in its way and eventually she was packed and composed enough to come downstairs, once Murray had checked that the coast was clear. She helped her with her suitcases and as she saw her off, she handed her one of her cards. 'That's my direct line. I'm going back to Edinburgh tonight but tomorrow if you're worried about anything, call me.'

Oriole didn't linger. Murray could only hope that she could see enough out of her swollen eyes to drive safely.

'Where is he?' Strang said into the phone.

'Kinloch Rannoch, sir. There's been a break-in at a shooting lodge and he's heading that so he's likely to be there a while.'

'I see. Thanks.' He put down the phone. 'How far is that, Hamish?'

'A little under three hours, traffic permitting,' Campbell said.

'Three hours. Well, nothing's going to happen in that time that hasn't happened already.'

Campbell looked at him curiously. 'Not following, boss.'

'Murray's discovered that he's been hunting for Jay. Yes, I know we all are, but I don't like it that this has been a bit of private enterprise.'

'Bit odd. Not quite sure what it could mean.'

'No, I'm not sure either. But what's worrying me is that

no one's seen the boy at all after he ran away from Glover. He wasn't managing on his own before she picked him up and I can't see he could be doing better now. Where the hell is he?'

'You don't think Drummond's actually got him? What for?'

'Shall we put it this way, I don't think it's just for the good of his health. I'd go round right now and search his property if I thought there was an ice-cube's chance in hell that a JP would give me a warrant.'

He realised he wasn't taking Campbell with him any more than he had taken Murray, and for the moment he was prepared to leave it there.

'I'm going to have to call DCS Borthwick to bring her up to date. Can you find a way of discreetly checking that Drummond is where he's supposed to be?'

'No problem' was one of Campbell's favourite phrases and he employed it now, but he was looking puzzled as he went out.

Campbell was a good man, but Strang was troubled by what he'd said about the force locally. Drummond seemed to have quite a following whom Campbell clearly believed were thoroughly corrupt. If the new DCS was going to be turning over stones, there would be some dangerously worried men.

At least on the face of it Drummond was safely occupied for the next bit and Strang could take time to get his thoughts in order before he rang JB. She wasn't going to be pleased about all this either.

* * *

It was only at 6 p.m. that Steve Christie summoned up enough energy to go and see Oriole. He'd felt guilty about spending far too much time skulking in his flat but even there he'd felt a sort of itchy awareness of her presence in the building, waiting to pounce on him when he appeared. It was the way he imagined a cat might feel with someone constantly stroking its fur the wrong way.

Added to that, he knew the staff were laughing at him. Senga had made some very snide comments, and he was afraid she might have overheard him when he was protesting to Keith – he knew she'd ears like a bat!

It wasn't kind to take his own discomfort out on Oriole, who had never been anything other than keen to please. She'd sat, uncomplaining, all by herself all day and it was about time he did his duty.

There would be glasses in the room. He grabbed a bottle of wine and set off for room 104 and tapped on the door.

She didn't reply – perhaps the poor soul was so bored she'd fallen asleep. He opened the door, calling, 'Oriole, love! How are you? Ready for a little—'

The room was empty. There were signs of her previous occupancy – magazines on the table, dirty dishes on the tray by the basin waiting for the cleaner and the bedcover was rumpled. A wardrobe door was standing open and coat hangers had been dropped randomly around the floor.

No clothes. No suitcases. She hadn't just emerged to look for company. She'd gone.

He felt so dizzy he had to go and sit down on one of the chairs placed to take advantage of the view. The sun was starting to go down and the red and cloudy sky was particularly dramatic, if he'd been in any mood to notice it.

This was a complete disaster. Immediately he thought of Senga's little veiled remarks – surely even she wouldn't have repeated directly to Oriole what she might have overheard? She probably wouldn't scruple to do it; she'd always had a pick against Oriole because she reckoned she was 'posh'. The terrible thing was it really was all he could think of to explain Oriole's departure.

So now, he supposed, he'd have to tell Keith. He gave a faint, despairing groan at the thought of his fury. Disaster, indeed – but for God's sake, why should it be? He knew Keith was adamant that Oriole be kept away from the house, but he didn't know the reason. He'd never asked what it was.

Steve's determination not to know things had always been his defence mechanism. He'd had enough sleepless nights just worrying about what Keith and his pals were up to; he'd never have slept at all if he hadn't made sure he wasn't directly involved. This time it was becoming borne in upon him that he was in too deep.

Poor, harmless Oriole! He knew what this would do to her – she would be utterly broken, and he despised himself. He was by nature someone who liked to be kind, charming, cheerful, but he aspired to the elegances of life that his own lack of business sense had prevented him from enjoying. Keith's plans had offered him what he'd always wanted, all for the price of doing what he was told and not asking questions.

Of course, he'd have to phone Oriole and persuade her

to return. If he couldn't convince her, he'd need to call Keith and warn him that she was back at Drumdalloch House.

Warn him? *Warn him?* What did that say about what was going on? All the danger lights were flashing and it was time he bailed out.

With shaking hands Steve Christie opened the bottle of wine, fetched a glass and sat and watched the sunset until he had enough command of himself to go downstairs and play the genial mine host.

His mouth was so dry that when he peeled his tongue off the roof of his mouth it felt almost as if he'd taken the skin off. His lips were cracked, his eyes felt as if there were lead weights on top of them and his head was one sick, dull, fuzzy ache. Was he even awake, or was he just dreaming? It felt unreal, and when he tried to put his hand to his head it somehow didn't work properly.

There was a strange smell, damp and fusty but with a sort of bonfire taint. He puzzled briefly over that, but he couldn't remember anything about where he was or think what he expected to see, if he could manage to raise those heavy lids, and he drifted off for a few more minutes.

It was a hunger pang that roused him. He was hungry, very, very hungry, and so thirsty. Yes, water first.

Jay Forsyth opened his eyes, and screamed. It was daylight, but the shadows were lengthening. He was on the edge of some sort of ledge, high, high up, with nothing below him but space. If he'd turned the wrong way as he woke up, he would have fallen straight down, past the charred beams and the broken staircases and the gutted bedrooms on the floor below, right on to the encaustic tiles of the hall of the burnt-out wing.

His heart racing, he clumsily edged further back, though there wasn't much space to move to. He was, he at last worked out, in what had been one of the maids' rooms in the attic floor; there was still an iron bedstead at the back with a heap of charred rags on top, but the wall was missing – not only that, but there was a great jagged hole where half of the floor should have been.

It was a dream – it must be. He'd often frightened himself playing crazy dangerous games around the ruin and it had featured in dreams, when he would wake up just before something awful was going to happen.

But he was awake. This was real. It felt sort of silly to actually shout, 'Help!' but he did, and then he did again, and then he went on till his throat was sore.

No one heard him. Or if they did, they didn't come.

CHAPTER TWENTY

'What are you trying to tell me, Kelso?'

DCS Jane Borthwick, who had sounded stressed before, sounded even worse today – almost weary, and unlike her usual confident self. Pressure from above, DI Strang diagnosed – hardly surprising when Jay Forsyth had dominated the Scottish news for days – and it didn't make him feel any happier about what he was going to tell her.

'Rebecca Glover is being released. If you remember, I said to you her confession was likely an attempt to cover up for her nephew.'

Borthwick said, 'Yes, you did. But does that get us any further forward, Kelso? Do you think it means that he did it?'

It was getting worse every minute. 'Not necessarily. It only means she thinks he did.'

He heard her sigh. 'And I take it she didn't tell you where to find him?'

'No. He disappeared without telling her anything.' Now came the hard part. 'It seems that one of the Inverness DIs has been trying to find him on his own initiative and I'm not sure what his motive is.'

There was silence at the other end of the phone and then Borthwick said, 'Please God, that doesn't mean what I think it means?'

'He is the driving force in the consortium I mentioned that aims to develop a luxury hotel on the Drumdalloch site. They have the enthusiastic support of the current part-owner and if the child will go along with it, it will be straightforward. If he won't, there's a problem.'

'I see.'

When you knew someone well, it wasn't hard to interpret their silences. He could see her eyebrows rising, her manicured fingernails tapping on the desk as she thought.

'Luxury hotels are expensive. Where's the serious money going to come from?'

She was good, there was no doubt about it. 'The third partner would sell his hotel. From personal experience, it's not very successful and, I judge, deeply indebted.'

'So?'

'Logic would suggest an investor who sees it as an opportunity of some sort. Greed's usually the driver but in this case the main attraction just could be its capacity to shield money from prying eyes. Expensive accountants can put you beyond the reach of the law.

'We know that one of the problems with the modern police force is that too many of them are closer to the neds than to the ordinary decent citizens and they forget what the real job is. They need somewhere to sink their illicit gains and it's sounding to me as if this fits the bill – a good way to launder it, no questions asked. It may even have become urgent, with the threat of a purge looming in Inverness.'

There was another silence. She said, 'I shouldn't have tempted the gods by saying it was someone else's problem. Look, Kelso, I think you need to tell me exactly what you're thinking.'

Strang drew a deep breath. 'I think Jay Forsyth is quite likely to be found dead, in some situation where it could be assumed it is suicide because after killing his father there is nowhere for him to go. My guess is that he has probably told Drummond that there is no way he'll agree to anything except the woods being left wild. If that's the case, he's in serious danger.

'I'm proceeding on that basis and the only thing that gives me comfort is that we know Drummond is on the other side of Scotland and until he gets back Jay should be safe.' Then he added sombrely, 'If he hasn't killed him already.'

He infinitely preferred face-to-face meetings. This particular silence was harder to interpret than the last. Then she said, 'So are we working on him being Forsyth's killer too?'

'There's a problem, unfortunately. He has a rock-solid alibi – in the hours between the last sighting of Forsyth and the time he was found dead he was on duty.'

'Awkward. So then we go back to the basics, don't we? Means, motive and opportunity?'

'Yes, but . . . that's Jay or the sister, Oriole. All very

well, but in such a rural area anyone could be moving around unseen. We've no hard evidence from the crime scene and there's so far only one major suspect cleared by the CCTV on the Kessock Bridge, and they're working through the night hours footage now, which may, or may not, exonerate another. And we have to keep in mind that local information suggests there is quite a number of people with a grudge against Forsyth who aren't even on the radar.'

'I like the sister,' Borthwick said firmly. 'They've been at daggers drawn, right? Wouldn't be hard for her.'

'Not going to argue. But unless something further emerges, we could never make a case against her.'

Borthwick sighed again. 'Kelso, I have to tell you we have a serious problem with this one. Unless we can get a solid result soon, we're in trouble.'

'I know. I was saying today they'll be looking at another force being brought in. I wouldn't like it, but if they can spot something I haven't—'

'I don't think you understand. You've always been resented in some quarters, largely because you've produced better results than the more orthodox forces. The threat isn't to the conduct of this investigation – it's a threat to the SRCS itself.'

After DS Murray had seen Oriole Forsyth into her car, she went back to the treatment room where she'd left DCI Strang with DI Campbell. There was no one there and she stood pondering her next move.

She'd been going to tell the boss about the situation with Oriole but it wasn't really important enough to phone him about – just an insight into the dirty tactics of Drummond and Co.

As far as she knew, Strang was staying here overnight. She, on the other hand, would be driving back, in the absence of further instructions. It went against the grain, though, to leave just when it looked as if things were starting to happen.

It would make sense to get something to eat before she set off – at least, she told herself it would, even if she'd get home quicker if she picked up a sandwich in a petrol station. Here, though, there was a chance that Campbell or even Strang might be doing the same thing.

The bar was busy and the barmaid was being assisted by an older man who was doing a lot of glad-handing. Steve Christie, presumably: she hadn't seen him before, and she looked now with great interest as she waited for her Diet Coke.

He was quite fit, with a very warm and pleasant manner and as he came to take her order she could quite understand why Oriole might be smitten. 'Now, what can I get you?' he said as he turned to look at her. She saw his face change; it was clear that though she didn't know him, he knew her. He didn't say anything, though, as he turned aside to fetch her Diet Coke.

He brought it back and took her order for a burger with a smile and a friendly word, though he didn't meet her eyes and when he brought the terminal for payment she could see his hand was shaking slightly.

But it wasn't the moment to ask him questions, with the bar full of journos discussing the case. They weren't being very flattering about the failure to find Jay Forsyth;

Murray even heard one saying, 'They'll probably only get him when he manages to kill someone else.' Clearly they weren't far from using the 'Killer Kid' headline.

When the burger arrived, she took it over to a table and ate it thoughtfully. Could they be right? Jay Forsyth certainly had gone to stay with Lachie at the relevant time and the earlier attack on Oriole was particularly nasty; it could easily have killed her. It could even be that it had been his first attempt on Perry's life. Kids weren't all dear little innocents – though in fact there was often an odd sort of innocence in an outlook that saw black and white and nothing in between.

Kelso seemed to think Drummond was a threat to Jay, and the boss had a good record of being right. If Drummond had lashed out at Forsyth, in a fit of temper, say, he might feel Jay's denials might be believed and he had to be shut up until he could be threatened, or even bribed into admitting guilt. But saddling yourself with a body to dispose of was a mug's game and Drummond was no mug.

Anyway, Drummond had been out at a fire in Fort William and there were witnesses. So, back to the drawing-board.

Murray sighed; there was no sign of either Kelso or Hamish and there was still the A9 ahead. She got up and was on her way out when Steve Christie intercepted her.

'Er, I wonder if you have a minute, Officer?'

He seemed painfully nervous. 'Of course,' she said. 'You're Mr Christie, yes?'

'That's right. Come this way.'

He led her into a small office. He didn't sit down, but began immediately, 'I'm not going to take up too much of your time. It's just, I think you know Oriole Forsyth? I'm worried about her. She was staying here but something seems to have upset her and she left without saying anything. I think she'll have gone back to Drumdalloch House and I wondered if you could drop in and check on her? I don't mean she's suicidal or anything, really, but I wouldn't want to take that risk.'

'I've spoken to her already, sir. She was hurt by something that was said to her, but she seemed perfectly rational. I don't get the impression that she's the hysterical type.'

It clearly wasn't the answer he wanted, for some reason. 'No, I'm sure that's right. But it would reassure me if you just went—'

It had been a long day and anyway she reckoned that Oriole would have gone straight to bed when she got home, exhausted by the emotional tempest. 'I'm sorry, Mr Christie, I'm afraid I'm off duty with a long drive ahead. Perhaps you could call her for a chat and reassure yourself that she's all right.'

A man wracked by serious guilt, she reckoned as she got into the car. As well he might be!

Well, he'd tried. He'd failed, but at least if it came to it Steve could claim that far from assisting Keith, he had tried to send the police out to stop him doing whatever it was he had in mind. He was afraid it wouldn't count for that much but at least it was something that might let him believe that while he was weak, he wasn't actually evil.

Oriole Forsyth cried herself out as she drove miserably back to Drumdalloch House and parked round in front of the kitchen. She was glad to have got back in daylight; with a livid sky it was starting to get dark quite early. She could hear the wind getting up too – it had been so changeable lately and it looked like being another stormy night.

Inside the house was bitterly cold. Having thought she'd be away for some time – for ever, just maybe? – she'd switched off the heating and even the Aga, and now she had to go round starting everything up again, with another sob for her shattered hopes. Keeping her coat on, she dumped her cases in the kitchen and stood thinking dismally about what to do now.

She'd just been going to fetch her tea when everything went so wrong and she was hungry now. With the Aga only just beginning to warm up she went to the cupboard to find the emergency kettle and put some bread in the toaster.

At least the tea was hot but the toast tasted like sawdust and the room was still freezing. She was feeling weary and sort of hollow; if she could drag herself up to bed, she could at least hope that sleep would blot out the grinding misery. She'd nothing better to do anyway.

Oriole filled a hot-water bottle and set off up the stairs with her cases. As she reached her room at the end of the landing, she heard a thin wail – the wind rising, as she had thought it would, and now she could hear rain battering the windows too – another of the stormy nights she hated. With so many draughts and leaks it would be noisy when what she wanted so desperately was peace and the chance of oblivion. She hurried along to her room and shut the door.

* * *

Jay had sunk back into a drug-ridden sleep, but this time as he started coming to, the fear hit him before he opened his eyes. It was almost dark and it was pouring, with the wind finding gaps in the roof and driving the rain through. It was falling on his face and he caught it on his tongue, grateful for the relief to his parched throat. He was cold, though, horribly cold, and his hunger was a physical pain now.

He was frightened to move; he'd been weirdly clumsy before, but he remembered the pile of ragged blankets on the bedstead and thought there might be more shelter further in under what was left of the roof. Just as he sat up a crash startled him, but then he realised it was just a dislodged roof tile and he embarked on his cautious crawling journey.

The blankets had charred edges and stank of smoke and dust but at least they offered some protection against the gusts of wind while he tried to work out what had happened. How could he have got all the way up here, for a start? It was still just light enough to look around and there, leaning against the farther wall, was one of the solid wooden extending ladders they used sometimes when there was a problem with one of the giant trees.

Someone had brought him up here and left him, then. It helped to be able to work out something that made sense because terrifyingly, nothing else did. The more he worked at remembering what had happened to him, the worse it felt. His head was empty as a drum. He gave a wail of desperation.

A memory at last came back to him, something that felt a long time before: he'd been having a row with Keith Drummond. He could remember him shouting, and shouting himself. And he could remember what Grandpa had said, much longer ago, that the woods were a heritage, and that was what Jay had been shouting.

That was a start, at least. But then . . . nothing. Nothing at all. Had he hit his head and passed out, or something? He certainly felt woozy. Drugged, he suddenly thought. Drummond had drugged him – there were things people could give you that made you forget everything. Like when they spiked someone's drink.

Working that out had occupied his mind. Now what was left was space for the stark terror he had been keeping at bay to take hold. He started to cry, helpless tears as if he was three-years-old again. There was no point in trying to think how he could get out of this because there wasn't anything he could do. Except fall.

Cat Fleming looked at her watch. She hadn't heard anything from Kelso all day and here it was 6 p.m.; usually he'd have touched base during the day and certainly by now he'd have been letting her know whether he might manage to get home tonight. He'd hinted the day before that they might be running out of reasons for him to stay over and she'd had her fingers crossed all day.

It was no surprise that he'd been busy; with her obsessive news habit she'd caught the bulletin that said the person arrested the previous day had been released, just as Kelso had said, but later bulletins gave no hint that they were nearer to finding the boy.

She'd made a practice of not calling him while he was working so she didn't pick up the phone herself, but she couldn't settle to anything. At last, she decided to ring her mother who might even have an inside track and know more – she still had a surprising number of contacts.

'Mum, do you know anything about what's going on? I haven't heard from Kelso at all today so I think things must be a bit hectic his end.'

Marjory Fleming said, 'If I'd had any real news about the investigation I'd have let you know. All I can tell you is that the suspect has been released, which you probably knew already.'

'Yes, of course. I check the bulletins like I have a nervous tic. If it was you, what would you be doing next?'

'Cat, I can't possibly answer that – I don't have any of the evidence in front of me, and anyway I'm not Kelso. There's no point in speculating. You'll just have to be patient – he's got a lot to deal with.'

'I suppose that's sensible. I certainly don't want to nag him – I just wish I could have some idea of how things are going, if there's any progress. What do you think will happen, if they can't find the boy?'

'Cat, I told you there's no point in my speculating. Go and text him, why don't you, so he can phone in his own time.'

'Yes,' she said, 'I suppose I could do that. OK, speak soon.'

Cat put down the phone, feeling somehow uneasy. That wasn't like her mother; it felt as if she just wanted to get Cat off the phone. Maybe she was busy – had something on the stove or a neighbour had dropped in or even was waiting for another call – but she'd normally have given a reason for trying to end the conversation.

The more she thought about it, the more uncomfortable

she felt. She'd phoned Marjory precisely because her contacts might have given her inside knowledge that wasn't being released to the media – though, of course, if it really was under wraps, she wouldn't tell Cat anyway.

That fitted, with the tone of the conversation. But surely, if there had been good news, she'd have sort of hinted, along the lines of, 'Oh, don't worry, everything's going fine, it just takes time.' She most definitely hadn't done that.

It wasn't good to be sitting here alone on a stormy night with the windows rattling, wondering what was going wrong, and Cat had been blessed – or cursed – with a lively imagination.

When she reached the point where Kelso had been caught up in one of the terrible incidents that all too often happen and Marjory had been informed but wasn't telling her until they knew how bad it was, she took a grip of herself and sent a chirpy text just hoping he was OK and sending lots of love.

Then she waited with the phone in her hand, willing it to ring. Instead, a text almost immediately pinged back. 'Sorry, sorry, sorry, sweetheart. It's a bit pressured this end. Will call when I can. Love you.'

She was a copper's daughter. Marjory loved Bill, but when had she ever taken time out to send him reassuring messages when she was in the thick of it – like, never ever. Cat needed to shape up, find something to watch on Netflix and stop staring at the phone in case it made it feel too self-conscious to ring.

Oriole Forsyth had crashed out when she got to bed but what followed was shallow sleep beset with anxious dreams and half-awakenings. It was perhaps inevitable that The Dream would feature eventually – the one where the monster that lived in the burnt-out wing would creep through to attack her.

She could hear him now, groaning and thumping, coming closer and closer until his strangling hands were reaching for her throat but she was choking to death with fright before she even turned her head to see the awful face with its bulging eyes and sharpened teeth – and then she wakened with a scream and a racing heart, coughing.

It's just The Dream, it's just The Dream, she told herself, sinking back into her pillows. She was coughing because she'd been lying on her back with her mouth open, snoring, probably. Sweet reason couldn't stop her feeling shaken though; she'd always dreaded getting upset as a child, because The Dream usually followed and it took a long time afterwards to throw off the slimy feel of it.

And now the horrors of yesterday came flooding back. She mustn't try to escape again into sleep because The Dream might return; she had to find something to do, to stop herself running it all over again in her head.

Make a cup of tea – the recommended answer to all life's difficulties. As if, she thought drearily, but she might as well and she put on her dressing-gown and went along the upper hall to the stairs.

Then she heard the sounds again, coming from the bricked-up doorway to the ruined wing: the groans and thumps of the monster. She froze. Was he about to burst through it right now? Was this real or was she still dreaming, trapped in a waking nightmare?

Of course she wasn't. She knew she wasn't, she was wide awake, wearing her dressing-gown and slippers and going to make herself a cup of tea. And she hadn't dreamt the noise; there it was again. Someone was in there, moving around.

And Oriole realised at once who it must be. Jay had always been fascinated by the ruin and had several times got himself into trouble, breaking in through the nailed-over doors and windows to climb around when of course the whole structure was unreliable – he'd even broken a collarbone sliding down a banister that collapsed. So it wasn't surprising he'd think of it when he wanted to disappear, though he must have kept very quiet; she hadn't heard noises before.

Now he was definitely sounding distressed, but she didn't know what to do. It was pitch-dark, and even if she could manage to find a way in past the barred doors with a torch, she wasn't at all sure how he'd react. Maybe she was just being cowardly, but he'd tried, at the very least, to harm her before. He might do it again and that would be disastrous for him as well as her. She felt real rage when she thought of what had been done to the loving little boy he had once been to make him what he was now.

What if he'd hurt himself again, hurt himself badly? She'd never forgive herself if she waited for daylight to assess the situation and something terrible happened. Jay might have wanted to evade the police but look where that had ended! He couldn't run for ever; he needed help now and she didn't doubt that calling them in was in his best interests. She had to do it right now.

Keith Drummond's card was in her handbag. She'd

never liked him and she liked him even less now, after what he and Steve had done to her, but though she had the nice woman detective's number too, she was in Edinburgh while Keith lived just down the road and could get here in minutes. With great reluctance, and with shaking hands, she dialled his number.

CHAPTER TWENTY-ONE

It had been nearly 8 p.m. when Kelso got round to phoning Cat. The conversation with JB had gone on at some length, and after that Hamish Campbell had come in to confirm that Drummond was indeed in Kinloch Rannoch and, depressingly, to report that nothing new had come in.

He couldn't talk to Cat about the threat to the SRCS that was uppermost in his mind, and it would hardly be kind to send her to bed burdened with his fears for the missing child, so it was a fairly short call. At least he'd been able to tell her he wasn't likely to be staying on in Kilbain after tomorrow, without adding that this was more down to cutting the budget than anything else.

Sitting in his incongruously pink bedroom, he'd eaten the indifferent pizza they'd sent up, with nothing else to do but shake out his problems one by one.

Of course the SRCS was threatened; if everything was to be dealt with centrally, whatever manpower there was on-site would be utilised even if their skills were inadequate. Justice had to take a back seat when it came to the power of the bottom line.

Perry Forsyth's murder: there was no doubt he'd broken his agreement with the consortium – had totally done them over, in fact. A man like Drummond would be incandescent – but surely a man like him would also have been smart enough to know that an informal agreement was likely to be broken when it no longer suited the interests of the other party. A reluctance to put things down on paper was understandable, but why had Drummond been so sure that Forsyth wouldn't do the dirty?

That report from the PIRC committee, Kelso had thought suddenly. It had put a question mark over the integrity of the investigation Drummond had headed into Helena Forsyth's death.

It was there on his laptop. He scrolled through it to the autopsy report that had enabled two doctors to authorise a cremation. The wound to the head had wood detritus embedded in it, bark and lichens that matched with the oak Helena had allegedly fallen on to. DI Drummond had accepted this as an accident without question and without further investigation.

Oriole had told Livvy Murray how bad the Forsyths' marriage had been. One piece of wood taken from the same tree would be much like another. Could Drummond have done a favour for his murderous friend that made him feel he had a permanent hold over him? It looked as if Drummond had underestimated him – but Drummond was ruthless too.

He'd had personal evidence of Drummond's temper, and it was easy enough to see him coming back to Drumdalloch later, pursuing Forsyth through the forest as he checked his plans for the next visit from the woodcutters, trying again to change his mind, failing, then in fury striking the blow that had killed him. A convincing scenario. Apart from the alibi.

He sighed. And when it came to Jay's disappearance, there was evidence that Drummond had at the very least withheld information, but nothing more than that – and the man had a ready tongue. If the boy had actually managed to evade him, somehow they'd just have to make sure once Drummond came back from Kinloch Rannoch he'd have no further chance of doing him harm – but Jay would still be missing.

Tomorrow he'd be going back to Edinburgh to join JB in a fight to save the SRCS that they were both so proud of and it looked as if he'd be having to admit that this whole investigation was heading for a dead end – or even, a million times worse, a dead child.

He was sure, though, that there was dirty money involved in the hotel project, and if Inverness did indeed start digging around, something more might emerge – like who would have had an interest in seeing that it went ahead. With the authorities breathing down their necks, could one of Drummond's chums even have obliged, while Drummond set up his perfect alibi? Forsyth being killed with a straightforward blow certainly suggested someone simply losing it and lashing out, but on the other hand it could suggest a sophisticated awareness that getting solid evidence from that method would be hard.

But it was far-fetched and only theoretically possible and didn't get them any further forward anyway. It was late; tomorrow would be a heavy day and fretting any more about what lay ahead was pointless. Fortunately, he'd retained the army habit of sleeping whatever the circumstances, and by midnight he was dead to the world.

DI Drummond answered abruptly, but when she said 'Keith, it's Oriole,' his tone changed. Sounding kindly, concerned, he said, 'Are you all right? Goodness, it's the middle of the night – are you not tucked up in your cosy bed? Where's Steve?'

'I don't know,' she said stiffly. 'I'm back at home.'

'You're what!' He wasn't sounding kindly any more.

'The thing is, there's someone moving about in the ruined wing of the house. I may be wrong, but I think it's perhaps Jay.'

There was a pause, and then he said, 'Right. The really important thing is not to go near him. Don't try to talk to him, even; he's highly dangerous and if he knew you were there he could come round to attack you again. Lock your doors and keep away – if you went near him he'd probably kill you this time. I've been in Kinloch Rannoch but I'm coming now as fast as I can – be patient and don't worry. We'll deal with it all very carefully I can promise – kid gloves stuff. He's only a child, after all.'

'I suppose you will,' Oriole said uncertainly. 'Yes, all right.'

'That's a good girl.' He was sounding kindly again. 'Just remember this is in his best interests.'

Those were the very words she'd used herself, but that

didn't stop her feeling a traitor. Huddled next to the Aga, she settled down to wait in an agony of misery.

Drummond erupted into rage as he flicked the switch to end the call, yelling and thumping the steering wheel with his fists. He had pulled rank to make sure he was demonstrably well away from anything that might happen at Drumdalloch tonight, joining the investigation of a common-or-garden break-in at a shooting-lodge to the surprise and unvoiced indignation of the DS who was perfectly capable of handling it himself.

To general dissatisfaction, he had dragged out the interview with the suspect with previous, whom they had lifted immediately, and had left only when he would be in nice time to report in at the station in Inverness in the early morning and could check for any developments overnight.

He'd taken care to see to it that there shouldn't be. And once Strang was called back to Edinburgh having failed, he would then suggest taking another look at the abandoned wing to see that the barriers hadn't been tampered with since they were checked just after Perry's death.

What he hadn't allowed for was this. How could Steve have managed to let the hen-witted female go back home? By now there should be a ring virtually on her finger and with Jay dead there would be nothing to stop them. This was unimaginably bad, the worst – he was right in the frame.

If he'd managed to scare her into doing as she was told, he could maybe survive as long as he could get into the place alone and take care of things. A big 'if'.

He was more than two hours away and the bloody woman could take it into her head to do anything. He turned on the blue lights and the siren and took off through the darkness, his jaw set and planning the painful revenge he was going to inflict on the moronic Steve Christie.

Livvy Murray had driven back south feeling tired and frustrated. She'd lots of ideas but there'd been no opportunity to share them.

She was still burning with indignation about poor Oriole, and the sordid little plan that had left her so publicly humiliated. She didn't deserve that; she'd tried so hard all these years with her uncaring family and the unwanted burden of the legacy of those awful woods too. Presumably the whole hotel project had crashed and burnt now; Drummond was an idiot to have blown it by trying this on when Oriole had been so totally in favour of it anyway.

Jay might have been a problem, though; Oriole had told her about Jay's attitude to the woods. As Perry's heir – always supposing he hadn't actually killed his father, of course – he could certainly mess things up, and what the boss had said about Drummond hunting for Jay came back to her. At the time it had sounded sort of doom-laden and a bit OTT – dead bodies, even when buried or dropped into the sea, had a way of turning up later and causing trouble, and she couldn't really see what he'd gain by it.

Then gradually she realised: of course, with Christie married to Oriole and Jay conveniently out of the way the consortium would be all set, Perry having been removed already.

She'd always fancied Drummond as the killer, but his was a solid alibi – recorded as out on a job with officers ready to swear to it. Then she remembered something – something that Hamish had said when first they met. What was it exactly? Something about an illicit brotherhood that would work together to give cover when needed? That was probably close to the old sin of believing something because she'd like it to be true.

But she could get hold of the details of the officers who had vouched for him and ask Hamish if they were members. Of course, admitting they'd lied for him would be a career-ending mistake, so it was unlikely that they would.

Feeling that here was just a hint of some sort of breakthrough, Livvy was feeling more cheerful as she reached the Edinburgh bypass. It was late, though, and she gave a huge yawn. Straight to bed, set the alarm for an early start and hope that maybe Kelso would be coming down to Edinburgh tomorrow and she wouldn't have to face the effing A9 again.

The hands on the kitchen clock must be sticking; it was showing that it was half an hour since Oriole had made the phone call but it felt an awful lot longer.

She was getting more frantic by the minute. It was true Jay could pose a threat to her – she'd thought that herself – but the way Keith had talked about him had been unfeeling, ugly. Jay was only a child, after all – a damaged child. She'd locked her door as Keith had told her, but as she did that, she'd heard Jay sobbing and felt awful about going back into the kitchen where she couldn't hear him any more.

It couldn't do any real harm, surely, to call to him through the wall, ask him what was wrong, ask if he was hurt. She could explain that the police were on their way and he mustn't be afraid because she'd look after him, if he'd let her. She'd said to someone that she supposed she would be his guardian now that Perry was dead, so she could make sure they treated him properly.

She'd feel better once she'd done that. She stood up just as the phone rang – Keith again. It was a short call; he said he wouldn't be long now and checked that she was obeying his instructions.

'Yes,' she said, and he rang off. Well, she had, so far. But she'd made up her mind now.

The sobbing seemed to have stopped. Her heart gave a little jump – what did the silence mean? Had he had some terrible accident and she hadn't helped him because she was scared?

'Jay!' she called. 'Jay! Are you there?'

She was holding her breath when the reply came. 'Is – is that you, Aunt Rorie?'

Her heart melted. 'Yes, it is. Are you all right? What's happened?'

He started crying again. 'Please, please help me! I'm so frightened!'

And then, between bouts of sobbing, he told her, and her blood ran cold.

It was well after midnight when DS Livvy Murray had got to bed with the result that she was sunk in that deep first sleep when her phone went, ringing five times before she got to it and even then she was woozy.

It didn't help that the woman at the other end was hysterical. 'Who is this?' she managed to say at last.

'It's Oriole, Oriole Forsyth. You've got to help me – I've done the most terrible thing!'

Suddenly she was wide awake. 'Oriole! What do you mean?'

'I didn't know, you see, and it seemed the best thing to do. Jay's here in the old wing and he's been put on a ledge up high where he can't get down, and I called Keith Drummond for help because I was frightened Jay was hurt or something. Then Jay told me it was Keith put him there and now he's coming as fast as he can, and I think he's going to try to kill Jay now. What am I to do? What can I do?'

Murray tried to gather her wits. 'Take a deep breath and try to be calm. I need you to tell me how soon he's likely to get there.'

'I don't know! He said he'd been in Kinloch Rannoch but he didn't say where he was when he phoned. But you couldn't get here from Edinburgh in time. Should I phone 999?'

Knowing the two cars they had available on night duty to cover a vast territory she'd no confidence that there would be a prompt response. 'No,' she said, 'leave it with me. I'm ringing off now but I'll call back shortly. Don't panic.'

Another legacy of DCI Strang's army service was the ability to be instantly responsive when wakened suddenly and what DS Murray told him was guaranteed to shake off the last vestiges of sleep.

Five minutes later, he was running down the stairs through the silent hotel and out to his car. Siren or no siren? The sound of help approaching might reassure Oriole and even Jay, but it could also be a sort of here-I-come-ready-or-not warning when he was relying on Drummond not being ready.

He switched on the blues for the sake of legality as he broke every speed limit. Murray would even now be calling for backup with top priority, but when it would arrive depended on the locality of response cars. If they were close they might even arrive before him, but it was much more likely he'd be in the front line on his own.

At least the worst hadn't happened – yet. Jay was still alive and now there was a witness to what Drummond had done. There was no indication of how far away he'd been when Oriole phoned, so all Strang could do was floor the pedal and hope he reached there first.

This early, there was almost nothing on the twisting road. He gave a burst of siren when he came up behind a trundling delivery lorry that swerved so abruptly out of his way that he had to check his mirror to make sure it hadn't gone into the ditch, and pressed on.

It was getting lighter and the first pale indication of dawn was glimmering through the trees as he went down the drive to Drumdalloch House. Had he made it in time, or was Drummond's car parked in front?

No. With a sigh of relief, Strang drove along beyond the house and parked out of sight, then leapt out and ran to the front door.

Murray had planned to contact Hamish Campbell direct, but when she called the number he'd given her it was switched off. There was no reason for him to be on duty, but she swore even so. At least she had the number for the Inverness switchboard and could demand emergency response, but after that it took some time to find her a detective who could get there more quickly.

DS Andy Munro didn't seem ready to leap into action. When she mentioned Drumdalloch House he said instantly, 'I can get hold of DI Drummond for you, if it's urgent. He's just round the corner.'

She hadn't expected that. 'I've reason to believe he isn't,' she said awkwardly. 'It's top priority. I need emergency backup for DCI Strang, who's on his way there.'

The response wasn't enthusiastic, but he agreed he'd get on to it. 'What's the situation, anyway?' he asked.

'Developing,' she said, putting the phone down. She wasn't happy, but there wasn't much else she could do, except call Oriole and do her best to keep her in the picture.

The call came in just as Drummond neared the Kessock Bridge. 'Just warning you, mate. Strang's on his way to Drumdalloch House. I've been called in, but I have to tell you, you're on your own.'

He didn't scream or swear this time. He snarled, 'That's what you think,' and switched off.

Oriole, of course. He knew she was scared of him, and he'd counted on that; not scared enough, it seemed. Her and Steve Christie – feeble folk both, yet they'd done for him. That galled. Jail for a police officer, surrounded by inmates with scores to settle, was by any standards brutal.

He was finished now, at least in this country. Hatred

that was more powerful than any rage possessed him; he'd take them all down with him, every last one, and the first was going to be that sneering bastard who'd already, apparently, positioned himself in the line of fire.

Not far now. He switched off the siren and blue light and drove through Kilbain at a decorous thirty miles an hour while he groped in the glovebox for the neat Czech Vz.15 that had happened to come his way and that he'd kept. Just in case.

Still huddled on the iron bedstead, Jay had waited in the growing light, stiff with fear but not crying any longer. He was trying to figure out something he could do if Drummond arrived first when there was a mighty crash and far below him the front door shuddered as an axe splintered it.

A couple of strokes later a man appeared through the gap he'd made, shouting, 'Police! Stay where you are – you're all right now.'

Jay sat up. His head was still spinning but he called, 'I'm here! There's a ladder over there – put it up and I can climb down.'

The man followed where he was pointing and pulled it over immediately, adjusting the extensions as he set it up. 'Now be very careful – I'll come up to help you.'

With the surge of adrenaline that hit Jay, he almost felt he could just fly down. 'I'm fine,' he called, standing up as the ladder reached him and taking a step towards the edge.

His legs, unused for twenty-four hours, buckled.

Dear God! The boy was going to fall!

'Fling yourself backwards,' Strang yelled, starting up the ladder. 'Keep calm, it's all right.'

If he staggered, he'd be over the edge. But after one panic-stricken cry, Jay had kept his head and landed on his bottom with a thump. A moment later Strang reached him.

'I'm going to give you a fireman's lift, all right? Don't try to stand again – crawl towards me till I can get hold of you, then just cooperate. Don't look down and keep still, OK?'

He was carefully not looking down himself. The Victorian house had high ceilings and from where he was standing now, on what would have been the attic floor, it must be almost forty feet to the ground.

At least the ladder was solidly made and it stood to reason that it had held the weight of a man and a boy since that was how Jay must have been put there. He could only hope that the broken edge of the floor it was propped against would hold firm and hadn't been weakened further already.

As Strang manoeuvred him over his shoulder, Jay was able to help by adjusting his position, making him lighter than the dead weight they'd practised on all those years ago in training, but he was tall for his age and weighty enough. Breathing heavily, Strang was descending, feeling for each step with infinite care.

They were still twelve feet off the ground when Jay, upside down and facing the door, gave a gasp. 'It's him!' he said as Drummond appeared through the gap in the door. 'He's got a gun!'

'Yes, I have,' Drummond shouted. 'Freeze!'

Facing the other way, Strang couldn't see him. 'Don't be a fool,' he yelled. 'I have backup coming and what you've done has been reported already. You can't possibly get away with this.'

'You think I don't know? The clock's ticking and I'm not going to waste my time talking.'

Before Strang could draw breath to say something, Drummond charged straight at the ladder, knocking it so that it swung away and crashed to the ground.

Crushed by the weight of the ladder and the boy on his back, Strang felt a searing pain in his leg, then his head hit the encaustic tiles of the floor. Jay had fared better but was too shocked to move.

Drummond laughed. 'Well, it's a start. And an immobile target – ideal. It's a while since I used this, and I wouldn't have liked to miss or anything.'

He came towards Strang, raised the pistol and as Jay screamed at him, he fired.

He turned his head. 'And you're next. Then I'm off.'

Oriole hadn't been idle. It wasn't easy to carry on a conversation through a wall, so apart from telling Jay, with an assurance she didn't feel, that he'd be all right and help would be coming any time now, she'd got busy.

She hurried out into the greenish pre-dawn light, listening for the sound of a car – friend or foe – approaching but all she could hear were the birds waking up, stirring and muttering, as she went to the woodshed and picked up an axe. DS Murray had pointed out that when the police arrived they wouldn't have time to hunt round for whatever entry Drummond had made and that she should find something they could use to break through the barrier across the door. Now she had this to hand to them if they arrived first. *When* they arrived first, Oriole told herself firmly.

But what if they didn't? The last thing Murray had said to her was, 'Remember he's dangerous.' If Drummond arrived to kill Jay, she wasn't going to stand back and let him do it. She'd been passive far too long.

She looked around the shed for a weapon of some kind; there was a heavy spade, but it was unwieldy. She hurried back into the house, looking wildly about her for something – anything – easier to use.

And there it was, her forebears' idea of rustic decor: the display of antique swords that had been gathering dust on the wall by the stairs for years. She couldn't see herself plunging in a sword, but she could use one like a club, if necessary. Better than nothing, certainly. She fetched pliers and went up the stairs to attack the fixings of the one with a big, ornate hilt.

It was heavier than she expected and even after all these years the blade was sharp when she tested it, so she had to fetch a dishtowel as padding. After a few sweeping practice strokes so that she wouldn't stagger when she had to use it, she was satisfied. When Drummond arrived and went into the wing, she would creep silently up behind him and strike him on the head.

After all, that had worked pretty well before.

She went back to watch. Only minutes later she saw Strang arrive, gave him the axe and heard the blows as he attacked the door, holding her breath as she listened. She did hear a sharp cry from Jay, but it sounded like alarm not pain, and she couldn't hear any agitation afterwards. Perhaps she'd actually been telling the truth when she'd said to Jay that it would be all right—

But then, there was Drummond's car nosing its way along the drive and her heart skipped a beat. She'd no way of warning Strang; she could only wait until it stopped and he leapt out, not even shutting the car door, and strode towards the wing. She slipped out of the house and clutching the sword by the blade she followed him.

She had just reached the door when she heard a crash, then Drummond shouting, then a shot.

She didn't hesitate. She came from behind, then putting into her strike the full force of the venom she felt towards this evil man, she swung the Highland basket-hilted sword at his head and watched him fall.

CHAPTER TWENTY-TWO

There was a wide, bloody wound on the back of Keith Drummond's head, and with horror Oriole saw DCI Strang, white and still, and with a bleeding chest wound, lying on the floor beside him. Jay, a livid bruise on his head, was getting up and levering himself away from the ladder.

He sounded panic-stricken. 'I think he's dead. Keith shot him.' And as Oriole stood, mute with shock, he said, looking at Drummond, 'I think you've killed him too.'

While they stood there, still as actors in a tableau, they heard the sound of a distant siren and to their horror, Drummond stirred and started scrambling unsteadily to his feet. He made for the gun he'd dropped but Jay shrieked, 'No! No!' and flung himself on top of it.

For a moment Drummond hesitated, but the siren was louder now, and roaring like a wounded bull, he staggered to the door. Seconds later, they heard his car being gunned down the drive.

He must have passed the police car just along the main road. Minutes later it arrived with uniformed officers, followed by a car with two detectives, and the tableau morphed into a scene of frantic activity: an officer running to kneel beside Strang, another calling for an ambulance, a detective speaking urgently into his phone. Oriole heard him say, 'Man down,' as a woman PC shepherded her and Jay towards the door.

The kitchen when they reached it seemed weirdly normal to her. How could it still look the same after all that had happened just through the wall? The constable was fussing around them, talking about tea and trying to persuade them to sit down.

Jay, trembling uncontrollably, slumped on a kitchen chair and asked for water. Oriole, rigid with shock, said only, 'Is he dead?'

The woman was looking shocked herself, but she said brightly, 'Don't you worry, the ambulance will be here in a minute. He'll be fine.'

But she didn't believe her.

Not waiting for any order, DS Murray had set out for Inverness once she finished talking to Oriole, sick with apprehension; even if Strang reached them before Drummond did it would be pretty much a *mano a mano* confrontation, the very thing every police officer is trained to avoid. It all hung on unknowables – how far Drummond had come on his journey from Kinloch Rannoch, where in their vast territory the nearest car was and how urgently DS Andy Munro would respond. She wasn't sure about that last.

It was just starting to get light when an anxious Hamish Campbell phoned her. An early riser, he'd found messages on his phone along with the ones she'd left for him, saying there was an emergency at Drumdalloch House, but he had no further information.

She briefed him rapidly and was reassured to know he was on his way there, though she'd a dreadful feeling that by now the outcome would be settled one way or another. At least the A9 was quiet, and for once it was dry and not blowing a gale so she'd made very good time. She should be able to shave quarter of an hour off the last journey she'd done.

She should never have allowed herself to think that. It was common knowledge that saying traffic was light guaranteed an obstruction round the next corner – and there it was.

She came up with the stoppage just before the Granish junction – one of the A9 accident black spots. Another idiot overtaking, no doubt, and it had happened not long ago; she could hear the scream of sirens coming up behind her from the south. With a groan she settled back to wait. There was nothing else to do, but by the time two ambulances and three police cars had gone through she realised she was going to have to wait a long time.

It was as the air ambulance helicopter went overhead that Campbell called her back. The minute she heard his voice she could tell it was bad news.

'The boy?' she said bleakly.

'No, he's all right. It's the boss.'

So she had to sit there, with nothing to do but think about Kelso, lying in Raigmore Hospital intensive care with a bullet in his chest and a head injury. Not good, Hamish had said, but not the worst. He hadn't said, 'Yet', but she had no doubt that they both had thought it.

At last, as the helicopter headed back south and the cars began to move, she reached the site of the collision – nasty, an Audi Q7 upside down in the ditch and a large black Ford, smashed beyond repair.

She recognised the number plate. She had last seen the car parked outside Keith Drummond's house in Kilbain.

They came for her at the Sheriff Court, the standard two uniformed officers, a male sergeant and a woman PC. Cat was standing chatting to her client's solicitor as they waited for the verdict on an armed robbery.

The police are a normal sight in the courts; it was only as they came right up to her and said, 'Catriona Fleming?' that she realised what their presence meant and she went cold.

'Kelso?' she said.

'I'm afraid there's been an incident,' the sergeant said. The constable chipped in hastily, 'Don't worry – they've got him to hospital and he's being well looked after.'

Cat could see they were looking distressed. 'You said, "Don't worry", not, "He's OK." That means it's bad, right?' She could see the answer in the glance that went between them. 'What happened?'

'We don't know the details,' the sergeant said. 'There was a shot fired, apparently, but he's in intensive care now in Raigmore Hospital and they'll be pulling out all the stops, I can promise you that.'

The solicitor who'd been talking to her moved to put

an arm round her shoulders. 'Are you all right, Cat? You'd maybe better sit down.'

She felt strangely calm. 'Thanks, but I'm just going. Make my apologies to your client.' How odd that she couldn't remember the man's name! She turned to the police.

'I'll get my car now. There isn't anything more you need from me, is there?'

'We've been authorised to take you up there,' the sergeant said, adding as she looked uncertain, 'It'll be quicker.'

She collected her coat and her bag and followed them out obediently. Somehow she seemed to be thinking very slowly – shock, perhaps? It was only as they were slicing their way through the Edinburgh traffic that she understood the implications.

It wasn't distress she'd seen on their faces, it was pity. If they didn't get her there quickly enough, it might be too late for her to say goodbye.

It was Senga who told Steve Christie about all the police cars going through Kilbain during the night and this morning.

'Don't know where they've all come from – just try getting one when someone's broken into your house. And my mum said she saw an ambulance too.'

Christie looked at her in horror. 'Where were they going?'

Senga shrugged. 'Don't know. Maybe they've found that boy they were looking for. No doubt we'll hear soon enough.'

Trying to sound offhand, he said, 'No doubt,' retreated into his office and shut the door. He had felt the clouds gathering; now it looked as if the storm was breaking. He dialled Keith's number, got no reply and left a terse message.

He struggled to produce his usual cheerful bonhomie as guests checked out and other guests set off for their day's activities while police cars drew up outside and a steady stream of officers went down the corridor to the incident room. When at last his phone rang, he took it in his office.

But it wasn't Keith. It was Oriole's name that came up.

Before he could say, 'Oriole, love!' she launched in. 'I just want you to know what your friend Keith has done. He's killed a police officer, right? And before that, he tried to kill my nephew. And guess who else was in on the whole thing? You, as I've been telling every policeman that would listen.

'You are despicable scum and it revolts me to think I was stupid enough to be taken in by your lies. He's taken off now, probably for South America or somewhere, so you've been left carrying the can. You can expect the police to breeze into reception any time now and I hope they lock you up for the next hundred years.'

The line went dead as he collapsed into a chair. Even in those sleepless nights when he'd worried about the games Keith and his pals were playing, his darkest imaginings had never envisaged anything like this.

If he got in first, told them all he knew, it could help. Plea-bargaining, didn't they call it? He had a whole list of names he could give them, Keith's colleagues who'd been in it from the start. He himself had just been a sock puppet, not really involved – they had to see that.

There'd be a price on his head afterwards, but the crisis was today. His legs were shaky as he walked out and along the corridor, ignoring Senga's, 'Here! What's going on, Steve?'

When Marjory Fleming's phone rang, she was in the kitchen brushing Scott who considered this a particularly entertaining game. Seeing Cat's name she answered it laughing.

'I'm trying to tame a wild beast here. He's taken the brush from me twice – Scott, will you come here! Sorry, darling – how are you?'

There was silence and, suddenly sobered, she said, 'Cat, what's wrong?'

Her daughter's voice was flat and emotionless. 'It's Kelso. He's been shot.'

Every day, every single day, police officers faced that risk. And every so often, someone was given the news that Cat was having to deal with now.

'How bad?'

'Not good. He's in theatre now. Concussion, broken leg, but they're not worried about those. It's the chest wound – they've avoiding all my questions about that.'

'Oh Cat! But they're very clever now, you know, and he's made it this far. How are you coping?'

That flat, emotionless voice said, 'I'm holding it together. Of course I am. He spelt out the risk of loving him from the very start. I'm all right.'

She didn't sound all right; she sounded in a state of

shock. 'We'll be on our way right now,' Marjory said. 'What is it – four hours or so to Inverness?'

'No!' There was an edge of anguish to the voice. 'Don't come! Like I said, I'm all right – if I see you, I could fall apart. He doesn't need that.'

'If that's what you want,' Marjory said. 'I'll keep my phone beside me. Love and prayers.'

She rang off just as her husband came into the room. 'That was Cat,' she said.

'How is—' Then, seeing her face, he broke off. 'What's happened?'

She told him. 'Now get whatever you need – we're going up there. She says she doesn't want us because she's bottling it up and trying not to cry – somehow she thinks Kelso would want her to keep a stiff upper lip, which is rubbish – that's the shock speaking. When we arrive she can always tell us to go away but if the worst happens she'll need us.'

'It's a mug's game, being a police officer today,' Bill said angrily.

'It always was,' Marjory said. 'More guns around now, certainly, but there was the occasional one in the old days too, and they didn't have the medical skills they've got now. We have to tell ourselves he's going to be all right.'

'Aye, maybe,' he said, but as Marjory phoned Cameron to tell him what had happened he ordered the dog to its basket with a savagery that surprised that pampered animal.

It took a long time for DS Murray to complete her journey, having stopped to inform Traffic about the identity of one of the crash victims.

'There were two others – a woman killed as well, a man badly injured. That's something else to add to the bastard's score sheet,' she told DI Campbell when she at last reached the treatment room. 'A back seat passenger claims he came straight across the road and slammed into them.

'Anyway – the boss?' She'd been agonising about him all the time, with tears not far away.

'Nothing new, beyond them operating on him. They've brought up his girlfriend and she's at the hospital.'

'Oh God, poor girl! Is someone with her?'

'A woman PC came up with her from Edinburgh – it's all we can do.'

That was true. Murray knew just what Cat Fleming would be feeling – the churning gut, the huge lump in the throat, the looming dread – but it would be an impertinence to intrude.

Sounding determinedly businesslike, she said, 'So, give me the details. Jay and Oriole – are they all right?'

'He's traumatised, of course, but just bruised and dehydrated. She's fine – set about Drummond with some old sword at just the right moment. She's insisted on making a formal statement immediately.

'Best of all, we've had Steve Christie, singing like a canary. Naive kind of guy, thinks that grassing on everyone else will get him off – touching, really. Now there's a few of my colleagues here with their hat on a shoogly peg and the air'll be a lot cleaner without them.'

'Drummond's always looked a fit for the murder, apart from the alibi. How many of those were his witnesses?'

He gave her a quizzical look. 'Two, I think. But there

was another one as well – me.'

'You mean – he couldn't have done it?'

He shook his head. 'Big fire. Drummond was in charge, there all night.'

She looked stricken. 'I was so sure that was false witness. So . . . Who, then?'

Campbell grimaced. 'It's take-a-pin time, isn't it? Someone took a bough, clobbered the man and got rid of it. No witnesses, no distinctive footprints. One of the brotherhood, drafted in? Wouldn't choke on my scone. And the boy's still in the picture – hated his father, violent tendencies, around at the time, then scarpered. Then of course . . . there's Oriole.'

'She's headed the suspect list all along,' Murray said, 'but she just doesn't act guilty: eager to cooperate, open about her movements, concealing the attack Jay had made on her earlier rather than using it to divert suspicion from her – and remember, if he was convicted, she'd inherit all the money, but she didn't even try. Then she confirmed Michael Erskine's story when she could well have dropped him in it – and anyway, she'd worked out how to stop the loggers and stymie Perry's plans. There was no need to kill him. My gut instinct tells me she didn't do it.'

'Their lordships don't go a lot on gut instinct,' Campbell said. 'But the media will go big on Drummond's crimes so we can dial it down now. We've other problems enough.'

'Yes,' she said heavily. Waiting for news was tough.

'DCS Anderson came in earlier and I showed him the list. He was looking trauchled – well, you would be a bit beaten down, discovering you're living in a viper's nest.'

Murray nodded. 'Bummer, right enough. Anyway, you

won't be needing me – you're in charge now.' She sketched a salute. 'So – orders, sir?'

He smiled. 'I leave it to your own good judgement.'

'I might just go and see Oriole. We're chums now, you know, and I'll get her talking. See if my gut is still telling me the same thing.'

The relatives' waiting room in the intensive care unit at Raigmore Hospital had been arranged with care to make it look homely, but somehow the atmosphere felt charged with the intensity of the varied emotions that had been felt here, Marjory Fleming thought as she and Bill walked in.

The only person there was their daughter, sitting bolt upright, staring into space and mindlessly wringing her hands. Her head flicked round the moment she heard someone coming in, but it wasn't a white-coated person and for a second her gaze slipped over them.

Then her chin wobbled and with a cry she ran across and cast herself on her father, sobbing. 'It's been so long – they won't tell me anything – just bring me cups of tea! Make them tell me!'

As Bill clasped his daughter close Marjory saw his eyes fill at the childhood cry – 'Daddy, make it better!' – and she couldn't speak herself for a moment, stricken with the pain of every parent with a suffering child. Cat wasn't wanting them to tell her, she was wanting them to tell her Kelso was all right. Not the same thing.

As they sat together, their arms round her, Cat's painful rigidity relaxed and at last with a handful of tissues from the box on the table beside the despised tea trays she mopped her eyes and blew her nose.

'I told you it would make me cry if you came,' Cat said to her mother with a hint of reproach, 'but I'm glad you did. It's been so long and it gets terribly lonely sitting waiting when you're so scared.'

'Kelso wouldn't expect you to be inhumanly brave,' Marjory said. 'We're all in this with you. And it's a good sign that it's taking time – bad news travels fast.'

The attempt at optimism fell like a pebble into a well, but Cat said dutifully, 'I suppose it does,' as they settled down again to wait.

What was also on Marjory's mind was what all this would do to the reputation of the SRCS, so much Kelso's baby. There had been rumours going around that the top brass were labelling it an expensive luxury and a drama like this was unfortunate to say the least.

'Thank you, DI Campbell, that's been quite extraordinarily helpful.'

DCS Jane Borthwick put down the phone, looking very thoughtful and turned to the computer terminal, where Hamish Campbell had posted his report on the interview with Steve Christie. She had been dreading her upcoming meeting with the chief constable, but armed with that – and, now she considered it, that earlier PIRC case – she could see a powerful way to advance her argument in favour of the SRCS.

She should have been able to discuss tactics with Kelso, to draw on his skill for finessing any situation. Since she couldn't, she needed to channel the rage she was feeling now about that into making her case, and she went to her meeting ready to give as good as she got.

The chief constable was more than sympathetic. They were all family, he said, and she believed him sincere, to the extent that when a police officer fell, you didn't need to know for whom the bell tolled. But it wasn't going to stop him pursuing the cost-cutting notion he'd been so taken with.

'This whole Drumdalloch business seems to have been something of a disaster,' he said. 'Delay, false confessions, drama – oh, the media can no doubt be fed the story of the hero cop saving the child at the possible expense of his own life – no more word, I take it?'

'No, I've told them to contact me here,' she said, tight-lipped.

'We'll keep hoping. But as I was saying, this sort of mess doesn't present a very good picture of your SRCS, Jane.'

'Oh? Now oddly enough I see it rather differently, sir.' She held out a piece of paper. 'I've run this off to give you so that you can look at it while we talk. This is from a source reporting to DI Campbell, seconded to the SRCS under DCI Strang, and it gives a list of corrupt officers within the local force with close links to DI Drummond, who planned and executed the kidnap and attempted murder of Jay Forsyth.'

She saw a red flush coming into his face as he read through the list. 'This has all been going on locally?' he said.

'For some years, apparently. The business agreement which is behind all of this was meant to give them safe harbour for funds illicitly obtained, and of course it was given immediacy by the purge you've been promoting in view of our increasing problems with bent coppers and rotten apples.'

'Ah yes. Yes, of course.' He nodded, and the flush died down. She congratulated herself privately; Kelso would have been proud of that. She went on, 'You see, had this been handled by the local force, it could all have been swept under the carpet until someone noticed – as I have reason to think happened some years ago. There was that PIRC report . . .'

She filled him in on that too and his confidence that disbanding the SRCS would be a sound idea dwindled before her eyes like a deflating balloon.

'It could have happened again,' she said. 'You can see the SRCS as an important way of keeping investigations honest and free of undesirable local influence – you know how powerful that can be. And, of course, it's not only homicides – the SRCS has had considerable success in other serious crime investigations too.'

'Yes, indeed,' he said. 'Theft of farm equipment – Strang's done well on that. I take your point, Jane. Until my initiative for cleaning up the problems within the force has had a chance to take full effect, I can see that it may justify the additional expense.'

Seizing her opportunity, Borthwick said, 'I think some of the delay you mentioned came from the budget cuts that meant we were not funding our own force to be on site. I know that DS Murray, a very useful officer in previous cases, has wasted hours driving to and fro on the A9.'

Not liking where that was going, he seized on the mention of the A9. 'What about the accident at Granish then? Have you a clear picture yet?'

'From the initial medical inspection, it seems Drummond was dead before the collision. Result of the blow to his head that Oriole Forsyth inflicted, most likely.'

The chief constable winced. 'Oh dear. Another enquiry. But can we assume that he was also responsible for Perry Forsyth's murder?'

Borthwick said blandly, 'I don't think we can assume anything, sir. We will, of course, be pursuing our enquiries. But with the nature of the crime and the lack of hard evidence, we have no obvious leads at the moment.'

The phone in her pocket rang. 'May I?' she said, taking it out. 'It's the hospital.'

As Cat, who had burst into tears all over again, was taken into the intensive care unit for a glimpse of her husband who was, they had assured her, doing as well as could be expected after a long and tricky operation, Marjory and Bill clung together for a moment.

'You know, it's bad enough being a parent without taking on extras like Kelso and Cammie's Annelise,' Marjory said. 'He's like a son to me and I'm worrying already about her having the next baby when it's six months away.'

'She'll be fine, and he will too,' Bill said stoutly. 'But he won't be conscious before tomorrow and at least we're here to see that Cat gets something to eat now. Let's go and prospect. An empty stomach makes everything feel worse.'

'You're not exactly an expert. Can't remember the last time you had one of those,' Marjory said drily, and followed smiling as Bill set off on his mission.

* * *

On the drive to Drumdalloch House DS Murray kept looking at her phone as if she was trying to compel it to ring; five hours now without news.

By way of distraction, she considered what Oriole might do now. Jay's aunt Rebecca had been prepared to sacrifice herself to protect him; would Oriole, now she and Jay were sharing top billing on the suspect list, keep quiet if she was guilty, having tried so hard to protect him before?

There was an almost childlike naivety about Oriole; she loved to talk. As Murray listened she needed to focus on that gut feeling – would it still be there?

Oriole welcomed her warmly, greeting her with a hug, and over a mug of coffee regaled her with the morning's events in some detail.

'Such a dreadful thing to have to do.' she said at last. 'Horrible! His head – and when he fell . . .' She shuddered. 'But the detective who took my statement was very nice and reassuring that I did the right thing. And I can't help feeling the world will be a better place without Keith Drummond.'

No guilt there, then – understandable enough. Murray said, 'Well, it's been a sad and difficult time for you, with Perry's death as well.'

Oriole nodded, bowing her head. 'More dreadful for poor Jay – as if losing his father wasn't enough, to be kidnapped and threatened with death in that terrible way!'

'He and his father didn't get on though, did they?' Murray said, and without warning the warm atmosphere changed to the sort you could chip into ice blocks.

'I don't know what you're implying. Jay had nothing

to do with his father's death – you can ask him yourself, as no doubt you will. He didn't even know about it until old Lachie told him.'

'Right,' Murray said. 'But you must understand that the enquiry will be ongoing until we have an answer.'

'I'm sure.' Oriole said, getting up, 'and I hope you get one. But if you don't mind, I'm really feeling rather tired, with everything.'

She'd overplayed her hand. Stupid! She said hopefully, 'Perhaps we could have a chat again later . . .'

'I'm afraid my lawyer has advised me to say nothing in answer to any future questioning apart from "No comment". I'm sorry, especially as you were so kind yesterday and such an absolute lifeline this morning.'

Politely but inexorably, Murray was ushered out. She was thinking furiously as she got back in the car. Oriole couldn't have thought that would be it; of course they'd go on trying to make a case against her brother's killer that would hold up. If they could.

It was only then it dawned on her. They hadn't so far, and Oriole had believed all along that they never would. There were endless unsolved cases lying neglected in police files.

No wonder Oriole hadn't shown any signs of guilt; she didn't feel it about Perry, any more than she did about Drummond. To her it had been a black-and-white issue: the list of his sins was extensive – he'd been a bad son, a bad brother, a bad husband and father and a false friend.

Murray gave a deep sigh as she drove away. Did Oriole know that Helena's death might not have been an accident? Which of course it could have been – and now this looked destined to be one of those intensely frustrating cases where you knew who the killer was but hadn't a hope of proof.

With a twinge of pain, she thought Kelso would say that wasn't knowing, that was a gut feeling, and however sure she might feel, her gut feelings about Oriole had pointed her in the wrong direction, hadn't they?

Just at that moment her phone rang, and it seemed as if Kelso was going to be all right after all – which made it a good day, and there had in a primitive way been justice for Perry Forsyth, even if it might not be the kind officially recognised by the High Court of Justiciary.

EPILOGUE

Cat Fleming was told Kelso was conscious and able to talk, and the staff had been confident that he was recovering well – remarkably well, his nurse had said – but it was still a shock to see him with a bandage turban on his head and strapping across his chest. He was attached to a spaghetti of tubes and machine wires, with a disconcerting screen beside him showing wiggly lines that looked as if they could flatline at any moment.

She could see signs of pain marking his face, pain that she felt inside herself, as if a hand had roughly squeezed her heart. His eyes were closed, but when she tentatively spoke, they opened immediately and he smiled.

'Sorry, sorry,' he said. 'My bad. Should be old enough by now to know how not to get in the way of a man with a gun.'

His voice was weak but he sounded – just normal, himself. Cat had never been a crier and it infuriated her that this brought tears to her eyes again – last thing he needed was a watering-pot.

She was almost afraid to touch him but when she kissed him gingerly and took his hand, his grip was surprisingly firm.

'Yeah, you should,' she said. 'I bet they have classes for that on the internet. We can look them up together.'

He smiled. 'Probably a good idea. Are you all right, my love?'

They hadn't the strength at the moment for drama. 'Oh, I'm tough, me,' she lied brightly. 'Nasty moment or two I have to admit, but I took the job on with you.' Seeing his face when she said that, she went on hastily, 'We need to plan the next bit. They've told me you're going to be signed off for a good spell and apart from the physio, that'll be time off.'

Kelso pulled a face. 'Not very good at time off.'

'No,' she agreed. 'That was why I had a thought. It would be a good time for a honeymoon. I think it's time you made an honest woman of me and after all this you'd probably hesitate to suggest it yourself.'

She could see him struggling with emotion again. 'I'm not what you'd call an enticing prospect, am I?'

Neither of them needed tears. 'Depends how you look at it, really. With your great pension arrangements, you're pretty tempting for a struggling advocate living on her wits.'

Surprised into laughter, he winced. 'Ouch! You know, I think I'd sort of thought proposals were more romantic than this – at an expensive restaurant say, or in some exotic location with a sunset . . . Someone down on one knee, maybe . . .'

'I was working within our limitations, but I do quite fancy that. We can do that bit when you actually agree. If you agree.'

'Sounds good to me. Maybe, once I've done enough physio, I can even be the one to do the down-on-one-knee bit.'

'It's absolutely killing me not being able to hug you, but I don't suppose you'd exactly welcome it,' she said.

'In one sense, no. I'm working on deep breaths at the moment. I hope to contemplate clearing my throat shortly.'

'Oh love!'

They'd kept it so carefully light, but as she leant forward to kiss him again, he said, gripping her hand so hard that it hurt, 'Dear God, I've been lucky, and it's brought it home to me that we don't have all the time in the world, we've only got now.

'And we can't cling to the past, either. That's always going to be there with its memories, but I've been thinking for a long time I should get them to smooth out the scar on my face.'

Cat only said, 'Whatever you want to do is fine.' She'd said she'd never be jealous of poor Alexa and she had meant it; she owed her. Alexa had taught Kelso how to be a good partner, but the visible mark of mourning had been a sign of looking back and they had to be looking forward now. With a loving thought directed towards that gentle ghost, she said briskly, 'We've a lot to schedule, then. What precise sort of exotic location had you in mind?'

Acknowledgements

My thanks go, as always, to my agent Jane Conway-Gordon, to my publisher Susie Dunlop, to Fliss Bage and all at Allison & Busby, and to Philip Templeton for his patience in responding to my endless legal queries.

ALINE TEMPLETON grew up in the fishing village of Anstruther, in the East Neuk of Fife. She has worked in education and broadcasting and was a Justice of the Peace for ten years. She has been a Chair of the Society of Authors in Scotland and a director of the Crime Writers' Association. Married, with a son and a daughter and four grandchildren, she lived in Edinburgh for many years but now lives in Kent.

alinetempleton.co.uk
@Aline Templeton